Windmaster's Bane

To Beverly

Enjoy!

Tom Deitz

Other books by Tom Deitz

Tales of David Sullivan

Windmaster's Bane (1986)
Fireshaper's Doom (1987)
Darkthunder's Way (1989)
Sunshaker's War (1990)
Stoneskin's Revenge (1991)
Ghostcountry's Wrath (1995)
Dreamseeker's Road (1995)
Landslayer's Law (1997)
Warstalker's Track(1999)

Also

The Gryphon King

The Soulsmith Trilogy

Tales of Thurderbird O'Connor

The Angen Chronicles

Windmaster's Bane

by

Tom Deitz

Book One of the Tales of David Sullivan

High Country Publishers

INGALLS PUBLISHING GROUP, INC.
Boone NC

High Country Publishers

INGALLS PUBLISHING GROUP, INC.
197 New Market Center, #135
Boone, NC 28607
www.ingallspublishinggroup.com
www.highcountrypublishers.com

Cover design by James Geary, from a
Painting by Val and Ron Lindahn
Text design by schuyler kaufman
Illustrations by the author
Incidental design elements from p22 type foundery

Library of Congress Cataloging-in-Publication Data
Deitz, Tom.
      Windmaster's bane / by Tom Deitz.
          p. cm. -- (The tales of David Sullivan ; bk. 1)
    ISBN-13: 978-1-932158-71-7 (alk. paper)
    ISBN-10: 1-932158-71-5 (alk. paper)
    ISBN-13: 978-1-932158-72-4 (trade pbk. : alk. paper)
    ISBN-10: 1-932158-72-3 (trade pbk. : alk. paper)
    I. Title.
    PS3554.E425W56 2006
    813'.54--dc22
                               2006001105

First printing: July 2006

for Louise:
who started it —
and now, twenty years later,
in tribute to that talented lady.

for Vickie:
who sustained it — and showed me
all manner of marvelous folk,
both in song and story.

for Sharon:
who said what she thought —
and never stopped saying it.
and,
in memory of Jack Hunter Daves:
who left us far too early.

acknowledgments

thanks to:
Mary Ellen Brooks and Barbara Brown
Joseph Coté and Louise DeVere
Linda Gilbert and Mark Golden
Gilbert Head and Margaret Dowdle-Head
Christie Johnson and Lin McNickle-Odend'hal
Klon Newell and James Robert Nicholson
Charles Pou and James Pratt
William Provost and Paul Schleifer
Vickie Sharp and Mike Stevens
Sharon Webb and Leann Willcox

... and now, twenty years later ...

Judith Geary and Barbara Ingalls
Bob Ingalls and Nate Kretzchmar
Buck Marchinton and Sharyn McCrumb
Paige McKnight and Stewart Russell
Bryan Visconti and Ronny Whitener

and especially,
Stephen Wood

inτRoducτion

1 αm a lucky son-of-a-gun.

Not only was I lucky enough to actually get a novel published – the year *Windmaster's Bane* came out there were, I think, something like fifty first novels published in the entire fantasy field – but I've also been lucky enough to have an opportunity to revisit work I did, in some cases, very close to twenty-five years ago.

Thing is, I've learned a lot about writing in recent years, so I feel compelled to at least mention some of the things that readers of that first iteration may find different.

First of all, don't panic. The bones and most of the meat of the story are still there. In fact, there's a little more meat, because I've taken this opportunity to add a few scenes from the points-of-view of Alec, Liz, and Uncle Dale – scenes that I trust don't slow the original narrative, but expand on their characters a bit. There are also a few scenes at the beginning that are intended to foreshadow events at the end that hindsight tends to render a tad too serendipitous. Nothing of substance has been cut; in fact, a few scenes are now longer and more detailed. And no really substantive changes have been made in the overall content or concept.

Except one.

Windmaster's Bane had its origins in the late 1970s and early 1980s, and I'm fond enough of specific details that I included specific details of – especially – the music and cars typical of that time. Unfortunately, some of those details now render the original work a bit more of a period piece than I'd like, and since I hope this book will reach – and appeal to – a new generation of younger readers, I didn't want it to seem too old fashioned, especially since many aspects of the culture depicted were already mired in a past that was passing away even as I wrote about them. So I made a few changes in terms of musical and automotive references, though I kept David's fondness for The Byrds – because that's one of the things he and I share. It's just that he now thinks of them as even older oldies than when he first discovered them. I don't even need to mention (but I will) that there was no way I was going to update the "Mustang-of-Death."

And then there's the matter of technology.

Cell phones and the internet are now givens of society – and exactly the sorts of things that folks like David and Alec and Liz would have embraced as a matter of course while growing up. So if I wanted my young heroes to seem at all contemporary, I had to allow for the presence of those two things. Happily, I'd already established that a lot of tech doesn't work in David's neck of the woods, so I was able – I hope – to allow for the existence-but-absence of "tech" without disrupting the overall logic and flow of the book too much. I'll let you readers (especially you readers who have read the older version) decide if it works.

Finally, on what I hope are a toned-up set of muscle-and-bones, I've applied a spiffy new skin.

As I said, I think I've learned a lot about writing in twenty-five years – a lot about style, in any case. And many of my preferences in terms of style have changed. What this means in the real world is that I've cut about half the original adverbs and generally adopted stronger verb forms throughout. And I've given the whole thing a thorough going over for consistency, for punctuation, and for sentence rhythm (which is very important to me, and which I hope readers will appreciate if they try to read this aloud). Along the way I've had valuable input from Judith Geary, whose primary complaint about the original was that it was "adverb happy" – and who, in the process of editing this edition, helped me excise even more of the wretched things than I already had.

The upshot is, I hope, fresher, more detailed, more up-to-date, and generally better written that that first novel I began, all unknowing, back there in 1980 (or whenever): a novel that retains all that was good about the initial version, while still incorporating changes that – I hope – make it richer, more enjoyable for those of you who've taken the journey with me, and a more accessible, more contemporary experience for those of you who are entering my imaginary world for the first time.

I hope you all enjoy it.

Welcome to Enotah County!

Tom Deitz
Oakwood, Georgia
January 2006

 PART 1

Prologue 1

Tir-nan-og
(high summer)

... a sound ...

... a sound of Power ...

... a low-pitched thrum, like an immense golden harp string plucked once and left to stand echoing in an empty place ...

And then, ten breaths later, another ...

But it was the ancient Straight Tracks that thrummed along their sparkling lengths, as they sometimes did for no reason the Danaans could discover – and they had been trying, essentially, for*ever*. Success still eluded them, though; for those half-seen ribbons of shimmering, sliding light that webbed the tangled woods and treacherous seas of Tir-Nan-Og – and which here and there rose through the skies themselves like the trunks of immense, fiery trees were not of Danaan making at all, nor, except nominally, of their World.

In some Worlds they were seen differently. And in some – like the nearby Lands of Men – they were not seen. That much the Danaans knew and little more, save how to travel upon them – and that was best done only at certain times and seasons.

Yet the Tracks – the *Ways* as some folk called them – were there in all Worlds. And they had Power in all Worlds. For Power was the thing of which they were chiefly wrought.

It was the half-heard humming of that Power murmuring through the high-arched windows and thick stone walls of the twelve-towered palace of Lugh Samildinach that awakened Ailill MacAngus shortly before sunset one day in Faerie's endless summer.

At first he did not know it as sound, for the thrum of the Track was as much felt in the body as heard with the ear. Like a swarm of furious tiny bees, it was: bees trapped in his teeth and bones. *Or* like a tingling in the blood, perhaps, like the bubbles in artfully made wine. *Or* maybe a dull tension in the air itself, that sang to him alone.

A smile twitched the corners of his mouth. It had been a long time since the Tracks had put forth a humming with which his *own* Power could harmonize.

Not that he lacked Power, of course; that wasn't the problem at all. Nay, Power was as much a part of him as his coal-black hair and night-blue eyes; as his tall, lean body and devious wit. But when Power came from without as well as within, one was wise to seize it at once and wrest it to one's will on the spot – or risk the consequences. For Power loose in the World was danger and waste alike, as all Danaans knew from bitter experience. Indeed, it had been another such random tolling of the Tracks that uncounted years gone by had wrenched their entire Eldritch tribe from the Northern Isles and set them wandering the Ways to this World, where they had founded Tir-Nan-Og and Erenn and Annwyn and the other realms of Faerie that lay scattered in the web-work of the Tracks like the glittering, airless wings of dead insects.

No, Power unbound was not to be ignored – no more than Ailill was one to ignore that Power in whatever form it manifested.

He sighed reflectively and folded his arms behind his head, where he lay on a low couch before a narrow window. The time for action was not yet. Sunset would be better and midnight best of all – assuming this particular sounding lasted that long. It would not, of course, so sunset it had better be. Which was just as well, for tomorrow would come the Riding of the Road, and that he dared not forego – in spite of certain ... apprehensions.

Meanwhile, he studied his quarters: those apartments high in the easternmost tower of Lugh's most splendid palace, that tradition set aside for the Ambassador from Erenn. In particular, his eyes were drawn to the high-relief sculptures worked into the four square panels of cast bronze set deep in the pale stone above the door: Earth and Water, Fire and Air. *Human work* he noted, as always, with a frown. *And wondrously well done for all that. Why can we Danaans not do such things?*

A rampant horse there was first, in sinister chief, to represent Earth, which was substance. And to its right, a leaping salmon for Water, which was the force that bound substance together and let it work. And below them, their mirrors: the displayed eagle of Air for spirit; and for Fire, for that which bound spirit together and allowed it to act, the two-legged dragon called a wyvern. Finally, framing all four was a rectangular border that bore the endlessly interlaced serpent of Time that enclosed all things.

Earth and Water, Fire and Air – and Time: of those five elements all the Worlds were made.

And the greatest of those is Fire, which manifests as Power, and of Power I am very fond, indeed.

Ailill arose then, and dressed in a long loose robe of iron-black velvet, lead-gray wool, and silver leather, all pieced together in narrow lozenges. A fur-fringed cloak of heavy black silk covered it, while a thumb-wide silver circlet bearing a procession of attenuated eagles worked in rubies bound his long hair off his face.

That accomplished, he took himself outside by way of the least-used portal, subtly relieved to find himself once more in the open air. A close-grown grove of splendid redwoods soared about him, their crowns yet less lofty than even Lugh's lesser walls. From the several available, he chose a narrow gravel path that ran downward and west through a tightly woven stand of stunted hazel trees, whose tortured branches twisted and twined like the knotwork brooches that bound his cloak to both shoulders. As the sun sank ever lower, he increased his pace in turn, Power now crackling through his flesh like bolts of summer lightning.

So it was that his lengthening strides brought him to the low, embattled wall that bordered the grove on the sunset side. Impulsively, he leapt atop that barrier and stood transfixed, as the empty immensity of scarlet sky exploded before him. *Glorious!* He shouted in his mind alone. *Absolutely glorious!* He smiled, but no good showed in the sensual curve of those thin lips. Careless, he stepped closer to the edge of the white marble merlon, let the rising wind set the shining silk cloak flapping behind him like the wings of the Morrigu in one of her corvine aspects. He did not fear to fall, for he could put on eagle's shape and ride the breezes into the High Air – far, far higher than the palace that crowned the wood-wrapped peak behind him.

Power! he confirmed, in body and mind alike, as he edged closer to the brink. Power raw as rocks. Free for the taking, free for the shaping. *But what should I do with it, I wonder?* His eyes narrowed and his brows lowered thoughtfully.

And then he knew.

Reaching into the air, he drew on the force he felt coiling there, shaped it into the storm it wanted to become, and held it poised in an indignant froth of wind-whipped clouds and latent lightning as he called upon the Power and looked between the Worlds to the homely splatter of silver lakes, gray-green mountains, and plain white houses that patterned the Lands of Men. The sun setting behind him in both Worlds today, which happened but four times a year, cast a shimmer of scarlet upon the landscape. Yet even to Danaan sight the shapes twisted and blurred like a torch seen in unquiet water, obscured by the same shifting glamour Lugh long ago had raised to shield his realm from mortal eyes in those places where the World Walls grew thin.

That would be an excellent place for his storm, he decided with a chuckle – even as tingling sparks shot from his fingertips and thunder rumbled among those lesser peaks.

And so he made it happen.

Windmaster, they called him, and with good reason. Windmaster, Stormmaker, Rainbringer – the names had attached themselves to him, and he gloried in every one. His mother, she who had been a queen in Erenn before his father had put her away, had told him that storms had raged in both Worlds on the night of his birth; thus, just as one's Power was strongest at the time that had watched one into a life, so did one feel closest to the weather that had heralded that arrival. He shrugged. Whatever their source, it was the storms themselves that mattered. He was a storm child; the storms he forged were his children: truer reflections of himself than the single son of his body could ever be. And this was an especially fine one.

For a long while he listened to the echoes of his handiwork crack and boom as it frolicked in that lesser World below. Indeed, he barely noted when the tolling of the Straight Tracks ended and they called to his blood no longer. Thus freed of that insistent tension, he relaxed into reverie, lulled by the dying storm's distant grumble.

Gradually, however, another sound crept through the grove to disturb his contemplation: the distant, muffled crunch of soft leather boots on the path that threaded the wood a short way behind him. It was a very faint sound, but clear to one of Ailill's lineage.

With the sound came the urge to follow those footfalls. And so he did, leaping with easy recklessness from merlon to merlon as the battlements spiraled down the mountainside until at last a clearing appeared among the dark shadows of the ancient oaks to his left. He paused at the edge, masked by a gnarled gray branch that grew close against the wall. And he saw who came there, tall, golden-haired, and dressed in white: Nuada Airgetlam – who, if not quite his enemy, was certainly not his friend – and who would not like his storm.

Pointless, that one would say. *Irresponsible.* The World shaped itself in its own good time and purpose. To impose one's will upon it without reason was to set oneself above the Laws of Dana. It was always the same tiresome litany.

Nuada had knelt and was plying a hand among the ivory blossoms of an unfamiliar shrub that flowered in the glade when Ailill sprang from the wall behind him, silent as leaf-fall. Nuada looked up, frowning, as Ailill's shadow fell dark upon him.

"Well, Windmaster, do you like it?" Nuada inquired, when Ailill did not speak. "A Cherokee rose, mortals call it. I have but newly brought it from the Lands of Men."

"I like it better like this," Ailill replied, languidly extending his left hand in an apparently careless gesture.

Blue flames enfolded the pale blossoms – flames in which the flowers nonetheless bloomed unscathed.

Nuada did not reply, but the slanted brows lowered above his sea-blue eyes like clouds above deep water, and he scratched his clean-angled chin with a right hand that gleamed of silver

"Or maybe this way?" Ailill continued, as a subtle shift of his first two fingers quenched the flames and encased the flowers in crystals of sparkling ice.

"Or like this?" And the roses burned like summer suns on one side and glittered like cold winter stars on the other.

"I like it like this," said Nuada, with an absent flick of his wrist. And fire and ice were gone.

Ailill sighed and leaned back against the mossy parapet, arms folded across his chest. He shook his head in weary resignation. "What is it with you, Airgetlam, that you favor the dross of dull mortality above the Power that is born in us, to use as we see fit?"

Slowly, deliberately, Nuada stood and turned to face Ailill, eyes narrowed to inky slits. "Ours to use, not misuse, MacAngus. And as for the dullness of mortality, do you not find immortality dull? Were it not for mortal men I would long since have quit this life from boredom."

"I find mortal men most boring of all!" Ailill snorted, glancing skyward in avoidance of the other's searching stare. "It is seldom they do anything worth noting."

"We shall see," Nuada gave back, eyes shining red in the reflected light of sunset. "For as the moons of our two Worlds align ever closer to midnight and the strength of the Erenn Road waxes in its turn, time draws near for this quarter's Riding. Who knows what may happen then?"

"That Track passes too near the Lands of Men," Ailill snapped. "This I have told Lugh before. I do not see why he endures it."

"This is not Erenn, Windmaster – nor Annwyn, either," Nuada retorted. "What was it? Five hundred years at Arawn's court, which hardly touches the Lands of Men at all – and that in what seems to us here to be their past? And then straight to Tir-Nan-Og? Much can change in five hundred years, let me assure you, and mortal men most of all. Granted, their works intrude – but no place is free from that now. And one thing, at least, may be said in their favor: They do not make storms. As to the Riding: You do not have to go. I ride as Lugh's vanguard this Lughnasadh."

Ailill did not reply. The sun had passed from sight. From somewhere in the towers above a fanfare of trumpets split the air to herald evening.

Nuada fixed Ailill with one final searching stare and returned to his roses.

Ailill frowned as he stole from the glade. He paused once at its edge, looked back, and softly snapped his fingers.

The roses turned the color of blood.

prologue II

in the lands of men
(friday, july 31)

THERE was a new crow in the cornfield, though the owners of that field would not have known that, nor cared much if they had. And even if it had gained their attention, they would only have noticed its unusual size, graceful ambulation, impeccably groomed feathers, exceptional blackness, and just possibly the way the other crows gave it a rather wide berth.

No one did notice, however, though that was not entirely the owners' failing.

And so it perched on the split pine railing at the edge of this season's stand of corn and watched the sunlight banish the shadows that were but the least troublesome legacy of two weeks of tempestuous weather that had largely precluded these visits. It seemed to the crow that the land sparkled, every new-washed blade and twig and leaf had turned to emerald and topaz, and every stone to silver and gold. Some of the latter were even steaming, as mid-summer sun blazed forth with a splendor that should have reminded the field's owners of their ancient heritage as worshipers of that same sun.

Should have, but did not.

Except, perhaps, for one.

That one the crow did not see. Nor the other owners, for that matter. Only a muddy road and a grassy hill and a mighty mound of mountain behind the lot. Only a white house and a graying barn, a handsome herd of cattle, and three ... *cars* she thought they were called.

Still, the crow considered, anyone as old as she was could spend as long as she liked at watching.

Chapter 1

a funeral seen
(friday, july 31)

death was fast approaching – and it was approaching them both. Yet Patrick the priest was not concerned: not when death came in the form of old age, which was one of mankind's burdens, and certainly not when there remained any chance of salvation for the tall old man seated on the stone beside him. Oisin was stubborn, and his arguments were cunning; but he was a pagan, and had once been a warrior: a son of Finn mac Cumaill, in fact, who had been the greatest champion in Ireland. Just now Oisin was defending Finn's prowess on the field of battle. His boasts were a study in Gaelic eloquence.

So much eloquence, in fact, that they fairly leapt from the page of the worn blue volume David Sullivan held open in his lap.

He could practically see them, the two old men: one thin and frail, robed and hooded like a monk; the other yet well-muscled, mail and helm and sword shining bright in the morning light. It was a marvelous image.

"Daaaavy!"

The image shattered. Footsteps pounded up the rickety barn stairs behind him. *Cursed be younger brothers,* he grumbled silently. *Won't even leave you alone for thirty minutes.* He scowled at the book in grim determination.

Oisin sang now of the virtues of Finn: no longer merely as a warlord, but as a man skilled in every art. It was getting good. The pagan was winning.

"Pa got the tractor stuck just like Ma said he would," Little Billy announced as he galloped past to stand perilously close to the hayloft's open door.

David grunted. He rearranged himself in the dusty old rocking chair, adjusted his wire-framed glasses, scratched his chin where a trace of stubble had *finally* begun to grow and returned to his reading.

"That sure is a big black station wagon," Little Billy continued, peering out the door and down the hill.

David ignored him.

"There sure are a lot of cars behind it, and all of 'em have their lights on, and it ain't even dark yet!"

David shook a stray lock of unruly blond hair out of his eyes and glanced up reluctantly, surprised to see patchy blue sky and scattered shafts of sunlight where but a short while before clouds had held uncontested sovereignty above the furtive river bottoms and high, rolling ridges of the north Georgia farm he called home. Wisps of clouds still hung wraithlike among the dark green hollows across the cove. *Just like Ireland must be*, he suspected – until he lowered his gaze toward the muddy gravel road at the foot of the hill, where a line of cars crept reverently along behind a hulking black vehicle.

"It's a funeral procession," he said matter-of-factly.

Only a couple more lines ...

"A funeral procession?"

"A funeral procession," David repeated. "You oughta know that, old as you are. And if you ask me any more questions, you'll have firsthand knowledge of one – from inside the hearse." The last words hung in the air, ominous as a circling buzzard.

"What's a hearse?"

"That big black station wagon. Except it's not a station wagon: bigger for one thing, and higher in the back; built on a stretched Lincoln frame, usually. They're only used for funerals. Now please be quiet; I've only got three more pages."

Little Billy was quiet for exactly three lines. "They're goin' in that old graveyard across the road. Are they gonna *bury* somebody?"

David slammed the book shut with a sound like a tiny thunderclap.

Little Billy jumped, uttered a yip of surprise, and dropped the handful of straw he'd been fidgeting with into the muddy earth below. He looked up at his older brother, and their eyes met, and they both knew he was in trouble.

David erupted from the rocker, setting it into riotous motion on the rough old boards. Billy was quicker, however, and darted down the narrow aisle between the hay bales.

"I'm gonna get you, squirt!" David hollered. He pursued his brother until he saw the boy's head disappear down the stairs that led to the barn's ground floor, then halted and tiptoed back, to jog noisily in place by the hayloft door. His mother's Friday wash flapped optimistically on the backyard line. And directly below ...

Little Billy bounded out into the broken sunlight of late afternoon and paused, gaping in obvious confusion, then glanced back into the gloom.

"Whoooeeeee!" David yelled, as he leapt from the hayloft in a sweeping arc that landed him directly behind his little brother. He made one frantic grab for the boy, but miscalculated and stumbled forward on his knees in the mud.

Little Billy shrieked, but his feet were already carrying him through the laundry and down the hill beside the house.

David recovered quickly and dodged left, skirting between his pa's four-wheel-drive Ford pickup and his own heirloom '66 Mustang, hoping to ambush Little Billy as he came around the other side. Little Billy saw him at the last moment, however; squealed joyously; and threw his luck into one last wild, reckless dash toward the road, where the slow parade of cars continued to pass.

David caught him halfway there, grasped him neatly by his hips, and jerked him into the air. He locked his elbows and held the little boy above his head, kicking furiously in five-year-old indignation.

"Now that I've got you, what should I do with you, I wonder?" David glanced meaningfully at the procession, then up at his brother, wincing as a flailing sneaker grazed his head.

"Maybe I'll take you down the hill and give you to the undertaker and tell him to put you on ice. Would you like that, Little Billy?"

Little Billy shook his head.

"Maybe I'll take you up to the house, then, and hang you from the rooftop first. Would that suit you better?"

"You better quit it, or I'm gonna tell Pa!"

"Pa's not here!" David smirked as he lowered his brother athwart his shoulders and strode off up the slope.

Little Billy tried to escape by his standard expedient of crawling headfirst down the front of David's body, but his efforts only resulted in David snaring him by the ankles as they passed and lowering him until his head was bobbing up and down between David's shins. It was not an efficient mode of travel, David realized before he had managed three steps. He stopped and began to swing his brother pendulum-like between his wide-braced legs, lowering him just enough that his white-blond hair brushed the rough-mown grass.

Little Billy alternately screamed and giggled, but David could feel his grip slipping. He made one final sweep and released his brother at the end of the arc, to send the little boy scooting back down the hill.

On the follow-through, David found himself peering between his knees at the bright-eyed face of a very smug Little Billy propped up on his elbows. He suddenly felt very foolish.

Little Billy laughed. "You sure do look funny with your butt up in the air and your face down by your feet!"

"You'll look funnier when I get through with you, you little –"

David started to straighten, but paused, blinking, as the air around his head suddenly seemed to hum, as though invisible mosquitoes swarmed there. The hair on the back of his neck began to prickle. He froze, still bent over.

The air pulsed again. David felt his eyes fill up with darkness, as sometimes happened when he stood up too fast from a hot bath. His head swam, and he felt dizzy. He blinked again, but the darkness lingered. *Oh my God!* he thought for a panicked instant, *I've been struck blind!*

But that was ridiculous! Yet his whole body was tingling now; he could feel the hair on his arms and legs stiffen as chill after chill raced over him. And then the darkness was burned away by a hot light, as if he stared straight into the sun, but with no pain.

Another blink, and the world returned to normal, leaving only a faint, itchy tingle in his eyes. He shrugged, executed a lopsided somersault, and got up to chase Little Billy.

They had nearly reached the rambling old farmhouse when their mother hollered from the western back porch that David had a telephone call.

"I'll get you yet, squirt," David shouted, as he bounded up the porch steps, leaving his brother to seek shelter in the barn.

"I just washed them pants," his mother groaned as he passed. The screen door slammed behind him.

The phone – one of the old kind that still had a cord; there had always been reception problems in Sullivan Cove – hung on the kitchen wall beside the back door. David took a deep breath and picked up the receiver. Probably his father calling from Uncle Dale's place, wanting him to come help with the stuck tractor.

"Hello?" he began tentatively.

"'Bout time you picked up, Sullivan! What're you doing, anyway?" came a voice young as his own, but slower and smoother; more like a lowland river than a mountain stream: his best friend, Alec McLean. An undercurrent of irritation surfaced on the last few words.

"Oh, it's you," David panted, glancing out the back door. "I was just trying to impose a little control on my brat of a younger brother."

"Well, why don't you impose a little control on yourself while you're at it, and check the time every day or two? You were supposed to pick me up half an hour ago."

David shot a glance at the yellow electric clock on the wall above the stove and grimaced in dismay: It was nearly six o'clock. He rubbed his eyes absently.

Alec went on relentlessly. "Camping? Remember? If it quit raining? Got me out of bed to ask?"

"Son-of-a-gun!" David groaned, smacking himself on the forehead. "Sorry. I'll be right over. I just got so engrossed in what I was reading I lost track of time."

Alec sounded unconvinced. "I thought you were controlling your brother. I'd suggest a rack, thumbscrews –"

"Before that, stooge. No, really; it was one of those books from that batch the library was throwing away: *Gods and Fighting Men*, by Lady Gregory. It's great stuff – Irish mythology. You know, like that other book I was telling you about last week: the one about Cuchulain, only –"

"Not now, Davy," Alec broke in. "I'm sure I'll hear more about it than I want to before long. At least it's not werewolves this time," he added slyly.

"You got something against werewolves?"

"I do when my best friend tries to turn himself into one, like you did last time we went camping."

"Alec, my lad, I would prefer to forget that unfortunate episode. I'm at least a month older and infinitely wiser now."

"Well, I prefer to remember it – in all its embarrassing glory. I mean, how could I forget you prancing around up on Lookout Rock, stark naked except for the fur collar off one of your mother's old coats, smeared all over with fat from a dead 'possum you'd found beside the road, muttering incantations out of another one of those old library books? That, my friend, is not an image that dies easily. Nor was it a smell that died easily, either – and I don't plan to let you forget it."

David sighed. "I thought you were my friend."

"I am," Alec replied dryly. "If I wasn't, I'd have sold the pictures."

"There are pictures?"

"Wouldn't you like to know?"

"Long as they don't show up on the Net."

"Hmm, good idea."

"In that case *I'd* want a cut of the profits – I'd suggest one of the Fortean sites."

Silence.

"But seriously," David went on, "This is just an ordinary camping trip – a celebration of the end of all that confounded rain, if we need an excuse. And if I time it right, I may get out of havin' to help Pa. Uncle Dale got his truck stuck, and Pa went over with the tractor and got stuck too, and –"

"David?"

"Yeah?"

"Shut up and come get me."

"Oh, right. Sorry. Be there in twenty minutes."

"You can't get to MacTyrie in twenty minutes."

"I can."

"You comin' in a jet or something?"

"Nah, just my Mustang."

"That's what I was afraid of. Well, try not to set the mountains on fire in transit."

"It's been raining for two weeks solid, McLean. The mountains are very, very wet." David's voice dripped sarcasm.

Alec turned serious. "Yeah, well, but Mom almost didn't let me go this time, 'cause of what she's heard about your driving – not from me, of course –"

"Of course."

"But then Dad came in and said, 'Get! No telling what that wild-eyed maniac will do if you don't!'"

David rolled his eyes toward the dingy ceiling. "Your dad thinks I'm a wild-eyed maniac?"

"He likes you anyway – otherwise he wouldn't have asked y'all to put me up while they're at that conference next weekend."

David nodded. "Uh-huh. No doubt he thinks you'll be a good influence on me."

"Something to that effect."

"Boy, is he mistaken!"

"Huh?"

"Never mind, old man. Gotta go. We're burning daylight."

David hung up the phone and flopped back against the doorjamb, grinning mischievously. *Damn, I feel good!* he chuckled to himself.

One reason, of course, was the impending return of good weather – even a little real sunshine did wonders for his state of mind. Partly, too, it was the promise of getting out of the house and off the farm for a while: away from the mind-numbing normality of his parents. And of course there was the anticipation of good fellowship. He and Alec hadn't had a good long bull session in ages, and there were things that needed discussing.

But there was something deeper underlying it all, he realized, as he started down the hall to pack. It was that rare and almost mystical elation that accompanied the discovery of some new thing that he instinctively knew would be of lasting significance for the rest of his life. On those rare occasions when that occurred, it was like the opening of a door in a high stone wall; and this particular door had opened when he'd begun *Gods and Fighting Men* the previous morning. From its first ringing line, that book had filled him with that same wild, unexpected joy he had felt when he'd first read *The Lord of the Rings* four years back. That work had given him "a new metaphor for existence," to use the phrase Alec's English-teacher father was fond of throwing around. And now, he suspected, he had another.

He grinned again in fiendish anticipation. He would tell Infidel Alec all about it – whether he wanted to know or not.

David's slim, blond mother was leaning against one of the back porch posts when he emerged from the house five minutes later. A frosted glass of iced tea tinkled in one hand; white flour patterned her faded blue Levis, indicative of a supper that was, atypically, running late. She looked tired. "Somebody's dead," she observed flatly, pointing down the hill.

"Somebody's always dead."

She frowned, which made the crow's-feet in the tanned skin around her eyes deepen. "Don't get smart, boy!"

"Oh, I already am; got it from my mother." David flashed her his most dazzling smile as he leapt from the shadowed gloom of the porch into the glare of sun-dappled yard. His worn knapsack flopped on his back as he sprinted toward the car. Little Billy was nowhere in sight.

In the suddenly harsh light, the Mustang seemed even redder than usual, as if the steel stampings that comprised its body had been heated in some smith-god's forge instead of merely the afternoon sunshine. Its narrow chrome bumpers glittered so brightly they actually made David's eyes water. Indeed, the very air seemed to sparkle in some uncanny way, as if every floating mote were a minute, perfectly-faceted diamond that had materialized out of nowhere to gyrate crazily before him in a swirl of multicolored particles like iridescent dust thrown before a wind, briefly outlining every tree and leaf and blade of grass with a glittering halo of burning, scintillating color.

David froze dead in his tracks, mouth agape, then wrenched off his glasses and stared at them in perplexity. Though the lenses appeared clean, he wiped them on the tail of his T-shirt and glanced up again, blinking.

The effect had ended.

A shrug. "Too hot, or something," he told himself.

Little Billy emerged from where he had been lurking behind the car. He peered at David uncertainly, then extended the copy of Lady Gregory. "Here's your book, Davy. I'm sorry I bothered you."

David blinked again, smiled absently, and ruffled his brother's tousled hair. "No problem, kid."

Little Billy's blue eyes were wide and hopeful. "You're not really gonna give me to the undertaker, are you?"

"Couldn't get enough for you, squirt," David grinned. "No, of course not. But thanks for gettin' this for me."

As he unslung the knapsack to stuff the book inside, David glimpsed the name neatly stenciled on the faded khaki canvas.

SULLIVAN, D.

A chill passed over him. He shivered and looked up, to see the crowd of people still clustered among the weathered tombstones and scruffy oaks across the road. It was startling how clear the air had become, how much more sharply focused everything seemed. It was as if he could read the names carved on those headstones, count the leaves on the trees, see the tears glistening on those grief-stricken faces.

And then he remembered another funeral three years gone by.

SULLIVAN D.

Not himself, but that other David Sullivan: his father's youngest brother, after whom he had been named. *David-the-Elder*, Uncle Dale had called him, to distinguish the two when David himself had been born.

David-the-Elder had embraced life with a burning enthusiasm not often seen in their normally cautious family – and had found a sympathetic outlet for that enthusiasm in his precocious young nephew, whom he had taught to read by the age of four, and how to fish and hunt and camp and wrestle and swim and drive and a hundred other rural survival skills before that same nephew turned thirteen.

Then he had joined the army.

"It'll pay for college," he'd said.

Two years later, he was dead, blown to pieces where he walked off-duty on a Middle-Eastern street. "An unprovoked terrorist attack," the government called it. A twenty-minute funeral had marked barely twenty years of life. But that night twenty-one shots had sounded over the family cemetery at Uncle Dale's farm, and a clench-jawed David-the-Younger had fired every one into the star-filled sky. It had been the least he could do. David felt his eyes misting as he fished for his car keys. Once they had been David-the-Elder's keys.

"You okay?" Little Billy ventured, concern shadowing his small features.

David shook his head as if to clear it, and smiled wanly, feeling too good to keep long company with such dark thoughts. "Yeah, sure."

He got in the car, cranked it, revved the little V-8 a couple of times from sheer high spirits, then turned on the radio. The nasal twang of some nameless female country singer berating her long-suffering husband about "drinkin' and runnin' around" that suddenly assailed his ears sent him hastily fumbling in the glove box for a CD instead.

U-2 maybe? Or Enya? No, that wasn't quite what he wanted. Tom Petty and the Heartbreakers? Closer, but perhaps something even older, though still with a folky heart, interesting instrumentation, and lyrics that really were lyrics. Ah! He knew just the thing.

A moment later, the familiar twelve-string intro to the classic Byrds cover of "Mr. Tambourine Man" jangled through the car. David found himself singing along as he paid token obeisance to the stop sign at the end of the Sullivan Cove road and turned left onto the long straightaway that passed through his father's river bottom on its way from Atlanta to the resorts of Tennessee and North Carolina. His tires chirped softly, leaving twin black streaks as he headed north to a rendezvous with Highway 76. There was a buzz in one of his rear speakers. He had already forgotten the funeral.

Nine minutes later, David slid the car to a halt at the intersection of Georgia 76 and MacTyrie Road, which marked the center of downtown Enotah. Signs pointed ahead – west – toward Hiawassee; east, back the way he had come – toward Clayton; and south toward MacTyrie. To his left, a hundred-year-old courthouse raised crumbling Gothic spires toward an unimpressed heaven. The only traffic light in Enotah county blinked balefully overhead. The car's engine stumbled ominously. "Damn," he growled, as he glanced at his gas gauge. It barely registered.

Fortunately, he was in sight of Berrong's Texaco, where he had worked the previous summer pumping gas. He pulled in beside the self-service pump, got out, and unscrewed the round chrome cap between the taillights. Behind the pyramid of oil cans visible through the station's plate glass window David saw chubby Earl Berrong nod and give him a thumbs-up. He grinned in turn, unhitched the nozzle, and inserted it into the gas filler, drumming his fingers on the deck lid as he watched the numbers loaf by. Always something when he was in a hurry; he'd never make MacTyrie in twenty minutes now.

A Tricia Yearwood song blared from a tinny speaker in the litter-strewn parking lot of the Enotah Burger across the highway, mingling discordantly with a car radio playing something heavy and dark – Creed, perhaps, or Nickelback – and the voices of the several youthful loiterers lounging by the take-out window.

One of that crew laughed loudly, and they all looked in David's direction. A female voice called out something that David didn't catch, and then the view was blocked by the bulk of a brand new black Ford pickup that pulled into the lane beside him.

His face lit up when the passenger's window powered down and a slender, red-haired girl stuck her head through the opening.

"Well, hello, David Sullivan! How're you a-doin'?" the girl drawled, her slightly pointed features and emerald green eyes sparkling with amused self-mockery. It was the way she always began conversations with him.

David took up the ritual greeting in his best mountain twang. "Well, Liz Hughes! I ain't seen you in a coon's age!"

He was at once delighted to see a friendly face, especially Liz's, and a tad uncomfortable about the proximity of the group across the road who might get ideas he was not ready for them to have yet. Liz had been a recurring theme in his thoughts of late, and he found that ... disconcerting. She had always been a friend, but he'd recently started noticing things like the fact that, unlike most other redheads he'd known, who tended to be pale and freckled, Liz's skin was tanned golden – which made a nice compliment to the auburn hair that now gleamed almost copper in the afternoon sunlight.

Beyond her, David could see Liz's mother talking animatedly to a red-faced Earl Berrong, who looked as though he would like to head for the hills but didn't dare.

"What's up?" David asked after an awkward pause.

"Nothing much," Liz replied promptly. "What're you doing?"

"Goin' camping with Alec – and I'm late."He paused again. He and Liz had been friends since elementary school, but her parents had separated the previous spring, and she had spent most of this summer with her father in Gainesville, sixty miles away. He was therefore not quite certain how things stood between them or where to direct the conversation.

Liz solved the problem for him. "Gonna take me to the fair?" she asked abruptly, eyes a-twinkle.

David glanced at the gas pump: eleven gallons. "I thought you might take *me* to the fair."

"Ha! Just 'cause I've got a driver's license now doesn't mean I'm gonna haul you around – though, now I think of it, I might ought to at that; we'd probably both live longer, considering your driving."

"What's wrong with my driving?" David glared at her as he drew himself up to his full five-foot-six then spoiled the effect by "yowing" as a froth of gas shot out of the filler and onto his hands. He blushed furiously and looked around frantically for something to wipe them on, but had to settle on his jeans.

Liz raised an amused eyebrow. "Oh, there's nothing wrong with it – if you happen to live in Daytona or Talladega or some place like that. But don't change the subject. When you gonna take me to the fair?"

"When you wanta go?"

"Last time you asked me that we still went when you wanted to."

"Beggars can't be–"

"Hush, David. I want to go Sunday and catch the bluegrass show."

"Oh, come on, Liz. You know I can't stand that stuff."

"It's our heritage, David."

"Your heritage, maybe."

"Yours, too!"

"Look, Liz," David sighed, "I don't feel like arguing right now. But if it'll make you happy, we can go, I guess – but I get to play my whole Byrds CD on the way."

"Ugh," Liz snorted – mostly to tease him, David suspected, since he knew she did not find the music at all offensive. "You limit yourself too much. But it's a fair trade, I reckon."

"Limit myself indeed!"

Liz's mother peered through the window behind her daughter, her face obscured by a cloud of dyed black hair. "Hi, Davy, how're you doin'?" she called loud enough to make Liz flinch. "Liz'll be livin' with me for the summer, so why don't you come see her some?" She winked at him.

"Mother!" Liz hissed, face reddening, but she still turned back to

David. "Oh, and David, this little trip's just you and me, okay? None of your shadows."

David looked confused. "My shadows?"

"Little Billy, young Master McLean or any of the rest of your ... gang."

"My brother, my almost-brother, and my quasi-brothers? You got something against my brothers?"

It was Liz's turn to look off-kilter. "Not overall," she managed finally, "but at some times and places, maybe. Sometimes."

"Liz, if I didn't know better –"

"Hush, David, not now. I'll have to check show times and get back to you. Just be sure to bring plenty of money."

"I don't have plenty of money."

"Well, enchant some leaves or something. You're the one who's always calling himself the Sorcerer of Sullivan Cove!" She had to shout the last few words as the pickup roared to life and rumbled away.

"Nice lookin' girl," Earl Berrong observed.

David nodded thoughtfully. "She is for a fact – and gettin' better all the time." He handed Earl a pair of wrinkled bills, fruit of the begrudged work on the farm that kept him in gas, CDs, and comic books.

"Sullivan's got a girlfriend!" a male voice jeered from across the road as David climbed into the car.

He turned on the ignition and revved the engine, drowning voices in the growl of dual exhausts and the Byrds singing "Eight Miles High."

"Alec, my lad," he announced to nobody, as he shifted into second, "we gonna get nearly that high tonight, just by walking up an old dirt road. High on life, I mean."

Eleven minutes later – courtesy of a dawdling logging truck, whose snail-like pace had set David cursing between his teeth – David crested the gap between two small mountains and beheld the tiny college town of MacTyrie drowsing in the valley below. A network of fields and tree-lined streams surrounded its northern and eastern reaches, while west and south were shadowed by the flat-topped mass of Huggins Ridge, its lesser slopes bracketing the village like protective arms. Expensive vacation homes made incongruous warts along the lower ridgelines.

Closer in, a long, curved bridge spanned one arm of a man-made lake that sent cold fingers probing among the dreaming mountains. Many a once-sunny hollow lay drowned forever beneath that dark water, giving the otherwise pastoral landscape a quality of ominous mystery that appealed to David even when he saw it in the bright light of day. He slowed reflexively, captivated by the image. It was as if he saw the whole valley with new clarity: The edges of objects seemed somehow crisper and more sharply defined; their shapes more three-dimensional; their colors richer beneath the clear blue sky.

And how remarkably blue that sky had become! It was almost like a sheet of stained glass framed by encircling mountains. A solitary bird floated there, drifting in a lazy circle half as wide as the heavens: something almost unbelievably huge. An eagle perhaps – if there were eagles in Georgia. David blinked, and the bird was gone – as if it had never existed.

A shudder shook him as he flung the Mustang down the mountain curves and sped onto the bridge. A second tremor followed, token of another kind of fear he suppressed so deeply he did not truly admit it even to himself:

He was afraid of bridges.

Unfortunately, there was no way to reach MacTyrie without crossing one of the wretched things, or else going miles out of the way. The solution was therefore to cross them as quickly as possible. With that in mind, David floored the accelerator and gazed out at the water, half expecting to see an arm clothed in white samite flourishing a fabled sword above that silver surface. He held his breath until he was back on regular turf. A roadside sign read: MacTyrie: 2 Miles.

Alec's house was the third right on the first street on the left, a regionally incongruous Cape Cod with dormer windows and a green-shingled roof. Ivy covered most of the street side and flanked the driveway.

A regiment of dogwoods that were Dr. McLean's pride screened the rest. There was precious little real yard.

Alec himself was waiting beside the driveway, his backpack and tightly rolled sleeping bag stacked carefully beside him. Clad in clean jeans, hiking boots, and an immaculate black "Days of the New" T-shirt, he was tall – taller than David, anyway – slender, and topped with spiky dark hair. And as perpetually neat as ever, David observed, as he brought the Mustang to a halt behind Dr. McLean's latest maroon Volvo. He didn't think he'd ever seen Alec really disheveled, even after a week in the woods. As he got out of the car he cast a bemused glance down at his own clothing: a faded denim jacket from which he had ripped the sleeves, worn over his customary plain white T-shirt and much-mended jeans.

Alec was holding the hiking stick that David had given him for Christmas the year before. A runestaff, David had called it; having laboriously composed an appropriate verse, translated it into Norse runes using the dictionary as a guide, and then carved them on a three-foot length of ash:

> "whoever holds to hinder here
> from road that's right, from quest that's clear,
> think not to trick with tongue untrue,
> nor veil the vision, nor the view;
> look not to lose, nor lead astray
> who wields this warden of the way."

As an afterthought he had added two more lines:

> "these runes were wrought; these spells were spun
> by david kevin sullivan."

David had capped the ends with iron in shop class, to his teacher's bemusement, and had wrapped the grip with leather. Alec had not quite known what to make of it, but had been proud nonetheless, for whatever else it was, it was made well and with affection. And, as Dr. McLean had observed through a cloud of pipe smoke, he was probably the only person in the country to get a runestaff for Christmas.

"Glad you could make it, old man," David began in a properly clipped British accent as he popped the trunk. He was good at accents – and at languages in general – another skill David-the-Elder had catalyzed.

As David stuffed Alec's gear into the cramped compartment, he noticed his own staff, a near twin to the one in Alec's hand, almost hidden amid the clutter. True to form, Alec did a bit of rearranging, then slammed the deck lid – too hard, so that David winced.

"And only an hour late," Alec chided. "You did set the mountains on fire, didn't you? Tell me, oh Human Torch, will the headline in next week's *Mouth of the Mountains* read 'Air Force Jets Scramble as Unidentified Red Blur Terrorizes County'?"

David regarded him solemnly. "I was delayed, Alec. Had to get gas ... saw Liz Hughes."

"Liz Hughes, huh?"

David nodded. "Wanted me to take her to the bluegrass show at the fair."

"The fair, huh?" Alec raised a neat black eyebrow.

David jingled the keys. "You said something about being in a hurry?"

"Liz the one who spilt gas on you?"

David inhaled deeply, wrinkling his nose as he and Alec climbed into the car. "Sulfurous and tormenting fumes."

Alec's forehead wrinkled.

"Hamlet, sort of."

"Shakespeare! Yecch! That's what I go camping to escape!"

"Infidel! Heretic!"

"You don't have to live with it all the time."

David looked Alec squarely in the eye. "For every minute you sit there profaning the Bard, I will drive five miles an hour over the speed limit."

Alec fell instantly silent.

"Harpier cries: 'Tis time, 'tis time!'" David hissed nasally in his best Peter Lorre impression.

Alec bit his lower lip to keep from laughing as the Mustang roared to life.

Interlude 1

In the lands of men

"**You're** awful quiet about something," Nora Hughes opined, from where she was hustling her brand new F-150 along a barely paved road at a rate that would've done Ward Burton proud, assorted pithy comments about David Sullivan's driving (which she knew about mostly from hearsay) notwithstanding. Neatly isolated from her by the center armrest, which provided a real as well as psychological barrier between them, Liz was staring out the window.

"I'm not being quiet," Liz murmured. "I'm thinking."

"About what?"

"Nothing."

"Does 'nothing' have blond hair that could use a trim and a pair of jeans in need of patching?"

Silence.

"He's not bad looking, you know, if he was cleaned up a little."

"He is clean, just ... scruffy. His priorities are just ... somewhere else. He's not into trying to impress people being something he's not."

"Well, whether he wants to or not, he's apparently impressed some folks anyway. I hear tell he's one of the smartest young men in the county."

Liz snorted. "He's *the* smartest young man in the county ... though I don't think he thinks of himself as a young man." She paused, considering. "Nope, I think he still thinks he's a boy."

Nora peered at her long enough to run wide on a curve, which prompted a hasty – and jerky – correction and gasps from both of them,

35

as assorted hardwoods suddenly loomed far too close for comfort.

"That could be good or not, depending."

"On what?"

"On what you think he should be."

Liz scowled at the passing landscape. "Yeah, well, that's what I was trying to figure out just now."

It was Nora's turn to hesitate. Then: "You could do a whole lot worse, but I'm not sure you could do much better."

Liz fixed her with an icy stare. "I'd prefer not to talk about it, if you don't mind. I've still got to do some thinking.

Nora had to suppress a smirk as she swung the pickup into the gravel-track-between-pines that served as the Hughes's driveway. "Something tells me you're not the only one that's going to be thinking, either."

"Mother!" Liz growled. And let silence supply the rest of the conversation.

Chapter 11

trumpets heard

Alec closed his eyes and held his breath around one last curve before David's Mustang hit the long straightaway through the river bottom below the Sullivans' homestead. When his stomach told him it might be safe to open them again, he was greeted with the familiar vista of the turn-of-the-last-century farmhouse, with its single front and dual side porches, squatting halfway up a steep, treeless hill; the irregular line of outbuildings behind it seeming the only rampart between it and the forest that commanded the mountain beyond.

David slammed on the brakes at the last possible instant and turned right.

"We *are* going to Lookout Rock, aren't we?" Alec asked shakily, as the car lurched to a halt amid a hail of gravel. "You haven't changed your mind or anything, have you?"

David grinned at him across the console. "And where else would we go? It is my Place of Power, after all."

Alec relaxed visibly. "Well, that's good; I don't think I could face going anywhere else in your car."

David ignored the jibe, but shot his friend a good-natured glare as he opened the door. "Nope, we'll go afoot. I just need to retrieve a few things here." He tossed the keys to Alec and sprinted toward the house, leaving his friend to unload.

Little Billy met him in the yard, grinning like a 'possum. "Pa says next time you run off like that when he's got work for you to do, he's gonna wear you out!"

"Have to catch me first!" David snorted as he bounded up the steps – just as his father ambled out of the kitchen and onto the porch.

Stocky and shirtless, Big Billy Sullivan was covered with red mud from the neck on down: mud nearly the color of his sunburned skin and not much different from his auburn hair. *A fire elemental,* David thought, as the westering sunlight struck full upon him. *Or a storm giant,* he added, as he noticed Big Billy's scowl. He slowed reluctantly.

"I don't recall you askin' if you could run off to MacTyrie," Big Billy rumbled.

"I was in a hurry, Pa. This is the first halfway clear day we've had in weeks, and I told you that me and Alec were goin' campin' as soon as there was decent weather."

"Or if I didn't have anything for you to do – which I did. You knowed I needed help gettin' Dale's truck outta the mud. But soon as you thought I might be thinkin' 'bout sendin' for you, off you went." Big Billy folded his arms across his impressive chest and squinted into the yard, where Alec continued to unload the car.

"I'm sorry, Pa, I –"

"I don't wanta hear it. But since you got your buddy here, you may as well run on – this time. Better be back early in the mornin', though, 'cause I'm gonna work your butt good tomorrow."

"I gather Papa Sullivan was not pleased with his oldest boy," Alec chuckled when David returned a few minutes later.

David grimaced and shook his head, but did not elaborate. He flourished several small packages wrapped in brown paper. "Venison."

"All right!" Alec exclaimed, his face breaking into a smile. "David, my friend, there are some things you do well and some things you do not do well, but one of the former, I am glad to have been a party to, is your cooking of venison."

David laid an arm across Alec's shoulders and bent his head close to whisper conspiratorially. "My pa taught me, and he learned it from his pa. There's a secret that the men of our family share. The women don't know and won't know. I'll pass it on to my sons after me."

Alec raised arched eyebrows. "Your sons? Didn't know you had any!"

"None to speak of, anyway!"

"Didn't think so ... unless you and old Leigh Hamilton?"

"Not likely!"

"Or Debbie Long?"

"I can do better than that!"

"Randi Huggins?"

"I wish."

"So does she – so I hear."

"But she's not really my type."

Alec's eyes narrowed slyly. "Liz Hughes?"

"Alec! That would be like – like incest!"

"But they say incest is best."

"Well, it's something to think about, anyway."

"If I were you, I'd do more than think."

"Ha!"

"You brought it up."

"But can you keep it up?" David giggled and slapped his friend on the back.

Alec ignored him. "Just keeping my database current."

David began collecting his gear. "Maybe so, but I didn't expect to have to compose a dissertation on the topic. If anything changes, I'll let you know. Now, if you're through analyzing my sex life, can we get down to business?"

Alec grinned again, then nodded.

David shouldered his pack and pointed up the mountain with his staff. "That way, old man."

They began to walk – past the barn and the corn crib and the car shed, following the driveway until it turned into the dirt logging road that marked the lower terminus of their route. There were signs of "civilization" at first: beer cans and food wrappers left by parking couples in defiance of Big Billy's POSTED signs, but they soon petered out. David stopped at the first sharp curve in the road and gazed back down the mountain to where the family farm lay, framed by the dark and dreaming pines: a patch of light between the shadowed trunks. He checked his watch: almost seven o'clock. They turned and climbed higher, soon lost the sound of the cars on the highway. The air became cooler: crisp and clean and scented with pine.

Somewhere around 8:45 they reached their destination. Halfway up the mountain, a spur trail broke off to the right, running more or less level beneath overhanging trees for roughly a quarter mile before opening into an almost circular clearing atop a rock outcrop that shouldered out from the body of the mountain proper.

Once trilobites lived here, David mused, as he glanced left, to where the hard stone of the mountain pushed through the encircling pines like the old bones of the earth wearing through the thin, tree-clad skin. A shimmering waterfall slid in what seemed like unnaturally slow motion down those black rocks to create, at its bottom, a small deep pool maybe twenty yards across. Mountain-born, it was always cold, even in high summer.

Without a word, the boys picked their way among lichen-covered boulders and fallen tree trunks to the precipitous ledge that gave Lookout Rock its name. David's eyes misted, as they always did when he beheld the expanse of furry-looking mountains, now shading with red and purple as the sun lowered. Enotah and MacTyrie were invisible behind intervening ridges, but here and there bits of connecting highway showed like a network of scars. The dark silver mirror of the lake lay silent and mysterious in this least populated end of the county. David's own Sullivan grandparents four greats back had built a cabin that now lay beneath a hundred feet of that cold water. Their graves were there too. He wondered what they dreamed.

A lot of things have changed since then, he reflected, as he busied himself building a small fire, setting up his battered but well-loved cooking pot, and putting the almost frozen venison on to simmer with mushrooms, onions, carrots, potatoes, a single can of Miller beer – and a limp brown packet of the secret family seasonings. The odor mingled with the scent of pine trees and wet leaves as the first breeze of evening brought a hint of chill creeping around the mountainside. It could get a little nippy on Lookout Rock, even in July.

Alec had finished setting up the lean-to in the traditional place at the edge of the clearing and made his way over to stand beside David, wiping dirty hands on his jeans as he came. He was sweating lightly. "You don't suppose it's warm enough to go swimming, do you?" He nodded toward the pool.

David rose from tending the fire and looked Alec straight in the eye. "It *is* July," he said. "It doesn't get any warmer than that. And besides, my vainly hopeful friend, it has never been too cold for me to pay due respect to my Place of Power. Of course we're goin' swimming! We must placate the spirits of this place by offering our bodies naked to the water."

Alec rolled his eyes. "Now?"

David slapped him roughly on the back. "Won't get any warmer. We've done it in April; what's to worry about July?"

The wind shifted, whistling through the trees. The harsh cry of what could've been either a crow or a raven crackled in the air. Suddenly David's eyes were itching furiously. He rubbed them and shook his head from side to side. *Smoke must be gettin' to 'em*, he decided.

"That wind feels like fall," Alec sighed. "We'll have to swim quick if we don't want to freeze our butts off." But he was already dragging a towel out of his pack. A moment later, he was heading for the pool. He looked around for David, as if expecting to find him already at waterside and bare-assed, but David had not moved. Rather, he was staring toward the overlook, his brows lowered thoughtfully. "Davy?" Alec called. "Last one in's a rotten 'possum."

"My eyes keep tingling," David whispered, mostly to himself, as he slowly followed Alec to the water's edge. He felt strange, he realized: almost dizzy. Things seemed to slip in and out of focus. The sensation was like having new glasses, as if something were forcing his vision, tugging at his eyes.

"Some of this cold water'll do wonders for 'em," Alec called over his shoulder, as he skinned out of his T-shirt and sat down to attack the laces of his hiking boots.

"I hope so," David muttered. He cast one last backward glance toward the precipice and doffed his T-shirt as well. A moment later both boys stood naked by the water: Alec taller, slimmer, and fairly pale; David shorter, efficiently muscled, and tan. Dark hair and fair. Grey eyes and blue. They hesitated for a moment, feeling the sly nip of wind against bare skin and knowing that the water was far, far colder. Still, there was tradition to consider – and honor.

"After you," David offered.

"Your Place of Power," Alec returned.

David frowned. Somehow that idea did not appeal to him just then, though he had no idea why. He'd used that phrase himself only moments before, had found it in some fantasy novel or other and appropriated it to designate his special place: that private place of beauty and contemplation he had claimed for his own and shared with no one else save by his own choosing. But now, for no apparent reason, such casual usage seemed frivolous, almost sacrilegious.

Alec cleared his throat. "Your Place of Power, I say."

David bit his lip and nodded decisively. "Right. Together then, and none of this sissy wading stuff: Jump in like men. Come on, race you to the falls."

Alec nodded in turn, and he and David launched themselves in flat, shallow dives into the darkening water. David came up gasping as the cold stole his breath, then ducked again, opening his eyes to let the water have a go at the annoying tingle. His hand brushed Alec's kicking leg and he struck off in the direction of the falls. Seconds later, his fingers touched mossy rock, and he broke surface, to see Alec's sleek, dark head emerge beside him, spitting water. They both took deep breaths and started back.

David soon found himself intensely uncomfortable, and not only from the chill of the water. The tingle in his eyes seemed to be getting worse. It was almost a burning now, and he was seeing bright flashes in the water around him. "Too cold for my blood," he gasped as he emerged from the pool, his skin a shimmering sheet of goose bumps. He gathered up his clothes and stalked back to the fire to dry off and dress.

Alec did two more laps, then followed. Wrapping his towel around his waist, he made his way across the clearing, shivering visibly all the way. David had returned to the edge of the lookout when he got there, and was gazing off into space again. He'd donned his pants, but that was all. The fading sunlight cast red highlights on his bare shoulders.

"You look like a barbarian," Alec observed, as he tugged on skivvies and jeans and applied the towel to his hair. "You know: like on one of those Conan covers. All you need is a sword and a beautiful maiden and a fearful monster."

"And about ninety pounds of muscle and nine inches of height," David added offhand. Beyond him the sun touched the horizon.

"Stew smells good," Alec ventured.

David did not respond. He was gazing through empty air at the next high mountain over, a mountain whose nether slopes were entirely ringed by the lake: an island, but a mountain nonetheless.

Bloody Bald, they called it, though it had a name in Cherokee. Bloody Bald, because the naked rock outcrops on its eastern and western flanks caught the first red rays of dawn and the last red rays of sunset.

Abruptly the half-heard, half-felt buzz was back, like an insect humming before David's face. His eyes misted again, worse than ever; they were also tingling badly. He rubbed them with his fingers, squinted, and stared once more into space, motionless.

For Bloody Bald shimmered as he looked at it, seeming at once to fade and rise higher into a symmetrical cone almost as perilously pointed as – as the steeple of a church, he decided. Misty, gray-green trees shrouded the lower reaches, merging into a twisting haze of pastel colors that obscured the place where the shoreline should have been. Higher up, shadowy gardens now overlaid the naked rocks, weaving in and out of a ghostly filigree of embattled white walls that in turn gave way to the slender, fluted towers that crowned the peak like the clustered facets of some rare crystal. Pale banners flickered from the golden roofs of those tenuous pinnacles, and faint but clear came the sound of trumpets blowing.

It was like a watercolor seen through a screen of fog; like a sculpture seen in a dream, shaped by the mind alone. Or by the spirit.

David stood immobile, caught up.

Alec eased up beside him and turned to follow David's enraptured stare, peering uncertainly into the increasing gloom, brow furrowed, clearly seeing nothing. "Davy? Are you all right?"

David shook his head, wrenched off his glasses and rubbed his eyes, gazed at the ground, then back into the air. He shook his head again and frowned.

"Davy?"

David turned to face his friend – and felt the tension flow out of him like water, leaving a residue of incredulity – or was it fear?

"Strangest thing, Alec – I think I just had an hallucination."

"An hallucination? What kind of hallucination?"

"I could've sworn that old Blood Top over there had a castle on it just now."

Alec folded his arms and nodded. "Been reading Tolkien again, haven't you? Finally affected your mind."

"I'm serious, Alec. It looked real. I mean really real – like a mixture of Mad Ludwig's castle, a Gothic cathedral, and a really nice hunk of quartz crystal. But now I look again, I don't see a thing." David replaced his glasses and shook his head. "Must've been a trick of light or something – but damn, it seemed so real!"

"Well, I didn't see anything, that's for sure."

"A trick of light," David repeated, though he did not sound convinced.

Abruptly the wind shifted, and the smell of venison stew filled their nostrils with the scent of history and ancient ritual and the wild. Hunger became uppermost in both their minds.

While David occupied himself with toasting the garlic bread that would accompany the stew, Alec noted the blue volume protruding from David's pack, fished it out, and flipped through it. "This the one you were telling me about?" he asked a little too casually.

David squinted across the glare of firelight, then nodded. "That would be it. I never had a chance to finish it. Irish mythology."

"Irish, huh? You've worn out Greek and Roman and Norse and who knows what else, so you're starting on another one now?"

David seemed to have shaken off his recent ... episode. "That's about it. I wish I'd run into it earlier. It's great stuff – if you can pronounce the names. Got more magic than Greek and not as grim as Norse. The Irish believed in fairies – human-sized fairies, kind of like Tolkien's elves. Still do, in fact, or so I gather from reading that. Actually, they call them the *Tuatha de Danaan*, or the Men of Dea, or the shee – spelled s-i-d-h-e, by the way, but pronounced shee, like in banshee, I think."

"You're starting to sound like my dad."

"Sorry. 'Tis me Irish blood a'talkin'. Now, laddie, would ye be havin' some o' me venison stew here? 'Tis made o' the flesh o' an Irish elk me mammy found in a peat bog, to which she was led by phoukas."

Alec laughed loudly. "I'd rather have some of that deer your daddy shot last year out of season."

"I've got some of that too, but it doesn't taste as good."

David read to Alec after supper – not that Alec really wanted him to, but David seemed to be himself again, and was off on another one of his weird tangents, so there was really nothing Alec could do but lie back and listen. David really did read well. Alec watched him for a long time as his friend droned on about the coming of the old gods to Ireland, about their wars with the Fir Bolg and the Fomorians and the Milesians. The firelight cast ruddy gold on the blond hair that brushed the collar of the sleeveless denim jacket David now wore over bare skin; laid flickering high-relief shadows on his stubby nose, strong cheekbones, and clearly-drawn jaw and chin; and darkened his already dark brows and lashes, so that, in spite of the glasses, Alec could imagine his friend with sword in hand and checked tunic belted about his waist, marching off to fight what seemed like an endless stream of Ireland's invaders.

Eventually David closed the book and looked over at Alec, who lay full length by the fire, eyes slitted closed, mouth slightly open.

David rose, walked over to him, and kicked him on the sole of a boot. "Up, thou rump-fed runion!" he cried. "I didn't bring you up here to saw logs."

"Aw, shucks! I was hoping you'd think I was really asleep and leave me alone, like a considerate person would."

"No way!"

They talked for a long time, then: about Irish mythology, first; and then about the next school year and the tyranny of their respective fathers and what to make of Liz Hughes. But there was something disquieting about the way David's conversation jumped from subject to subject – something a little forced, as if he sought to disguise some underlying tension. It worried Alec, but he suppressed his concern, and then an unshakable drowsiness overtook him, and he crept off to the lean-to, leaving David awake with the stars.

A long time later Alec awoke and found David still absent. He leaned up on his elbow and saw his friend still sitting near the ledge, gazing northwest toward Bloody Bald. It was almost dark of the moon, and the night sky glittered with the constellations of summer, Cygnus foremost among them.

"Still seeing castles in the air?" Alec yawned, stumbling up to crouch beside David.

"It was on the ground, not in the air; and no, I don't see it. I must've been seeing things. But damn, Alec, it was so real!" David pounded the ground with his fist.

"Well, it could have been some kind of mirage or something; you know: reflecting part of Atlanta onto the mountains, or something like that." He paused. "I've never heard of mirages on a mountain, though."

"Yeah, well, I've never heard of castles on Georgia mountains, either. All that cold water must've done something to my eyes."

Alec clapped an arm on his shoulder and shook him gently. "No use losing sleep over."

"I guess not." David sighed. He rose, stretched, yawned, and returned to the lean-to, where he flopped down atop his sleeping bag and lay thinking about the magic of Ireland, trying to picture in his mind's eye the coming of the Tuatha de Danaan "out of the air and the high air," to use Lady Gregory's remarkable line. But another image kept intruding in his thoughts, refusing to give way: an ephemeral castle on a mountaintop.

Sleep claimed him eventually, but he awoke again shortly before sunrise, to lie with his face by the edge of the sleeping platform, looking out into the swirls of white mist awaiting banishment by the sun. A trace of unseasonable coolness remained in the air, and he snuggled gratefully into his sleeping bag, heard Alec groan and roll onto his back.

Yeah, just a couple more minutes and he would get up and watch the sunrise from his Place of Power. It was the Irish thing to do; he had learned that much from what he'd read already: that the Irish had ordered the year a particular way, and certain days and times of day had power – including dusk and dawn. What better way to connect with that ancient tradition than by watching the sun come up?

But still, it was warm in the sleeping bag, and he had stayed up very late waiting or hoping or simply being – he was not certain which. He yawned. Five minutes more.

The sun had already broken the horizon when he woke again. He sat up in the shelter and cursed himself. His eyes were burning like fire, and he thought he could make out the last fading call of trumpets. He rushed from the lean-to, gazed out into mist-filled space – and saw ...

Nothing

The burning faded as quickly as it had come. Suddenly he felt very foolish. He yawned and stretched, yawned again, and crawled back into the shelter. When he awoke once more, it was to Alec kicking him none too gently in the ribs and reminding him that Big Billy had a busy day planned for him, and if he wanted anything to eat, he'd better get up right then, or there wouldn't be anything left.

David groaned. That was always the way of it. His pa always had something for him to do, especially when there was something else he wanted to do more – like ponder the disquieting events of the last day, for instance. Maybe tonight he'd take another look at Bloody Bald.

Fat chance, he told himself. Big Billy would keep him busy clear up until dark; he always did. Well, David decided, he'd best get up and see what Alec had muddled up for breakfast; maybe see if he could con his buddy into a morning swim. It would be the last fun he'd have that day; that was for certain.

Alec McLean's Journal

(Saturday, August 1)

Well, oh, most trusted journal of mine, I guess I should start by saying that it's the day after the night before, and that it's because of that aforesaid night that I'm writing now, when I haven't bothered to update this thing in months, mostly because there's been nothing worth updating. I mean, all I've done this summer is read (*The Holographic Universe*, for one thing), fuss with the parental units about the usual stuff, and for the last two weeks watch it rain. Okay, I've surfed the Net some, and sent assorted emails of little consequence. I've also hung out with the M-gang but they're all heading out for camp or other parts unknown, as of this coming Monday. And I've watched some movies on DVD and video, but can't remember the names of any of them, so none of them must have moved me and of course I've buddied around with David when his schedule allowed, which hasn't been often, courtesy of that slave driver that claims to be his father.

And naturally I've bitched and moaned about the fact that he doesn't have email (what else is new?), but it's not like that's his fault. I mean, he's tried, but for whatever reason, he's in an electronic dead spot. It's like he can get online, but something out there fries modems like they were breakfast eggs. I'm told that they're lucky the phone works and that's only because they've got an old-fashioned phone with old fashioned wiring in an old-fashioned house. I know my cell doesn't work out there, and neither does anyone else's. Oh, and apparently the only reason they get TV is 'cause they've got an old-style antenna. Forget cable.

But enough of that. I was actually starting to write here because ... well, to address myself:

"Alec, my lad, have you ever known something was 'up' with somebody, but had no idea what that 'up' was, and you weren't even sure there *was* an 'up,' only you'd been around that person so much they were almost like your other self, only suddenly something changed and you didn't know what it was, but there was suddenly some kind of weird-ass distance thing? I mean, to cut to the chase, David said he saw something weird while we were camping, but I didn't see a damned thing out of the ordinary, but from the time he saw it, he was different. It was like he was play-acting. Like he was ... tolerating me, or something, and really wanted to be doing something else, or that his mind was a million miles away or whatever. Actually, he was that way before he saw this something – a castle on a mountain top, so he says but only for a little while before. I've tried to pinpoint the exact moment where he went strange(er) and I can't, except that it was somewhere between the time we got to the Rock and the time we went swimming. I don't know; it was just weird. Or maybe I was. Maybe there was some kind of funky mushroom in the stew and I'm just imagining all this. Maybe. Anyway ... Damn! Gotta go. Mom's just called me to lunch, and you know how that is. You know because you're me. You're not gonna go all weird and strange on me, are you? See you."

Chapter III

music in the night

Uncle Dale Sullivan, whose long dead youngest brother had been Big Billy's father, owned the next farm up the hollow that the Post Office called Sullivan Cove and often "just thought he'd drop by" his nephew's house around suppertime. Full of pork chops and mashed potatoes, he and Big Billy were sitting on the eastern side-porch – the one that overlooked the highway – discussing their day's work and watching evening creep into the valley. The soft clicking of dishes being washed in the adjoining kitchen made a tidy counterpoint to the rhythmic squeaking of their rockers.

Bone tired from his day's begrudged labor, David slumped out of the kitchen and flopped down on the concrete steps, where he sat staring vacantly down the hill. The long, neat rows of glossy corn at its foot stirred in the soft evening breeze, their froth of tassels pale against the blue-green leaves like foam on a dirty sea. He could hear the occasional whoosh of a car as it cleared the last curve off the mountain to the right and accelerated on the straightaway that split the river bottom. But he found himself straining his hearing for other sounds as well – sounds he was no longer sure he had heard. And his eyes tingled almost constantly now. He was still not sure what he had seen on the mountain – if he had actually seen anything at all – but he was beginning to get concerned.

Big Billy gestured broadly with a stubby right hand. "I swear, Uncle Dale, I never could see why in the hell Papaw let them put that there highway through the middle of his river bottom like that." He took a healthy swig from the can of Miller that sat atop a copy of *The Progressive Farmer* on the floor beside him. "Nosiree," he continued, "if I had any idea why he done that, I'd sure say, but I don't. He was a strange old feller, so Daddy said."

"He was a strange 'un, all right," Dale nodded. "But he told me he let them put that road through there 'cause they wasn't nothin' would grow there that was worth anything to anybody anyway. He'd plant corn or cane, and it'd grow up fine and straight 'cept in that one place he'd get mornin' glories and sweet peas that'd strangle the life outta the crops – either them, or briars."

"Always did have trouble with briars down there," Big Billy acknowledged.

"So when the railroad folks come along, he let 'em follow that route, and the highway folks come after. It was the straightest way, I reckon."

"Yeah, Papaw always said that there was an old Indian trail down there way back before they was even a wagon road; I know I've found a good many arrowheads 'round there."

Dale leaned forward in his rocker; his voice took on a darker coloring. "Yep, Paw told me about that when I was a boy. But he told me something else, too, Bill. He said that the Indians that was here before our folks settled said that trail was made by the Moon-eyed People. You know, them spooky folks the Cherokees say was here afore them – that built them walls down on Fort Mountain, some say."

"I heard those walls were built by Prince Madoc in the year 1170," David inserted from the steps.

"That boy's a lot like his great-grandpaw was," Dale chuckled, as if David were not there – though his eyes showed a gleam when they sought his grand-nephew. "Not as interested in this world as in the next – or at least in some part besides the north Georgia mountains."

"I like the mountains fine," David retorted. "I just don't like all the tourists we get nowadays."

"Them tourist folks brings trade, and trade brings money, boy," Big Billy said brusquely. "Speakin' of which: Dale, did I tell you I was thinkin' of switchin' to sorghum in the lower bottom too? The tourists love it, and old Webster Bryant over in Blairsville says he'll buy all I can work. Too late this year, but I may just take him up on it next time around."

Dale didn't answer. He was looking at David. He rocked back in his wooden rocker and crossed his ankles on the porch railing. David glanced up to see three inches of thin, white, hairless leg between the old man's socks and khaki work pants. He peered down at his own tanned, lightly-haired legs, took off his glasses, and rubbed his eyes absently.

"Prince Madoc," Dale mused at length, ignoring Big Billy. "I've heard Paw mention him once or twice, but he didn't put much stock in that story. One thing he did say about that old Indian trail, though, is that it's bordered with briars as far as he ever followed it – and that's a right smart piece. He's right, too; they may be little and scraggly and close in or far out, but they're there. And another thing he told me is that it goes on straight as a stick, right on over wood and water; says he got on it a huntin' one night and it like to scared him to death."

David was suddenly alert. "Did he say why?"

"Shore didn't – though I do know his dogs never come back with him that night. He made us boys and girls swear on the Bible not to go on it ourselves, 'specially not at night, and we never did. He got most of us so scared we never even mentioned it to our young'uns – 'course we was nearly all married and gone by then anyway. Yore paw ever tell you about it, Bill?"

"Hell no," Big Billy muttered sourly. He took another swig of beer and wiped his mouth on his hand. "Damn it, Dale, I ain't got time for fairytale nonsense. You're as bad as the boys. Now, about that sorghum ... I been meanin' to ask you –"

Little Billy pranced around the back corner of the house with an enormous piece of fried apple pie in one hand – which he stuffed into his mouth as soon as he saw David. "Davy says that fairies are as big as people and twice as beautiful," he announced, once he had managed to swallow.

David rolled his eyes skyward.

"Damn it, and double damn it!" Big Billy exploded, slamming his fist down hard on the arm of his rocker. "I don't know what's worse: havin' boys that won't keep their mouths shut and that won't mind their own business when grown folks is talkin', or boys that won't work and just sets around all day with their noses in books. I don't give a tinker's damn about fairies and how big they are. They ain't no such things, and you both know it. If you'd read yore Bible 'stead of them funny books, you'd find that out." He picked up the copy of *The Progressive Farmer* from beside his chair, rolled it into a tube, and tossed it at David. "Here, if you want to read somethin' that'll be worth somethin' to you, read that."

The projectile unrolled itself in flight and landed in an untidy heap at David's feet.

David picked it up, shook it distastefully and then, very pointedly turned it upside down and proceeded to peruse it with exaggerated care.

"You're readin' it upside down," Little Billy observed from the yard beside him.

David lowered the magazine, fixed his eyes on his younger brother, drew his lips back slowly, clicked his teeth precisely together one time – and looked back down at the inverted print. His eyes tingled ever so slightly but, he realized for the first time, it felt good.

"Davy, could you turn the radio off?" Billy mumbled into the darkness of David's bedroom, several hours later. "I can't sleep."

David grunted and dragged his eyes open, to see his little brother silhouetted in the open doorway. A glance at his bedside clock showed that it was nearly midnight.

"I don't have it on," he muttered, turning over and pulling a pillow over his head.

"You do so! I can hear it!"

"I do not! Now get back to bed."

"Da-a-a-a-vy!"

"It's David," said David. "It must be the TV. Ma must be up watching Leno. I guess she's having another one of her restless spells."

"It ain't the TV! It's comin' from your side of the house."

David levered himself up on his elbow and glared at the silhouette. "I-do-not-have-the-radio-on!"

Little Billy shifted from foot to foot. "Maybe it's outside, then."

David paused, listening. "Now you mention it, I do hear something like music outside. Must be a couple parkin' down by the turn-off with the stereo on loud. Pa'll have a fit if he finds out.

Little Billy's nose wrinkled thoughtfully. "Don't sound like a radio no more."

David strained his own hearing. "That's true." He sat up in bed, drew the window curtains aside, and looked out. A warm breeze floated over him – as warm that night as it had been cool the night before. He could see the solitary security light in the yard casting its circle of blue-white radiance onto the grass that sloped down to the cornfield. Away to the left he could make out the juncture of the Sullivan Cove Road and the main highway. He could hear the music more clearly, too, and it was strange music: not rock, nor yet folk or country, nor what his pa called "that long-hair stuff." No, it was different: soft and sweet and low, with a hint of flutes and maybe something like guitars and a gentle jingling like bells. More than anything else, it sounded vaguely Celtic, but with a little bit of the soundtrack to *The Last of the Mohicans* mixed in, and a thousand times more strange. Strange, yet somehow familiar.

"Somethin's goin' on," David announced. "I'm gonna take a look."

"Not without me!" Little Billy shot back a little too loudly, as his brother slipped out of bed.

"Oh no you don't! You're staying right here. I'm in enough trouble 'cause of you already." David tugged on jeans, sneakers, and T-shirt, and headed for the door.

"I'll follow you anyway," Little Billy warned.

David frowned, then sighed. "Okay, you can come, but please be quiet. And if you say one word about this, I swear I'll cut a spancel out of your hide."

"What's a spancel?"

"A strip of skin cut from a corpse."

"But I ain't dead."

"You will be if you tell on me."

"I'll be quiet."

"You'd better."

David followed Little Billy into the hall. A floorboard squeaked like an alarm. He winced and gritted his teeth, but no sounds came from the rest of the house. He stood guard uneasily while Little Billy dashed into his own room to change.

A moment later they had eased out the eastern back door and paused in the yard. The mercury vapor light turned their skins an eerie green and their lips and nails blue.

"You look like Frankenstein," Little Billy whispered.

"And you look like Dracula's grandson. Now be quiet." David cocked his head. "Do you hear it? Louder – from down by the highway. Come on!"

They trotted down the long slope of hill, halting at the irregular tangle of blackberry briars that fringed the bank above the cornfield. All at once the music became louder yet, the jingle of bells more evident. David could now make out what sounded like voices singing. He screwed up his eyes until they hurt, staring vainly into the darkness in search of he knew not what.

And then at the far side of that part of the field that lay beyond the highway he saw ... *something*. A file of pale yellow lights winked in and out among the trees that bordered the small stream that marked the property line, maybe an eighth of a mile away.

He inhaled sharply.

Little Billy stared up at him.

"Can you see anything?" David murmured.

Little Billy squinted into the gloom. "I can see a buncha lightnin' bugs flyin' along in a line over by the creek. Is that what you're talkin' about? Makes my eyes hurt. An' I can sorta hear some kinda singin', too." His voice trembled slightly.

"Come on! Let's take a closer look."

Little Billy hung back, doubt a shadow among shadows on his face, but followed dutifully as his brother pushed through the briars, careful of the tiny thorns. They scooted down the clay slope and slipped into the welcome cover of the towering corn. As they thrust their way between the knobby stalks, the hard-edged leaves cut at their exposed skin like green knives. Eventually they shouldered through the last row and crouched breathlessly among the weeds and beer cans in the shallow ditch below the shoulder of the highway.

David eased up cautiously.

Pain filled his eyes. Pain or light, he could not tell which, subsiding as quickly as it had come, into an itching so intense he wrenched off his glasses and rubbed his lids furiously.

When he looked up again, the lights were both closer and brighter, following the line of the highway, but a little way beyond it and angling toward a point farther to the right where the road and the fields and the mountain all converged.

"They're headin' for the woods behind our house – toward that old Indian trail Uncle Dale was talking about, I bet! Quick, maybe we can get a better view up there!"

David ducked back into the cornfield, with Little Billy following reluctantly. Together, they loped along between the last row and the bank, gradually drawing ahead of the lights, which were fast approaching the highway to their left. Finally they halted at the base of a steeper, rockier slope, above which the forest began in earnest. A barricade of young maple trees and more blackberry briars marked its edge, save at one place farther on, where a dark gap showed in the leafy barrier – almost like an archway.

David hesitated, suddenly wary of the gap. He glanced back, saw the lights still approaching, brighter and brighter – and made his decision.

"Up the bank, Little Billy. Quick."

Little Billy grabbed David's pant leg. "I don't wanta. I'm scared."

David grasped his brother roughly by the shoulders. "You want me to leave you alone in this cornfield in the middle of the night?" The harshness of the words surprised him.

Little Billy stared at the ground. "No, Davy."

"Then shinny up that bank!"

Little Billy set his chin. "You first."

David scowled. "No runnin' off?"

"Promise."

David scrambled up the bank, pausing before the thorny barrier at the top to hoist his brother the final few feet. The briars were thicker than they had first appeared, but he kicked recklessly through them and entered the forest proper – directly above the sharp curve where the highway bent due east and began its torturous climb up to Franks Gap. They were barely a quarter mile from home, so David knew he must have been in that place before, but in the bright moonbeams of the summer night it seemed different somehow, as if transfigured by that radiance. *Transfigured – or maybe damned:* The thought was a flickering ghost in his mind as he glanced around and saw the familiar trunks of pines and maples, the dark clumps of rhododendron and laurel. And the briars – more briars than he had ever seen, weaving in and out among the trees to the right, forming a subtle prickly barrier between himself and home, whose yard light he could dimly discern like a distant will-o'-the-wisp.

But to his left the ground was clearer, and he could see that there was a sort of trail coming on straight up between the trees, like a continuation of the straight part of the highway. It was covered with moss and pine needles, but nothing else grew there. Indeed, it was that lack of growth that most clearly defined it, though now David examined it closely, it seemed to be overlaid by a ribbon-like glaze of golden luminescence that did not quite lie upon the ground. He could almost make out patterns, too: forming and reforming along that numinous surface. But looking at it made the tingle in his eyes edge toward pain, and he felt a strange reluctance to walk there. Instead, he dragged Little Billy along beside it until their way was blocked, maybe a hundred yards up the mountain, by the half-rotted trunk of a fallen tree.

David sat down on the log and pulled his brother down beside him. And then realization struck him like a blow: There could be no moonlight – for the moon had been full two weeks ago! Why, just the night before he had remarked to Alec about it being dark of the moon. Yet there was a cold, sourceless brightness in that place – like a snowfield seen in starlight – everywhere but on the trail itself. A shiver ran up his spine. The lights ... the moon ... the briars ... this place ...

Something was very wrong.

But at that moment a whisper of music reached his ears, and the first yellow lights became visible at the top of the bank.

His eyes felt as if they were on fire. His vision sharpened, blurred, sharpened again. He was sweating, too, and could feel the short hairs on the back of his neck rise one by one as more and more of the lights entered the forest, brightening as they came, before coalescing finally into a nimbus of golden light that enfolded in its heart ...

People.

If people they were: a great host of stern-faced men and women riding in solemn procession astride great black or white horses, or horses whose smooth hides gleamed like polished steel or burnished copper or new-wrought gold. A few of those steeds appeared to be scaled, and many sported fantastic horns or antlers, though whether these grew from the beasts themselves or were some work of artifice upon their chamfrons, David could not tell.

But it was the appearance of the riders themselves that made David's mouth fall open in wonder, for he had never witnessed such a display of color, texture, and form as now passed before him like a dream from another age.

They were a tall people – men and women alike – and beautiful beyond reason: slim of build, narrow of chin, slanted of brow, with long, shining hair, most frequently black, and flashing eyes that seemed at once menacing and remote.

Long, jewel-toned gowns of a heavy napped fabric like velvet accentuated the proud carriage of most of the women, though here and there rode one clad in strangely cut garb patterned in elaborate plaids or checks. The majority of the men wore long hose, high boots, and short, tight tunics with flowing sleeves, but an occasional one was dressed in a longer robe or in clothing of a much simpler, looser style and rougher texture. A fair number of both sexes wore plate armor or glittering mail. Tassels and jewels and feathers and fringes were everywhere; and equally common was the glint of shiny metal blades and golden crowns. The host had stopped singing now, but from the bells on their clothing and their horse trappings rang out a gentle, constant melody, taking its rhythm from their tread.

At their head rode a man clad in silver armor wrought of overlapping ridged plates like fish scales, each one rayed with a blazing filigree of golden wire. His eyes were the color of deep, still water, and the long fair hair that flowed like silk from beneath a plain silver circlet shone like the sun. He sat astride a long-limbed white stallion and bore a naked sword across the saddle before him. A white cloak swept from his shoulders, its golden fringe rippling about his ankles. The light came strongest from him.

David felt Little Billy's hand tense in his own. A quick downward glance showed the little boy staring not at the spectacle on the trail but at David himself. A disturbing thought struck David. "See anything ... odd?" he whispered.

Little Billy shook his head. "Just lights. Bright lights, like the air was shinin'."

David felt his breath catch. The copper taste of fear filled his mouth. He started to stand, to run away, but something held him back. He was seeing something strange, uncanny – even, quite possibly, dangerous. But no power on earth would have moved him.

"I want to go home, Davy!"

"Hang on just a minute more. There's something I want to check out."

"Davy –"

"Hush!"

The procession drew nearer. The leader passed the boys as if they were not there. Indeed, few of the lords and ladies paid them any heed, though some did spare them brief, amused glances, and one or two looked slightly puzzled. But another – a man dressed more simply than most in a long robe of silver and black – reined his black horse to a slow walk and stared at them intently through eyes narrowed to baleful slits. "Hail, Children of Death," he called, in a voice as cold as frozen steel.

The words filled David's ears like sounds heard underwater: more felt in the mind than heard with the body. Chill after chill danced upon him. He swallowed hard and rose, as if by instinct, yanking Little Billy up beside him, then took a step forward. "Hello ... Sir?" he managed to croak to the other's departing back.

Little Billy stared at David in bewilderment. "Who're you talkin' to, Davy? I don't see nobody. You're scarin' me! I wanna go *home!*"

"Be quiet!" David growled out of the corner of his mouth.

The black-clad figure reined his horse to a dead stop and twisted around in his saddle. "You can see us!" he said fiercely, his voice almost a hiss. He turned to the black-haired, crimson-clad woman who rode next behind him. An enormous black crow perched arrogantly on her shoulder. "The man-child can see us!"

David suddenly felt very uneasy, but he steeled himself. "Of c-course I can see you," he stammered. "You're here, aren't you?"

"*Who's* here, Davy? You better quit scarin' me, or I'm gonna tell Pa!" Little Billy kicked at David's right foot. "C'mon, let's go!"

David winced but did not move, as a buzz of anticipation spread through the host like the swarming of bees. By ones and twos the mounted figures began to stop, turn, and gather round the boys until the tall shapes loomed above them like the towers of some sinister citadel.

David began backing away, partly in response to fear, partly in response to his brother's insistent tugs – only to discover that he could go so far and no farther. Something stopped him: a vague paralysis in his legs, an unyielding surface in the very air itself. He glanced down and saw that the golden glimmer now lay beneath his feet. Somehow, in spite of his intentions, he had blundered onto the track. *Oh my God!* he thought. *We're trapped by their magic!*

Little Billy screamed: a forlorn sound in the night, as if he, too, felt that barrier press against his back. "I can't move, Davy!" he wailed. "My legs is froze!" He released his grip on David's arm and tried to run, only to fall flat on his face and lie sobbing upon the moss.

David squatted beside him and helped him up, all the while keeping a wary eye on the encircling host. "Hang on, kid," he murmured desperately into his brother's ear.

The black-clad man brought his horse to stand directly in front of the boys. "And who are you, mortals, to gaze upon the Tuatha de Danaan?" he barked. "That dare to question the Hosts of Faerie when they are about their Riding?" His nostrils flared, and more than a touch of malice colored his voice.

"You're the *Tuatha de Danaan?*" David gasped as he took Little Billy in his arms and rose. "I thought you lived in Ireland."

"Do you question my word?" the man snapped. "Would you have me unsoul you here and now?" His eyes burned like coals.

But then a shadow flashed across the man's face and his chiseled features softened abruptly. He smiled a little too eagerly. "Ah, but I forgot myself, mortal lad, for time passes and we have a great distance to travel tonight. Come with us, if you like. Long has it been since we have taken two sons of men into our number. We grow bored with our own company." He cast a dark glance toward the head of the line. "Some of us, anyway." He extended a black-gloved hand – which, David saw, was covered with tiny metal plates that tinkled slightly as he moved; minute jewels winked from their surfaces.

"Come back in a few years, then," David retorted. He tried to sound brave, but felt a point of fear awaken in the middle of his back and slowly spread throughout his body. His pulse raced.

The man's face hardened. "Then you should know, *human*, to see us is ... unfortunate. It is likely we will curse you for your impertinence. It is even likely you will die and your brother as well."

"Not Little Billy," David cried. "He hasn't done anything. I don't think he can even see you."

"See who, Davy?" came a trembling whisper from where Little Billy's face was pressed against David's shoulder. "Done what? Who're you talkin' to? I want to go *home!*" The last word rose to a shriek. The little boy began pounding his brother's face and shoulders with his fists, so that David had to shift his grip to maintain his hold.

"Be still!" he hissed through gritted teeth. "I'm not doing this for fun, believe me!"

The Faery-lord raised a thoughtful eyebrow, haughtily oblivious to the little boy's fear. He stared absently at David. "The little one cannot see us," he mused. "Yet you can. ... But none of your kind can see us unless we will it or unless ..."

David caught the muttered words. "Unless?"

The dark man's eyes narrowed again, but he did not answer. "We could take him with us anyway, you know, and leave a changeling." He chuckled in a way that held no hint of mirth. "Or we could take you instead, or both of you."

"Don't take Little Billy; he's my mama's favorite."

"Take me *where?*" the little boy shrieked. "You ain't takin' me nowhere." With that, he sank his teeth into David's ear, striking out with renewed fury and twisting in David's arms like an enraged cat.

David could not maintain his hold. Little Billy thrust himself free and half jumped, half fell from his brother's grasp. He hit the shimmering surface of the track with both feet together – and crumpled at once into a motionless heap.

David flung himself forward and knelt beside the still form, feeling for a pulse at his throat. He glared up at the Faery lord. "What've you done to him?" he shouted. "If you've hurt him, I'll ... I'll –"

"You will what?" the dark man asked silkily. "Nothing, I imagine, but he is only sleeping. I am tired of being interrupted at my bargaining. Now, we were discussing what you have to offer in exchange for the small one's freedom. For you should know that no one meets our kind without paying the price of that encounter." He folded his arms across the high pommel of his saddle and glared intently down at David like a snake regarding an egg it intended to swallow. David could not return that stare.

"I don't think I've got anything you'd want," David replied in a small voice. "Let me see ..." He began searching his pockets, only to find them empty. Reluctantly, he took his brother in his arms and stood up, despair a mask upon his face.

"Well, then, it must be yourself," the man retorted with a malicious smile.

The woman with the crow spoke then, her voice colder even than the black-clad man's, and carrying with it more than a hint of anger. "Do not forget the Laws of Dana, Windmaster. They are mightier than any of us. You may not impose your will on the boy unless you give him some chance for escape.

A scowl clouded the man's features; his mouth hardened to a thin line, but at last he spoke. "So be it, then. I will make you a bargain, boy. If you can answer three questions, I will let you go free, and your brother as well."

David was suddenly wary. "Just as we are? Not changed or enchanted or anything?"

The man looked amused. "If that is your will, exactly as you came here."

"And if I lose?"

"Then you will come with us."

David took a deep breath and nodded grimly. "I've ... I've got a request to make too – if I win."

The black-clad man laughed derisively. "So you would now crave favors of the Danaans? Well, if nothing else, you are brave, mortal lad brave or a fool."

"It is his right," the crimson-clad woman observed pointedly.

"Ask, then," the man snapped. "We can but say yes or no."

David shot the woman an uncertain smile and cleared his throat. "If I lose, you'll gain control over me, right? But if I win, I'll gain nothing but memory that I may not trust as I get older. So I'd like to have something, you know, *real* from you all, so that I'll know I'm not havin' a dream or anything. And I'd like to ask you all some questions – three, I guess – in return. After all, I may not get a chance to see you folks again."

"Do you forget that you will be gaining your freedom?" the man snapped. "That is reward enough for most men, and those who win it deem themselves fortunate. Yet it is ever the way with you mortals that you desire more than is your right. But since you are a mortal and thus not likely to win, I will agree."

David swallowed hard. "Then I accept, I guess. Any time you're ready." He shifted his sleeping brother to a more comfortable position and squared his shoulders, but he had to clamp his jaws together to keep his teeth from chattering.

The black-clad man looked thoughtful for a moment, then spoke: "Name the stars in the sky."

David felt as if cold lightning had pierced his heart. "That's not a fair question!" he blurted out.

"Indeed, it is not," the crow-woman broke in. "You do know the rules, do you not, Windmaster? For if you do not, you insult the honor of the trial. You must ask only questions to which the answers are known among those you ask, if they have the learning for it. And since you yourself cannot answer that one, I think you had better find another question – or I will find one for you."

The dark Faery dipped his head mockingly. "As you will, Mistress of Battles. If I am to deal with fools, then I must ask foolish questions." He looked back at David.

"What animal did Queen Maeve of Connacht most love, and what animal did she most hate? Does that satisfy you, Morrigu?"

A low murmur rose within the host behind him, and knowing smiles crossed those beautiful, remote faces, as if the question was a familiar opening gambit in some ancient game of strategy.

"That's not a fair question either!" David protested. "That's two questions."

"A coin may have two faces and yet be one coin," the dark man replied coldly. "I do not think even Morrigu will argue that. Now answer – or come with us."

David closed his eyes, his thoughts racing frantically. The question wasn't as difficult as he had feared; the answer was in something he'd read recently; he knew it was. *Okay, focus, Sullivan, focus,* he told himself. He knew that Queen Maeve was a character in another book Lady Gregory had written, one about the *Tain Bo Cuailnge*, The Cattle Raid of Cooley. He had read it last week, right before *Gods and Fighting Men*, but what was it called? *Cuchulain of Muirthme*? And he knew that Queen Maeve had gone to war over a bull, so that was probably the answer to the first part. As for the second – well, the answer to that wasn't nearly as obvious.

"I'm not sure about the animal she most loved," he said at last, his voice quivering. "But the one she most wanted was the Brown Bull of Cooley. As to which one she most hated, I'm not sure about that either; I don't think the book I read said. ... But wait a minute! Cuchulain means 'the Hound of Culaign,' or something like that, doesn't it? He was called that because he volunteered to take the place of somebody's watchdog he killed. Is that it? It must be! He was Maeve's worst enemy, in battle at least. You were trying to trick me! You must have been! The answer must be Cuchulain!"

Behind the dark man a woman in a silver coronet bent her head toward the gray-robed lady who rode beside her and whispered, "The boy has some wit about him, a rare thing on this shore indeed."

"You are correct so far," the Faery lord conceded. "But I have a second question, and this one will not be so easy."

"I'm ready any time," David retorted, trying to keep his voice steady, his bold words belying the fear that threatened to overwhelm him. His only comfort was the warmth of Little Billy's body pressed against his own.

The Faery lord paused but an instant. "What four treasures did the Tuatha de Danaan bring with them when first they came to Ireland?"

David's face brightened in spite of his fear. This was one he knew right off. It was in Lady Gregory, too; he'd read the section to Alec only the night before. He took a deep breath. "Let's see," he began, looking down at the pine needles on the ground. "There was a cauldron, as I recall; and a spear – a magic spear. And a sword – magic, too. And a stone that cried out when the true king stepped on it. I'm glad you didn't ask me their names, though, 'cause I sure couldn't have told you."

"I will be more careful how I phrase my questions," the Faery lord replied archly, "but you are correct." A faint, ironic smile played about his lips; an eyebrow lifted slightly, but only for a moment before his forehead furrowed again and his brows lowered over eyes that flashed like black diamonds. "Let me see; this is my last chance for a changeling, so I must succeed with this one."

Before he could continue, however, a disturbance arose among the close-packed host. The white-cloaked leader had turned his horse and now rode back down the milling ranks toward the black-clad man. His searching glance barely brushed the brothers as he came to face the other. It was as if the two bright stars in Orion strove for supremacy in the night sky. The very air seemed to withdraw from between them.

"What are you doing, Ailill?" the white-clad man demanded. "I did not think you interested in mortals."

"And I thought you so interested in them that you might want a pair to observe – perhaps to plant in your garden," Ailill shot back. "Besides, the older one has the Sight. So I play the Question Game with him, the stakes being freedom for himself and his brother."

"I have seen my share of mortals," the new comer observed coolly, "and these do not seem particularly remarkable. But you are correct about the older one." He pointed toward David. "He does seem to have the Sight; it shows in his eyes. He also seems to have both wit and courage to his credit, maybe even a little of the stuff of heroes. But I wonder at your reasoning, Ailill. Do you really think I want a changeling, particularly one of your choosing? Or are you simply trying to incite trouble between the Danaans and mortal men – trouble we do not need? Might you even be trying to contrive a confrontation with me? Since you know Lugh chose not to ride with us tonight, do you test my authority as his second? What would Finvarra say, whose ambassador you are – or have you so soon forgotten?"

"I have only your best interests in mind," Ailill answered smoothly, though his tone belied the words. "That, and our brief amusement on this tiresome journey through the Lands of Men."

"Then you will not mind giving the last question to me?"

Ailill's hands strayed toward his sword hilt. He said nothing, but his white skin took on a flush of anger, and his eyes grew as dark as his hair. David saw him open his mouth as if to voice some bitter retort, then take a firmer set.

"You came perilously close to breaking the Rules on the first question," the Morrigu noted. "I would be careful what I did now."

"Nor, I think, would Finvarra be pleased," the white-clad man appended. "He, at least, is a man of honor."

"I seem to have no choice, then," Ailill hissed, a trace of uncertainty coloring his tone. "If it is the will of the mortal lad, I will relinquish my last question. It is, after all, his decision."

David breathed a mental sigh of relief, though why he thought he was better off with this new turn of affairs, he had no idea. "If that's what you folks want; that's how it'll have to be, I guess. Go on and ask – and get it over with."

"Standard Rules, I presume?" the white-clad man asked the crow-woman, before turning back to David and Little Billy.

"The Rules as proclaimed by Dana," the woman affirmed.

The man nodded, then dropped the reins of his white horse and folded his arms across his armored chest.

"So you think you know something about the Tuatha de Danaan, mortal lad?" the Faery said. "So you think what you have read in mortal books will suffice to save you? Well, then, let us see how clever you really are. Since you were spared having to name the stars in the sky, I will ask you a simpler question: What is *my* name?"

Out of the frying pan, David thought in dismay. *How should I know his name? I might as well try to name the stars; much good it would do me. Now I know how Gollum felt when Bilbo asked what he had in his pocket. Still, there must be a way; they said that if I had the right learning I would know – but they all look alike to me!*

David studied the man carefully, taking in every detail of the beautiful silver armor and the elegant face and form – but could make out no special insignia, no distinctive marks that might offer some clue to his identity. The man began drumming his fingers on his upper arms, as if impatient. David noticed the movement, slight though it was, and looked more closely at the man's hands. They were not the same, he realized: The left one was encased in an articulated silver gauntlet that came up over the wrist in an elaborate flare. But the one on the right ... the workmanship there seemed more delicate, more like a real hand. And then he recalled that a king of the Tuatha de Danaan had lost an arm in battle, and a new one had been made for him out of silver. All at once David knew the answer to the third question.

"Your name is Nuada of the Silver Hand," he said, "or however you pronounce it. I hope that's close enough."

The man nodded and glanced back at the assembled host, then stared straight at Ailill, whose diamond eyes now glinted with hints of ruby flame, though the white-clad man bore the brunt of that anger.

"You gave it away, Nuada. You helped him," the black-clad man snapped.

"I helped him? You gave me the question, so it is no longer your concern, is it? He is free now." Nuada flashed a triumphant grin at his adversary and turned back to David. "You have won the contest," he continued with unexpected gentleness. "You are free to go."

David exhaled a long soft sigh; his knees sagged as the tension flowed from his body so swiftly that he nearly collapsed. Much of his fear had fallen away as well, and in its place came the return of some of his old cockiness.

He looked up at Nuada, faced him eye to eye. "Don't I get three questions now?"

Nuada's head snapped around. "You promised him that, Ailill? You are a fool."

"I did," Ailill snorted. "I did not plan on his winning."

"A fool twice over, then. But still, he has won fairly, and so we are bound." Nuada turned back to David. "Ask, mortal," he said, as if intoning an ancient ritual, "and if it is within our power to answer, we will. But be warned that if you seek to learn the future, only ill can come of it."

"Oh, I don't want to know the future," David replied airily. "I just want to satisfy my curiosity. After all, you don't come upon the ... Fair Folk, I guess you are, riding through your daddy's back forty every day. And you were trespassing – by our laws."

"And not by ours, which are older. But ask."

"I'll put it in one sentence then: Who are you, exactly; why are you here; and where're you going?" They were not the best questions he could have asked, he knew instantly; but he hadn't really considered what would happen if he won the contest.

Nuada took a deep breath and began. "As Ailill has doubtless told you, we are the Tuatha de Danaan – or, if you like, the Danaans or the

Men of Dea; or, as we do not like, but as your kind now call us, the Faeries or the Sidhe, though once they called us gods, long ago in Ireland and elsewhere. Since you have not asked our separate names, I will not give them to you, though you may have mine, as you have won it, and Ailill has forfeited his, so you may have it as well. As to what we are, that is beyond the scope of your question.

"But as to why we are here, by which I assume you mean in this place and not some other; that is a thing both easy to know and hard to tell. Perhaps it is best simply to say that only in very few places does the World in which we customarily dwell touch your own, and only in those places can we find true rest from our wanderings on the Straight Tracks among the Worlds. Alas! Not all such places are the same; some are more firmly rooted to your World than others, and once there were many more than now remain. But all such resting places we cherish, and this is one of them. Tir-Nan-Og, we call it: the Land of the Young."

David looked puzzled and opened his mouth to speak, but Nuada went on, oblivious.

"And to answer your third question: Many of our kind still dwell in Erenn, which touches what mortal men call Ireland; and many there have kindred here. The Road we presently ride connects the two, yet that passage becomes ever more difficult as more and more the works of men breach the Walls between the Worlds. Yet there are still certain times of year – four of them, to be precise, of which this is one – when the Road is strongest and the journey less perilous. Those times we follow the Way to the Eastern Sea to greet those who have chosen to come here. That is why we ride tonight, and where."

Nuada paused, as if considering whether or not to continue, and the strength of his gaze made David feel as if his soul were being read. "You have a sympathy for the old things, David Sullivan, that I can tell already. It is a rare youth indeed, in this or any other land, who has heard of the Tuatha de Danaan, much less of Cuchulain or Nuada Airgetlam. And you have the Second Sight, as well – and that is a gift both precious and perilous. Now farewell, David Sullivan, for the Track calls us, and the Track may not be denied."

David felt his eyes tingle again. Little Billy snored softly. All at once David felt very sleepy himself. He took a step backward, then another. The barrier was gone; the paralysis had lifted.

Nuada extended his silver hand, then raised it above his head in salute before gathering up his reins. He shook them once, so that the silver bells chimed, and then again, and with that the surrounding host took up the rhythm with other bells, and with tambourines and flutes and pipes and recorders. Even the golden Track beneath them began to pulse gently. Old, that music sounded – older than man, David suspected – and filled with a heart-rending longing.

Little Billy slept quietly. David watched until the last rider had vanished among the trees. Where the host had passed, the moss was unbroken, the pine needles unstirred. Only a faint golden glimmer remained to mark their passage, and then that too faded. He yawned again and began the trek home, his brother a comforting weight in his arms.

As he came to the line of briars, David paused. They seemed lower, less densely tangled, less ... vigilant. He was back in his own world again, back in his own night. It was dark, too – moonless, like it ought to be.

But as the last light faded behind him, he did not see Ailill draw a needlelike dagger from a sheath at his waist and discreetly prick his palm, which he then shook so that three drops of blood fell to a single oak leaf that lay on the otherwise naked earth.

Nor did he see another member of the company, who had fallen unobtrusively back to ride near the end of the procession, rein his gray horse to a halt and turn empty silver eyes in David's wake, and with practiced precision inscribe a circle in the air with the ringed fourth finger of his many-ringed right hand.

Interlude II

in the lands of men
(sunday, august 2)

dale Sullivan was asleep. And then, abruptly, he wasn't.

Something was nagging at him, like an itch down there deep between his shoulder blades where he couldn't reach it. Or like a scrap of Joanne's fried pork chops caught between his hind teeth – and he still had all of 'em, too, which was something to be proud of at his age. Except when you found yourself worrying at something caught between 'em with your tongue.

But this was something he was worrying about with a different part of himself entirely. He'd gone to sleep the way he liked to: tired, full, every so slightly tipsy on his own homemade brand of 'shine and without a care in the world, since everything he owned was paid for, and everyone he cared about – everyone that was still alive, at least –was no more than ten minutes away – and that was if one was inclined to walking.

And then he'd awakened with a memory playing around his head like a dream that didn't want to be forgotten, but that he knew would be forgotten in the morning if he didn't do something about it right now. A memory that nagged at him and told him that it had been forgotten for more years than he wanted to try to figure out just then, but that didn't want to stay hidden anymore because it was more important than any of the other chores that marked Dale Sullivan's comfortable daily routine.

Sighing, Dale rose in the dark, felt his way to the adjoining living room – living in a place for sixty years pretty much assured a reasonable amount of intrinsic radar, or if not, then familiarity did – and followed the lone plug-in security light he'd got at Wal-Mart to the little white table on which sat his phone. A tattered yellow notepad rested there, along with a Bic pen with the familiar blue cap. Yawning, he jotted down the two words that wouldn't let him sleep.

He paused then, wondering if he should just stay up since he was already awake, but a glance at the clock told him it was 1:00 a.m. and decided him against it. Yawning mightily, he flopped back against the doorframe between the living room and the bedroom and used it as a backscratcher the way a cat or dog might do. He wished Hattie was here to scratch his back the way she used to. But she was gone all these many years just like David-the-Elder, whose death, though he was no blood kin to her, had seemed to take all the starch out of her, so that she'd had no urge to fight the cancer any longer.

But that was then; this was now, and there was David-the-Younger to consider. David-the-Younger who was, though Dale had no idea how or why, tied up with the phrase he had jotted down when it had come to him out of the realms of slumber.

Daddy's journal.

And that would be enough. Tomorrow he would start looking.

As for tonight ... sleep beckoned.

Sleep found him, too, and he didn't dream again, as far as he could tell. But he did think, for one moment, when he awoke again sometime between three and four by the luminous dial of the alarm clock, that he had heard something that sounded remarkably like bells.

Chapter IV

The Ring of the Sidhe

"**I have** seen the Sidhe!" David said to himself, flopping back against his pillow, arms folded behind his head.

It was not the first time those words had chimed in his thoughts that night; he had whispered them over and over as he passed wraithlike through the dark forest, across the yard, into the silent house – never certain if he walked or ran or moved by some remnant of supernatural power that lingered yet about him. He had seen but still could not quite believe; his mind recoiled from what it had witnessed. Already his body was falling asleep around him as he strove to make sense of what he had experienced.

He had seen the Sidhe!

The Sidhe.

Impossible.

Or was it?

That castle on Bloody Bald – the one he had almost convinced himself had been a hallucination or the work of an overly active imagination – it was real! He had seen it, had heard the horns of Elfland greeting dusk and dawn.

And his eye problem: the recurring itchy tingle. Was that what had enabled him to look into that other world? They had called it Second Sight. But how did it work? More to the point, how had he acquired it? He hadn't always had it; that was for certain.

He yawned, stretched luxuriously, and gazed across the room to the door where his brother had appeared before everything had ... changed.

Abruptly he had a troubling thought: *How much had Little Billy seen? What would he remember?* The little boy had seen the lights and heard the music; that much was clear. Yet he had not seemed to see anything during the actual encounter, at least not if his responses to David's actions were any indication. And the Sidhe had said they were visible to mortals – it was funny to think of oneself as a "mortal" – only if they chose. Or, he supposed, if the mortal in question had the Sight. For that matter, why had Little Billy not awakened, even when David laid him in bed? Was that more Faery magic? Or – as David was beginning to fear – something worse? He wished he'd thought to ask Nuada a few more questions, but it was too late now. He was probably lucky to have escaped with his skin. What had they got themselves into?

Lord, he was tired, he realized, as consciousness faded farther – not entirely of his own volition. But something still lingered in the back of his mind: one more thing that he needed to recall before he could sleep – something important. But whatever it was hovered tantalizingly just beyond recall and would not manifest. And as his mind dropped its guard to follow that elusive something, sleep found him instead.

Certainly it was not enough sleep, but when his mother hollered through the door that breakfast was ready and he'd better get it while it was hot because she was going to church and wasn't going to cook but once, David woke immediately, unexpectedly refreshed. At the same time, he realized what had been bothering him the night before. It pranced into his consciousness and sat there clear as day: He had forgotten to ask the Sidhe for the promised token of their meeting.

"Crap," he said aloud, as he climbed out of bed and pulled on his jeans, noting a few briars still caught in the worn denim. He paused to look in on Little Billy, who slept peacefully, a blissful smile upon his face, seeming none the worse for wear, then padded barefoot into the bathroom, where he splashed cold water on his face and ran a comb through his tangled hair.

And was just picking up his toothbrush when he felt a burning pain against his right thigh, like when Mike Wheeler had put a red hot penny down the back of his pants in the eighth grade. Reflex made him look down, half expecting to see either smoke or a spider. He saw neither, but the pain persisted. He stuck his hand into his right front pocket – and found the source of the heat. And felt it grow cooler even as he fished it out.

It was a silver ring, almost a quarter of an inch wide, entirely plain except for an indentation running completely around the circumference. Before he thought about it, he slid it onto his left ring finger. It fit perfectly.

Raising it to eye level, he examined it more closely. It was not as plain as he had thought; there was a pattern in the indentation: an intricate filigree of interlacing lines that passed over and under each other in an endless looping circle that he now recognized as an impossibly complex variation of Celtic knotwork. He found his gaze following that pattern. Simple it was, and yet fabulously complex. And beautiful – the most beautiful thing he had ever seen. It never occurred to him to wonder where it had come from. "I have seen the Sidhe!" he told the shirtless, tow-headed, awestruck boy in the mirror, who no longer seemed to be himself.

Little Billy ambled into the bathroom, yawning hugely and rubbing his eyes with his fists. David whirled around, glaring, and jerked his hand behind his back. "Don't you ever knock?"

"Door wasn't locked. Now get; I gotta go. Ma's lookin' for you."

"So what else is new?"

Behind his back David tugged at the ring. At first it didn't budge, then it came free too quickly – and slipped capriciously from his grasp to fall to the beige tile floor with a gentle *ping*. He snatched it on the second bounce and stuffed it back into his pocket, realizing as he did that trying to hide it was absolutely the wrong thing to do.

"What's that?" Little Billy demanded.

"Oh, just a ring." David tried to change the subject. "Did you sleep okay last night?"

"Yeah. Had some funny dreams, though."

Well, that's a relief! David thought.

Little Billy stared at him solemnly. "Where'd you get that ring?"

"Found it. What'd you dream about?"

"Nothin' much. Where'd you find it?"

"Up in the woods."

"When?"

"When–" David hesitated. He was not ready for this, not when there was so much else he needed to sort out. "– when me and Alec went campin' night before last," he finished lamely.

Little Billy's eyes narrowed. "Then how come I never seen it before? How come you never showed it to me?"

David was not pleased with his brother's persistence. "I'll show you my hand on your backside if you don't hush."

"You're hidin' somethin', ain't you, Davy? You didn't find that ol' ring, did you?"

71

David thought desperately. "I got it from the – from a – from a girl," he mumbled finally, making up the best excuse possible on such short notice, immediately aware of how lame it sounded.

Little Billy raised dubious eyebrows. "You got a girlfriend?"

"Don't tell. Please?"

"Okay," Little Billy agreed, a tad too quickly.

"Promise?"

"Yeah."

"Good. Oh, and thanks."

So much was whirling through David's mind as he drifted down the hall to breakfast that he felt numb. There was the night before to consider, of course, when things he had thought unreal – or at best safely distanced – had suddenly crowded hard and near upon him, so that the entire composition of reality had shifted around him. And there was the matter of the ring and the lie had had just told Little Billy and already regretted. He had always preferred telling as much of the truth as possible when in a difficult situation; it made getting caught harder. *Oh well,* he thought, as he slumped into the kitchen and sank down at the table that dominated the center of the room, *maybe the kid's already forgotten about it. At least he doesn't seem to remember last night. Thank heavens for that!*

That!

The encounter with the Sidhe!

Had it really happened? Well, this ring had to have come from somewhere, but still ... A chill raced down his back.

If things had not gone as they had – if he had not won the question game – he would not be sitting down to breakfast now. All at once he saw his parents with a new appreciation – and with a trace of sadness as well, for the drabness of their lives. He knew his own would never be drab again.

Still, David felt certain they would instantly pounce upon him as he pulled out his customary chair. God knew they had plenty of reason, if they suspected what he'd been up to – if they could understand it at all. Instead, his mother laid a shiny new romance novel facedown by the butter dish and got up to stick a couple more slices of bread in the toaster. Nothing out of the ordinary there. Big Billy was drinking strong black coffee with his bacon and eggs and reading the Sunday edition of the *Atlanta Journal and Constitution*. Business-as-usual there, too. David's guilt was still his own.

Little Billy bounced in, sat down across from him, and helped himself to a pile of bacon, eggs, and toast nearly as big as he was, with homemade blackberry jelly for the toast.

"You goin' to church this morning?" Big Billy asked loudly, without looking up.

The question so startled David from the apprehensive stupor into which he had lapsed that he nearly fell out of his chair. Fortunately, nobody noticed. "Hadn't planned to," he replied as nonchalantly as he could, pouring himself a cup of coffee – black for a change.

"Way you was talkin' yesterday, you better go," Big Billy rumbled in turn.

David suppressed the urge to respond with the inevitable observation that Big Billy didn't go either, but held his tongue. He had more important things on his mind just then than rehashing that tired old argument.

"David's got a girlfriend," Little Billy mumbled through a mouthful of toast.

David tried to look daggers in two directions at once and found he couldn't. Too much too fast. What had possessed his brother to blurt out his secret like that? It was not even a real secret, either, just a hastily contrived fabrication that could not stand close inspection, never mind cross-examination. He needed time to sort things out, to get his stories straight, or he'd get so far in he'd never get out again. Maybe his pa had a point; maybe he *should* go to church. Now that he had proof that at least some supernatural creatures existed, didn't it follow that there could be others?

Suddenly God was in his Heaven and all wasn't right in David's world at all. His ambivalent agnosticism was hanging in tatters like the scrambled eggs hanging from his fork.

"Don't talk with your mouth full, Little Billy," his mother warned. "Now don't let me tell you again!"

Little Billy chewed noisily for at least half a minute.

"I said David's got a girlfriend!" he repeated, looking so smug it took all David's willpower to keep from pushing his face down into his breakfast then and there.

Big Billy slowly lowered his paper and looked up incredulously, as though it had taken a while for the words to sink in.

David kicked at Little Billy under the table, missed, and got a chair leg instead. He grimaced and pretended interest in a slice of bacon.

"He's got a ring and everything," Little Billy went on, clearly delighted by David's discomfort. David discovered to his horror that he was wearing the ring again; there it sat, in plain sight, big as life. Big Billy was staring straight at it.

"Son-of-a-gun!" Big Billy exclaimed with unexpected good humor. "It's about time!" He set his coffee cup down hard and laughed. "Sneaky

73

little son-of-a-gun – like his daddy. Who is she, boy?" he continued conspiratorially. David was more than a little taken aback by his interest.

"Uh ... you don't know her. She's a girl ... a girl at school."

"You ain't been to school this summer," Little Billy pointed out.

"I didn't say it was this summer," David snapped, feeling as if he were digging his own grave.

"A girl!" Big Billy repeated. "Well, I'll be damned! You may make a man yet! But who is she? Don't do to be ashamed of your woman." His eyes narrowed. "You ain't done nothin' you'd be sorry for, have you?"

David looked horrified. Suddenly he felt *very* uneasy.

His mother seemed surprisingly unconcerned. She picked up her coffee and her romance novel, shuffled into the den, and turned on the TV. The raucous noise of cartoons sounded for a moment, followed quickly by the cracking hiss of fuzzing wavelengths and then somebody with an oil-on-water voice telling a nation of wretched sinners about Jee-ee-uh-sus-uh.

Big Billy changed tactics. "What's her name, Little Billy? Who's your brother's gal?"

Little Billy shrugged. "I dunno. All I know is he's got a ring he's been tryin' to hide, and I could hear him mumblin' last night about seein' the she."

David rolled his eyes skyward in complete dismay. Had he talked in his sleep as well? And so loud Little Billy could hear him from his room? Lord, he hoped not!

"A ring and everything! Must be serious. You give her one too, boy? Goin' steady?"

"Uh, not yet," David lied. Things were getting worse by the moment. "She just happened to have this one, so she gave it to me; it was sudden – unexpected, you know. I met her down in Atlanta at that Beta Club convention back before school was out. Nothing serious ... really," he added lamely.

"But you just said she was a girl at school," Little Billy noted.

"Maybe I *will* go to church," David announced, grasping at anything to change the subject and get away from the breakfast table. "I haven't been in a while."

"That might be a good idea," Big Billy affirmed, returning to his paper. "Get yourself some practice," he added, "before that Atlanta gal drags you there for another reason."

David got up and took a long cold shower – long because he needed to think, and cold because his wits were obviously still muddled, or he never would have got himself in such a fix. Neither helped. In the end church seemed the best option. Any assistance would do now.

Worse and worse, David groaned to himself, as he eased his mother's latest Crown Victoria into the gravel parking lot of the First Antioch and Damascus Baptist Church ten miles up the main highway, too late to sneak in unobtrusively. Normally, when he went to church at all, he accompanied Alec to the much more liberal MacTyrie Methodist; but that was usually when he'd spent Saturday night at Alec's house. David hadn't been to services in a Baptist church in easily three years.

As soon as the car had stopped moving, Little Billy was out of the backseat and off to play with some of his friends.

His mother got out with considerably more grace, and David couldn't help noticing that she did cut a fine figure – when she wanted to, and spent half the morning putting it on. It was also apparent that she was utterly delighted to be seen at church with her delinquent older son, since her husband – despite his talk – had not set foot inside a church in eighteen years except for weddings and funerals.

David took a deep breath, straightened his tie, and opened his door. Some girls he knew from school were standing on the semi-circle of steps at the entrance to the white frame building, watching his arrival with considerable interest and no little surprise. One of them pointed, and there was a chorus of giggles behind hands. David felt ridiculously self-conscious and wondered what sin they imagined he had committed that was bad enough to bring him to church. An even worse thought struck him, then, and he glanced down to check his fly, breathing a small sigh of relief that it was still securely fastened. He stuffed his hands into the pockets of his dark blue suit – it was getting a little tight through the armpits, he noted – and felt the coolness of the ring on his finger.

His mother was waiting for him at the foot of the steps. She smiled as he shuffled up the walk. "I ain't had a chance to be escorted into church by my handsome oldest son in a long time," she said, "not since he got to be taller'n me and – I'm gonna take it." She offered her arm, and he could not refuse, though he did mutter a sullen, "Yeah, tall, all right," under his breath as they stepped inside.

David paid even less attention to the sermon than he usually did. Instead, he spent literally every second trying to puzzle out a consistent story about the nameless girl from Atlanta he had so precipitously invented – and kept getting tangled up in it, especially as he had told two different versions of the story already. *And the confounded ring would not come off!* His knuckle had swollen just enough to make it stick. It sat there on his finger gleaming brightly, looking as smug as Little Billy had when he'd blurted out David's supposed secret at the breakfast table. And what could possibly have possessed his brother to tell that? He was usually reliable about secrets.

As David scanned the congregation, he noticed something else he didn't like. There was Little Billy sitting over on the other side with several of his Sunday school cronies, whispering together, giggling, and pointing at David.

Does everybody have to do that? David folded his arms and stared straight ahead while trying to work the ring off under his armpit. But it still would not budge. And to make matters worse, his mother expected him to hold the hymnal open for her every time there was a song or a responsive reading, which seemed to be about every other minute. He rather believed he'd prefer sitting there stark naked to sitting there with that silver ring on just then. It was not that he didn't want it; he just didn't want it on now, in church; didn't want folks to see it. But he had a feeling it was too late for that already.

He glared at Little Billy as his brother whispered into the ear of one of his cronies. Soon as they got home, he would give that little boy a talking-to he wouldn't soon forget. It was his fault, for telling everything. *No, it wasn't,* David knew full well; it was his own – for not being straight with the kid, among other things, and for the lack of self-control, which had led him into the woods in the first place. He was jealous, too, he realized: jealous of his actual secret. But he might warm Little Billy's bottom anyway. And he wanted to take another look at that trail up in the woods, this time by daylight.

But he didn't get the chance.

Because Liz phoned practically as he came in the kitchen door, to tell him the music show started at two, and to ask when he would be by to pick her up, and would not hear his excuses for not wanting to go.

And then it started to rain.

And then lunch was ready.

And right after lunch the phone rang again.

"Is this Lover Boy Sullivan?" came Alec McLean's familiar drawl.

David nearly hung up in disgust. "Sorry, there's nobody of that name here."

"That's not what I heard."

"What *did* you hear, then? I mean news travels fast an' all, but *that* fast?"

"Then you admit there is news?"

Damn, David thought, *should've kept my mouth shut.*

"I have my sources," Alec continued slyly.

"So do I, but I haven't heard anything."

"Sure. Sure."

"There's nothing to hear, Alec."

"That's not what your brother said at church this morning."

"I really should have given him to the undertaker," David muttered.

"What's that?"

David cleared his throat. "Little Billy has a way of ... exaggerating."

"He also has a way of telling the truth when it'll get you in trouble," Alec went on complacently.

"Look, Alec, level with me. What did you hear? From whom? And how?"

"What is this? The Spanish Inquisition? No, okay, seriously: Your brother told Buster Smith, who told his sister Carolyn, who told one of her crew, who told a mutual friend of ours who shall remain nameless, as I need my spies, who told me that you were sporting a ring at church this morning: a ring you said you got from a girl down in Atlanta – at Beta Club Convention, as a matter of fact."

So Little Billy's decided to believe that story. Well, it's easier to substantiate – or disprove.

"I'd hardly call it 'sporting'," David growled.

"Now, David," Alec continued gleefully, "it so happens that I was with you in Atlanta on the aforementioned occasion, and I don't recall you seeing any particular girl while we were there."

"You weren't with me every minute, either," David shot back – and could've kicked himself. Here he was again, building a maze of lies around the story – lies that intensified his dilemma rather than dispelling it. He had intended to try to be as honest with Alec as he could, given the circumstances. He just hoped Alec didn't invoke the MacTyrie Gang's oath never to lie to another member of the Gang.

"That's true. But if you're that fast a worker – well, there's a side of you I haven't seen before. No, you're not leveling with me, bro; something's going on." He sounded hurt.

David sighed. "Look, Alec, this is too complex to go into on the phone, and besides, walls have ears, if you know what I mean – and, anyway, I've got to take Liz to the bluegrass show this afternoon."

"Oh, right, I remember you telling me about that. Well, maybe we can talk about it then; Dad's got to go anyway, to help man the gate. I can catch a ride with him."

"Uh, Alec ... Liz," David faltered. He could tell he'd hurt Alec by not being straight with him; no need to make things worse.

"What?"

"Never mind. Look, Alec, I promise I'll give you the straight scoop the first chance we get. You won't believe it, but I'll give it to you. Now I really do have to go – all I need is to have Liz on my case."

"Sure – just one more thing: Aikin's trying to get the M-Gang together tonight for one more Risk marathon before him and Darrell go off to band camp and Gary heads out for vacation with his folks. You interested?"

"Oh man – jeeze! Any other time, I'd say 'don't start without me' but this time ... Yeah, I'm gonna do the smart thing and say 'I don't think so.' I doubt I'll be back from the fair until late, for one thing, and – well, I've got some other things I need to do. Sorry."

"It's okay."

"See you later, then."

David hung up the phone and squared his shoulders. Well, he had made one decision in the last thirty seconds: he would not lie anymore. To Alec, at least, he would tell the truth – as much as could be believed. If he told him that he had found the ring, which was literally true, he wouldn't be lying, at least not technically, and maybe he could by slow degrees initiate Alec into the rest of the mystery. It would take some doing, though. And there was still Liz to worry about. He tugged at the ring irritably, and was more than a little surprised when it slipped off. He started to take it back to his room, thinking that perhaps the best thing to do was simply to put it in a drawer and forget about it. But he suddenly found the idea of being separated from it incredibly disturbing, as if the ring had somehow bonded with him, to become almost a part of his own body.

On the other hand, if he put the ring on a chain around his neck, he'd still have it with him but it wouldn't show, and he wouldn't be tempted to put it on every five minutes, as would be the case if he carried it in his pocket. He went to look for a chain he remembered seeing in one of his dresser drawers. One problem solved. But there was still the matter of what to tell Alec – and Liz.

Liz Hughes's Diary

(Saturday, August 1)

Dear Diary,

   I'm sitting here wondering if I just made a fool of myself.
How did I do that? you ask. By calling David Sullivan just
now to remind him that we were going to the Bluegrass show
at the fair. Nothing major just a simple phone call to somebody
I've know for years, but ... I just don't know. I mean, he was
nice and all, and I was nice and all (of course), but I just never
know how to act around him(me being gone for the last school
year hasn't helped, either). But as I was saying ... I really
don't know how to act around boys in general, because frankly,
the Gainesville boys just left me cold, 'cause they were too busy
trying to be cool so I therefore ignored them, but there aren't
any boys around these parts that I'm interested in knowing well
enough to phone, much less almost ask out on a date. I can just
about count 'em on the fingers of one hand, in fact.

   Actually, I can. There's David, who counts as three, and
if I push came to shove, there's Alec McLean. Actually, he is a
friend and somebody I'd call, it's just that I'm also jealous of him
being David's best friend and it really drives me crazy sometimes

79

just thinking about all the time they spend together, and all the
"guy" things they do together, and I don't mean just "guy" things
like hiking and camping and stuff, I mean things like all night
bull sessions and sleeping over at each other's houses, and stuff.
And skinny dipping, which I really don't want to think about
because it makes me think about David without any clothes on
(see, I can't even write the word 'naked' here, let me try … naked,
naked, naked), and that's something I'm not quite ready to think
about yet. What I've seen looks pretty good, and the rest … well,
Maybe I'll find out someday.

But anyway, I guess Alec is a friend, and I guess he's
somebody I could at least try to be interested in. I mean, he's smart
(but not smart like David's smart, which is just smart because
he's curious about everything, apparently — but more 'geek' smart
like in 'making good grades' smart, but not really wondering about
anything), and he's not hard to look at, either, and he does have
more sense of style than David has, which is to say he has one,
whereas David appears to have none at all and would probably
wear jeans and T-shirts until they fell apart if it wasn't for his
mom. And he's fun to talk to, sometimes, and to see movies with,
and stuff. But when he and I are together, it's like the jealousy
thing, plus I'm always comparing him to David, and that's just
not fair to him. So I guess what I'm saying is that if David was
out of the picture somehow, I could get interested in Alec. But I
don't want to think about David being out of the picture.

And that still leaves one finger, which would have to be
Aikin Daniels, but in Aik's case, I could just take what I said
about Alec and ditto most of it, except that Aikin's even shorter
than David, and David is almost too short himself but I'm
hoping he'll still grow an inch or two, which is certainly possible,
given he's only sixteen. Oh, and except for the fact that at least
Alec will talk. Aikin won't unless it's something he's suddenly

got into at the moment, but even then it's mostly to the darned MacTyrie Gang. I think he's got the word 'enigmatic' tattooed on his butt. I guess the Gang would know. (See reference to skinnydipping.)

As for the rest of the aforementioned 'darned MacTyrie Gang,' (though I don't know why I even bother), Gary (as in Gary Hudson) has a nice bod and drives a nice car and is rich, but he also knows it (all three 'its'), plus he thinks he's God's gift to women, which rumor says he might be, but only in one certain way I am not going to mention even in my diary. Bottom line: too many girls have told him he looks like Tom Cruise. And sometimes their mothers have, too, which is really creepy.

Which leaves Darrell — that would be Darrell Buchanan, BTW. And he's just a goof. A sweet goof, sometimes, but still basically a goof. He'd fit in perfectly in 1960's California; unfortunately, he lives in Enotah County. I can't even imagine going out with him, even if he didn't have that equally goofy VW van he thinks is so cool. Actually, the only thing really cool about it is its name, Apocalypse Now, and I think David actually thought of that, so that brings us back to him.

And since I just noticed that it's nearly 2:00, I guess I'd better go make myself beautiful. Maybe If I'm lucky, David will even notice I'm a girl. He'd better.

Interlude III

In Tir-nan-og
(high summer)

Three drops of blood glittering on a fallen oak leaf.
Still bright, still liquid after half a day in the Lands of Men.
A black ant samples one and turns at once to ash.
Faery blood.
The blood of Ailill.

It had taken an absurd amount of effort to arrive at the place where Ailill found himself two days after the Riding of the Road on Lughnasadh – two days by the sun of Tir-Nan-Og; though scarce twelve hours had passed in the Lands of Men, for the cycles of the Worlds no longer coursed in tandem, nor would again until Samhain brought them once more into confluence: three months hence – by human time.

He had wasted the day after the Riding in fruitless contention with Nuada: words first, ever more heated, and then a trial of strength. Arm wrestling it had been, though not by Ailill's choice, but by Morrigu's suggestion and Lugh's consent, which he could not refuse. His left arm still ached from that encounter, too. Silverhand was strong, and the match had lasted from dawn until dusk with no victor, at which time Lugh had commanded them to call off their quarrel and each pursue his own ends and come back in a year and a day for judgment.

But Ailill could not wait that long for revenge. It had taken most of another day to find a place where he could work his summons undetected, and that was enough time wasted. He would begin now, at midnight on the second day: midnight, when his Power was at its peak.

The lakeshore where he stood would have been beautiful if he had spared time to look at it. It was framed by a beach of black sand on which tiny waves slapped with an oily sluggishness that suggested something more than water. The stuff smelled vaguely of cloves, and the handful he had dripped from his fingers sparkled amber in the moonlight, though he had had no desire to taste it.

The lake itself opened out behind him until its glittering surface merged with the starlit sky, which it mirrored perfectly. Steep slopes ringed that water on the sinister side, and tall warrior pines marched up them to stand in file at the crest like the soldiers for which they were named: the sparse cones of branches at their crowns for helmets and the curling strips of hard gray bark that frayed from their trunks in ring-like semicircles standing in for mail.

The only sound was the blurred whisper of the wind on the water and the forlorn cry of selkies among the rocks to the north.

Ailill glanced at the sky and nodded.

Midnight.

Time to begin the summoning.

It was too bad he could not work openly; too bad he could not work from the Track itself. But his kinsmen in Tir-Nan-Og seemed to have more regard for mortal men than he was accustomed to, and he had reason to suspect that any open hostility against the boy would stand him in poor stead with his hosts.

He would have to play a careful game, then, and one of great subtlety, for he had heard much of Lugh Samildinach and knew him to be a man of unbending nobility. Lugh would be a staunch opponent of his plan, if it came to his knowledge; for even Ailill's own lord and brother, Finvarra, did not know all the dark thoughts that filled the secret places of his mind. Not that he cared, really; the war would come anyway – *his* war: the war with humankind. But if he could capture the boy without Lugh's awareness – rob the humans of what little initiative the boy's knowledge might provide – the start of that war might be delayed until Ailill could orchestrate it to his best advantage and give him what he had for so many centuries wanted: the Kingship of the Danaans in Tir-Nan-Og and Erenn alike.

Turning to face northeast, he drew four deep breaths and closed his eyes. His brow furrowed briefly, and then he shook his head and crabwalked a dozen paces to his right, where he repeated the procedure. *This was it; this was the place!* This time he was in perfect alignment with the blood trace he had left on the Track and that human house where another kind of Power told him the mortal boy dwelt.

Kneeling on the damp sand, he closed his eyes again, took four more breaths, and set his Power to insinuating his consciousness through the World Walls. A moment only, that took: like feeling his way through a densely leaved forest shrouded in thick fog. Once through, however, it was a simple matter to locate the residue of Power that still clung to those three drops of blood.

He cleared his mind, extended his Power, called into being a bridge of thought linking himself with that tiny fragment of his own essence he had left as a focus.

Found it! Connected! Good!

Now to send the Power seeking its victim.

Ailill summoned the boy's image to his mind: shorter than most mortal men his age; solidly built, yet supple, like a tumbler or a swimmer; handsome for a human, with thick fair hair almost to his shoulders, dark brows, blue eyes, and fine white teeth in a full-lipped mouth that would grin too easily. The image brightened and sharpened. Ailill felt the line of Power grow taut, exerting a firm but gentle tug against his will. He would enter the boy's mind now, fix the line of Power, and draw him from his own World, as a fisherman would reel in a catch.

The image was clear. The boy was standing on the porch of that hovel that for his kind passed as housing. Now to touch the mind, to fix the Power, just so –

NO! There was other Power there! Power that felt his touch and raced to meet it like flames cast upon threads of raw silk. Coming toward him. Coming nearer. Hotter and hotter. And he could not break free of that Power greater than his own that had appeared from nowhere to shield the boy.

It was almost on him. He must break the link. He must break the link. Now! Now! Now! Now! Now!

He failed.

That other Power had him, ripped his spirit free of his control, filled it with a twisting, crisping agony so intense it seemed his soul itself were aflame.

Pain. Pain. Pain. Pain. Pain.

And then oblivion.

It was morning when the tentative nibblings of a twelve-legged crab upon his outflung hand returned Ailill to consciousness. He was not happy. The boy was protected; that much he now knew by bitter experience.

Protected by what, he did not know, though he intended to find out. There would be no more summoning from afar – of that he was very sure indeed. But perhaps there were other methods.

On the floor of a forest path less than half a mile from David Sullivan's home in rural northeast Georgia, three wisps of smoke rose from the blackened powder that had once been an oak leaf. The leaves touched by that smoke withered.

Chapter V

Fortunes

A combination regional fair, fiddlers' convention, livestock show, and arts-and-crafts exhibition, the Enotah Mountain Fair was held on the grounds of the county high school and lasted an entire week plus the weekends on either side.

For that brief period tiny, rural Enotah County boasted the same population as Atlanta, or so it appeared to those few residents who tried to follow their normal routines amid the steady stream of motor homes, SUVs, minivans, and premium imports. For the rest, mundane life slowed to a virtual standstill, as the locals indulged themselves in the biggest taste of outside reality – or fantasy, depending on how one defined it – many of them ever had.

It didn't take David and Liz long to explore the exhibits. They were both proud to see their culture on display, of course, but they'd seen it all before – often the exact same items year after year – and the bluegrass show developed a glitch in the sound system, so they gave up on it about seven o'clock and went to get something to eat and soak themselves in the sensory overload of the midway. David didn't really like that either; that is, he didn't like the crowds that jostled and pushed and grunted along in interminable lines, getting cotton candy on everybody and spilling popcorn all over the ground, where a thick layer of mud from the earlier shower had already made walking treacherous. It reminded him of what he had read about the La Brea Tar Pits, and he half expected to come upon a human hand sticking up out of the ooze, going down for the third and final time.

They met Alec while standing in line for the Trabant.

"I thought you guys were going to the music show," Alec said, staring intently at David, oblivious to the sour scowl that had darkened Liz's features.

David scowled as well. "We were, but the P.A. system went out, so we came down here to numb our senses with sight and sound and smell – and rather too much of the latter," he added, wrinkling his nose in the general direction of what purported to be a petting zoo, complete with undergroomed llamas. "I thought you were playing Risk with the M-Gang."

Alec glanced at his watch. "Not until eight. Gary can't make it until then." He looked at David expectantly.

David took a deep breath. "So, you want to join us?" He cast a furtive glance at Liz, then looked back at Alec and caught his friend's eyes in a subtle contact that said, *Bear with me and bide your time.*

Liz delivered a hard but unobtrusive kick to his shin, but it was too late.

David grunted and gestured at the Trabant, which spun before them like a giddily drunken top. "We're gonna ride this next."

Alec managed what was clearly a forced grin and produced a free pass, courtesy of his father. Liz didn't say anything at all. David guessed she had resigned herself to a threesome.

They were finally beginning to catch the rhythm of the ride's dips, plunges, and sudden changes in altitude, so that they could anticipate – and indeed enhance – the periodic weightless sensation they got when the Trabant would indulge in one of its precipitous dives, when the first raindrops fell.

At first David thought it was light-addled bugs, or someone's Coke brought illegally on the ride – it was impossible to see the drops themselves beyond the perimeter of pink and white lights that surrounded the ride, or to hear any sound above the shrill roar of four huge speakers that blared out soulless versions of tunes that had been popular five years earlier – but before long it was raining in earnest.

The operator tugged at the long red control lever and brought the ride to a halt before the passengers got entirely soaked.

"Let's go somewhere dry!" Liz cried, wiping a strand of sodden red hair from her face. "And fast!"

David pulled up the hood of his light nylon windbreaker and pointed toward a dull green tent that was marked outside by a hand-painted sign depicting a crystal ball beneath an upraised open palm. "There's a fortune teller. Maybe we could go in there. It doesn't look too busy."

In spite of the rain, they hesitated.

"Always wanted to get my fortune told," Alec ventured at last.

"I always wanted to see if they were as fake as they're supposed to be," Liz countered.

"I predict," David said, hunching over as the rain fell harder still and people began to drift toward overhanging awnings, "that we will soon meet a tall, dark fortuneteller. In fact, I think we'll do it *now!*"

He grabbed Liz's hand, and they sprinted the five or so yards, deftly sidestepping people and leaping half-submerged power cables as they went, leaving Alec to follow with his customary deliberation.

David was caught off guard by the sudden cessation of sound and water beneath the awning, though he could still see beyond it into a world now largely masked by the silver-lit curtain of water cascading off the scalloped edge as the shower became a downpour.

He also thought it a little strange that no one was selling tickets, but even as he was about to voice that thought, a vertical slit opened in the tent wall beside the open-palmed sign, and a very short, very fat woman with frizzy red hair and heavily made-up eyes came out and stood before them. She folded her arms imperiously and looked them up and down.

"Come in, my children," she said in a tone that left no room for refusal. The accent was not entirely convincing – something between Bela Lugosi and the Bronx, New York.

The three friends looked at each other and shrugged in unison.

"How much?" Alec asked, ever the pragmatist. "It doesn't say out here."

The woman shrugged, jingling a good ten pounds of silver-and-turquoise jewelry on her arms. "That depends on your fortune: no more than five dollars, no less than one."

Alec shot David a troubled look. "You got an extra fiver?"

"If I need to, yes."

Alec sighed and nodded.

"Okay," David said finally. "We'll all come, then."

"Yes, you will," the fortuneteller agreed. She turned and led the way into her tent.

"So much for a tall, dark fortuneteller," Alec muttered into David's ear.

They found themselves in a small, square anteroom whose walls were hung with stained and faded red velvet drapes probably pirated from a defunct theater. A cheap fake-Persian rug covered the canvas floor, and there were several low couches upholstered in red plush and heavily scarred with cigarette burns.

The fortuneteller gestured them into one of the cleaner sofas, and studied each of them for a long time, one hand cupping her chin, index finger extended along her jaw. She looked longest at David, then sighed and pointed at Alec. "You first."

Alec held back. "Can't we all go together?"

The woman's eyes narrowed. "I don't want to confuse the spirits. Now come or not. Will you know your fate, or deny it?"

Alec rose reluctantly, and the woman motioned him through a slit in the back wall of the anteroom.

David scratched his ring finger unconsciously. It was itching, though the ring itself now hung upon a cheap pot-metal chain around his neck.

"Well, she's not your typical gypsy, anyway," Liz whispered. "I wonder if she reads palms, or uses cards, or crystal balls, or the Tarot, or what."

"Or Second Sight?" David suggested quietly.

"What's that?"

"The ability to see things not in this world. Some folks in Scotland and Ireland claim to have it: the ones who say they've seen the Faeries, among others."

Before David could continue, the slit parted and Alec rejoined them, peering doubtfully at his palm.

"So what did she tell you?" Liz asked, looking up.

"She said for you to go next – by name, as a matter of fact, which I find interesting – and beyond that I will say no more until we're out of here and can all tell the tale one time and get it over with."

Liz got up and rather self-consciously passed through the slit. Alec sat opposite David, hands draped between his knees, a pointing finger tracing the pattern on the rug.

"Very strange," he murmured. "Very strange."

David didn't reply.

Alec continued to stare at the rug. "I don't think Liz likes me," he whispered after a while.

"I think she has another problem with you, but that's a discussion for another time and place. Let's not talk about it now, okay?"

"Okay," Alec conceded glumly. He looked at David. "So ... let's see the famous ring."

David sighed, fingering the chain. "Famous or infamous, I'm not sure which."

"Come on, let's see it."

David grimaced and fished the ring out of his shirtfront. Alec took it on his palm and examined it carefully, but said nothing. He looked puzzled.

"You sure you got this from a girl?"

"That's what I need to talk to you about," David murmured as he secreted the chain again.

"So talk."

"I don't quite know where to begin –"

"Next," Liz interrupted as she pushed through the curtain, a troubled expression clouding her face.

David got up and parted the barrier, aware at once of the difference in temperature between the muggy outer room and the cooler inner one; aware as well of the overwhelming scent of incense mixed with cigarette smoke, and of the uncertain light cast by four dark-blue candles that stood atop knobby brass pedestals in the corners of the chamber. But most of all he was aware that he could hear absolutely nothing of the outside world. He might have been transported to deep space or the bottom of the sea. He felt the ring warm slightly on his chest.

The fortuneteller sat behind a small round table draped with black velvet, on which, true to expectation, sat a bowling-ball-sized globe of some transparent substance. Oddly, it did not look like plastic, or really like glass. Half-seen shapes seemed to swirl within it, making David's eyes itch. Next to the ball was stacked a worn deck of Tarot cards with the top card turned face up to show the Magician. Lying on the velvet beside it was the Knight of Wands.

"Come in, David ... Sullivan, I believe?" The woman closed her eyes and extended a plump hand in his direction, as if hoping to find confirmation written on the air in Braille.

"Right!" David cried, genuinely surprised, as he seated himself on the small stool opposite. "How did you know?"

"I'm a fortuneteller; I'm supposed to know." The Bela Lugosi part of the accent had faded. She paused, staring more intently at David, then nodded. "For you there will be no charge."

"Why not? Just out of curiosity, I mean?"

The woman threw up her hands theatrically, setting the jewelry to jingling again. "Is it not obvious, my son, that it is I who should seek guidance from you? It is many years since I have met one with the Sight."

"How could you tell?" David gasped.

The woman's manner of speech began to change imperceptibly, as if she drew from parts of herself she did not normally access.

"Your eyes: They do not merely look; they see. And they have a gleam of silver about them, if you know how to look for it. I have not the Sight myself, but my mother did. It was she who taught me to recognize the signs."

"But I don't even know how I got it. Everything was normal until two days ago, and then ... all hell broke loose."

"Tell me!"

"You'd think I'm crazy."

"If I had not wanted to know, I would not have asked."

"I've seen ... things."

"What kind of things?"

"A ... a ... castle on a mountaintop, for one."

"But more than that? Something more frightening?"

"Yes."

"And you've never seen such things before?"

"Never. But I would've liked to – and that's what bothers me. I have such a strong imagination that I thought –"

"You were wrong. You have the Sight, and you have acquired it recently, and there are only a very few ways that could have happened without you intending it." She looked at David, as if to read the unasked question on his face, then said, "Wait here."

With that, she rose and disappeared through a rift in the curtains opposite the entrance. When she returned, she held an ancient brown book, as weathered as an old leaf, and almost as small.

"This is *The Secret Common-Wealth*," she said. "My mother gave it to me, and she had it from her mother, and so on back to Scotland. I have no children, nor am likely to have any, now. You are the one to take the book. It may contain answers – *some* answers to your questions. Whether what it contains is true, I cannot say, but my mother believed it, and she had no reason to lie."

David hesitated before touching the volume, awed by the magnificence of such a gift from a total stranger. "I can't accept this!" he whispered.

"Your fate may depend on it."

Reluctantly David took the book and secreted it in the pouch-pocket of his windbreaker. "I have to confess," he said, feeling rather awkward and squirming a little on the stool, "that I thought you were a fraud." He cleared his throat. "Well, actually, I thought that all carnival fortunetellers were frauds – but I'm not so sure about you now."

"Oh, I am a fraud," the woman replied matter-of-factly, clearly undisturbed by David's bluntness. "Certainly a fraud compared to you, if you chose to use your power – which I see you do not. But most people have so little fortune – real fortune, that is – that there is nothing for even the gifted to see. All they want to know about is love and death and money, so that's what I tell them. But one in ten thousand, maybe, has a fortune that I can read – and such a one are you."

"What about Liz and Alec?"

"Their fortunes are bound up with yours. They can tell you what I told them if they so choose." She removed a cigarette from a tarnished silver case behind the table but did not light it.

"What about my fortune? Can you tell me anything?"

The woman leaned forward. "Let me see your hand."

David laid his right hand on the table.

"No, not that one; the left one. That is the hand where your fate is written."

David laid his left hand palm-up on the black velvet beside the crystal ball.

"Can I see the ring as well?" the woman asked after a moment.

David was at once suspicious. "What ring?"

"This finger wants to wear a ring."

Frowning, David slipped the chain over his head and placed the ring on the table where, to his surprise, it glowed softly.

Equally surprising, the fortuneteller picked up the crystal ball and set it on the floor, as if fearing some reaction between the two. A long time passed as she looked at David's hand, but not once did she touch it. Neither did she touch the ring. Finally she spoke.

"It's all threes and sixes," she declared. "And one. You are one of the three, and the three are stronger than one, yet the one is mightiest of the three. Six people you love, and those six people will cause you pain for the pain you bring on them. Three weeks – the next three weeks will see you tested: a testing such as you have never experienced before."

She paused and studied his hand more carefully, following each line to its termination, examining each mound and hollow, her red-lacquered nail always a hair's breadth above his flesh. "Three years will pass, and maybe three again, before all is done and you may rest, your labors ended. But remember, David, that among these threes and sixes you are one, prime and indivisible, and thus strong. You will have to find the pattern, but if you can survive the next three weeks and remain as you are, you will grow stronger. But, David Sullivan, if you choose the wrong road at the end, there may be no more roads for you at all."

David felt his throat go dry. "You mean I might die?"

The woman shrugged. "Death is always a possibility. He sits beside all of us, near or far. He is everywhere, if you look, but you are untrained in the looking, and I caution you not to try. Yet you will see Death sitting beside someone close to you in less than two weeks' time: of that I am certain. That is all I can tell you."

The fortuneteller picked up the ring by its chain, lowered it into

David's palm, and folded his hand around it. Then she took a deep breath and forced a smile. "Thank you for letting me meet you," she said. "Long has it been since I met one like you, and never in this short-sighted land. As I have told you, I ask no payment, but if you would touch your ring to the crystal here, I would be grateful." She stooped to retrieve the glassy sphere. "It won't hurt the ring and it might help the ball. If nothing else, maybe I'll be able to see something in it besides cheating husbands and new cars." She lit her cigarette and, after David had complied with her request, winked at him one last time before waving him away with her free hand, her metal-linked bracelets tinkling softly.

David reached out impulsively, clasped her pudgy hand, and kissed it with awkward chivalry. "Thanks," he whispered. Then, more loudly: "If you're here next year, I'll return the book. I promise."

The woman smiled. "If I am here next year, perhaps I will accept it. But for now, take it, read it, study it. It may be your only strength or your only shield. Now go! Compare notes with your friends."

"Well ... ? Well ... ?" Alec asked eagerly as David returned to the anteroom.

"Well?" Liz echoed. "You sure were in there a long time, compared to us. What were you doing?"

"Talking shop," David replied a little too lightly. "I was getting a few pointers on lycanthropy."

Liz frowned. "Huh?"

"Becoming a werewolf," Alec chuckled.

"Not really," David continued. "But let's not talk here."

They went back outside, blinking into the glare of gaudy lights. The rain had stopped, and the crowds were fumbling their way back to the rides. The rich soup of mud was even worse than before.

"Ugh!" Liz growled. "We gotta walk through that?"

"Let's take our shoes off; we can wash our feet before we leave," David said.

"Ugh," Liz repeated.

"Why, Liz, don't you like the feel of mud squishing up between your toes?" Alec teased.

"I'll squish mud up against your nose if you don't shut up, McLean!" Liz flared, and then broke into laughter over her inadvertent rhyme.

David hunkered down, untied his sneakers, and picked them up.

"I'm takin' mine off, anyway. Anybody rides in my car has gotta have clean feet." He stalked off, leaving Alec and Liz frantically pulling laces in the mud.

Fifteen minutes later, they had found a place where they could talk without fear of surveillance: the unused chemistry lab of the high school building. Alec had been a lab assistant the year before and possessed a key no one had asked him to return, so they had crept in and were now sitting on the floor below window level, the room illuminated only by a blue mercury vapor lamp outside, exactly like the one at David's house.

"So spill it," Alec burst out.

David didn't want to lie to his friends, but knew he couldn't tell them the entire truth, either – at least not yet. Fortunately, he'd had time to decide on a ploy during their trek up to the lab. "There's not really much to tell," he began. "She just told me we'd be seeing a lot of each other for the next few weeks, and that our fates were bound up together."

Alec's eyes narrowed. "Is that all? You talked longer than that."

"Well, she told me some crap about marriage and death and cars, but nothing very specific – as you'd expect. What did she tell you guys?"

"There you go again, David," Alec grumbled, "not being straight with us – though I guess I'll have to live with it. But I think she told you a lot more than you're saying – serious stuff, too, judging by your expression when you came out." He slapped the metal leg of a lab stool before continuing. "All she told me was to help you during the next few weeks as much as I could: that you were under a sore trial but didn't know it yet and would need my aid."

Liz looked up in surprise. "That's almost exactly what she told me: that three were mightier than one, but one was mightiest of the three – but that none would survive without the other two. That ... was weird."

David looked straight into her eyes and smiled. "All the same B.S."

"What did you expect from a fortuneteller?"

"I dunno. Never been to one."

"I'm not going back, either," Liz said. "Gave me the creeps. But I think she was serious. It didn't sound like what I expected to hear. It just felt ... right."

Alec nodded. "Yes, it did."

"You'll get no argument from me there," David agreed. "Now, let's go wash off this mud and go home. We can use the restrooms up here."

95

David decided to drop by the Risk game after all. He really did owe it to his second, third, and fourth best buddies, with the result that it was very late indeed when he finally got back to Sullivan Cove. Happily, no one was up, which meant he finally had some time to himself. He grabbed a fresh bag of sour-cream-and-onion Ruffles from the kitchen and crawled into bed with the fortuneteller's book. He'd waited long enough for answers, and he was going to get them now.

Before diving into the text, however, he examined the book itself, noting for the first time – and with some bemusement – its complete title:

the secret common-wealth;
or, a treatise displaying the chief curiosities among the people of scotland as they are in use to this day.

It was a brittle old volume and very thin – almost a pamphlet, really – and written in an archaic style that was often difficult to decipher not surprising when he learned that it had been composed in 1692. The author, a Reverend Robert Kirk, had been a Scottish minister who had become so interested in the local fairy lore that he had written the first serious study of the fair-folk, and had apparently come to believe in them himself.

David flipped the pages rapidly. Halfway through a passage caught his eye:

"There be odd solemnities at investing a man with the priviledges of the whol Misterie of this Second Sight. He must run a tedder of hair (which bound a Corps to the Beir) in a Helix about his midle from end to end, then bow his head downward: (as did Elijah in I King 18.42.) and look back thorow his legs untill he see a funerall advance, till the people cross two Marches; or look thus back thorow a hole where was a knot of fir. But if the wind change points while the hair tedder is ty'd about him, he is in peril of his Lyfe. The usuall method for a curious person to get a transient sight of this otherwise invisible crew of Subterraneans (if impotently and over-rashly sought) is to put his foot on the Seers foot, and the Seers hand is put on the Inquirers head, who is to look over the Wizards right shoulder (which hes an ill appearance, as if by this ceremonie, an implicite surrender were made of all betwixt the Wizard's foot and his hand ere the person can be admitted a privado to the art.)

"Then will he see a multitude of Wights like furious hardie men flocking to him hastily from all quarters, as thick as the atomes in the air, which are no nonentities or phantasm, creatures, proceeding from ane affrighted apprehensione confused or crazed sense, but Realities, appearing to a stable man in his awaking sense and enduring a rational tryal of their being ..."

There were a slew of footnotes giving additional Biblical quotations cited by Reverend Kirk. David scanned them all, but did not truly absorb what he read.

So! He smiled in satisfaction. *It must've been the funeral procession Little Billy and I saw.* He had definitely seen it from between his legs. And had felt very strange indeed immediately thereafter.

But that was a difficult concept for a rational man to accept. There was simply no logical connection between the two events that he could see, not even the most tenuous sort of cause-and-effect. And then there was that business about a "tether that has bound a corpse to a bier." He had certainly done no such thing – yet he just as certainly had the Sight. Which didn't make sense, unless the bit about the tether was just a piece of nonsense to keep people from trying the process willy-nilly. Which *did* make sense, if the folk with the Sight had enjoyed a special position in the community and didn't want everybody muscling in on the act – and had therefore made up a complicated bit of mumbo-jumbo to obscure the actual process.

It would take some doing, after all, to bind a corpse to a bier with a tether of hair and then remove it later. And what kind of hair would be long and strong enough for that, or to wind in a helix about one's middle? Surely nothing human! He giggled. It seemed he knew something that Reverend Kirk hadn't.

Even more interesting was that bit about giving the Sight to someone else. Now that was something he probably ought to try – on Alec, maybe, or Little Billy. He reread that section to be certain he had it right, then checked the footnotes, which he had skipped earlier. Apparently the main thing was that the would-be seer was supposed to surrender himself completely to the control of the experienced one. The experienced seer would then assert his physical domination by the method Kirk had described, while at the same time confirming his control by proclaiming "Everything between my hands and my feet is mine," or some similar phrase.

Well, that's interesting, David said to himself. *Very interesting indeed.*

He spent most of the next hour examining parts of the book he had slighted earlier. Along the way he learned how Reverend Kirk's body had been found atop a supposed fairy mound, and how some people had said he had been taken by the fair-folk and a changeling left in his place; and that there had been various attempts at setting him free, all of which had failed. He shuddered at that last, thinking how perilously close he had come to that same fate.

His eyes had grown tired by then, for it was very late, so he turned out the light and snuggled down under the covers – only to realize that his mouth tasted far too strongly of the chips he'd been eating. Wearily, he got up and went into the bathroom to brush his teeth.

He had just found his toothbrush and reached for a tube of Crest when he felt a flash of heat from where the ring lay on his bare chest. At the same time, he became aware of a voice: but a voice like none he had ever heard. It was so low as to seem almost subliminal, but it was harsh, too, not unlike a growl. And it was strangely inflected, as if the mouth that shaped it was unaccustomed to the subtleties of human speech. Sweat sprang out on his body as he gazed about the tiny room in search of the source of those half-heard words, but not until it spoke again could he pinpoint its origin.

The darkness beyond the bathroom window.

A chill raced down between his shoulder blades and lodged at the base of his spine. His muscles tensed. His heart double-thumped. Finally, he took a deep breath and eased the curtain aside, keeping his eyes slitted, dreading what he might see.

It was as he feared.

No man's shape greeted him there. Rather, the massive head and front paws of an immense white dog stood out against the yard light's glow. Its claws rested on the windowsill; its enormous eyes burned like red-hot coals.

They stared at each other for a timeless moment, and then the dog began to speak again, and this time he could understand its words. "One of your own kind, David Sullivan, has said that a little knowledge is a dangerous thing. And so it is. You have a little knowledge, and you seek to make it more, and so it is a dangerous thing."

David started to reply, but found that his mouth was so dry he couldn't speak. He swallowed clumsily. The toothbrush slipped from his fingers and fell to the floor with a plastic clatter.

"Now it is well known among Faery-kind," the dog continued, "that certain ... things have become known to mortal men – certain shards of a greater knowledge that are perhaps not entirely appropriate for them to possess. Many have sought that knowledge, but few have found it, and fewer still have profited by that lore.

"But where you are different is that you have knowledge backed by proof: the proof that lies gleaming upon your chest. And such knowledge places you in a dangerous position indeed: dangerous both to yourself – for in Ailill Windmaster you have made a powerful enemy – and to certain others who sometimes share your World."

The dog hesitated, though its gaze never left David. "Thus it is," it went on at last, "that you have two choices: If you end this quest for knowledge now, when it is scarcely begun, and try to forget what you have seen and turn your thoughts to other paths, there may still be time to forestall Ailill's intervention. But if you continue as you are, never again will your life be as it has been heretofore. Do not seek to know more than you do or prepare to pay the price of that knowledge."

And it was gone.

David felt the hair prickle once again on his neck and arms. He picked up the toothbrush and rinsed it off mechanically, but he found that no matter how hard he tried, he could not hold his hands steady. The ring continued to send forth pulses of low heat, and to glow softly. A final shudder shook him, and the coiled fear began to disperse.

Well, he thought, *maybe I'd better leave that trail alone for a while.*
Or, he added, *maybe I should memorize the fortuneteller's book.*

Alec McLean's Journal

(Sunday, August 2)

Well, oh, most trusted journal, we meet again! And let me just get right to the point and say something really strange just happened.

Short form: David was acting even weirder today than he was on Friday, namely that he's suddenly acquired a girlfriend when there's no way in the world he can have acquired a girlfriend, unless he's twins, or something, and to cut to the chase (I'll fill in details later, 'cause I don't' feel like writing boring stuff when I've got interesting stuff burning holes in my fingertips), I decided the smart thing to do was for me to meet him at the fair.

So I did.

Of course Liz was with him, and she wasn't exactly a model of hospitality, though I guess I can kind of understand where she's coming from, given that I can be pretty jealous of folks hanging out with my number one buddy as well. But anyway, he wound up coming by Aikin's place after he dropped Liz off after we'd all kind of been zapped by the fortuneteller at the fair, and actually, he was pretty much himself, at least in the sense that he played his standard Risk game: piling armies in Australia 'til it wouldn't hold any more, while Gary did the same in South America, and then playing the plague card (we've added a few cards to try to spice up the game, like requiring double damage when you fight across certain boundaries, and all that), so that Gary lost half his armies.

But anyway, he was pretty much his old self.

Which means I was pretty much *my* old self. Or maybe I wasn't, since Gary had snuck some brews out of his daddy's stash, and I'd kind of got into them a little more than I usually do, which is why what I think is strange might not have been strange at all.

Basically, when David left, I remembered that I'd forgotten to pay him back the five bucks I owed him for the fortuneteller, so I ran out to give it to him, only he was already too far gone by then to see or hear me. But what's weird is that there was this really enormous white dog chasing along behind him. Only there aren't any dogs like that in Aik's neighborhood, as far as I know.

But anyway, I yelled at David (which I wouldn't usually have done, but I had been drinking just a little), and what's really weird is that David didn't slow down, but the dog did: just stopped dead in its tracks and turned and looked at me. And I swear it spoke. And when it spoke, it said, "You do not see me; you will forget you ever saw me, your mind will not accept that I exist."

And it felt just then like whatever I'd had to drink was, like, ten times as much. So I headed back here, which is to say home, and immediately sat down to write this stuff down while I'm still thinking about it, like I used to write down dreams, or whatever.

Or whatever.

What am I writing, anyway?

(Monday, August 3)

Strangest thing just happened. I just sat down to do a routine check on some emails I'd sent yesterday, and to add some stuff about the game to my journal, only to find that I'd apparently deleted every last thing I wrote last night instead of saving it. What's worse is that I can't remember what I did write; it's like my brain just slips sideways from it. I must've had more booze than I thought – have to watch that, I guess. There was some phrase David used yesterday that I was gonna look up on the 'Net, too, but I don't remember what that was, either.

I'm supposed to spend next weekend over there anyway, so maybe it'll come to me then.

Maybe.

I hope I'm not going bonkers.

 PART II

prologue III

In Tir-nan-og

It *is good to be an eagle,* thought Ailill, who now wore that shape. Wings longer than his man's form was tall swept from his shoulders, caressing the air like the fingers of the most sensuous of lovers. Feathers black as his hair covered his body; eyes sharp as his devious wit peered over a beak cruel as the desire for vengeance that burned like a coal in his heart.

It is good to fly, Ailill added to himself. *It is good to rule the air, to ride winds no mortal bird could dare, to breathe air too thin for their ill-made lungs, to fly so high that stars appear, so high the curve of the mortal World shows when I look down.*

It is good to gaze upon the Lands of Men and think how it would be to crush them, to beat them into the iron-sodden dirt from whence they came. Or better yet, to hurl them into the cold blackness that surrounds them. Tenuous indeed is their hold on that World – if they only knew.

He blinked his yellow eyes and spiraled higher on the merest hint of an updraft, then drew upon his Power and looked down again, to see both Worlds – the round Lands of Men clustered close and thick and fearful, bound all unknowing within the less easily described shapes of the far-rung Realms of Faerie, all laced about by the glittering golden lattice of the Tracks that wrapped all Worlds and rose past him into space – and time as well – binding them all together in ways at once too complex and too subtle for even the Men of Dea to comprehend. Though not *of* Faerie, the Faerie-born could travel upon them – if they dared – and mortal men as well, if they had the art, as none now did, save perhaps that detestable boy Nuada had virtually snatched from his grasp, and who had cost him considerable trouble and no little pain in the bargain.

Nuada!

The tendons that worked Ailill's claws tightened when that name entered his thoughts. He ground the edges of his beak together, then vented a harsh shriek of rage into the cold empty air that surrounded him.

Nuada Airgetlam, whom men called Silverhand. Once King of the Danaans in Erenn; once disarmed in the most literal sense by a blade of Fir Bolg iron; once healed, then slain by a king of the Fomori, half in Faerie, half in the Lands of Men; and then once more reborn, though oddly enough without the iron-cursed arm – and yet another barrier between Ailill and the war he desired between the two Worlds: between men and gods, if men chose to call them that. But there was another thing Ailill wanted now, and that was vengeance: vengeance against Nuada, who had thwarted his plan and made him look the fool in the bargain; and against the mortal boy, David Sullivan, who somehow bore some arcane protection whose nature Ailill could not discover, nor his Power break.

He was the unknown, the unloaded die, the rogue element in the plan Ailill was forming.

He is the one I must master; he is the one whose blood this body would taste this day if I gave myself to it, and if someone – or something – did not prevent it. That is what I must discover, and if it is an object that protects him, then that object I must either possess or destroy.

The eagle spoke to him then, in that part of his mind where instincts had their dwelling. And what it spoke of was hunger.

Ailill gazed about himself: at the glitter of stars in the black sky, then at the Worlds – both Worlds – spread below, gleaming in the embrace of the golden lattice of the Tracks.

And then he narrowed the focus of his vision, so that he gazed only into the Lands of Men.

And there he saw what his eagle-body sought. He folded his wings and dived, felt the air thicken about him, felt his feathers grow warm from the force of that fall, knowing that if he put upon himself the substance of the Mortal World, as he must do to remain there for more than a brief time, the thing men called friction would burn him to ash before he reached his goal.

But he was not of that substance. This body, like his man-body, was formed of the stuff of Faerie, and so was bound by the laws of that World now.

The land spread wide below him: the distant coast a thin-edged glimmer on one horizon, the mountains faint wrinkles on another.

And still he fell.

Fields and rivers took form, and those same mountains rose around him. Trees became distinct, and then the leaves that clothed them. He saw only with the eagle's eyes now, and let the raptor's own small mind claim ascendancy, so that instincts burned in the place of thoughts.

The eagle saw its quarry: long-eared, brown-furred, white tuft a marker of despair at its tail. Red became the color of the eagle's thoughts, as the hidden part that was Ailill called upon his Power and wrapped his eagle-shape in the substance of the Lands of Men. Only thus could it feed there.

The rabbit moved beneath him, running, frantic, sensing the black-winged doom that was suddenly falling toward it out of a clear blue sky.

Now! Wings out! Tail fanned! Brake! Brake! Legs down, talons extended!

There was impact and a squeaking, and then the muffled sound of feathers brushing against dry grass.

An eagle's shape is an excellent shape for certain purposes, Ailill affirmed, as he prepared to feed. But there are even better shapes a clever man might wear to achieve his goals.

He gave himself to the eagle then – and red became the color of the grass as Ailill, who was the eagle, feasted.

Chapter VI

swimming
(saturday. august 8)

"IT'S hot," Alec McLean announced from where he half-sat, half-sprawled on the edge of the Sullivans' front porch. "Too hot to spend three hours helping your dad pull the engine out of that old wreck of a truck he just bought."

"This is Georgia in August; it's supposed to be hot," David retorted, taking a long draught from a Dr. Pepper before setting it down beside him in the porch swing. Down the hill and across the cornfield he could see a steady stream of traffic flashing by, as it would for the next four months. Tourist season had begun with the fair, and there was nothing he could do about it. "Wildwood Flower" would resonate in his mental ears for months.

"This is the Georgia mountains in August," Alec countered obstinately. "It's not supposed to be a hundred degrees in the shade!"

"At least there *is* shade." David gestured around the porch. "And, anyway, who are you to tell me what it's supposed to be like up here? I was born here; you're a flatland ferriner."

A large yellow tomcat jumped unexpectedly into the swing, upsetting the Dr. Pepper into David's lap.

Alec's face contorted with laughter. "Still wettin' your pants, are you, *hillbilly!*"

"Damn."

"Better not let your mom hear that!"

"Damn!" David repeated, louder, as he got up and disappeared into the house, to return a moment later with a wet dishrag, with which he swabbed the swing and the floor beneath, where the soda had leaked through. He had not changed his sodden jeans.

He grinned at Alec. "Leastwise part of me's cool now."

"Some way to get cool!"

Silence fell on their conversation. The air stilled. The only sounds were the muffled roar of the cars on the highway and the soft creaking of the swing. They did not look at each other. David stared into space over Alec's head; Alec methodically dismembered a daisy from one of the pots perched precariously along the porch railing.

"You've been acting funny lately," Alec ventured at last. "Besides the business with the ring, I mean, which is another matter entirely. I've given up trying to get the straight scoop on *that*, and Lord knows I've been trying all week."

The petals continued to fall. He looked up at his friend and their gazes met: blue and gray. Alec's tone was soft, but something about it hit David like a blow, as if he'd just heard one of his secrets told aloud in church.

David frowned and blinked, breaking the contact. "I always act funny; it's the way I am."

"I know that," Alec replied, folding his arms across his chest and stretching his legs along the top step. "Like when you tried to turn yourself into a werewolf that time. But that's not what I mean. Thing is, I can't really tell you exactly what I *do* mean, except that – well, it's like … like you're not all here, or something. You seem distracted a lot, or … whatever."

He paused, swallowed, felt for the wall behind him before continuing. "I can't explain it any better, but you – you stare into space a lot more than you used to, and I see you looking at things funny sometimes – like you've never seen 'em before, or something."

David did not reply, but he began to rock the swing gently.

"You're doing it now, Davy. You're not half listening to me. It's like we can kid around and all, like we were just doing; but then suddenly you're off somewhere." He swallowed again and took a deep breath. "I mean, look, Sullivan; we've been friends practically forever and never kept anything from each other – even before we started the MacTyrie Gang – and now something's bothering you – or something's happening to you – or has happened to you – and you won't tell me what it is. It's like you're going somewhere I can't follow: like a barrier where there's never been one – and I don't like it!"

He flung the completely dismembered daisy far down into the yard. The yellow tomcat made a tentative dash toward it before retreating into the shadows under the house.

"I'm sorry," David sighed. "Would it help if I did something weird now?"

"You *are* doing something weird!" Alec snorted, looking up, with an expression of hurt on his face that shocked David. "You're not being straight with me, and you've never done that – not this way."

"If I told you, you'd never believe me."

"I've heard that line before – and never believed *it*!"

David took a deep breath. "I have seen the Sidhe."

His eyes flashed for a moment as his gaze again locked with Alec's and broke as suddenly. The line of his mouth was set.

Alec shook his head and looked down. "You're right. I don't believe you."

"Then you won't believe that I got the ring from them."

Alec stood up and began to pace the length of the porch, hands clinched into white-knuckled fists. Damn it, Sullivan," he spat, "Will you never tell me the truth about that bleeding ring? 'You got it from a girl.' 'You got it from the fairies.' Next you'll be saying you got it from a frigging man from mars! For Pete's sake, Davy, don't you see? I don't know what to believe anymore. I might've believed you if that was the story you told first, but it's not – so can you blame me for not believing you now?"

He whirled around abruptly and stood glowering at David. He was shaking. The swing had stopped.

"I don't blame you," David said softly. "Sometimes I don't believe it myself. But I've got to do something about it. It's about to drive me crazy."

"That's your problem," Alec snapped. "You're the one who's been flashing it around like it was the crown jewels. I'd have kept it quiet if I didn't want people to know about it, and I sure as hell wouldn't have told my loud-mouthed baby brother." He pounded the porch rail, but the white heat of his anger was already subsiding. From the depths of the house came the sound of the telephone ringing.

"Twenty-twenty hindsight."

"You could, of course, just get rid of it and say that everything's over. That's what I'd do."

David chuckled grimly. "I've actually considered that – but I feel really uncomfortable without it, like something awful will happen if I don't have it with me, or if I lose it. I nearly get sick to my stomach just thinking about it. The chain's a compromise."

"Well, don't complain to me. You've made your bed; you can lie in it."

"David! Telephone!" David's mother called from inside.

"Crap," David muttered – and disappeared through the front door as Alec broke off a second daisy.

"Well, David Sullivan," Liz's voice crackled, distorted by a recurrence of the frequent and apparently incurable static that seemed to plague all electronics in Sullivan Cove. "You haven't called me since the fair, so I'm taking matters into my own hands."

Her voice was firm rather than flirtatious, and David couldn't help but grin. Liz had a way about her: a plain, honest, straightforward way. That was what he liked best about her, in fact. She always said what she meant, and if it was tactful, fine; and if it wasn't, fine; and if it made her look like a fool, well, that didn't bother her too much, either. He wished he could be as forthright, but on the other hand, Liz hadn't seen the Sidhe.

"Sorry," David replied. "I've had things on my mind – and, besides, it's not even been a week."

There was a flustered pause. "So what are you doing now, Davy?"

"It's *David*, Liz – with a D, like in dammit. And I'm not doing anything except sitting on the porch complaining about the heat and fussing with Alec."

"Well, I can't help with your fussing, except to ask you not to get a black eye if you can help it. I don't want to be seen with a boy with a black eye."

"It's not that kind of fussing. Call it a gentlemans' disagreement."

"You two? Gentlemen? Ha! You won't even call a girl, and Alec never can seem to figure out when he's not wanted. But as far as the heat's concerned, maybe I can help with that – if you'd like to go swimming down in the lake behind my mom's house. I'll even be nice and let you bring young Mr. McLean."

David grinned. "That's good, 'cause he's stayin' here this weekend, and I'd hate to have to leave him to the tender mercies of my pa – or, even worse, Little Billy."

"Your folks might as well adopt him, much as he's over there."

"Actually, his folks're out of town at a literature conference up at Appalachian State, and asked us to take custody. I doubt the rugged rural life would agree with him in the long run."

"Well, that's good. There are other people who'd like some of your time once in a while – just in case you were wondering."

"Anybody I know?"

"Never mind, Davy, just get your butt over here."

"Can I bring the rest of me too?"

"That was the general idea."

"But you said –"

A flustered sigh. "David!"

"Right."

"See you in a little while."

"Right ..." David hesitated, not quite knowing how to end the conversation – which, he realized, could have continued for hours in endless exchange of taunts and inanities. Still, he'd left an unhappy best friend on the porch and wanted to resolve that. It was ironic in any case, since before Alec's mad spell had soured the afternoon, he's been on the verge of proposing a dip in the cove anyway. This wouldn't be that much different, all things considered – except for the obvious part.

"Bye," he finished awkwardly, and hung up.

The door slammed behind him as David returned to the porch. Alec looked up, raised an inquiring eyebrow, then scowled into his third daisy.

"That was Liz wantin' to know if we wanted to go swimmin' over at her place."

"So what'd you tell her?" There was no trace of Alec's former hostility, as if he had regained control of his emotions – or suppressed them.

"I told her 'yes,' of course. I presume you do want to go, considering how much you were complaining about the heat just now. Maybe some lake water'll wash a little of the mad off you."

Alec grimaced. "I'm not mad; I'm just ... confused – and hurt, a little, to be completely honest." He smiled wanly as he levered himself to his feet. "But I guess you really do mean well, even if you are crazy. At least I know you didn't get that ring from Liz; it's not her style."

"As a matter of fact she hasn't even seen it," David replied darkly. "I'd as soon she didn't, either; but there's not much I can do about it, if we're goin' swimming."

"If you say so," Alec agreed with careful neutrality. "You got any swimming togs I can borrow? Somehow I don't think skinny-dipping would be appropriate, and that's all I came prepared for."

"Might be interesting, though!" David laughed. He laid an arm across Alec's shoulders and steered him into the house. "Come on, fool of a Scotsman, I can probably find you something. We'd best get goin', though, before Liz changes her mind."

David took as many back roads as possible in transit to Liz's place – ostensibly to avoid traffic, but also so he could try to puzzle out a few things. Alec spent most of the trip with his eyes closed and his hands trying to strangle his seatbelt. Even so, it was barely twenty minutes before they sighted the house: an almost-new brick ranch sprawling amid a stand of pines at the end of a long gravel driveway.

Liz was waiting for them in the front yard, an incredibly large, white towel draped around her body. Her auburn hair fell atop it like dark copper wire. She had always had nice hair, David reckoned. A purple two-piece bathing suit — not quite a bikini — peeked from beneath the sweep of terrycloth.

"Well," she drawled in a tone of mock irritation, "it took you long enough!"

"Don't say that!" Alec yelped. "I'd hate for him to take up hurrying. It's bad enough when he's just taking it easy."

David shot Alec a scathing glare and threw a friendly punch at his shoulder.

"All right, boys!" Liz said firmly. "I don't allow no fightin' 'round here."

"Yes ma'am," they replied as one, extravagantly repentant.

They had to pass through a small pinewood to reach the designated arm of the lake, which was maybe a quarter mile behind Liz's house. The air there was cool and clean-smelling. As they threaded their way among the oaks and ashes, they saw at least half-a-dozen squirrels and two chipmunks, the latter of which darted frantically about, as if they had just popped into existence and didn't quite know what to make of finding themselves suddenly alive.

"I hope there aren't any 'possums around," Alec whispered wickedly.

David elbowed him in the ribs.

Alec parried the elbow with a wrist. "Alive *or* dead."

"What's this about 'possums?" Liz inquired from the head of the file. Beyond her the gray-green shimmer of the lake was becoming visible.

Alec snickered. "David tried to turn himself into a werepossum back in June."

"Alec!" David growled. "Shut up!"

"A werepossum?" Liz's tone was serious.

"Don't ask," David mumbled.

"I don't need to," Liz called back. "I'm sure Alec will tell me all I want to know. Right, Alec?"

Alec started, as if surprised to find his existence acknowledged. "Definitely," he replied, grinning smugly at David and raising his brows.

They had reached the shore by then. The land there descended in a series of red clay shelves to a thread of sandy beach Liz's father had trucked in as a birthday present years before. The water was clear and smooth, reflecting the blue sky and the surrounding pines, along with the three tanned faces that stared into it.

"A werepossum," Liz repeated, as if to herself, though David knew it was a prompt, if not a very subtle one.

"Never mind." He gritted his teeth. "Did we come here to talk or to swim?"

"I came to swim," Liz cried, dropping her towel and running fifteen or so feet into the lake before thrusting her head smoothly under water.

"She's filled out some this summer," Alec observed.

David nodded appreciatively. "She has for a fact. Now come on, let's go find a bush and change."

"If you weren't so picky about that damned car, we wouldn't have to do this in the woods," Alec grumbled as he followed David toward a clump of laurel at the top of the bank.

"If Liz had been thinking and had offered her house, we wouldn't have to anyway," David shot back.

Once reasonably secluded, they dumped their duffle bags and commenced stripping. David paused with his shirt off and his jeans around his ankles, fingering the ring that hung from its chain: cold silver against his warm, tan chest.

"What's the matter now?" Alec asked, still T-shirted, but bare-assed.

"I don't know what to do with this."

Alec shrugged and reached for the cut-offs David had leant him. "Seems reasonable to me. Leave it alone, wear it on your finger, or stick it in a pocket and stash it with your clothes."

David actually shivered at the latter possibility. "If I wear it on the chain I might lose it "

"Wear it on your finger, then. I mean, Liz is gonna see it anyway, if that's what you're worried about."

Still David hesitated.

"Well, is it?"

"Maybe," he muttered at last. "I guess I'd better wear it, then; at least that way it'd be safe and maybe not attract as much attention."

Alec chuckled. "Oh, she'll notice. Girls always notice things like that, believe me."

"A lot you know!"

"As much as you — at least experientially."

David sighed and transferred the ring to his finger, then finished changing. Alec was waiting for him when he finished. He tested the waistband of his borrowed togs dubiously. "Remind me to bring a belt next time. These things are gonna fall off if I'm not careful."

"At least it'd give Liz a thrill," David laughed. "I, of course, would be completely underwhelmed."

Alec snorted. "Somehow I think she'd like it better if it was you."

David glared at him.

Alec grinned.

A few minutes later the three friends stood together on the muddy bottom, water waist-deep about their bodies, hair slicked back, beads of moisture dewlike on their limbs, lashes stuck together.

All at once Liz snatched David's hand from under the surface, bringing it up in a cloud of spray that set Alec flinching. "So this is the famous ring!" she cried, grasping David firmly by the wrist while she turned his hand this way and that, as the water glittered on the silver circle.

David rolled his eyes at Alec in a "save me" gesture. Alec shrugged noncommittally, leaving David to fend for himself.

"Who is she?" Liz asked.

"I found it."

"Oh, *another* story," Alec muttered.

"That's not what Little Billy told my brother Marvin at Bible school," Liz said calmly.

David blushed. "That's practically ancient history now, Liz. And, besides, Little Billy's a kid. Who you gonna believe, him or me?"

"Don't ask me!" from Alec.

"Shit!" David growled, staring absently at the water lapping in and out of his navel. "Who *hasn't* he told about that?"

"Your guess," Liz chuckled. "I've heard from three different people that you'd said you had a girlfriend but wouldn't give her name."

"Good grief!" David sighed. "Can't I do anything without it being front page news? And, Alec, how many people have you told about me and a little trip up the mountain? Will I read about that in the paper next week? 'Local Boy Tries to Become Werewolf; Fails; Parents Horrified.' Or maybe, 'Local Boy Sees Castle, then Psychiatrist'?"

Alec feigned dumbness, pointing to his closed mouth and gesticulating wildly. Abruptly he stiffened and fell backward into the water, only to emerge a moment later, grinning, his hair slicked into his eyes like an inky skullcap.

"You know," Liz continued, peering intently at the ring, "I get kind of a funny feeling about this thing – like it was really old, or something." She shook her head. "No, I don't think you got this from any girl around here; it's too ... esoteric for anybody up here."

"I told you! He got it from a girl in Atlanta."

David wrenched his hand away from Liz and thrust it in a pocket. "Oh, come on, McLean, let it die. Where would I have met a girl in

Atlanta? I'd never been there without my folks but once before the convention, and I was with you then. And, besides, would I be here if I had a girl in Atlanta?" David's eyes twinkled, but he knew he was treading on dangerous ground – for several reasons.

Both Alec and Liz looked confused.

David started to speak again: something off topic – or anything to divert the conversation. But just as he opened his mouth – having no idea what might come out – Alec uttered a startled "Yow!" and pointed shoreward. David and Liz turned, following the line of his pointing finger.

"A white squirrel!" Liz gasped.

The animal in question lay precariously on the tip of a pine bough that overhung the water: a patch of brilliant, almost snow-like white amid the prickly green, like a spike of winter thrust into summer's warm body. Unfortunately, it reminded David a little too *much* of winter, which was his least favorite season. Goosebumps rose on his back and chest and shoulders.

The squirrel did not move; rather, it seemed to be watching them. The branch swayed gently under its weight.

"Is it an albino, you reckon?" Liz wondered.

"Most white animals in this part of the country are," David replied, relieved to be on safer ground, if only by comparison. "Unless they're naturally white – which doesn't make sense, if you think about it. I mean albinos *are* natural."

"Not likely to live long, though," Alec observed. "Stands out too clearly. Easy prey for a hawk."

"Somehow I don't think so," David retorted, scratching his chin – and flinched, for the ring had suddenly grown hot on his hand. Looking down, he saw that it was blazing with light.

"What was that?" Alec yipped.

"What was what?"

"That glitter."

"Sun on the water, probably," Liz said, "if you saw what I saw."

"Weird."

In the old-fashioned sense, David conceded, as he ducked beneath the surface of the lake. He entered a brown-green world marked by the pale shapes of his friends' legs, the white cutoffs he had lent Alec, and Liz's purple suit. When his head broke water again, the squirrel was gone.

"Where'd it go?" he gasped through a face-full of water.

Alec shrugged. "I dunno. You splashed; I blinked and it wasn't there. Simple as that."

"Yeah," Liz agreed, looking troubled. "Simple as that."

David could only stare at her.

Alec was shaking his head. "That's weird."

"What is?" from David.

Alec shrugged again. "Oh, nothing; it's just that for a minute I thought of something that squirrel reminded me of but then suddenly whatever it was had vanished, like it just slipped sideways out of my mind."

"If you didn't keep so much *in* your mind that wouldn't happen," David retorted.

Alec merely growled, but his face still looked troubled.

"Let me have another look at that ring," Liz said abruptly, reaching for David's hand.

David snatched it behind his back, fearful they would see the glow, though he knew from its diminished heat that it was fading. He counted to five and held it up reluctantly.

"I wonder if I can get some vibrations off it," Liz mused, puffing her cheeks.

"Oh for heaven's sake," Alec snorted, turning his back and folding his arms dramatically. "Is everybody I know crazy as a bedbug? Vibrations! Liz, come on! Not you too!"

"Well, Alec McLean, you were acting pretty strange yourself just now, but the fact is, sometimes I can pick up vibrations – impressions, whatever you want to call 'em. My granny taught me how to do it before she died. Well, she didn't exactly teach me; she just told me to be aware of what was there and to trust my feelings about things, and I do and it works, most of the time. And right now I've got a feeling about David's ring."

"What are you gonna do?" David asked, both fascinated and surprised.

He'd known Liz for years and never suspected she was in any way interested in arcane matters, though she had listened to him go on about his various fixations with something besides the bemused glances he usually got from his buddies in the MacTyrie Gang, and did occasionally ask a penetrating question. Maybe she *was* a little bit psychic. In that case, it certainly wouldn't hurt to indulge her; at least that way maybe he could find out ... something. Taking a deep breath, he extended his hand.

She closed her eyes and placed her hands on his, one over and one under; then took a deep breath of her own. David and Alec merely gaped.

She was silent for quite a while, but her dark lashes fluttered, and her breath became shallow. When she finally opened her eyes, they were wide and filled with an odd light in their green depths.

"I don't know what just happened, but it was ... strange."

"Strange?" Alec breathed. "How strange?"

Liz shook her head. "I – I just tried to picture the ring, and then to be aware of whatever images came into my mind, and I got this incredibly sharp picture of an old man in gray robes looking at me, and then of two men, one in black and one in white, fighting with each other. Well, not exactly fighting, but *contending* somehow. And then they looked at me, and I got scared and quit. I've had ... impressions before, but this was like television!"

"What did – ?" David began.

A sound cut him off: a sound like the howling of a thousand wolves heard from a great distance. But it was the sound of the wind: a strange wind that swept suddenly out of the high, still air and flowed among the pines on the far bank, then raced across the glassy water, stirring up a miniature tsunami in its wake, before finally fleeing up the nearer shore – but not until it had whirled and eddied about the three friends so violently they had to dive clear to the bottom to avoid its touch, which was like deadly ice.

"I ... don't think ... I want to swim anymore today," Liz whispered, when they all had surfaced.

"Nonsense!" Alec laughed, if somewhat nervously. He immediately did a back flip and swam out into the again-smooth water. David followed, and so reluctantly did Liz, though her eyes looked troubled and her mouth was set in a thin, hard line. For a good while they sported about, diving the fifteen or so feet to the bottom and rising again, pulling each other's legs in an effort to relieve the tension that the eerie wind had wrought. David considered yanking Alec's too-loose cut-offs down, but decided he'd put his best friend through enough for one day.

Eventually Alec's head broke water next to David. He blew runoff from his mouth and nose. His eyes were huge.

"Did you see that?" he sputtered.

"See what?"

"The white fish."

"White fish?" David was treading water, but faltered in his stroke. "Are you kidding?"

"He's not kidding," Liz sputtered in turn, emerging beside them, "if he's talking about the white trout I just saw."

David took a gulp of air and dove, peering past his friend's lazily churning legs to where a white trout did, indeed, swim rapidly in a tight circle just beyond them. At the same time, he felt of a burning on his finger so sudden and intense that he almost gasped out his lungful of air.

The ring was glowing white-hot, flaring like a magnesium torch. It hurt to look at it, even underwater.

Abruptly, the trout darted straight toward him. He jerked back, but not before it grazed his ring finger and, in an apparently deliberate gesture, swam directly toward shore. The ring was hotter than ever, hotter than David had ever felt it – so hot that he wanted to take it off. But he knew that he would be the rankest sort of fool if he did.

He held what remained of his breath as long as he could, then surfaced and looked around. Liz and Alec were where he had left them. But maybe fifty yards across the lake behind them he could now see the head and upper body of what appeared to be an enormous black horse swimming toward them. It was utterly silent, and its eyes glowed red in a way that made David shiver. He thought he saw steam issuing from its nostrils.

"Come on, you guys!" he shouted, stroking frantically toward shore. "There's a horse coming straight toward us. And it doesn't look friendly!"

Alec glanced over his shoulder. "Son-of-a-bitch!" he yelped and followed David's example. Liz merely swam. Behind them, David could hear the horse's heavy breathing and the splash of the water against its head and neck as it increased its pace. More than once he thought he could feel its hot breath on his back. And was it his imagination, or did a faint stench like burning sulfur taint the air?

They swam until they could stand and run clumsily in the shallows, mud welling up between their toes, water sucking at their legs, hampering their escape. They had not turned once to look back, but the snuffling hiss of labored breathing sounded closer every instant, and the dull, heavy splashing of the black horse's knees breaking the surface as it entered shallow water became clearer by the second.

Breathless, they heaved themselves onto dry land and scrambled up the bank. Once in the more tangible safety of the trees, they turned as one, fearing what they might see.

And gasped again.

For in the shallows below them a great black horse stared malevolently up the bank toward them – stared, but made no move to leave the water that lapped about its hocks. Moisture glistened on its flanks, but the devil light in its eyes had faded – at least to David's sight – to a dull, lifeless gray.

"Son-of-a-*bitch*!" Alec repeated.

The horse regarded them for a moment longer, then turned and swam off into the lake. The three friends watched it from the safety of the trees until it became a mere speck. Oddly, it did not move toward the bank on the other side of the cove; rather, it continued into the open water to the right, to disappear finally around an outthrust peninsula.

"That was scary!" Liz gasped breathlessly.

"I won't argue in the slightest!" David agreed, picking up his towel. Liz cautiously dashed back to the shore to fetch hers.

"Any idea whose horse that was?" David asked when she returned.

She shook her head. "Nobody around here has a black horse, and, anyway, I've never heard of a horse swimming in open water like that. I wonder if – Lord, I hope not! You don't reckon it might've had rabies or something, do you? I sure don't want to think about a rabid horse running around."

"Swimming around, you mean," Alec corrected. "You know, though, it was almost like it was in its natural habitat – and was chasing us off."

"Good thing you saw the fish when you did," David put in. "Or we might not have noticed till it was right on top of us."

"What fish?" Alec replied, looking blank.

"Yeah, what fish?" Liz echoed, looking equally puzzled. She shuddered and hugged her towel more closely about her. "Anyway," she continued, "between the horse and that strange gust of wind right before, all of a sudden I don't feel in the least like going back in the water."

"I know what you mean," David agreed though a shudder of his own that had less to do with either the horse or the temperature than with his friends' apparently lapses of memory – which he dared not pursue at the moment: not until he had a little more time to think about them. "It's about time for us to head out anyway. Got to get me and Master McLean home before supper – and I'd hate to have to take up hurrying." He shot Alec a fiendish grin, though it hid a darker concern.

As he and Alec found the clump of laurel bushes where they had left their clothes and began to change, David wondered if his eyes had deceived him, or if he had actually seen what he thought he'd seen at the ends of the horse's legs: not hooves but fins. He glanced down at the ring. It was its usual cold and shiny self. Beautiful, but in no other way remarkable – except, he was now absolutely convinced, it was magic.

Interlude IV

In Tir-nan-og
(high summer)

The boy had spent the night with a selkie woman. They had lain together twice: once on shore, when the boy had put on the seal shape that the woman preferred; and again in his boat, when she had shed her skin and coupled with him in more familiar fashion.

It was morning now; the woman was gone — and he was still in the boat. The low sun glimmered through pale tendrils of pink-tinged mist that rose from an expanse of water scarcely darker. To the north, the vague blue crenulations of the forested shore looked like the ghosts of trees. On every other side was water: motionless as ice and more silent.

A breeze stirred, twitching the fog from the angry eyes of the gilded dragon prow and causing the limp green sail to billow apprehensively. The thick red fur of the manticore hide with which the boy had wrapped his nakedness rippled, as though that hide sought to return to life. He might have been fifteen or twenty-one, though he was more than ten times either. With his flawless skin and delicate bones, he might also have been pretty, had not the line of his jaw and the angle of his chin and the set of his mouth and brows skewed him into handsome. A strand of hair as fair as spun sunlight blew into his face and tickled him awake.

Something moved at his bare feet: A scaly silver head on an arm-long neck writhed from under the fur and hissed hoarsely, its elaborate ear flares flicking elegantly as if they caught unseen sounds. The rest followed: close-furled wings, two clawed legs, and a tail whip-thin like a serpent's. The boy jerked a foot back under the cover as the wyvern made a dive for it. He grunted, slipped a hand over the low portside gunwale, and eased it into the water.

It took but a trickle of Power to call the fish: three of them. Each a hand long, they waited by the boat, tails undulating trustingly.

The first two he flung into his pet's waiting jaws. The third he cooked in his fist and ate himself, peeling the white flesh from the bones with perfect teeth, before washing it down with the remnants of a flagon of the previous evening's wine.

He was pondering the remaining flagon when he became aware of a change in the uncertain light.

"Too good to last, wasn't it, Dylan?" he grumbled, as he heaved himself up among the furs and tugged a gray silk tunic over his head. That accomplished, he stood unsteadily and squinted into the shimmering red haze of the rising sun.

There, to the east, maybe an arrow's shot away, a glimmering strip upon the water was resolving itself into a streak of burning golden light as a Way came awake beneath the tread of one of his kin.

Fionchadd! The name echoed in his mind alone: the call of Ailill, his father.

He frowned, but conjured a breeze to set the boat gliding across the lake toward that summoning.

The golden haze that was the Way floated just above the water, stretching arrow-straight north and south until it was lost in the mist, the rift between the Worlds above it casting flickering images upon the air itself that made him giddy to gaze upon.

And then the Way brightened gloriously at a certain point until it rivaled the sun. When Fionchadd could no longer look at it, Ailill stepped straight from that glow and onto the boat amidships. The craft rocked gently, so that Ailill had to grasp the single mast to steady himself before sitting down.

Fionchadd offered him the wine.

Ailill's gaze remained fixed upon the boy, as he took a long draught. "You do not look happy, my son," he observed.

"I do not like waiting."

Ailill shrugged and returned the flagon. "It was midnight when I left; it is sunrise now. That is not long, and you seem to have spent it well enough or is that not the stench of selkie I scent upon you?"

The boy looked away. "Did you learn what you set out to learn? What is there in the Lands of Men to interest you?"

"You know of the boy, do you not? The human boy?"

"The one who bested you in the Question Game?"

"The one who insulted me."

Fionchadd took a sip of wine. "I know of him."

"Do you know that he is protected? I tried to summon him, so as to settle accounts my own way. But when I worked the ritual, I met a Power greater than my own that almost consumed me. I have been in the Lands of Men since then, seeking to learn the nature of that protection."

Fionchadd frowned into his cup. "I spent a cold night on a cold lake with a cold woman so you could ensorcel a mortal boy?"

Ailill's brows lowered dangerously. "It is you who are answerable to me, not I to you."

"You could have told me what you were about."

"And you could then have told anyone who asked you where I was."

"I could have lied."

"You do not do that well, nor do you hide your thoughts with any skill. They are there on your face for anyone to read."

"Perhaps so. But then again, I have less to hide than you do. Now, are you going to tell me what you learned?"

Ailill sighed and regarded his son uneasily. *Just like his mother. Just like the Annwyn-born bitch I got him on. He even looks like her. Fair as sunlight. But of course he was born at dawn.*

"I learned some things, my son," Ailill said finally, "and I lay a geas upon you to reveal them to none." He traced a complex symbol in the air.

Fionchadd traced a matching glyph. "And what might those things be?"

Ailill made a cushion from the manticore pelt and leaned against it. "Very well: I went by the Water Road, since it is less frequently traveled. In that I was fortunate, for I came upon the boy swimming with his friends. I then put upon myself the shape of a black kepplian, thinking its strength and speed might be of use; also, I thought to test the boy's knowledge of such things. And I watched for a while, and then I threatened – to see if that which protects him shields his body as well as his mind."

"And does it?"

"It does. I could only approach so far, and then it was like a wall of flame about him. But I also saw what it is that effects this protection."

"And what is that?"

"A ring. "

"A ring?" Fionchadd raised a perfect eyebrow. "Interesting. I assume you mean to procure it. How do you propose to accomplish that?"

Ailill managed a small grim smile. "That is the problem, isn't it? I can approach only so closely, and I cannot summon him."

"Have you tried summoning one of his kinsmen? If you cannot touch him, perhaps you could touch one of them. Or you could take one as a hostage."

Ailill's face brightened. "Now you show yourself truly my son. But there may be a problem. I have tried summoning all those whose faces I saw graven in those parts of his mind where thoughts of the beloved dwell, but every time I tried, there was Fire – weaker than that which protects him, but still beyond my Power to quench. I fear the ring shields his loved ones equally."

Fionchadd regarded his father levelly. "What is it you want from me?"

"I want you to help me. I cannot touch the boy, and I cannot touch that which protects him. Nor do I dare absent myself from court too often or too long, for Lugh would become suspicious, or if not him, then Silverhand. But there is a possibility that the ring protects the boy from me alone. It might not hinder you."

"So you want me to help you capture this human?"

Ailill nodded. "If possible. At least I want you to see how close you can come to the ring. It would be best if you began now. Go into the Lands of Men. Watch. Listen. Use whichever arts seem good to you. And report to me. You do know how to operate the Tracks, do you not?"

"Oh, aye," Fionchadd agreed absently, as he summoned another fish. "My mother taught me *that* art very well indeed."

Chapter VII

oisin
(Friday, July 31)

"**Supper!**" JoAnne Sullivan called from the barbed wire fence at the top of the pasture Big Billy shared with Uncle Dale. "You men gonna stand there starin' at that sorghum patch all evenin'? Ain't gonna make it grow no faster!" She could see their silhouettes cut out against the lush green growth that filled the narrow strip of flat land between the pasture and the Sullivan Cove road: Big Billy, tall and heavy-set, stomach gone to fat from too much beer and good food, but still well muscled; Dale, taller still, rail-thin, and aged like a locust fence post; and beside him, in stair-step order: slender Alec; David, shorter but more solidly built; and Little Billy, who looked like he would beat them all.

"One more call's all you're gettin', and then I'm gonna eat this stuff myself – now get up here!"

"Yes, ma'am," Big Billy hollered back, smiling faintly.

As they trudged up the grassy slope, Alec and David fell behind. Alec clapped a hand good-naturedly on David's shoulder and bent close. "Sorry about this afternoon," he murmured.

David shrugged. "No problem. I appreciate your concern, but I'm just ... confused about some things, and haven't figured them out yet."

"That's the kind of stuff we used to work out together, bro."

David nodded grimly. "I know, and I hope we can work this out too. But not yet. Not quite yet."

They had reached the top of the hill by then, and David stretched the barbed wire up for Alec to climb through before following himself. Alec glanced up at his friend from the ditch beside the driveway, bit his lip, and nodded in resignation.

David paused at the fence line. "You go on up, I'll be there in a second."

Alec raised an eyebrow. "Your mom's probably given up on us already, and I, for one, am not one to miss your mom's cooking. So don't expect me to leave anything for you."

"I won't," David called to Alec's back, as he took off his glasses and rubbed his eyes, then turned to survey the landscape. Something was up again, he knew. But where? He checked east, toward the highway; north, toward the churchyard and the road; south, toward the mountains; and finally west, toward Uncle Dale's farm. And saw nothing untoward in any of those quarters. Shrugging, he followed his friend toward the house. The itching persisted, however, and for a long moment he stood in the side yard looking out across the intervening fields and pastures toward the silver-red glitter of the lake half a mile to the west – and then up the gravel road to the bulk of the mountain. His eyes were all but burning now; his hand unconsciously sought the ring.

And then he saw the source of that affliction: right at the limits of vision, so faint as to be almost invisible against the dark forest.

Just where the road marched in among the trees beyond the barn, he could barely make out the hazy figure of a man – an old man in flowing gray robes, who stared at him for a moment, then raised one thin arm and pointed up the mountain before continuing up the road. It seemed, too, that the man held a walking stick in his other hand: one with which he felt his way along. When the burning in his eyes forced David to blink, the man was gone.

David put down his glass of milk. "I think me and Alec are gonna hike up to Lookout Rock after supper," he announced, as he speared a slice of roast beef and looked quizzically over at Big Billy, who was applying himself vigorously to his own generous portion.

"We're gonna what?" cried an obviously shocked Alec through a mouthful of mashed potatoes. Little Billy giggled, but nobody noticed.

Alec slumped in his chair and glared at David through tired eyes. "David, my friend, I am weary to the bone," he sighed, pointing at himself with his fork. "All I want to do is take a long hot shower and go to bed. I don't know how I let you talk me into putting in the whole day following you around."

"We didn't do anything but talk and go swimming."

"And help your dad pull the engine out of that old pickup. Besides, hanging onto the seat while you took every curve between here and Liz's house on two wheels takes it out of a body."

David snorted. "Wimp."

"If you're so set on goin' up that mountain, why don't you take Little Billy," Uncle Dale suggested. "Me an' Alec'll play us a game or two of checkers. That be okay? You want to go hikin' up to the Rock with Davy, Little Billy?"

Little Billy looked up, wide-eyed. Milk had painted a white mustache on his upper lip. "Nope."

"Well, why not?" the old man asked.

"I don't like bein' in the woods."

Dale's eyes narrowed. "Any partic'lar reason?"

"They's boogers in there," the little boy said solemnly.

"Boogers!" Dale exclaimed. "Why, what kind of talk is that?" He shot David a sharp look. "Who's been tellin' you 'bout boogers?"

"Nobody. I seen one."

"Seen one!" Dale exclaimed again. "Well, what did it look like?"

"Like a shiny boy."

"A shiny boy? I never heard of boogers lookin' like shiny boys."

"Well, it did," Little Billy said stubbornly. "A shiny boy wearin' funny gray clothes."

David felt the hairs on the back of his neck rise one by one. Apparently his brother had seen one of the Sidhe. But if what Ailill had said was true: that the Sidhe could make themselves visible to anyone if such were their choice, then why had one shown himself to Little Billy? That didn't augur well at all. "Did he say anything?" David asked cautiously.

"Nope. Just stood up there by the barn an' looked at me."

"You won't go near him if you see him again, will you?" David laughed, trying to mask how much his brother's remark disturbed him.

Dale shot David another sharp glance.

"I ain't crazy," Little Billy replied, reaching for the plate of freshly baked oatmeal cookies that were desert.

"But you will stay close to home, won't you?" David insisted hopefully.

"I ain't crazy," Little Billy repeated.

In spite of David's suggestion of an evening hike, he and Alec retired to David's room at a surprisingly early hour. Alec, freshly showered and almost literally squeaky clean, was asleep as soon as he hit the covers, but David stayed up to read, hoping to find some key to the day's occurrence in *Gods and Fighting Men* or *The Secret Common-Wealth*. He'd read the latter cover to cover several times – it wasn't very long – but except for the business about Second Sight, which occupied almost half the book, there was very little in it that seemed relevant to his current situation. There were no magic rings, for instance, and no water horses. It was also difficult to reconcile Reverend Kirk's provincial "Subterraneans" with the sophisticated, urbane Faeries he had met. There were certainly some things in it worth knowing, but almost none of them were either pleasant or encouraging. The stuff about changelings was particularly disturbing, for instance.

I really do need to check out some of this stuff on the Net, he told himself. *If I can ever get to the Net, that is.* That was frustrating as hell, too; given that he had no computer of his own, and he already knew without asking that Alec's laptop would refuse to function if he brought it anywhere near Sullivan cove. Never mind the fact that the ones at school were locked away until school itself actually started, and the ones at the library had all been fried by lightning during one of the past week's thunderstorms.

All of which was just a shade too coincidental, David concluded through the evening's heaviest yawn. He wondered if he could get Alec to check some stuff for him without either asking too many questions – or worse yet, knowing what he was checking. For that matter, there was still that business of the white fish Alec had pointed out and then conveniently forgotten. Given the white dog he himself had seen, he didn't want to think about what that portended.

Another yawn found him; he sighed and returned to his reading. Before long, however, he found his eyes getting heavy. A fatigue he had not previously been aware of had fallen upon him, and as it claimed him, unconsciousness followed.

Two hours later, David was awake again. The clock on the dresser between the beds proclaimed it to be a few minutes before midnight. He glanced over at Alec, who was still sound asleep, breathing heavily through his mouth, one bare arm hanging off the bedside.

He'll put his arm to sleep for sure, David mused and lay back down, only to sit up again a moment later. *Jesus, he was restless!* What a predicament:

to be fully awake in the middle of the night and not be able to do anything about it for fear of waking others. He wondered if anyone else was up, but the only sound that reached his ears was the distant wind; there was no TV or radio. He looked out the window beside his bed and idly watched a single car accelerate down the highway.

"Crap," he muttered. "I was afraid it'd come to this."

Quietly he got up, slipped on a pair of jeans, tiptoed barefoot to the door, and soundlessly opened it, grateful he'd had the foresight to oil the hinges. He continued down the hall into the kitchen, and thence onto the western back porch, which more nearly faced the mountain. For a long moment he leaned against a post, staring out into the yard, oblivious to the chill wind that played about his bare shoulders and feet. Absently, he hugged his arms about himself and continued his vigil, not knowing what he sought, but knowing, too, with absolute conviction, that there was some reason for the sense of undirected urgency that filled him. Eventually, he became aware of a sort of sparkle in the grass, as if dew had fallen or autumn had sent a tentative vanguard of frost venturing in from the north. At the same time he sensed a new brightness in the air, as if the moon had risen. Impulsively, he leapt into the yard and raised his face skyward, seeking the source of that radiance.

It was the moon, all right, rising golden-yellow. Only ... something was wrong! Hadn't the moon been new the previous weekend? And now it was full! And wasn't it in the wrong part of the sky? And at the wrong time? The familiar tingle tickled his eyes. He grimaced and exhaled sharply. And knew what he had to do.

When he slipped back into his room a moment later, he found Alec sitting on the side of his bed calmly tugging on his socks.

"I'm going with you, of course," Alec whispered in response to David's scowl. "I could tell by that look in your eyes at supper that you'd go up that mountain tonight, with me or without me – and I'm just stupid enough to go with you. Maybe I'll get to the bottom of this foolishness yet."

David didn't say anything, merely crossed soundlessly to the closet and pulled out a long-sleeved flannel shirt. "Wait and put your shoes on outside," he told his friend. "No way you can walk quiet as me through the house, and Pa's a light sleeper."

Alec nodded. A moment later both boys sat on the back steps gazing out into the night.

"See anything funny?" David ventured, watching Alec's face.

Alec glanced at the sky, then back at David, as if noticing the scrutiny. "Am I *supposed* to see anything funny? It's night. Dark, mostly. Some stars. Land is darker than sky."

David continued to stare at his friend. "Any moon?"

Alec frowned and gazed back at the sky. "Nope. It's the wrong time of month for it, isn't it? Why?"

David took a deep breath. "How bright does it look out here to you?"

"What do you mean, 'how bright?'"

"I mean how bright. Bright enough to read by? Bright enough to barely feel your way around in if you're not in shadow? How bright?"

Alec returned David's stare. "Not bright enough to read by, that's for sure."

"Alec," David whispered very slowly, "I know you're not going to believe this, but ... I see a full moon."

"Made out of green cheese or painted blue?"

David sighed and flung his hands up in dismay. He rose, jumped off the steps, and strode toward the driveway, his paces long and deliberate. Alec had to run to catch up.

"Damn, Sullivan, what're you doing fumbling around out here in the dark? Aren't you at least gonna get a flashlight?"

David rounded on his friend but did not slow down. "I don't *need* a flashlight, Alec! I see a full moon, and I see by its light. If you want to come along, you're welcome, but don't slow me down; there's something I gotta do tonight. I don't know what it is yet, but something magic is cookin'; I know it. And maybe, just maybe, if you come with me, you'll see something too and believe me." His voice softened. "I don't like not having you believe me, Scotsboy. But you won't without proof, so maybe I can give you some!"

Alec glared at David as he followed him toward the logging road. "I just don't want you breaking your leg in the dark!"

"Ha!" came David's scornful voice at the point where the trees began to close in, making a sort of gate to the forest. "You're the one who needs to worry – especially if you don't catch up." His voice took on a lighter color. "There are werewolves in these woods, so I hear."

"Werepossums, anyway," came Alec's voice behind him.

Close to two hours later, they reached their destination. It was impossible to tell exactly how long the trip had taken because David discovered halfway there that his watch had stopped. It still registered a few minutes past midnight. The moon did seem to have moved, however, but somehow in not quite the proper manner. David shrugged it off. Time was the least of his worries.

As he and Alec made their way into the open space behind the lookout, David suppressed a chill as he recalled the last time they had been there. He glanced furtively at the sky before trotting forward to stand on the overlook itself.

There was the usual gut-wrenching sensation of being suddenly very high in the air, the more so because the wind was blowing fallen leaves around, blurring the distinction between earth and sky, even as the darkness itself did. The waterfall roared incessantly to the left, strangely loud as it poured into the pool, its edges fringed with more decaying brown leaves.

David and Alec found their customary ledge at the very edge of the overlook. Without a word they stretched out side-by-side, hands hooked behind their heads, gazing up at the stars. A meteor obligingly flashed out of the northwest. Alec pointed. "Did you see that?"

David nodded. "Nice one."

"You know, this old rock is pretty comfortable. I could almost go to sleep here."

"You'd freeze your butt off, too, and be stiff as rigor mortis in the morning." David levered himself up on his elbows. "Speaking of which, we'd best start back soon. I don't know why I wanted to come up here; I have no idea what I'd hoped to find."

"The Holy Grail?"

"This is serious."

Alec closed his eyes. "Just wake me in when you're ready."

David continued to watch the sky for a while, hoping to see another meteor — or something. Yet somehow, he could not seem to muster either the inclination or the energy to commence the trek back home. Or was it that he still felt that sense of anticipation, as if something important were about to happen? He sat up again, hunched over, wrapped his arms about his knees and rested his chin on them, wishing he'd brought a jacket.

"It is a little cold," came a voice behind him, a voice that sang in his ears like music. Though the phrase was in no way remarkable, David would never forget the first words he heard that voice speak.

He did not start when the voice sounded; rather, he very calmly and quietly stood up and looked back toward the mass of mountain — and was not surprised to see a robed figure sitting placidly on one of the larger rocks by the waterfall. His eyes tingled too, but he scarcely noticed, as he glanced down at Alec. His friend appeared to be sound asleep, a smile of almost abandoned pleasure curving the full lips above his pointed chin. David smiled in turn, then began to pick his way across the thirty or so feet between the overlook and the mysterious figure. It occurred to him, then, that he should not have been able to hear the man's voice above the roar of the waterfall yet the words had sounded clearly, like a whisper in an empty church.

Without truly deciding as much, David found himself sitting on a smaller rock opposite the man. Beneath the gray-white hood the man seemed to look at David, yet not at him; his gaze seemed fixed somewhere slightly above David's head. Slowly the man extended a hand, brushed his fingertips briefly against David's brow and as slowly withdrew them then raised both hands to the hood and flung it back.

David watched as if hypnotized, taking in every detail: the ancient, corded hands like old tree bark; the nails perfect and almost metallic-looking, a ring on each finger. No, on all fingers but *one* – each of them silver but all different. David couldn't make his eyes focus on the rest of the body, but he had an impression of a slender form shrouded in long gray-and-white robes of a soft, napped fabric like velvet. If moonlight was woven into cloth it would be like that, he decided.

And the face ... David hesitated to look full on it. But when he finally dared, he saw that it was the face of an old man, lined with a thousand wrinkles, yet still with its power and dignity about it, and still with the joy of youth playing about the lips and eyes. He realized then that the appearance of age lay mostly on the surface, for the muscles and bones kept their firmness; age was more like a patina on silver or the fine network of cracks on an old painting. The hair was white, too: white as the stars in the sky, long, infinitely fine, and sweeping back from a furrowed forehead. And the eyes! David didn't know how long he looked at those eyes as the man continued to smile softly in the silence. They were silver-colored: from edge to edge, dark silver. *Blind,* David knew instinctively, but beautiful, and infinitely strange.

"You will have to look a long time to read my whole story there, David Sullivan," the stranger said at last, and a hush fell about that place, as if the whole world stopped to listen.

"Who are you?" David managed to croak. "Why did you want me to come here?"

"Did I want you to come here?" the blind man asked calmly.

"Well, *someone* changed the moon down at my house," David managed, aware even as he spoke of how rude he probably sounded. "This isn't the real moon."

"I'm a blind man. How could I know that?"

"The same way I could hear your voice above the sound of the wind and the water," David replied more softly.

"Nicely said," the blind man retorted, smiling again. "And since I know your name, and thereby have power over you according to some, I will give you mine in return. When I last walked freely among mortal men I was called Oisin."

"Oisin," David gasped. It was a name he remembered from *Gods and Fighting Men*, and to hear it now filled him with a rush of wonder. Why, the very sound of it cast shadows in his mind: of the ocean, of endless leagues of dark water sailed by a silver boat under a moon that never waned, while harp music floated softly over the waves; and then of other things: of the Sidhe, and the banshee; and the soft, threatening sheen of cold steel weaponry well made.

"It is a name like any other," Oisin said quietly. "It conjures images like any other. Someday I may tell you what visions shine in my inner eye when I hear David Kevin Sullivan spoken aloud – or Suilleabhain, as it was in the tongue of your fathers."

David realized, then, that the language Oisin spoke was English, though strangely stressed and cadenced. There was none of that remote, heard-under-water quality he recalled from his encounters with the Sidhe. *That*, he suspected, had been their own language rendered intelligible in his mind alone.

Oisin rapped David on the knee with his cane so that David flinched. "But I did not come here to speak of words and languages, boy. I came to speak of deeds. And particularly of your deeds, once and future."

"Deeds?" David blurted out. "I don't plan any deeds. I just want to go on living a normal life, like I was living before –"

"Like you thought you were living, you mean," Oisin broke in sharply. "Few men in this age stay up nights reading anything at all, David, much less the sorts of things you read. And you have seen things no one in this land has seen – things no one may see and remain unchanged."

"You seem to know a great deal about me," David replied suspiciously. "But why should I trust you? What difference does it make to you what happens to me?"

Oisin turned his face toward the cold blue sky. "That would be obvious if you knew my tale. Indeed, I am surprised you do not, though perhaps men have forgotten that story. At times I forget it myself. Certainly few of the Men of Dea seem to recall that I was once a mortal man such as you; that iron-red blood like yours once coursed through my veins."

"Your tale ... ?" David ventured, wishing he'd read Lady Gregory a little more closely.

"I came to Tir-Nan-Og once, as a youth. Years uncounted I spent here, ageless and full of fire. And then a craving came on me to return to

Ireland. That grace the Lord Lugh granted me, but as soon as I touched the earth of that land, age fell upon me, and I withered where I stood. I can but recall with bitterness how I crept back here with my youth stricken from me by my own careless folly and by the Danaans' curse – how the Faery women would have naught to do with me because I was no longer a fit lover, and how the Faery men lost interest because I was no fit companion in their endless hunts, battles, and intrigues. I do not want that to happen to you, and it could easily – in spite of the protection that is now upon you."

David started to speak, but Oisin went on relentlessly.

"Nothing changes in Faerie, David: The dead do not stay dead; the living scarcely know they are alive. What passion there is, in love and hate, in pain and pleasure, has no heat behind it. It is only gratification of the moment; for when time does not matter, neither does anything else. The past is gone, yet the present is so like it that there is nothing to distinguish this year from one a thousand years gone by. To the Sidhe – as I prefer to call them – the Sons of Mil came yesterday; to them the sun will fade tomorrow. There is eternity in a moment, and a moment may span five centuries.

"Now look at me!" Oisin demanded fiercely. "Imagine your features cast upon mine, and ask yourself if anyone would wish this upon another of his own kind."

Unable to resist, though he equally feared to acquiesce, David found himself staring into the blazing silver emptiness of the old man's blind eyes. The force of the horror and regret he found there chilled him to the soul. Finally he blinked and tore his gaze away, to stare at the stony ground.

"Now do you see why I feel it my duty to speak to you?" Oisin asked, shifting his position. "But enough of this. I have some things to tell you, and some things to ask you, but first of all I have a warning, and that warning is this: Beware the wrath of Ailill. He is a dire threat to you and those you love."

"Tell me something I don't know," David snorted. "He's been after me at least once today already. Either him, or somebody, or some*thing* – that works for him. There was this black horse that came after me and two of my friends while we were swimming. If it hadn't been for all those white animals." He paused and regarded Oisin curiously. "They weren't you, were they?"

"White animals? No, I have not lately worn any shape but my own. Now tell me of these things." Urgency filled Oisin's voice.

"Well, last weekend there was a white dog, a talking white dog – and then today I saw a white squirrel, and a white trout which my friends conveniently forgot about, apparently – and –"

"Those would be Nuada, I think. Or some of his minions. He is of your faction."

"My faction? What faction?" David shook his head. "I don't understand."

"The Sidhe are of two minds about you, David," Oisin said. "One sept, of whom Ailill is chief, regards you as a threat. They say that when your people made the chariot road that passes near here, and it thus became easy for great numbers of men to come into these mountains, there was then no longer a possibility of peace between the Worlds; and unless the Sidhe make a stand very soon, the day is not far off when only the Deep Waters will remain where the immortals may walk freely – and there are no stars in the Deep Waters, and no moon. Ailill and his like fear you, yet they dare not slay you, if only in dread of the wrath of Nuada and Lugh. But they would be glad to have you safely in Tir-Nan-Og, so drunk on Faery wine that you never recall your own lands. This Ailill would have done on Lughnasadh had Nuada not thwarted him and had your answers not been so astute. Ailill did not like that at all, and he and Nuada have become great enemies because of it, and the rift between them grows wider by the day. Lugh is greatly vexed."

"Lugh is your king, right?"

Oisin nodded. "Lugh Samildinach, Ard Rhi – High King, you would say – for this time in Tir-Nan-Og. It was not always so, nor will it always be. Nuada was king once, though in Erenn; he may be again, and for your sake I hope that day is soon. It is his faction that feels you may be of service to us as you are: a youth largely untouched by the grosser things of this world." Again he rapped David on the knee. "Nuada feels that you may serve us best if you remain free among mortals, perhaps in time to become a sort of ambassador between Faery-kind and mortal men, working in both their interests."

"And how would I do that?" David snorted. "Go to Atlanta and tell the governor, 'I'm David Sullivan, and the Irish fairies said for you not to build any more roads in the mountains 'cause they were there first?' Shoot! They wouldn't listen to the Indians, the environmentalists, or anybody who's lived here longer than a month; they sure as hell won't listen to somebody they *can't* see!"

"The *Ani-Yunwiya* gave us no sorrow," Oisin mused wistfully. "The *Nunnihe*, they called us."

"But I've only seen a couple of things," David went on more calmly, "and already I'm fidgety all the time. I can't trust anything to be what it looks like. I don't mean Ailill any harm, Oisin! I don't want to hurt any of the Sidhe." He buried his face in his hands.

"And they wish that you — and all men of this land — would leave them alone." Oisin's response began harshly but faded to gentler tones. "Oh, it is true, lad, that no one may harbor ill will toward what he does not know exists, but the taint of mortal men nevertheless intrudes more and more into Faerie. The days of the Sidhe in the land you call Ireland are nearly done because of that intrusion. Here in these mountains the intrusion is both less and slower, yet this land, too, is becoming closed by such things as the iron tracks that once lay where the chariot road now lies. Fifty years they have been gone, yet their shadows remain, and their fire, and their stench. The Way is still very weak there, the Walls between the Worlds very thin. Indeed, for that brief distance the Sidhe must ride almost wholly in your World. And this year those Walls were thinner than ever before; only the thinnest veil of glamour remained. Anyone with a trace of Power could have heard our music and seen our lights. And such Power is in you — and in your brother as well, though it still sleeps in him. What has awakened it in you, I do not know — but we have more important things to discuss. You said you thought Ailill had been after you already?"

"If that really was him today that water-horse thing. And there was a weird wind, too. Could he have had something to do with that?"

Oisin shrugged. "Neither would surprise me. Ailill is fond of shapeshifting and is likewise a master of winds and tempests, though it seems strange that he would attack you by daylight, for his Power is greatest at night. As I said before, a protection has been laid upon you. I suspect he seeks to learn the source of that protection, and therefore uses the tools that he knows best. But, more importantly, he fears the threat he thinks you embody, and a frightened man can be very dangerous indeed."

David drummed his fingers on his thigh. "But what about the ring? I'm sure it's mixed up in this. Is it the protection you just mentioned?"

"Ah!" Oisin smiled. "The ring. I myself was among the host that you encountered on Lughnasadh, and even as we continued on our Riding, I reminded Ailill of the promise he had made to confer a token of your meeting and how it was an ill thing for him not to see that bargain fulfilled. Oh, he was in a black mood after his double defeats, let me tell you, and he dismissed me with a shrug, saying that if tokens were bestowed, someone else would do the bestowing.

"And then I bethought myself of these many rings I have, each given me by a Faery lover when I was young." Oisin spread his hands wide so that David could see the intricate metalwork and almost infinitely tiny gems that decorated a ring on every finger except one. "And how each of them *is* magic, but one alone was afforded protection against the Sidhe themselves, for it was forged by a druid of the Fir Bolg and once belonged to Eochaid their king. That ring I caused to be put on your finger."

"But how – ?"

Oisin smiled again. "One learns much in two-thousand years, even those of mortal birth, such as I was before Lugh took from me the substance of that World. For while mortality shortens our lives, it also quickens our wits."

David scowled. "You say the ring protects me?"

"It will protect you and those you love – those you *truly* love from anyone with even a trace of Faery blood or Faery Power. While you possess it, the Sidhe are unable to do you any physical harm, nor tamper with your mind or memory. They may not touch you against your will, and their magic will have no power over you. But the ring has limits, too. I still retain some control over it, for instance, such as I used to tempt you here. And the Straightways are a greater Power and older; even the Sidhe do not understand all their workings."

"But how will I know whom it protects?"

"You have but to observe, for you are not without Power yourself. Things have Power because you give them Power; do not forget that. Discover that Power! Use it! There are people, for instance, to whom you have given enough of yourself, knowing or unknowing, that part of your Power is in them. Just as there are objects like that, and places – Places of Power for you, like this one. There is part of you in that boy over there." Oisin pointed to the sleeping Alec. " – and in the red-haired girl."

"Liz? I don't love her."

"Do you not?"

"I don't think so," David added in a small voice.

"Then you may be surprised one day."

Suddenly David felt very uncomfortable. "Is there anything else I can do to ... play it safe?" he asked at last.

"Iron and ash may provide some aid," Oisin replied. "And the Sidhe may enter no dwelling unasked. Remember that. Nor does time run in Faerie as it does in the Lands of Men; thus the Sidhe are sometimes slow to act or to respond. That may be your strongest defense against them. Also, do not let anyone you care about be alone when you can prevent it, especially at night, for as I said, the ring has limitations. And take special care of your brother; he is a prize they covet. There is little Ailill would not do to have him in his grasp."

"Like ... what?" David asked slowly.

Oisin straightened and began to rise. "Would that I had time to tell you a tenth part of them. Surely you have heard something of Faerie's less favorable dealings with mortals. Much that has been written is true."

He extended a hand to help David up. "Now, I fear I must depart. Already I have stayed too long; for I suspect that I am watched, and with more than eyes. Ailill knows I favor you and will do all in his power to forestall our further meetings if he learns of this one. Yet if you find yourself truly in need of me, it may be that I can return at your bidding, for they would not expect that, though it is likely that I could return but once. Should that need arise, come into the forest and break a twig from an oak tree. But do so only if you have no alternative, for it is magic of a kind, and you should have as little to do with magic as possible." He turned and started toward the waterfall.

"Wait a minute, please, before you go. I want Alec to meet you."

Oisin shook his head. "That may not be. Your friend will recall nothing of this night's work. He is safer thus."

"But, Oisin – !"

Oisin twisted around to face David. "Do you want to see him imperiled? More than he already is? Even now I feel someone's thought creeping about the walls of my mind, so truly I must depart. I will leave you with a warning, however – one thing that should never be far from your thoughts if you would deal with the Sidhe: This land they have claimed for their own, for the eternity of their lives, and they will see that it remains theirs, even if they must make one last stand against mortal men! That time is not yet, but I fear it fast approaches, and when it arrives, it may fall upon you to choose with whom you cast your lot. You could be a valuable friend then, or a bitter foe. It is up to you. Now farewell, David Sullivan, most blessed of mortal men."

With that, he turned away and walked not into the woods, but directly into the pool and thence under the waterfall. David was not surprised when the waters did not bow his head.

Most blessed of mortal men. David snorted to himself. "Or most cursed," he added aloud, as he made his way back to the overlook.

Alec was stirring as David sank down beside him. He stretched languorously. "Darn! I didn't mean to go to sleep like that. Why didn't you wake me?"

David smiled cryptically. "I didn't notice at first; I was thinking about ... other things. And then ... you just looked so peaceful."

"Well, the only other thing I'm thinking about is a nice soft bed a couple of miles down the road, and the sooner the better. I hope you found whatever it was you were looking for – if you could see anything without moon or flashlight.

David glanced up reflexively. The Faery moon was gone. Magic had retreated from the night.

They didn't talk much on their way back down the mountain. Indeed, the cloud cover had become so heavy that they had to devote most of their attention simply to navigating the road without stumbling, tripping, or actually falling down.

Somehow they managed to get into the house without waking anyone, undressed in the dark, and crawled into bed. Just as he closed his eyes, David heard the grandfather clock in the living room toll once. He checked his watch's luminous readout from habit: five after one. *It's running again*, he realized. *But how could it only be one? We left just past midnight, and we've been gone hours and hours.* He started to wake Alec to tell him, then thought better of it. His friend was already snoring.

Chapter VIII

Running
(sunday, august 9)

david couldn't believe how good he felt the next morning. His eyes literally popped open at six a.m., and he had no urge whatever to remain in bed. That in spite of logic, which told him that he had, in fact, slept rather less than six hours; and emotion, which told him that he'd awakened with a great deal more to worry about than he'd gone to bed with the night before.

And, on top of everything else, it was threatening rain again, as a glance out his window showed. Heavy clouds loomed dark and ominous, promising the kind of sullen day he hated. If his father was a fire elemental, David mused, he must himself be a spirit of the air, for it was bright sunlight and clear, clean skies that made him feel most alive.

Still, in spite of logic, in spite of emotion, even in spite of the weather he was experiencing an almost embarrassing sense of well-being. It was as if some untapped spring of energy had overflowed into his mind and body alike. He felt – there was no other term for it – empowered. Empowered in the most positive, most literal sense imaginable – and there was no way to account for it. Unless, just possibly, it was some legacy of his meeting with Oisin.

He vaulted out of bed and stretched luxuriously, feeling every muscle, bone, and sinew slide sensuously into place. There was no trace of morning stiffness – none of the soreness he expected from the three hours he'd spent yesterday tugging on a block-and-tackle attached to a 390 cubic inch Ford V-8. What was present was pure, unadulterated, adolescent energy.

He glanced over at the amorphous mass of rumpled fabric that presumably concealed a still-sleeping Alec. A single bare foot protruded from the lower edge of a wadded sheet. He grabbed it, tugged, and twisted. A muffled cry was followed by a resounding thump as Alec flopped to the floor amid a tumble of pillow, linens, and bedspread.

"Rise and shine, Scotsboy," David cried, grinning.

"You gotta be kiddin'," Alec mumbled, trying unsuccessfully to extricate himself from the combination toga, sari, and cocoon into which he'd wound himself during the night.

David sat down on his own bed and watched with vast amusement as Alec disentangled himself from the pile, rose, and stretched in turn, fingers automatically trying to order his rumpled hair even before rubbing his eyes. "What's the matter, McLean? Not ready to face the day? I feel marvelous! Absolutely great. In fact, I don't think I can resist going for a run before breakfast. And you, of course, oh faithful partner, will accompany me."

Alec stumbled over to kneel on David's bed so as to peer out the window. "You've got to be kidding," he repeated through a yawn.

"Oh, come on, bro! Rigorous rural life not agreeing with you?"

"Not until after breakfast. I'll take a rain check then."

"Probably with real rain, too!"

"If I'm lucky," Alec muttered.

David cuffed him smartly, then slid off the bed and began scouring the piles of clothing on the floor for a pair of gym shorts he'd last worn two days before – which, once located, were followed by an ancient gray sweatshirt from which the sleeves and everything below the ribcage had been ripped, and a reasonably clean pair of socks – none of which he put on.

Alec stepped over him and peered groggily into the mirror on the closet door. "Those guys got any friends?" he called over his shoulder. "Preferably clean ones?"

"Not much of a boy scout, are you?" David grunted as he rummaged under his bed for a delinquent running shoe. "Never seem to be prepared. Fortunately I think Sullivan Outfitters can come up with something." He snared the shoe and reached for its twin.

"One condition."

"I make no promises."

"Coffee."

"Afterwards."

Alec flopped back onto his bed. "Before, or I don't go."

"It'll stunt your growth."

"For which you should be grateful, seeing how I'm taller than you already."

David threw a pillow at him.

Alec caught it in mid-flight and used it as a shield as he advanced on David, whom he caught off guard trying to find the front of the shorts, the telltale tag being absent. Giggling like idiots, they collapsed onto the bed with Alec on top, straddling David's stomach.

"Fool of a Scotsman!" David gasped. "Get off me!"

"Promise me something, first."

"I promise to beat your ass if you don't get off me."

"Two cups of coffee."

"I can't promise if I can't breathe."

"Two cups of coffee."

"Done. Now hurry up and get dressed, before Pa catches us and puts us to doing something obnoxious."

Alec released David instantly. "He works like that on Sunday?"

David looked startled. "It *is* Sunday, isn't it? Well, well."

Another search of the floor produced a pair of cutoffs, which David flung in Alec's general direction. His friend regarded them dubiously before sighing and tugging them on. "Well, well *what*?" he inquired.

David slipped a hand under the abbreviated shirt and fondled the ring. "I've had this for a whole week now."

"What?" a confused Alec repeated, as his head emerged through the neck of his T-shirt.

"Oh, nothing."

Alec frowned. "My butt."

"– Has as its primary function keeping your legs connected to your torso in a vain attempt to follow in my footsteps as I run fleet as a deer through the morning woods."

"Gimme a break, Sullivan. Nobody feels that good this early."

"Not everybody has a magic ring, either."

"I'll make you a deal," Alec said, suddenly serious. "If I can beat you in a race, you tell me the straight story, beginning to end."

David stared at him. "I *have* told you the straight story."

"Bull." Alec extended a hand, his face still serious, eyes trusting. "Deal?"

David took the hand reluctantly. "Deal – but only if you catch me."

Maybe I'll just run off in the woods and not come back!

David actually considered that, if briefly, as he burst into the backyard a few minutes later, with a still-groggy Alec trotting stiffly in tow. He'd follow the short course, he'd decided: maybe a mile-and-a-half (it wouldn't do to push Alec too hard): across the upper pasture first, just skirting the woods; then down the other side, then back up into the woods proper for half a mile or so, following a steep, winding path that gradually straightened and then paralleled the top edge of a precipitous bank behind Uncle Dale's place, where some over-ambitious relative had ripped a gash in the mountain to make a level place for a barn that had never been built – then finally back to civilization on the other side of Dale's farm, where the forest intersected the Sullivan Cove road at the lake. And then another half mile back along that road to the farm. A fair mix of terrain, all things considered. Challenging too, but not impossible for one less conditioned to running than he was.

Not that he was much of a jock, either, at least not in the conventional sense. The only sport he actually liked to participate in was volleyball, though he was an excellent swimmer, liked to wrestle with his buddies, and didn't mind watching gymnastics (a good sport for muscular little guys like him, plus he admired the fine control gymnasts had over their bodies). Unfortunately, rural Enotah County offered nothing along any of those lines, and driving fast didn't count, even if auto racing was also a sport. Still, he had grown more aware of his body of late, now that the eager upward rush of puberty seemed to be abating and giving his body time to fill out instead of up. A little more *up* would be nice, though, he thought wistfully, but at least his work on the farm over the summer had done some good: His ribs were sleek with muscles now, and his shirts were getting tight in the armpits. Still, he lacked the discipline to exercise on a regular basis. To compensate, he had started running a couple of months before – which was less like exercise than like religion: a becoming of one with the natural world.

As for other forms of exercise ... Well, a part of him wished he could study sword fighting, or at least fencing, but there was no way either would be possible in a place as remote from mainstream American culture as Sullivan Cove. It was tempting to imagine, though: himself in plate armor, swinging a two-handed broadsword in his gauntleted fists: a lord among men – like Nuada.

Joyfully, he vaulted the low barbed-wire fence at the edge of the pasture, then jogged back to lift a strand for Alec to climb through. This first part of the route ran gently uphill across the rounded crest of the upper pasture – maybe a hundred yards. David gloried in the feel of air rushing in his ears, the rhythm of his strides, the steady thud of his feet touching the springy ground. This early on there was no trace of fatigue, only the exhilaration of moving swiftly on soft grass, with the faint scent of pine needles coming in on every breath. Straight ahead, the stubborn sun broke through the glowering clouds with swords of light, dolloping the stubble of cow-mown grass with greenish gold and striking fire from the tin roof of Uncle Dale's old house, huddled in its hollow a quarter of a mile away.

Alec's dull, staccato tread and hissing breaths sounded behind him. *Poor guy*, he thought, as their route leveled out along an abandoned farm road before turning down the steeper slope on the far side of the pasture. It would be down this slope, in a now-broken rhythm, across (or under, or through) another barbed-wire fence at the bottom, and then sharply left and back uphill into the woods proper.

David more jumped than ran down the lower face of the slope, though he was careful not to twist an ankle in some unexpected gully, then leapt the fence one-handed and headed south, aiming for the gap between two lightning-blasted pines that marked the entrance to the wooded part of the route.

Soon enough, the forest closed about him, though the sun still sent pale shafts of light shooting between the branches: shafts so bright against the gloom they virtually seemed solid. David set himself a new pace, then; arms pumping vigorously, breath coming steadily but a little harder as he began to exert himself. Up ahead he could see another landmark tree, to which he called an absurd, if friendly, greeting as he passed. He could feel sweat forming on his chest and back now, rolling down between his shoulders to pool, tickling, at the waistband of his skivvies.

His thoughts began to wander as he slowed where the course became steeper and more crooked. A new-fallen limb lay athwart the trail, but he leapt over it and continued on. Behind him he could hear the steady thump-gasp, thump-gasp of a remarkably persistent Alec. He broke stride to venture a glance over his shoulder and saw his friend pounding grimly onward, dark hair sticking to his forehead in lieu of its usual spikes. Alec's gaze caught David's for an instant, and he bared his teeth in friendly menace.

David reestablished his pace, but he could hear Alec's breathing becoming harder and more forceful, though it was not yet labored. *He's like a little bull*, he thought. Alec was gaining, too – which wasn't good. Suppose David lost! Suppose Alec held him to his vow and demanded the whole preposterous story from him. How could he tell his friend that?

A branch slapped at his face, disrupting his reverie. He checked the trail ahead – he hadn't been this way in a while, and the landmarks were not as clear as he remembered them. Still, he quickened his pace, but the sound of Alec's running grew no fainter.

"You'd better run, Sullivan," Alec called behind him. "'Cause if I catch you, you ain't gonna like being caught!"

"What you gonna do, fool of a Scotsman?"

"Wring the truth out of you like a bagpipe!"

"Ha!" David cried. "Not bloody likely!"

But he nevertheless ran faster.

A dozen strides later, they veered west onto a short section that was both straight and level: an aisle among the oaks and maples. Ahead and to the right David glimpsed the roof of Uncle Dale's house, much closer now. Once on the straight, he increased his speed – but so did Alec.

Time to get serious, now. David withdrew into himself, concentrating, feeling only his blood racing, his legs pumping; hearing the air whistle between his glasses and his ears; noting that the lenses were steaming up. Where was the next landmark, anyway? The trail had become unclear. Oh yeah, there it was, over to the left.

The trail now bent upward into the steepest part they had yet confronted, the section that led most deeply into the forest before turning back on itself. David didn't remember it being quite so steep; then again it had been a while since he had used this route. And it was awfully straight, wasn't it? *Too* straight, in fact; maybe he'd made a wrong turn and wound up on one of those old logging roads that laced the woods. Up ahead he could see something pale moving alongside the trail: the telltale flag of a whitetail deer, perhaps? Probably – there were plenty of them hereabouts.

The trail widened again, and the air felt cooler. The green of the needles, the brown of the pine straw, even the gray patches of sky he occasionally glimpsed seemed subtly brighter, more clearly defined. David's eyes itched – but they did that most of the time now – and he was sweating profusely. He could still hear Alec behind him, though; kept expecting at any moment to see his friend pull even with him, or – worse – feel him grab him from behind to wrest from him the secret he was now honor-bound to reveal.

And then he felt the pain.

Not in his side, however – that he more or less expected – but on his chest! A burning from where the ring bounced up and down between his pecs. *Not good*, he told himself. *Not good at all.*

The trail leveled off once more, but the trees closed in ominously, and the shafts of sunlight vanished abruptly, like lamps turned off. He could still see the tantalizing pale flash up ahead, hear the muffled rustle of its passage through the woods, but the quality of both had shifted in a way David could not articulate, save that it disturbed him. He slowed, suddenly frightened. Something weird was going on. And then he knew.

He was on a Straight Track – or *Way, or whatever the Faeries called 'em.* And indeed the trail was arrow-straight, broken only by gentle undulations, but rising steadily to ... where? It was glowing softly golden, too, its margin marked by star-shaped white flowers of an unknown variety, which – David shuddered when he noticed – were also glowing. Now that he was aware of it, the fact that this was a Track was obvious, and he felt an utter fool not to have noticed earlier. Still, he was not exactly used to thinking in terms of such things, for all that his eyes were burning almost painfully. He tried to veer off, to turn aside from that place of subtly disturbing otherness. But as moved toward the side of the trail, he found that he could only go so far and no farther. It was as if he brushed up against a soft but infinitely strong barrier through which he could not pass: exactly the sort of barrier he had encountered the night he had met the Sidhe.

Oh, God! He thought, clutching at the ring, *I'm on one of their roads, like Great-grandpa got on, and I can't get off! It's some kind of trap! But I haven't done anything to them; they should know that. I haven't even told anybody about them except Alec, and he doesn't believe me. Shit! If they've got me, they've got him too!*

Behind him, David could still hear Alec wheezing along. "Where you goin', Sullivan?" his friend gasped. "You gone off the deep end or something? This ain't the course you described."

"Veer off, Alec!" David shouted, as panic began to replace rationality. "Veer off!"

But Alec did not veer off.

And David kept on running – though he wanted to stop, to fling Alec bodily from that path, if such a thing were possible. With that in mind, he actually tried to halt – and found that he could not. His legs continued to work, in spite of his intentions to the contrary. There was no alternative but to run.

In one brief instant David's whole world compressed to the sounds of footfalls and breath, and to alternating flashes of dark and light that were *too* dark and *too* light, as he sped past trees that grew thicker and taller than any Georgia tree had done since before man walked the earth. And there were certainly no familiar landmarks now; all that was certain was that he ran in a straight line. Up ahead the half-seen shape that he had thought might be a deer seemed to have paused beside the trail, but intervening branches masked a clearer view. Which was just as well. He doubted it was anything he wanted to encounter.

"I'll catch you sooner or later, Sullivan," he heard Alec pant. "You can't run forever."

"That may be exactly what we're doing," David shouted back.

He did run faster then; surely as fast as it was possible for him to move, so that the world became a whistling blur of dark green and pale gray centered on the pain on his chest where the ring burned white-hot. And as he passed a particularly thick and squatty live oak (*Live oak? Here, in north Georgia?*) he saw, with a small cry of dismay, that no woodland creature crouched there – nor any monster out of his worst fears, either. Rather, the phantom runner he had been pacing was a naked, pale-skinned, blond-haired boy who looked no older than himself, but whose slanted green eyes, slightly pointed ears, and unearthly grace of face and limb marked him surely as one of the Sidhe. As he passed the stranger, David saw the perfect lips open and a rather too wicked smile play about them, even as the boy reached toward him with one slim-fingered hand. David dodged left at the last possible instant and ran on, now doubly pursued.

Almost immediately, the Track began to slant downhill. Painful shocks raced up David's legs as his feet impacted the ground with ever-increasing force. Behind him, he could still hear Alec's consistent strides, and the softer but somehow more insidious tread of the Faery runner. David's heart rose for a moment, as an idea occurred to him. Alec was back there; Alec would see and believe.

But, no, his friend hadn't reacted when the boy appeared and surely he would have. His heart sank as quickly as hope had risen, for he very much feared Alec could not see their new companion.

Up ahead a light showed: a break in the trees – a goal, if nothing else. Perhaps with clear sky above, he could think of a solution.

The trail leveled off again, then sloped steeply downward, after which he would be there. What he would do when he reached that goal, he had no idea. Perhaps he would run onward until the Track ended or he died. Now, that would be some way to go! No one would write a song, though; no folk ballad would celebrate Mad Davy Sullivan who ran a footrace with the Sidhe. He chuckled grimly, reminded of the tune about the man lost forever on the Boston subway and then was jerked back to what passed for reality by the brush of hands against his abbreviated shirt.

"Got you now, Sullivan!" he heard Alec shout.

Alec! He was in as much danger as David himself, perhaps more, for his friend had no notion that this was anything but another one of David's mad indulgences. Alec was running for knowledge; David was quite literally running for his life indeed, quite possibly, for both their lives.

David exerted himself one last time, imagining himself as a deer pursued by two hounds, neither of which suspected the other's existence, yet both with teeth snapping at its heels, though each for a different reason. He could almost see mortal and Faery hands reaching toward him. But up ahead was the open place, the blue sky. *Blue sky?* He ran on down the slope toward that welcoming color.

And broke free into empty air.

A pain centered on his chest shattered his senses. Golden light exploded behind his eyes. A voice screamed his name.

And then there was no ground below him at all, merely thirty feet of space and a long, steep slope of blood-colored earth studded with bruised and broken rocks. Far below he could see the stream that flowed behind Uncle Dale's house.

In that one eternal second when he was sure he hung suspended in mid-air before gravity woke up to his presence there, he felt something brush the nape of his neck and twisted around to see an inhumanly white arm cross his field of vision. With it came another flash of pain, like a knife drawn across his throat.

And then he saw nothing at all except Alec's face frozen in an incredulous open-mouthed stare.

He began to fall.

He hit once. A staggering pain tore through his right thigh and hip, as the earth shredded the bare flesh there; a shoulder struck something hard; then he was sliding, rolling, trying to slow himself with hands that tore to tatters. And then it was his head that hit something, and then the air was knocked from his lungs. Something cold and wet enfolded him; water filled his nose and ears. And then oblivion seized his consciousness and reality disappeared.

He came to gazing up at that same ominous and strangely remote gray sky he remembered from earlier that morning. And then Alec's face swung into view closer in, dark against the glare. He looked concerned. A drop of sweat fell from his forehead onto David's cheek to become one with that much cooler wetness that tickled capriciously about him. He was dizzy; his head spun. His head *hurt*, he realized dimly. There was a darkness out there waiting for him. It would be so easy to fall into it, to let it stave off the pain. Stars. Stars and comets and the granddaddy of all meteor showers: his own private light show going on behind his eyes.

No!

David fought his way back to consciousness, opened his eyes and felt for his glasses – which, remarkably, still rested crookedly on his nose. But there was too much light, too much pain. He closed his eyes again, whether to return to that place of increasingly pleasant darkness or to steel himself to rise, he didn't know – until he found himself trying to sit up – and cried out, as agony exploded from his right shoulder to join other bursts from hip, legs, and hands. His whole body ached; an unpleasant stickiness oozed from his palms. He fell back into the water, gripping the bank with one hand, fingers digging small trenches among the pebbles.

"Davy! You okay?" It was Alec's voice that echoed metallically in his ears. Someone lifted his head; hands worked their way into his armpits.

"Easy, boy, let me help you here," a different voice crackled.

David forced his eyes open to see another face looming above him, this one crowned with silver hair escaping the dark halo of an ancient felt hat. The smell of tobacco reached his nostrils: Uncle Dale's own personal blend of homegrown.

The hands in his armpits shifted, and he found himself being dragged onto dry ground. Somebody picked up his feet, and he grunted at the pain. And then there was solid ground beneath him.

"David?" he could hear Uncle Dale's voice call. "Davy, boy; you hear me?" The old man sounded strangely calm. "Don't talk, just nod if you can hear me."

David opened his mouth but could only croak something he intended to be "hurt."

"You'll live, I reckon," Uncle Dale murmured. "Appears you've scraped yourself up some; yore butt looks like a side of bacon. Maybe got one of them concussions, too – leastwise you look like you're seein' stars. Now, then, you just lay there and get yore breath; I don't think nothin' else is wrong."

Wrong? David thought vaguely. *Wrong? Something must be wrong.* But he couldn't remember. All he could recall was running and getting lost in the woods, and running and running and running some more; and then falling for what seemed like forever. Only there was a burst of agony about every ten centuries, each in a different place. And there had been other runners ...

He tensed, felt pain again, and groaned dully as he tried to roll away from that discomfort, even as hands forced him once more onto his back. He heard some distant shaky voice that might've been Alec's say, "Here's a blanket," then add, "I can't believe he didn't see that bank. I just can't believe it."

No, this wasn't Alec's fault, David conceded dully, nor even his own; it was that other boy's: the one who'd been after him, who'd been after the ...

The ring!

David's fingers clutched for his throat, felt for the chain that should lie about his neck.

It was gone.

He brushed his hands across his chest, feeling for the ring that should lie atop his breastbone.

It was gone!

The Faeries had won it back; that he now knew of a certainty. It was gone. The most precious thing he owned; one of the great heirlooms of the world, perhaps – according to what Oisin had told him. Gone. Lost. Stolen.

And with that abandonment of hope, David abandoned consciousness as well and passed into an empty, falling blackness from which he did not return until much, much later.

The next thing David remembered clearly was waking up on the sofa in the dim light of Uncle Dale's living room. His scraped thigh and the raw ruin of his hands made themselves known by distant throbbings. Someone coughed softly, and David followed that sound through slitted lids to where Uncle Dale sat in his favorite rocker, looking seriously concerned. An ancient transistor radio beside him whispered banjo music. For no clear reason, David's attention was drawn to the stuffed deer head that hung above the fieldstone fireplace opposite the sofa.

Oh God, I hurt! he told himself. *But I can't stay here. The Faeries have my ring. I've got to find it.*

"I've got to find it!" he shouted aloud, trying to sit up. Firm hands on his shoulders restrained him. Uncle Dale could move amazingly fast when he needed to.

"Now, boy, don't go gettin' excited. You hit yore head a good'un, and I 'spect we'd better get a doctor to take a look at it. Alec's called the hospital and yore folks; he's in the kitchen makin' us some coffee right now. You hungry? Bet you ain't had breakfast yet." The old man stood up and started for the kitchen door.

"Hospital!" David started to protest to the old man's departing back, but the effort of opening his mouth that wide made pains shoot through his head that made a perfect counterpoint to the stars that returned to cloud his vision. "Hospital," he whispered. "I can't go to the hospital. I can't! I've got to find my ring!" His voice grew louder. "I gotta go look for my ring! You didn't find my ring, did you? Oh God!" His voice sank into a moan.

Alec padded in from the kitchen, barefoot, and with a steaming mug in his hand, which he started to pass to David. David grabbed his friend's wrist instead, oblivious to the agony it cost him. "Alec, you didn't find my ring, did you?"

Alec gently pried David's fingers loose. "No, sorry. I didn't even think about it."

David sat up, though it made his eyes fill up with darkness and his head spin. Thunder pounded between his ears.

"You didn't think about it? What *did* you think about?"

Alec gaped incredulously. "Why, you, of course! You're more important than any old ring."

"You sure about that?"

"Dammit, Sullivan, you could've drowned in that creek if I hadn't been right behind you when you decided to go bungee jumping without a cord. You think I'm gonna be worrying about jewelry when you've got blood all over you? You could've been dying for all I know."

"You don't understand, Alec, you really don't. It's a *magic* ring, and it's very, very important. You didn't even see the chain anywhere?

Alec shook his head. "Sorry."

Thunder rumbled ominously outside; the lights dimmed. Rain tinkled on the tin roof.

"Looks like we're in for a bad 'un," Uncle Dale opined, motioning toward the window with his pipe. "Just what you need to make you feel better, ain't it Davy boy?" He paused, eyes narrowed. "You think you oughta be settin' up like that?"

Thunder drowned David's grunted reply, and the lights dimmed again. Lightning flashed uncomfortably close by. The tempo of the rain increased, rattling on the roof like an infinity of marbles dropped from an impossible height. David glanced toward a window but could see only a silver shimmer.

"A real bad 'un," Uncle Dale repeated.

David stood up, swaying. "Uncle Dale, did you happen to see anything of my ring when you found me?"

"You mean that old ring you got from that gal? Nope, sure didn't. I ain't seen you wearin' it lately, so I figured you'd broke up with her."

David rolled his eyes, his gaze seeking Alec's. "I only had it a week!"

Dale spoke from beside the window. "A week's time enough to do nearly anything, if a man sets his mind to it – course a week of rain like this'd be more than enough for most people, though not for God, maybe.

But I'll tell you something, David. If that ring was anywhere on that bank before, it's plumb washed away by now."

Ailill is a master of winds and tempests. David recalled Oisin saying. Had he contrived this storm purely to confound David's efforts at recovering the ring? August rain usually consisted of brief afternoon showers: the day's electricity shorting itself out in a harmless display of self-indulgent pyrotechnics. Rain this hard so early in the day was well nigh unprecedented.

"No!" David cried suddenly. "No, I've got to find it. I've got to!"

He broke into a lurching run toward the door that led into the kitchen and thence onto the back porch. Alec grabbed at him as he passed, but David shoved him aside with so much force that his friend sprawled backward onto the floor. Coffee splattered across the linoleum.

David flung open the backdoor screen as another bolt of lightning struck nearby, followed almost at once by a blast of thunder that rang through the valley like a mile-high steel gong being smashed to slivers. The world turned white; the stars he had never stopped seeing were black cutouts against it. The stench of ozone filled the air. David's head throbbed abominably.

But he had to find the ring. It was his last chance his only chance.

He didn't notice the water that sheeted directly off the tin roof without benefit of gutters, for he was already soaked to the skin – and skin was mostly what he wore anyway. He began to run toward the bank, his head exploding with every footfall, his scraped leg sending its own insistent messages of protest. He didn't care. He had to find the ring. He *had* to find the ring!

The ring. The ring. The ring. The thoughts echoed the pounding of his feet. Behind him he could hear Alec and Uncle Dale calling to him.

The ring, the ring, the ring, the ring, the ring ...

Somehow David found himself by the creek but it was hardly recognizable, having become in a few scant minutes a swollen, frothing torrent, stained blood red by the sticky mud that scabbed the bank above it. A thousand tributary streams flowed into it, each with its own load of brown silt and red Georgia clay, any one of which perhaps was carrying his ring to some unreachable destination.

If the Sidhe didn't have it or get it first.

But he had to look; he *had* to.

David waded out into the creek and ran his fingers along the bottom, searching, feeling – to no avail. Dirty foam welled up around his forearms. Once he thought he'd found it, but it was only the tab from an old pop-top drink can, and the current swept it away before he could toss it. He waded a few yards downstream, following that current, which was unexpectedly strong for such a shallow creek. He felt for the bottom again, but found only coarse, rounded gravel amid larger, more jagged, rocks.

Another try, another failure. It was no use: There was too much to search and no time. Water was his enemy.

Another try.

Another failure.

The bank, then – as he heaved his aching body out of the stream and into the cleaner, though scarcely less dense, torrents that gushed from the swollen clouds above.

But the bank was a treacherous wall of mud, and David barely got two steps up it before he began to slip downward once more. It was almost too steep to climb at the best of times – and this wasn't one of them.

Lightning again, and thunder.

And rain.

Pain.

Noise.

His head hurt.

He had lost the ring.

He was defeated.

Wearily he slogged through the knee-high water, turning back toward the barely discernible shape of Uncle Dale's house. Two figures stood on the back porch.

David halted when he saw them and crumpled forward onto his knees in the mud. His hair was plastered to his head; his tattered clothes clung to his body like a wrinkled second skin. But the water that washed his face most fiercely bore the salt of his own tears.

Uncle Dale was in the yard beside him, with Alec close behind. Together they hoisted him up and helped him climb the steps onto the back porch. When they finally got him back into the living room, he flung his arms around the old man and began sobbing uncontrollably. "I've lost it," he choked. "It's gone!"

Alec draped a blanket around his best friend's shoulders and patted him awkwardly.

David glanced sideways at his buddy and said, with perfect lucidity, "It's gone, Alec and I don't even want to think about what might happen now."

Interlude V

In the lands of men

"**Well,** thank God," Dale Sullivan said, and hung up the phone.

"Who 'uz that?" Little Billy wondered, from where he was playing his latest portable video game at Dale's kitchen table.

Dale looked at him, as if seeing him for the first time – or, more properly, as if not quite sure who he was seeing. The Sullivan boys were starting to run together in his mind and memory now, what with all of them being handsome blond lads: David-the-Elder and then David-the-Younger, and now Little Billy. All had somehow wound up with blond hair, in spite of Big Billy's being red as fire, as Dale's own once had been. As his father's had also been. He guessed the hair came from their mothers.

But he bet if you lined 'em all up at the same age, they'd look just about like twins, or triplets, rather. Certainly the two Davids would, except for the Elder being a wee bit taller and leaner. Of course the jury was still out on that, as far as Little Billy was concerned.

"Who wuz, it, Uncle Dale?" Little Billy persisted.

Dale shook himself back to the present. "Just your daddy callin' to say David's okay. He's not got a concussion, or anything; just a bunch of scrapes and bruises."

"What's a con – con – ?"

"Hard hit on the head's enough for you to know right now," Dale said, leaning up against the wall by the telephone table. And since it was only the second time he'd actually had to use the phone in the last two weeks (the first time being a couple of hours back when he'd called

157

David's folks about the boy's fall), it was actually no surprise that it was the first time he'd been in a position to notice the note he'd written back Friday a week ago: the one that simply read, "Daddy's journal."

Even so, it took him a while to remember why he'd written it, and even then, he wasn't exactly certain.

Still, he must've thought it was important then, or it wouldn't be here now.

"Stay right there," he told Little Billy, who was sufficiently intent on his game he was likely to stay put.

And with that Dale betook himself to the closet in the tiny guest bedroom and dug down behind a rack of old clothes until he found the Christmas decorations he hadn't touched since Hattie died, and under them found an old footlocker.

He grunted as he dragged it out far enough to see, not much caring that the decorations slid back behind it.

Opening the lid, he sorted through an assortment of what were now less physical objects than memories of objects, until he found a small book bound in red leather.

With that he closed the lid (fearing, perhaps, that too many other memories would escape, as they seemed to have a tendency to do when he prowled around in his past for too long) and returned to the relative warmth of the kitchen. Warmth because the storm that had come up just about the time David had fallen seemed intent on washing every last trace of summer heat out of the air.

Little Billy hadn't moved more than his fingers when Dale returned. Without speaking, he made himself a cup of his trademark coffee-and-'shine, sat down opposite his younger grand-nephew and began to read.

It took him a while to find what he was looking for, but at least what he was looking for was actually there, which certainly hadn't been a given. But there it was, an entry from the year before Dale's younger brother – Big Billy's pa – had been born. He'd have been about ten then, himself. His daddy would've been in his early forties: old enough to tell the difference between what was real and what was not.

And then he started reading.

At first it was all notes about routine matters around the farm – the old farm, the one that had been drowned when the lake came in: stuff about hog-killing and such-like that pretty well set the time – the journal wasn't dated – as some time in the fall. But then halfway down the page he found what he had sought. Or what memory had conjured him to seek, better say.

"I'm not sure whether I should even write this down: what I'm about to say, cause I reckon folks might think I'm a crazy man if they read it. But since nobody's going to read this, at least while I'm alive (and after that, it won't matter what they think), I reckon I'll go ahead and write it down myself, since this is the kind of thing I suspect I might want to look back on sometime and see if it really happened, and if I've got stuff about it wrote down, then that'll be more proof than just my memory that I was neither drunk nor crazy that time.

So anyway, it goes like this.

Last night I decided I was up for a little coon hunting, so I got the dogs ready, and we headed out towards where the railroad tracks are, out where they've been talking about taking up the tracks and putting in one of them paved roads. Now granted, that's not the best place to start a coon hunt from, but I hadn't been out there in a while, cause frankly it pains me to see the land used like that, but I guess a man can only fight progress – if you can call it that – for so long. Anyway, I wanted to see if it was as bad as I remember it (it was), and having the dogs along gave me an excuse to think about something else later. I ain't no fool, or at least I didn't think I was.

But as I was saying, I took the dogs out. And I guess I should say now I wasn't really hunting – nothing I particularly wanted (though I wouldn't have said no to a brace of coons) – and you ain't supposed to hunt deer with dogs. I guess it was more pretend hunting, like my wife likes to go pretend fishing, which is to say she sits on the bank with a line in the water. Anyway, I followed the train tracks for a ways, but I kept noticing that the dogs didn't much like them, so I decided to just head straight up in the woods where the tracks curve east up that old Indian trail I've been hearing about all my life and never can quite remember to check out. I guess that's funny, if you think about it: something that interesting being close by all your life and you never checking it out, but I reckon folks get to thinking about certain things in certain ways and they forget there's any other way to think about them.

Well, anyway, I headed up the bank that was made by the railroad cut, and I swear to God I thought I was gonna have to whip them dogs to get them to move, but then all of a sudden I seems like all they changed their mind at once, and before I knowed it they was running up that bank like the Devil hisself was after them. Well, I followed, cause that's what a hunting man's supposed to do, and I wanted to see what they'd found that was so interesting. And Lord Jesus, I wish I'd brought a horse, cause they was already just about beyond earshot by then.

So anyway, I headed up the bank and got into the woods, and I sure enough found that old Indian trail, cause I'd always heard it was bounded by briars, and it really was: biggest old briars I ever seen, but I don't think they was blackberry briars. Funny thing, too, was that the trail was still so well marked after all these years, like folks was still using it or something, though I know they ain't. Funnier was the fact that it was straight as a stick, which should've told me something but didn't. So I started following it, just to see how long it would run straight. I felt okay about that, cause I could hear the hounds a hollering ahead of me.

And then all of a sudden they stopped: silent as the grave. And I guess they wasn't moving, cause I caught up with them a little later, and there they were at some kind of weird clearing, just nosing around like they were looking for something. And then I saw something that plumb put the wind up me. Best way to say it is just to say it.

It was a deer: a pure white deer, big old buck, it was, only it didn't look like the kinds of bucks we've got round here; it looked like one of them red deer they've got in Europe that I've seen pictures of. Only this one was pure, pure white.

And it run right into the clearing – come right up the way I'd just come, and it kept on running. Well, my dogs, being my dogs and good dogs, took one look at it and took off after it.

And I wish to the Lord they hadn't.

Cause right behind that deer come five of the strangest looking dogs I ever seen. They was big old dogs, can't quite say the breed, but they was long and rangy and hairy and frankly they looked a lot like wolves. And they was white as snow. White as snow, that is, except for their ears, and those ears was red as blood. And they took off after that deer like it was Sunday dinner and they hadn't eat for a month of Sundays. And I just stood there like a fool and watched them run past, and didn't even think until it was too late that those dogs probably wouldn't take much of a shine to my dogs if they run into them (as seemed likely, cause it looked to me like they was all on the self-same trail).

So I figured that maybe the smart thing to do was to round mine up and head home, and hopefully on the way I'd find whoever had them strange dogs and we could have a word or two, though I'm not sure now what that word might've been.

Well I'd just started on up the trail, when I heard hoof beats behind me, and I looked around, and I seen a man on a horse riding up the trail I'd been on (and never left), and that man was wearing all gray clothes, but they didn't look like our clothes, though I can't rightly say how they did look. His horse was gray, too, and he was setting a right good pace. But then he saw me, and he reined that horse back – though he didn't exactly stop it – and he looked down on me, and it looked to me like his eyes were on fire, and he said one thing that I'll never forget as long as I live. And what he said was, "Leave this place now, or never see home again."

Well, let me tell you, this wasn't the kind of man you want to argue with, so I just said something like, "Just let me get my dogs, and I'll do just that" but he just looked at me and I swear there was fire in his eyes and said, "Your dogs are my dogs now."

And I started to say something else, but he just looked at me again and said, "Hunt where you will, but do not hunt here – ever."

And then he kicked that gray horse of his and rode on off up the trail.

So I come home without my dogs, and I swore then I'd never tell a soul about what I seen, and I won't. But I guess I may have to explain what happened to my dogs, but damned if I know what I'm gonna say. I don't want to lie to my wife or the kids. But I'm surely damned if I'm gonna tell 'em the truth."

"Well, well, well," Dale whispered to the top of Little Billy's head, as he closed the book. "Well, well, well."

And then the phone rang again, jerking Dale firmly back to the present. It was Big Billy saying that David was fine and that they were heading back home right then, and that JoAnne wanted to know if he could pull some pork chops out of the freezer so they could start to thawing.

"Well, well, well," Dale repeated, as he got up to return his daddy's journal to its rightful place among vanished memories.

"Well, well, well."

 PART III

Prologue IV

In Tir-nan-og
(high summer)

Silverhand's *weed seems to be everywhere,* Ailill observed irritably, as he strode down the high-arched length of the Hall of Manannan in the southwest wing of Lugh's palace. Ten times a man's height those bone-white arches rose – appropriately, for each of those spans was made of the single bladelike rib of a species of leviathan that was now extinct in Faerie. Mosaics of lapis and malachite laid in a marine motif and overlaid with rock crystal patterned the walls, while the floors were tiled in alternating squares of ground coral and powdered pearls set in a matrix of glass.

Between every pair of arches was a waist-high vase in the shape of a giant purple murex. And in each of those vases grew a clump of those insipid flowers Nuada had brought from the Lands of Men.

And there he is himself, Ailill mused, as the fair-haired Danaan Lord stepped from the shadows of one of the arches with a handful of dead leaves in one hand – at which he was gazing in some perplexity.

"At the flowers, again?" Ailill inquired to Nuada's back. "Perhaps Lugh should make you his gardener instead of his warlord."

Nuada did not look up, but Ailill saw his back muscles tense beneath the dirty white velvet of his tunic. The sight pleased him considerably.

"Well," the dark Faery went on, "perhaps there is something to the study of the mortal lands after all. Perhaps you have had a favorable influence on me."

"I doubt that," Nuada observed archly, without turning.

Ailill moved his hand a certain way, and the rose nearest Nuada wilted.

Nuada whirled. A tiny dagger appeared, needlelike, in his hand — exactly where the leaves had been.

Ailill was not impressed. "For you see, Silverhand," he continued languidly, "I too have taken up the study of mortals — and a fascinating study I find it."

Nuada raised a skeptical eyebrow. "Indeed?"

"Yes," Ailill went on, "and one of the things I find most fascinating is how they can subsist without Power."

"Very well, I would say," Nuada retorted.

"Perhaps." Ailill looked idly at the bush, blinked thrice in succession, and sent as many blossoms crumbling into dust. "But consider an example here, Nuada. Suppose that one of us lost something. Why, then, all we have to do is to call upon the Power, and there are half a score ways we might recover it."

"That fact is not unknown to me," Nuada replied.

"Ah! But mortals cannot always find things when they lose them, and one of the things I have learned in the process of my recent activities is that mortals lose things very frequently — very frequently indeed. But they do not find them nearly as often."

Nuada tapped impatient fingers on his hip. "What, exactly, are you referencing?"

"A certain ring."

"A ring?"

"A particular ring that offers some slight protection against some forms of Power."

"A particular ring ..."

"That is no longer in a certain mortal boy's keeping."

"Nor in yours, either, I suspect," Nuada chuckled. "Or you would have taken special care to call it to my attention by now."

"Would I?"

Nuada glared at his adversary. "There are things about that ring you do not know, Ailill. There are things about that ring *I* do not know. Probably even things Oisin himself does not know. After all, we did not make it."

It was Ailill's turn to glare. "Indeed?"

"And besides," Nuada continued calmly, "there is protection beyond the ring: protection older and stronger."

Ailill raised a brow. "You would not be speaking of yourself, would you? You are certainly older than I, if not as old as the ring. As to stronger?" He shrugged. "It is not a boast I would make if I were you. I have not noticed that you have had remarkable success in protecting the boy."

"I am as successful as I need to be. My strength has never failed me. Can you say the same?"

"My Power has never failed me."

"Has it not? I was under the impression that a certain summoning of yours had not gone to your liking." Nuada paused. "Surely you see the foolishness of what you undertake, Windmaster. Whatever you may think, mankind is no docile foe; be assured of that. You may think the Sullivan boy easy prey, but that is not true, either – even without aid from our kind. And be assured, Ailill, that though I do not approve of intervention in the Lands of Men, I will do whatever I must to keep the Worlds apart. The boy will not be harmed."

"So you are a traitor?" Ailill sneered.

Nuada's eyes narrowed dangerously. "I would be careful how I used that word."

Ailill's eyes narrowed in turn. "I listened to you once, Silverhand, and have been put to much trouble because of it. I should have known that you could not study the ways of mortals as closely as you have and not be won to their cause."

"I have *not* been won to their cause," Nuada flared. "But I believe in making no enemies without reason, and in making allies where they might be of benefit. I have no more desire than you to return into the High Air, or to retreat into the Hollow Hills or the Deep Waters.

"But there are ways and ways of achieving one's ends," Nuada went on. "And I also believe one should study one's foes and learn from them and, if possible, seek their friendship. No war is declared between Mortalkind and Faerie, though I know you itch for battle. Yet mortal men do not know us as their enemy; they do not know us at all, except for one, and you yourself know that even his closest comrades think him either a madman or a liar. There is no honor in attacking the innocent and the ignorant, Ailill. And there is no honor in making war for your own glory. You despise mortals because they have no honor and have lost sight of truth, yet you behave no better. And so I must stand with the lad."

"But are you prepared to die with him?"

"It is unlikely I will have the opportunity."

"Do not be too certain of that."

"I have seen mortal men at war. You have not. That is worth remembering."

"Perhaps I will – if it suits me."

Nuada frowned. "Then perhaps there are a few other things you should remember while you are thus engaged: your status in this realm, for instance. You are a *guest* in this land, an ambassador of your brother,

Finvarra of Erenn. Lugh Samildinach reigns in Tir-Nan-Og, yet you have defied him a hundred times over in the short while since you came here. Lugh will tolerate only so much arrogance and even less interference."

"Interference may not be needed much longer," Ailill smiled.

"Nor may Finvarra's most current ambassador," Nuada shot back, as he returned to the Cherokee roses.

Chapter IX

hiking
(tuesday, august 11)

Though David had indeed been spared a concussion, he did have a headache of a different kind two days later – in the form of an early morning phone call from Liz Hughes. She had called simply to check on his recovery – which was progressing nicely – but things had quickly taken a more troublesome tack.

"No, Liz," David said firmly and for the third time, "you cannot go ginseng hunting with Uncle Dale and me."

The phone crackled ominously.

"But why not, Davy? I think your Uncle Dale is neat, and I've never even seen any ginseng, and I think this would be a good time to combine both – kill two birds with one stone, as it were."

David sighed and scratched his back against the doorjamb. "It's a matter of tradition, Liz. The men in my family have always been the ones who know the secret places where the ginseng grows – shoot, they're only now letting *me* know – and no Sullivan male has ever, ever taken a woman along."

"Except your Aunt Hattie," Uncle Dale corrected, as he sauntered into the kitchen from the hall.

David covered the phone with his hand and looked skeptically at his kinsman.

"Who is it?" the old man asked.

"Liz Hughes," David answered hurriedly. He spoke back into the phone. "Just a minute, Liz."

"What's she want?"

David lowered the receiver to waist level. "Oh, nothing; she just wants to go ginseng hunting with us tomorrow."

Uncle Dale pursed his lips; his eyes twinkled. "She does, does she? Well, we might oughta consider that."

"Uncle Dale, come on! I don't want her goin'!"

David could hear Liz calling his name from down by his hip.

"Better talk to her, son," Dale continued. "Don't want yore hikin' partner mad at you. Bad luck. I 'spect she'll be wantin' to go deer huntin' next, and it wouldn't do to be on her bad side – might get shot." His voice was pitched a shade too loud – deliberately, David suspected.

Reluctantly David returned the phone to his ear.

"What was that?" Liz demanded.

"Uncle Dale seems to think it might be all right for you to go," he said glumly. "Seems Aunt Hattie used to go with him."

"Great ! When do we leave?"

"Early, Liz. Before daylight. It's supposed to rain again tomorrow afternoon, and Uncle Dale wants to get an early start."

"So why doesn't he just wait till the weather's better?"

"That's what I asked him." David sighed in some annoyance, "and all he'd say was something about having to do it when the moon was in the right phase. Apparently you can find ginseng anytime, but only certain times are good to harvest it. And it's supposed to be most potent if you get it early in the morning while the dew's still on it, or something like that. Which means we gotta start before sunup." A pause. "Still want to go?" he added sarcastically.

"I'll be there when I need to be," Liz replied firmly, "and I'll be dressed right, and I'll have what I need, and I bet I find some ginseng before you do."

"Maybe you will and maybe you won't," David growled – and hung up before she could reply.

"That's some gal," Uncle Dale offered wryly, as he helped himself to a cup of the morning's coffee. "She really does remind me of yore great-aunt Hattie, rest her soul. Fine woman – 'course most of them Bonesteel women are; comes from living up to the name, I guess. Got up at four o'clock every mornin' of her married life and sent me off to the copper mines to work. Damn fine woman – and a sight better with a gun than I am, too, if the truth was known. You know that ten-pointer I got over my fireplace that I always said I shot?" He took David by the shoulder conspiratorially. "Well, she really got it – but I never told, and she let me have my glory. But why you reckon that Hughes gal wants to go huntin' 'seng with us?"

David studied the floor. "I dunno. Just being a pain, I guess."

Uncle Dale looked straight at him. "I think you do know."

David leaned up against the wall and folded his arms across his chest. "Well, she's into this back-to-nature thing and all – survival skills, wilderness living, herbs and all that. She's a walking Foxfire Book."

"That may be true," the old man laughed. "But there's some things to a woman's nature she's never far from. Trouble is, us menfolks are usually too late in findin' it out." He laughed again.

"I can run pretty fast," David shot back, through a scowl.

"Can you outrun one of Cupid's arrows, though? That what you was runnin' from the other day?"

David rolled his eyes. "You know I don't want you to go, either."

Dale looked as surprised as David had ever seen him. "Why, Davy boy! Why not? I been trompin' around in them woods for seventy-something years. I ain't gonna quit now."

You will see Death sitting beside someone close to you in less than two weeks' time: of that I am certain. The fortuneteller's words tolled in David's mind as he tried not to look at the calendar on the wall. "That's a good reason: them seventy-something years," he said aloud. "You ain't as young as you used to be."

"Well, that's a fact!" Dale agreed. "But them woods is a lot older'n I am, and they can still show a feller a good time."

David considered that unexpected piece of philosophy.

"But suppose something happened to you out there?"

The old man shrugged. "What can happen? I know every rock and tree and stream for ten square miles back where we're goin'. Been there every season and every weather. They ain't nothin' there can hurt me. Bears'll run – what few there are these days. Ain't no cougars no more – least not officially. Snakes you just gotta watch out for; Indians're gone a hundred fifty years; what else is there?"

"Oh, broken legs, sprained ankles –"

"– Heart attacks?"

"Now that you mention it."

"Look, Davy, us Sullivans 're long-lived folks. Takes a lot to kill us."

You oughta know that yoreself, considerin' how busted up you was just two days ago. That even put the wind up me, if you want to know the truth. But look at you now. Just a scab or two to show for a thirty foot fall. Few of us are ever sick more'n an aspirin'll cure, and when we die, it's usually 'cause we think it's time for us to die – none of this lingerin' in the hospital business. Shoot! Wars get more of us than anything else, and at that it takes some shootin' to catch a mortal spot."

David recalled how Uncle Dale's father had been wounded a couple of times in World War II, and he wasn't a young man then. He glanced into the yard, where a certain red Mustang gleamed, and recalled how another – if undeclared – war had claimed David-the-Elder – and nearly unleashed a bitter retort, but restrained himself.

Dale was looking at him intently. "So what else is there to be scared of?"

"Maybe there's things in the woods you can't see."

"You been at them weird books again, ain't you, boy?"

"They're not weird; they were written by learned people."

"As learned as you'll be one day, I've no doubt. But look, boy, I know they's things in the world besides what we know; I've been too close to some of 'em to disbelieve entirely, like when I seen yore grandpa's ghost that time – and I know you believe a darn sight more than I do – but I also believe I'm gonna be all right, and that they ain't nothin' to be scared of this year that ain't been there for seventy years before. ... At least not in broad daylight," he added after a pause that, while slight, David noted.

The old man poured himself another cup of coffee and buttered a cold biscuit. "Now you tell me somethin', boy: What're you scared of – or is it 'who'?"

"I'm not scared of anybody," David replied sulkily.

"You're the first man alive who ain't, then. That's part of life – that, and facin' up to it. But just remember who you are, what you are, and what you believe in. That's all it takes."

"Right-makes-might is easy if you're six-foot-two and one-eighty."

"Shoot, size don't matter none. Why, when I was yore age I was littler than you. I done all right."

"Oh, it's not that," David growled, drumming his fingers against the wall. I can fight okay if I have to. It's just the hassle that bothers me: having to put up with things that I can't control, but that try to control me. I've got a whole lot bothering me right now, and I'm gonna have to start back to school real soon, and that'll only make it worse. I can't stand this being in a bunch of worlds at once – like at school, where half the town kids won't hang out with me 'cause I'm 'too country'," he made quote marks with his fingers "and half the country kids won't 'cause I'm too 'city', and they all think I'm weird, and the girls –"

"Go on."

"Oh, nothing! I just wish I could go off and not come back."

"Do it, then. Nobody's stoppin' you."

"You know I can't."

"I know you won't. There's a difference." The old man's voice softened.

"Look, David, you are you: smart as a whip, good lookin', healthy as a moose, well-brought-up, honest. You've got a good turn, and I don't know what else – you're everything anybody'd want in a son. And you sit there talkin' like you ain't worth nothin'! That's a bunch of crap, boy. Now tell me, what's got you so bothered?"

"I'm afraid of words, I guess, of being hassled and made fun of ... and of something else I can't tell even you."

"There ain't never been much you couldn't tell me."

"This is one of those things, though; this is one of those things I can't even tell Alec."

Dale took a sip of coffee, but his gaze never left David. "It's about that ring, ain't it?"

David did not reply, but he could feel the weight of that stare.

Uncle Dale nodded. "I thought so. Just remember one thing, boy: You ain't the only one in the family that's ever lived here and been up in them woods of a summer night."

David looked up incredulously. "You?"

Uncle Dale shook his head almost sadly. "I told you, we didn't dare. But my pa did. He seen something not of this world, and, you know, that strangeness in his eyes was just like the one I been seein' in yore's lately – and it was there till the day he died."

"Uncle Dale –"

"Now's not the time, boy. You'd best be gettin' your gear together for tomorrow. Won't be no time for it then 'less you wanta get up real early."

Fog filled the lowlands the next morning, hiding the farms, the lakes, even a good part of the mountains. Ragged bits lingered higher up, too, hanging eerily among the oaks and maples. An unseasonable cold front had moved into north Georgia during the night, bringing with it record low temperatures and scattered reports of frost. David had had to get up in the wee hours to turn on the heat in his bedroom.

But it was still a splendid morning. Or would be when the sun rose, David conceded – even allowing for Liz, who'd been on time, and dressed appropriately, and had brought everything she was supposed to bring, and had even helped his mother make coffee. David wished he had another cup, too – as the three ginseng hunters pushed through a patch of rhododendron and paused for a rest atop a rock outcrop twenty or so feet high, from which they could look both out and down.

David sank down on his haunches with his runestaff braced across his knees and took in the view, huddling himself up in his blaze orange hunting jacket – the same color as the jaunty cap Uncle Dale was wearing. He could see his breath floating away in the morning air, reminding him of the fog below. To the east, the sun still hid sleepily just out of sight behind a fold of mountain.

"That sure is a pretty view," Liz observed.

"It is for a fact," Uncle Dale agreed. "I shot my first deer from up here, two days after Davy's grandpa was born."

"Was that before or after the Flood?" David teased, as he continued to contemplate the view. The first rays of sunrise cast a glitter into the air, and David found himself gazing across the fog-shrouded lake that filled the valley below to the nearly symmetrical cone of Bloody Bald, now completely ringed with white. Would it happen? he wondered. Would he see what he expected to see? Funny how nearly two weeks could pass without him ever getting time to catch Bloody Bald exactly at sunrise or sunset.

But he had his chance now, and even as he looked, his eyes took on the familiar tingle, and he saw that same mountain rise into an impossibly slender peak; saw it crowned with towers, battlements, buttresses, and arches – and dimly thought he could make out men on those battlements, and dimly, very dimly hear horns ringing in his ears to welcome the dawn.

And then he blinked and it was gone, replaced by the fuzzy gray bulk of the mundane mountain.

A rustle among the trees to their right made the ginseng hunters turn – to see three ravens take wing among the dark trunks. They watched the birds fly out into the open air, wheeling and circling above the fog.

David raised his runestaff to his shoulder like a rifle and aimed experimentally, oblivious to the pain that still lingered in his shoulder as one of several legacies of his fall.

Dale laid a hand on the smooth wood and slowly but firmly pushed it down. "Don't even think such things, boy. Shootin' ravens is bad luck."

"Just playin' around," David said testily.

Dale bent over to sight down the face of the rock, and as he did, the brilliant orange cap fell from his white hair and floated down, to land amid the brown leaves and moss at the bottom. It rolled to a stop at the base of an oak tree so ancient, gnarled, and covered with fungi it looked like something from a Brian Froud painting.

"I'll get it," David volunteered.

"I'll get it," Liz echoed, already on her way down the gentler slope to the left of the cliff.

"*I'll* get it," Dale said loudest. "I was the fool that lost it."

"Why don't we all go," David grumbled.

Dale cuffed him gently on the shoulder, but there was warning in the glance he shot his nephew. "And be quick about it. No sense wakin' up the whole woods arguin'."

So they all went – Liz down the southern slope, David and Dale down the steeper northern one. Dale picked up his cap and paused, peering at the ground where it had lain. Something showed in the soft earth there: the unmistakable print of a cloven hoof, pointed at the front. The old man stooped to check it.

"That's deer sign, and fresh," Dale said, straightening to look back toward the cliff. "But we ain't huntin' deer."

Liz led the way back up the gentler slope. To their left the sheer rock face jutted out, gray and crusted with lichens, crowned with a thicket of rhododendron and laurel. Their feet rustled the damp brown leaves. The footing was treacherous, too, and they slipped frequently. David slipped more than frequently, finally falling onto all fours in spite of his runestaff. When he straightened, he found himself facing Dale's back a few paces ahead of him.

Something twanged in David's ears then – or was it in his mind alone? Something hissed as it flew fast through the cool damp air. Something white flashed and then buried itself in Dale's chest with a dull thud. David cried out, lunged forward desperately, aware too late of the telltale burning in his eyes.

Dale slumped forward, clutching at his head. He uttered no sound; rather, he simply collapsed, twisting as he fell, to land on his side in the damp leaves.

Liz, a little higher up the slope, turned and stared at him, gasping, green eyes wide, face pale beneath her red hair.

As David scrambled toward the old man, he spared a glance at the cliff. And saw in plain view, making no move to hide himself, what looked to be a very young man clad in white, gray, and pale green clothing that was most certainly not consistent with the present-day time or place or world.

"Faery," David whispered. Fear grabbed at his heart and twisted.

Whoever – whatever – it was, he held a long white bow in his left hand, and the white fletching of the second arrow half-nocked in the other was identical to that of the short shaft that now protruded from the right side of Uncle Dale's torso. As David stood there gaping, the youth turned and pushed silently back into the bushes.

David remained frozen for at least five breaths, wondering if he should stay or follow, but a groan from his kinsman made that decision for him. Reluctantly, he knelt beside the old man and rolled him onto his back. Even as he reached for the arrow, it began to dissipate into the cold, crisp air. And then it was gone, as if it had never been.

Liz scooted down the slope to join them. "What is it? What's happened?"

"He's had a ... stroke, I think. – Maybe a heart attack, but probably a stroke."

Probably, hell! Only the tiniest hole was left in the old man's jacket, but David knew the damage was done. Why, the very word stroke itself was short for elf-stroke, because folks had once believed that people who suffered unexpected paralysis had in fact been struck by Faery arrows – usually stone-tipped ones, if he recalled what he'd read in *The Secret Common-Wealth* correctly. Evidently there was truth to the legend.

David laid his hand on his uncle's chest, moved it to his neck, his wrist, searching for a heartbeat, a pulse, anything to confirm he was still alive. Blessedly, both were present, if faint and uneven. And Dale was breathing shallowly.

The old man fought to rise, but his body wouldn't respond properly. His blue eyes sought David's, wide and panic-stricken; he tried to talk, raising his good left arm and pointing to his right side. But then his eyes rolled back, and he lost consciousness.

"Quick, Liz," David cried, "we've got to cover him up and get some help. There's nothing we can do here. It was a stroke, I think." He hesitated. "You go get help," he continued. "I'll stay here."

Liz stood up, obviously flustered. "You go, Davy; I don't know the way. I might get lost."

"He's my flesh and blood," David countered hotly. "I'm stayin' here. Just get to the top of this ridge and then follow it east. You'll come to the road that goes down by our house. It's not far, really. Get Pa, and call an ambulance."

"Should've brought my cell phone."

"Wouldn't have worked. They don't around here, remember."

"I could've tried."

"Liz–!" David warned.

"All right, Davy, all right – if you're sure there's nothing I can do here."

"Look," David all but shouted, "one of us has got to stay and one go. I've gotta stay. I want to be here in case. In case – well, just in case." Tears welled up in his eyes as he looked down at Uncle Dale lying flat on his back among the leaves.

David took off his jacket and spread it over the old man, then thought for a moment and added his shirt as well, leaving him shivering in a white

T-shirt. He frowned up at the top of the cliff, face set.

"Here, Liz," he sighed at last, tossing his runestaff toward her, "maybe this'll help."

Liz caught the staff easily – and to David's surprise, his eyes tingled and he thought he saw a faint white glow spread outward from where her hands grasped it.

Ash, Oisin had said, was supposed to afford some protection against the Sidhe – and there was iron on the ends, which was also good. There was no way he could protect both Liz and Uncle Dale, but he'd give Liz the best shot he could manage.

"Go on! Hurry!"

Liz shook her head, then turned and scrambled up the slope. She was gone from sight in an instant, but David could hear her crashing through underbrush for at least another minute. Even when silence found him again, he continued to stare emptily through the trees at the dissipating fog.

And then, though he feared it, back down at his kinsman.

You will see Death sitting beside someone close to you in less than two weeks' time: of that I am certain.

Was that what he was looking at now? The working out of a prophecy?

Maybe. But maybe not yet – apparently. For the old man didn't seem to be any worse – for all that he didn't seem to be any better.

Damn, David growled to himself, gazing up at the rock face again. *I knew I shouldn't have let him come.* He clenched his hands into fists, and had almost looked away before he saw the Faery reappear atop the outcrop.

David watched fascinated as, without the slightest hesitation, the youth leapt from the cliff and all but floated down from that height. It was as if he had not weight enough to fall at a normal speed. Bow still in hand, he landed in a bent-kneed crouch then calmly walked toward David.

David grabbed a broken branch from the forest floor and held it before him like a cudgel. A twinge of pain ran through his shoulder, but he ignored it.

The youth continued to approach. "That is not a good weapon against one such as I," he chuckled. "And at no time would it be simple for you to slay me in your World. You, on the other hand, do not appear to be as well protected as you have been, else my arrow would not have harmed the old man. Interesting. You haven't lost anything lately, have you? A ring, perhaps?" He lifted his bow and nocked another arrow.

"I'm more good to you alive," David growled, trying to stall for time.

The Faery laughed again, but there was a hollowness in the sound: a lack of conviction that did not quite ring true. He scowled for a moment, then lowered his bow and seated himself primly on a fallen log, motioning David to sit beside him.

It was all David could do to suppress his rage. This boy had hurt Uncle Dale – quite possibly killed him. And he had the nerve to ask David to sit beside him?

David gritted his teeth and glared helplessly, half a mind to swing his clumsy stick in that other's face again and again until one or the other broke, and then continue with his fists until those too-pretty features turned to bloody pulp. Iron and ash indeed! He'd give him flesh-and-blood fists!

But that would really solve nothing and probably be a futile effort in the bargain. Besides, there was more at stake here than simple revenge. The boy had returned for some reason, and David had to find out what it was. He risked a glance at Dale's prostrate form. The old man seemed to be no worse. David took a deep breath and lowered the stick but continued to stare at the youth. There was something disquietingly familiar about those clean-chiseled features and that sweep of shoulder-length silky blond hair.

"Well, have you seen enough?" the Faery asked wryly. "Should I stand up and turn around? Take my clothes off, perhaps? That form might be more familiar."

"I've seen enough," David said grimly, trying not to think about what the Faery's taunts implied. "One of your arrows in my uncle's chest. Why did you do that? What did he ever do to you?"

"I was ... following orders," the boy replied. "The old man is important to you; we have hurt him. He will not die unless he himself chooses, but he will never recover without Faery aid. We want only one thing in return for that healing. You."

David feigned innocence. "What's so special about me?"

"I thought Oisin made that clear: We want you where you can do no more harm."

"So you're one of Ailill's minions?"

The Faery's eyes narrowed. "I am my own man. But yes, I have some obligation to that one's service."

David sat down abruptly, finding it difficult to maintain anger toward someone so reasonable-sounding and fair-spoken. But then his glance touched Dale and he found his anger returning and harsh words coming more freely. He wondered distantly if there was some kind of glamour involved.

"So you're going to pick away at my loved ones until I give myself up?"

"That is the plan as it was revealed to me."

"What if I won't?"

"Then those you love will suffer." The Faery took a breath and continued, his voice earnest – sincerely so, David hoped. "You cannot be everywhere, David Sullivan – but you can be one place where those you love will be protected – and you, yourself as well." He rose and joined David on the ground, laid a hand on David's thigh in a way that made David shudder.

"Come with us; truly it is not as bad as you think. There are women wondrous fair and quick to lust, and food such as you have never tasted, and wine such as you have never drunk – but you have not drunk much wine, have you? Or tasted many women? And for sport, there is hunting! You think pursuing the beasts of this world a challenge? Wait until you have slain manticores or taken a kraken from the depths of the sea with Manannan MacLir! You can learn magic, David; see other worlds – even go beyond this poor round planet if you have the courage for it. You have but to come with us." The grip on David's leg grew tighter. "Come for a day only; we ask no more if Faerie does not please you."

"Yeah, and I know what a day can be like in Faerie," David shot back fiercely. "I'm not stupid. I've read about it and I've met Oisin."

A shadow crossed the Faery's face. "Oisin! Yes! A fine old man, though troublesome. He thought Ailill had forgotten he had once been mortal, but Ailill remembered and reminded Lugh of certain prohibitions. Lugh has forbidden Oisin to meet with you again."

David's heart sank, but he maintained his stoic facade. "Why did he have to do that?"

The Faery shrugged. "Lugh views this matter as a contest between Ailill and Nuada alone; he does not want others meddling."

"But isn't that what you're doing? Why don't you just kill me now and be done with it?"

"I think you know the answer to that as well as I do," the Faery replied. "Nuada is right about you, too: You do have the stuff of heroes in you – and something of Power as well; even I can see them. Killing you would be a waste. But it would be interesting to see whether the Power you hold flares to flame or passes into darkness – as your kinsman's life soon will, if you make the wrong decision."

David stopped listening. The Faery's words were more than he could bear. His gaze began to wander.

Something caught his attention then, out of the corner of his eye. He stared at it for a moment, then glanced quickly back at the Faery boy lest his reaction betray him. Fortunately, the lad was peering uneasily at a large raven perched on a limb above his head.

That was all David needed.

He lunged to his left – a long body-leap – and barely managed to grab the bow the Faery had laid aside. Even as he rose to his feet, he whirled back around, gripping the bow by one delicately filigreed end. Raising it above his head , he made as if to strike it against the trunk of the ancient oak that had caught his attention earlier.

The Faery likewise sprang, his slender body tense, a feral light in his emerald eyes. Panther-quick, he leapt at David.

David swung the bow around and down, but the Faery was on him before he could complete the arc. They fell to the ground, rolling over and over in a knot of arms and legs, with the bow between them, miraculously unbroken. All at once David found himself straddling the Faery. And though he could touch that Faery stranger's flesh and feel the solidity of his body beneath him, it was as if the Faery could not quite touch him in return, though he glared up at David with bared teeth, yellow sparks flashing in his green eyes, wet brown leaves sticking in his golden hair, soiling the white velvet tunic. Gritting his teeth, David grasped the bow with both hands and pressed it down across the Faery's throat. The boy grabbed it in turn, and they struggled, so evenly matched neither could gain the upper hand.

The Faery was surprisingly strong, for all he was more lightly built than David, but David could feel a cold fire boiling up from his innermost core. He thought about Uncle Dale lying unconscious behind him, of Liz wending her way down a mountain, probably scared to death and – slowly, inexorably, and oblivious to the pain that now shot through his injured shoulder – began to press the bow down toward the Faery's throat until it rested atop his windpipe.

"I told you, nothing you can do in this world can harm me – not for longer than it takes to heal," the Faery hissed.

"What if I break this bow?" David growled through gritted teeth. "It was when I began to threaten it that you attacked me. What's so great about this bow?"

"That is none of your concern."

"What's so great about this bow, dammit? Tell me now, or I'll break it."

The Faery's eyes flashed fire. "It was made for me by Goibniu, the smith of the Tuatha de Danaan from the last of the yew he brought out of Gorias. Rarely does he work in wood, but when he does, it is wonderful work indeed. I prize it above all things in the Worlds I have seen, for it never misses."

"Then tell me how to cure Uncle Dale, then, or I *will* break it."

The boy's face grew pale, almost fearful, and he grimaced. "That I may not do, mortal, much as I might now wish it, for I do not know the answer. I am a hunter, not a master of Power or of lore. I may slay a man in Faerie one day and be drinking with him again the next night, but such is not the case in your World, and the rules that govern that difference I do not entirely understand. Truly I cannot help you."

David's eyes blazed. "Swear that you can't?"

"If you like."

"On your bow?"

"If you like."

"Swear, then, that all Power may vanish from this bow, and that it will never again shoot true if you lie."

"I so swear. Now are you satisfied?"

"A little."

"Then let me up."

"Not yet. What do you know about my ring?"

"I know that you do not have it, but that its protection is still somewhat upon you." The Faery hesitated, took a deep breath. When he spoke it seemed he chose his words carefully. "I also know that he who was sent to procure it has failed."

David's eyes narrowed. It was as if the pauses and the subtly accented words of the Faery's speech were meant to convey some second, hidden, message that must remain unspoken.

"Well, if you folks don't have the ring, and I don't have it, where is it?"

"Somewhere in your World, I suppose."

"Swear? Damn it, *swear* it: swear that that's the truth."

"I swear that I do not know where the ring is. To make further oaths in ignorance would be foolish."

David grunted. "Are you sure?"

"It is as I have said. Now will you let me up? There is nothing more I can do to help you."

"I guess I'll have to take your word for it." David growled. His lips quirked in a smile as grimly suspicious as the Faery's. He withdrew the bow from the boy's throat and rose.

The Faery rose as well and brushed himself off. "You have bested me in a fight," he said, "and few have done that. I would offer you my aid, but it is sworn elsewhere and I may not break that oath. But when this song is ended, let us be friends. Maybe yet we will meet as comrades in Faerie." He paused and extended a slim right hand.

David didn't know what to do at first or why he did what he did do, but that phrase rang in his mind as something sacred, old, and honorable: beyond good and evil. Hadn't Bres, the champion of the Tuatha de Danaan, said something like that to Sreng, the Fir Bolg champion, when first they met in Ireland? He extended his own hand hesitantly and clasped that of the Faery youth.

They looked into each other's eyes for a long moment, then dropped hands. The Faery boy took his bow from David's now-lax fingers. "And now I must depart," he said. "Ailill has asked of me more than he knows. Farewell."

The boy had disappeared into the trees before David could think of anything to say. The leaves did not rustle under his tread, but the print of his back was still visible in the soft loam of the forest floor. David sat down by Uncle Dale and waited, staring at his hands, wondering whether he was a traitor.

Interlude VI

in the lands of men

Shit! Alec McLean said to himself. Then, "Damn!" aloud. He leaned back in his chair and stared at the computer screen, shook his head, and ran his hands through his hair, for once not concerned with neatness. He pursed is lips, then gnawed them. Ahead of him in the odd-angled room behind the dormer windows of his parents' house in MacTyrie, the computer was telling him, for the third time that morning, that his program had "performed an illegal operation and would be shut down."

"Once more into the breach," he gritted, and booted it up again. A moment later, he was logged on. A moment after that, he'd gone online and had summoned up his search-engine-of-the-moment. At the prompt, he typed in "second sight" and waited.

It seemed to take forever, and when he finally got the actual search results, it was hardly worth the wait, as only one link looked promising. "Apparent power to perceive things not present to the senses," was all that item told him and he already knew that much, from assorted bits he'd salvaged and filed away from random conversations with David. Granted, it did explain the weirdness up on Bloody Bald (which certainly hadn't been present to his senses) except for the small fact that seeing a castle on any mountain top in very non-medieval Georgia was a rather radical expression of that power as he perceived it – since, among other things, it implied that there really was a castle there, which was preposterous.

With a sigh, Alec clicked back a screen and continued his search. Unfortunately, all the other references seemed to be either to a video game he'd never heard of or a British TV series he'd never heard of either. A surprising number also seemed to be in foreign alphabets, notably Cyrillic.

He tried three screens, more or less at random, and gave up, at least for the moment. Later, when he was more patient, he'd try again.

Meanwhile, he rose, ambled over to the window and gazed outside, where his father was pruning the dogwoods. A glance at the sky showed an ominous gloom and the wind whipping up, swishing through the leaves of the yard's two sentinel maples to chill him where he stood. That wind also dislodged what was either a crow or a raven – probably the former, given that this was Georgia, but one never quite knew anymore, besides which ornithology wasn't his thing – from somewhere in the depths of one of the trees. It cried raucously and wheeled skyward, then seemed to change its mind and returned, to perch on his windowsill, looking in.

Alec raised a brow and returned that beady stare. "If you're expecting me to start quoting poetry," he told it, "you've got the wrong place. You want the Sullivan residence for that. Ask for David."

The bird, not unexpectedly, did not reply.

"If you're waiting for me to say, 'nevermore', you're going to be waiting a long time," Alec told it then realized his error. "And if *you* say 'nevermore' I'm outta here."

And with that, he turned his back, returned to his computer, and typed in "s-i-d-h-e" figuring that the word itself was sufficiently esoteric.

The machine growled and grumbled a little, then took him to a list that was only slightly more promising than "second sight" had been. At least this time there was a page with a clearly Celtic focus. He called it up, read what was there and scowled again. The page basically told him nothing David hadn't told him on their camping trip almost two weeks ago: the day Alec had first really tumbled to how serious David was about the 'Irish thing.'

Two more screens told him little more, except to confirm that *sidhe* meant, more or less, "people who live in (or under) hills" apparently in reference to a folk belief in Ireland that the original, more magical inhabitants – the Tuatha de Danaan, the site called them – had been forced to move underground when the ancestors of the present-day Irish had arrived. Rather like Cherokee, he supposed – which, he seemed to recall from an ancient term paper, was a name given to the local aborigines by Europeans. It meant "people who live in caves" or something like that. Their own name for themselves was Ani-something.

Gad, he told himself, what was happening to his memory?

In any case, the screen beckoned, promising answers to those questions and many more.

But by the time he called up a fourth, he'd become aware of a vague discomfort he could define no more clearly than that: a feeling of something ... watching him.

Turning abruptly, he saw that the crow or whatever it was was still sitting on the windowsill.

"Nevermore," he told it. Then, "Satisfied?"

To punctuate his remark, he rose and tapped on the window screen. The bird squawked and flew away.

Alec had just started to sit down at the computer again when his cell phone rang.

To his very great surprise, it was David. David, whose parents had conditioned him never to call anyone unless he had to.

"Alec," David said without preamble. "I've only got a second. We're on our way to the hospital. Something terrible's happened."

"What?"

"Short form, Uncle Dale's had ... a stroke."

"Long form?"

"No time now; you wouldn't understand anyway."

"David –"

"Just wanted to let you know. Check in if you can, but wait a while. Wait until there's something I can actually tell you."

"If you're sure –"

"I'm not sure of anything right now," David said. And either hung up or lost the connection.

Alec turned off the computer and went downstairs.

"Can I borrow the car?" he asked his father, who was still working in the yard.

"You mean my car?"

"That's the only one I see."

"I need it – or will, in about thirty minutes."

"What about Mom?"

"I have no idea. Said she'd be back in time for dinner, which I suppose we'll have to take on faith, as we usually do."

"And you really do have to have yours?"

Dr. McLean, who looked rather like a more wrinkled version of his son, but one whose hair had also exploded when it turned gray, shook his head. "I'm afraid, oh my son, that I do."

"Well," Alec said, as he tuned away. "Shit."

And for once he didn't care if his father heard him.

* * *

Chapter X

visitation

Little Billy looked up at David, who slumped beside him in the white-walled waiting room of the Enotah County Medical Center. "Will Uncle Dale die?" the little boy asked earnestly.

At least fifteen people were jammed up against the walls around the waiting room, but David didn't know any of them – nor care to just then. He wished they were all somewhere else – or that he was; he was feeling very alone at the moment. It was mid-afternoon, and his parents had not yet returned from securing affairs at Uncle Dale's farm. Liz had stayed for a while after they had first brought the old man in, but she'd eventually had to leave. Alec had phoned twice, both times apologizing for not being able to come over, but there was nothing to tell him. Nobody knew anything.

"Will Uncle Dale *die*, Davy?" Little Billy repeated, tugging on David's sleeve.

"I don't *know!*" David growled back, so harshly that Little Billy cowered down into his shirt collar. "I hope not," he added more softly, reaching over to ruffle his brother's hair, feeling how soft it was and realizing suddenly what a neat kid Little Billy was turning out to be. And then, deep in the pit of his stomach, rose the fear that had engulfed him after the Faery boy had left: the fear that the same fate that had claimed Uncle Dale awaited all those he cared about. David found himself clenching his fists.

A brown-haired nurse came out of the room into which they had taken Uncle Dale.

"Nurse?" David called shyly, looking up.

The woman glanced down irritably, obviously taken aback by the dirty woodsman's togs David still wore. "Yes?" she demanded.

"My uncle – Dale Sullivan – will he be all right?"

The nurse grimaced. "We ... think he's had a stroke, but Doctor Nesheim has him stabilized. He won't get any worse. But he shoulda known better'n to be running 'round in the woods at his age. 'Course it coulda been worse; coulda been a heart attack – but he still shoulda known better." She frowned at David, who felt himself cringe under the combination of her gaze and his own guilt. "Good thing you were with him," she added, before continuing down the corridor.

"Can I go see him?" David shouted after her.

"Not yet," she called back, still moving. "Maybe later."

David slumped back in his chair, folded his arms on his chest, and tried to sleep. He wished he had something to read, but he had already exhausted the waiting room's supply of outdated magazines and had hardly been in a position to snare anything at home before the trip to the hospital. Sleep was therefore the only way he could think of to speed the time until he found out something about Uncle Dale's condition – at least until his parents returned.

Two hours passed before a friendlier nurse – Talbot was the name on her plastic name tag – let David in to see Uncle Dale. His parents still had not returned, and he found himself alone in the hospital room with the old man. Dale lay propped up in bed, tubes running out of his nose, a bottle of some nameless clear fluid set up on a stand beside him, leading to needles taped into his arms. He was under heavy sedation and, the doctor had finally admitted, had probably lost the use of his right side. The real fear, however, was that knowing he was half paralyzed, he'd just give up and will himself to die. That didn't sound like Uncle Dale to David. But then again, he apparently didn't know as much about his kinsman as he had thought. *One thing for sure,* David decided, *I'll bet he never expected to die of elf-stroke.*

Dale was breathing more or less evenly, but his face showed a gray pallor that wasn't typical and emphasized the age that lay heavily upon him. Cautiously, David reached over and pulled down the covers. Curiosity had got the best of him; he had to check on something.

Keeping one eye on the door, he worked the hospital gown down on the side where the elf-arrow had struck – and saw some of what he expected: pale, flabby skin; stringy muscles like old ropes; stray coarse hairs. But look though he would, he could find no wound – yet he knew the damage was there: invisible to mortal eyes and – evidently – machines.

It occurred to him then, that there might be a third alternative: one accessible only to him. Taking a deep breath and straining his eyes in a way that could not precisely be explained, he tried to conjure the Sight – and was finally rewarded by the faintest glimpse of a pale red X-shaped mark exactly where he was looking for it: in the outer point of the triangular depression below the collarbone. He stared at it in mute resignation. There was nothing he could do. Help would have to come from some unorthodox source; certainly no human doctor could cure a wound born of Faery weaponry and Faery magic.

Abruptly a heavy arm fell across his shoulder. "We're back," Big Billy rumbled behind him. "Mama and me'll stay here tonight; you take Little Billy and go on home. We'll keep you posted."

David nodded reluctantly and shuffled out of the room, noticing through the hallway window outside that the threatened rain had arrived.

The glass in David's bedroom window rattled, struck by a not-so-gentle wind. He started, as the sound brought him full awake. He had been dozing – dreaming of the Sidhe – and now found himself trying to make sense of what Oisin had said, of what the Faery boy had told him.

They were *perilous*, David knew, and some of them had it in for him – but still, they were not truly evil, not by their own standards. He could even understand how they felt, a little; he felt the same way about the people who moved into the mountains from Atlanta and Florida and put up summer homes on the high places, spoiling everyone else's view and increasing the traffic for those natives who didn't want a million-dollar "cabin" on every mountaintop but preferred inviolate wilderness where a man could walk for hours and see no more sign of civilization than vapor trails in the sky.

It was crazy, he knew – considering what he'd been through – but part of him still wanted to see the Sidhe again. They were so beautiful, so heartbreakingly beautiful! If he could only watch without being seen – see them just one more time astride their long-limbed horses: black and silver, gold and frosty gray; see them in their silks and velvets and fine wool: wine-red and midnight-blue, forest-green and sunset-amber; see those tall, stern-faced women with hawks on their shoulders and braided hair to their knees, and the clean-faced warriors with their sharp spears and silver armor and rustling mail; see their ghost-thin greyhounds and their great hunting dogs that were close kin to wolves; see those banners that floated above them, unfurled by no wind of the Mortal World ...

One banner in particular he remembered, borne at the head of the procession. Maybe thirty feet long, it was, but narrow as his forearm was long, and held aloft on an ivory staff. It had been made of silk, or something as soft and shimmery, and was red as sunrise, cut at its trailing edge into flickering flame-like streamers so tenuous they might have *been* flames, and worked near the staff with the stylized image of the sun – a 'sun in splendor,' it was called; he'd learned that term while prowling through heraldry books. But this one glowed of its own light, its alternating straight and curved rays shrinking, expanding, and rotating in the figures of some obscure dance in praise of fire.

The wind rattled the window again, and a patter of rain sounded on the roof. He was not at all sleepy, he realized, as he got up, turned on the light, and settled himself to reread *Paradise Lost*.

So it was that he was still awake when he heard Little Billy talking quietly in his bedroom across the hall. He scowled, climbed wearily out of bed, and slipped into the hallway, to pause by the closed door to his brother's room. He could hear the little boy inside, talking as if in his sleep, but couldn't quite make out what he was saying. Gently, David opened the door and peeked inside.

Little Billy was kneeling on his bed, peering out the window, and as he watched, David could hear him saying, "But I can't let you in. We can't have dogs in the house. My mama won't allow 'em."

"Come outside, then," said a voice from the darkness beyond the window.

"I can't; I'm not allowed to go outside at night, and Davy told me special not to go outside tonight."

"Your brother is a fool," the unknown voice rasped.

David could contain himself no longer. He rushed into the shadowed room, lunged toward the window, and stared out above Little Billy's head.

And found the shape of an immense black dog glaring back at him: a shaggy black dog with its feet on the sill and its great black nose nearly touching – but *not* touching – the window screen. Its eyes were red as coal: an all-too-familiar red. The logical part of David's mind told him that the sill was at least seven feet off the ground. But then he recognized the voice. Even allowing for the alien physiognomy, there was no mistaking those mocking, if strangely beguiling tones.

It was Ailill – his enemy.

The dog growled through bared teeth. David caught a glimpse of fabulously long fangs, a black tongue, and a blood-red throat, from which small flames seemed to issue. And then it growled again – louder – and leapt away. David watched as it ran, wolf-like, toward the road up the mountain. And as it disappeared into the obscuring gray drizzle, he thought he saw it joined – and in none too friendly a fashion – by another dog, this one as white as bone. David glanced down at his little brother, who still knelt beside him, gazing quietly – *too* quietly – out the window.

"You saw that?" David choked. "Tell me what you saw, Little Billy; tell me what you remember."

Little Billy turned a white and tear-stained face toward David, a face so wracked with fear that David gasped.

David took his brother by the shoulders and held him firmly. "Look at me, kid," he whispered. "It's me, Davy. Now tell me what you saw. Don't worry; I'll believe you."

"I don't know!" Little Billy sobbed. "I woke up and saw these red lights shinin' in the window, and I got scared and hid under the covers. But then I heard a voice sayin' not to be afraid, and I looked out again and saw they was still there, but they was the eyes of this big black dog, and I got scared again, 'cause dogs can't talk. Only this one did; and I heard it say that it wasn't just any old dog, that it was a magic dog and would make me magic, too, if I'd come with it, and that I wouldn't ever have to go to school, but could do whatever I wanted to do, and could play all the time. And I said I couldn't do that unless Ma and Pa said I could; and it told me not to ask, 'cause if I wanted to go, I had to go right now."

"Did it ask you to let it in?"

"Yeah, and I told it we couldn't have animals in the house."

David couldn't help but smile at such simple but effective logic. But he wrapped his arms around his brother and held him tight.

"You did fine, kid. You did real good."

Little Billy was shaking, wracked with sobs, but David held him firm. "Tell you what," David whispered into his brother's sweat-soaked hair, "you can sleep with me tonight. I don't think I want to be alone, either."

Interlude VII

In Tir-nan-og
(high summer)

Fionchadd was shooting pomegranates out of his wyvern's mouth when Ailill found him practicing archery in the Court of the Kraken. He stepped into the shadow of a rough-hewn pillar and watched his son unseen. Fionchadd was almost full-grown now, but still a long way from the sort of manhood Ailill had hoped to see him achieve. *More of that Annwyn blood,* he grumbled. *I should never have acknowledged him.* Still, the lad was a skillful archer – as he noted the boy's confident stance and the purposeful tension of the bare arms revealed by his simple blue-and-white-checked tunic.

Fionchadd drew to the cheek and released. The arrow flew true to its mark, striking dead center in the rough red globe that Dylan held delicately in his needle-toothed beak. Instead of bearing the target away, however, the arrow was stopped in mid-flight, when, with exquisite timing, the creature snapped its jaws shut, trapping both fruit and skewer. The wyvern staggered under the impact but did not lose its footing. A loud crack and the drooping of the white fletching marked the final closure of its beak. Twin trails of red juice trickled across the silver cheek scales to drip in a starfish-shaped puddle at the suckered tip of a mosaic kraken arm that curled by the beast's taloned feet. Balancing precariously on one elegant limb, the creature neatly extracted the arrow halves with the other. It swallowed once, the fruit a visible lump in its supple neck, then spread its wings and glided forward to receive another pomegranate from its master.

"You have become a fine archer," Ailill murmured, emerging from the shadows where he'd stood.

Fionchadd's head snapped up, his expression clouding when he recognized his father. Dylan scurried behind him, to peer uncertainly from beneath the dark blue fringe of his tunic.

"I don't like being spied upon," the boy snapped.

"Then you should use the Power. Perhaps a glamour –"

"Why? Yours is stronger, so there's no point in that regard; and in the case of anybody else, there's no need." Fionchadd fumbled in his quiver for another arrow. "But you spy on everyone, don't you?"

Ailill laughed harshly. "Very nearly. But, then, everyone spies on me. Silverhand has been stalking me like a shadow."

"I understand you have been in the Lands of Men again," Fionchadd said as he nocked the arrow and drew experimental aim on a distant silver squirrel. "Did he follow you there?"

Ailill nodded. "Oh, aye; there have been more white animals than I can count. But there is little he can do to stop me."

The boy took aim. "That you know of."

Ailill's nostrils flared. "Sometimes I doubt your loyalty to me."

His son did not reply.

"Fionchadd?"

The boy lowered the bow and glared at his father. "Sometimes I doubt your loyalty to anyone at all – except yourself."

"Those are not good words to hear, nor are they good to say."

"Nonetheless, they are mine. They are all I have."

Ailill folded his arms and returned his son's glare. "Twice I have sent you into Lands of Men, and twice you have failed me."

"I have provided information," Fionchadd retorted, "which is the main thing you sent me for. And while I was your spy I missed two hunts and almost lost my bow."

"But you still failed at the tasks I set for you."

Fionchadd laid the bow carefully aside and turned to face his father. "I have *not* failed. I watched the mortal boy. I saw him meet with Oisin. I heard that one's words. When the power of the ring awakened the Track, I was there. I ran. I would have captured the ring, if only –"

"Yes?"

The boy's shoulders slumped. "If only the Power of the ring had not wrenched him from the Road."

"The chain broke, so you told me. Yet you did not see where the ring fell?"

"I did not expect the chain to be made of iron; it burned me. The boy was in his own World by the time I recovered from that shock. And then it took a moment to shift my Sight."

"And what of the old man?"

"I made the arrow as you instructed. My aim was true. You said not to kill him. You said the boy's concern for his family would drive him to us. Besides, the fact that I could wound the old man yet could not touch the boy confirms that the ring no longer protects anyone but the lad himself. I tried to get him to join us."

"You were not very persuasive."

"I am not a diplomat!"

Ailill smiled. "I do better than you, boy! I almost have the younger brother where I want him. There is a storm brewing in the Lands of Men, which I can augment to good advantage."

"Lugh will not like that," Fionchadd snorted. "He says you spend too much time there at the expense of your other duties. You missed his feast last night."

"I thought it more important to investigate threats to his realm than the food on his table."

"I am sure."

"My brother would think so."

"Uncle Finvarra would not care what you did as long as you were not underfoot. That is, after all, why he sent you here, is it not?"

Ailill's eyes narrowed dangerously. "So you know my brother's mind better than I do? If you would second-guess him, you tread on dangerous ground indeed."

Fionchadd raised an inquisitive eyebrow. "As do you, if you would challenge Lugh Samildinach. I have seen that much while I have been here. Shall we see who has the greater number of friends?"

"And which are you, boy? You give your oath everywhere; even to those you are sworn to seek."

Fionchadd's face reddened with indignation. "*Forced* to seek, more like it. Twice the boy has bested me in combat, Father: at running and at wrestling. It was the honorable thing to do. Even The Morrigu commended me."

"They were not fair fights, however; for the ring's protection was still upon the boy. The Mistress of Battles is a fool to say otherwise."

"A very powerful fool, however." Fionchadd chuckled.

Ailill raised his fist as if to strike his son, then lowered it again, though reluctantly. "Very well, boy. Since you are so concerned with the Rules, I also invoke them: You owe me one more attempt on David Sullivan."

Fionchadd's eyes blazed. "By what right?"

"By the Rule of Three," Ailill shot back. "Twice he has bested you. There must be a third."

"The boy is not my enemy!" Fionchadd shouted.

"Then you are not my son," Ailill replied, his voice chill as the space between the stars, and as soulless.

Chapter XI

what the lightning brings
(thursday, august 13)

"**So** what was it you wanted to talk to me about that was a big enough deal to make you offer me a ride home?" David asked, after Liz had eased her mother's F-150 out of Enotah County Medical's rearmost parking lot and onto rain-slick Highway 76. Curved tails of spray rose behind her as the vehicle splashed through the puddles that still remained from an earlier thunderstorm. Clouds hinted at more to come, and quickly. She was chauffeuring him home after a three-hour shift of Dale-watching after his parents had stranded him there.

"Not that I don't appreciate it," David added, "but it is a little out of character for you."

Liz frowned pensively. "Oh, I don't know where to start, David – Uncle Dale, I guess. What do you think's really wrong with him?"

David shrugged. "He's had a stroke, of course. You don't recover from one of those in two days."

"I know that, dummy. But why doesn't he want to fight back?"

David slumped down in the seat and fiddled with his seatbelt. "I wish I knew, Liz, I really wish I knew. But if I did, I'd sure do something about it, don't you think?" A pause, then: "So why are you so curious all of a sudden? I mean, you've known him for years and years – known who he was, anyway. And now all of sudden, it's like you're ... doing a documentary, or something."

Liz's frown deepened. "Don't you ever see anything, David?" she sighed, more than a trace of exasperation coloring her voice. "Does it all have to be spelled out to you? He's just got something ... special about him;

that's all I can say. He fits into the world. He's part of your father's world – the real world, the farmer's world – but he's got something more, too: a sort of ... magic, or something. The same kind of magic you have, in a way. I think you'll grow up to be a lot like him – personality-wise, I mean."

David cocked an eyebrow. "I didn't know you were interested in magic."

Liz shot him a sideways smirk. "Don't you have anything between your ears besides air, David? Air and imagination? I'm interested in a lot of things you don't know about. Some of 'em are even your fault, too – and I bet you didn't know that, either. But as a matter of fact, I've been interested in ... weird stuff for a long time. I told you about my granny."

"I wonder if she knew my grandpa or Uncle Dale."

Liz drummed her fingers on the steering wheel as a slower vehicle impeded their progress. "Probably. They all knew each other up here back then. But about your uncle: I just think he's a really neat guy. There aren't gonna be folks like him around much longer: folks who remember how it was before there was electricity up here; never mind folks who remember the old arts and crafts and stories."

"So you want to collect him like a piece of folklore?"

"I want to learn from him, Davy. Surely you can understand that. You're concerned with folklore and magic and all that yourself."

David plucked at the hem of his T-shirt where it was bunched up below the seatbelt. "Well, I don't think Uncle Dale knows any magic. And besides, what I'm interested in is mythology, especially Irish mythology, not mountain folklore. That's only a shadow of the real thing."

"Maybe so," Liz sniffed, "but it's your heritage – and it may not be as remote as you think."

He regarded her sharply. "What do you mean by that?"

"Oh, you're always goin' on about fairies and all, like they were real – but always in Ireland during the Dark Ages, or something. But my granny said she saw 'em when she was a little girl."

David raised a skeptical brow. "Was she Irish?"

Liz shrugged again and switched on the wipers. It had started misting again. "May have been. I don't think you have to be Irish to see fairies. She said she saw a couple playing in her yard when she was a little girl up in North Carolina."

"She say what they looked like?"

"Yeah, she said they were about a foot high; had wings and all."

David snorted and rubbed at his window. "Faeries don't look like that."

"And how do you know? Have you seen 'em?"

"If I told you yes, would you believe me?"

Liz hesitated. "I don't know. But I believed my granny. She never lied to me about anything else. And she'd have no cause to lie about something as 'out there' as that."

David turned to stare out his window at the sodden landscape: the whole world gone dull and flat, with the merest trace here and there of tired green, aged blue, or dim purple lurking among the shadows. A few clouds hung ominously lower than the rest, like vultures waiting to devour the day. He took a deep breath. "What would you say if I told you I thought the Faeries had caused Uncle Dale's stroke?"

Liz's mouth became a thin line. "I'd say that you were either telling the truth or were lying, and that if you were lying, either you knew you were, or you didn't. How's that?"

David smiled. "You sounded full of ancient wisdom just then."

Liz smiled back. "I got that phrase from my granny, too. She was full of ancient wisdom. But why would the fairies want to hurt Uncle Dale?"

"To get at me."

Liz risked a sideways glance at him, then kicked the wipers up a notch at the rain fell harder. "Why are you so important?"

"I saw them not two weeks ago. I accidentally got Second Sight, and the night after that, I met them and asked them for a token that the meeting was real. That's when I got the ring."

Liz slapped the steering wheel hard enough to make David start. "*Another* story about that ring," she cried, clearly exasperated. "David, please don't lie to me."

David wished he could melt into the seat. "I'm not!" he sighed. "I'm like the boy who cried wolf, I guess: I've told so many wild stories nobody will believe the truth when I do tell it. But I swear to you; I really do absolutely swear to you that I really did get the ring from the Faeries – well, the Sidhe more properly, or the Tuatha de Danaan, or whatever. The fortuneteller knew it, and she knew I have Second Sight."

Liz's hair fell forward, obscuring her expression. David wished he could see her face. "What is Second Sight? You've mentioned it a couple of times, now."

"The ability to see into the Otherworld, I guess you could call it. I might see a mountain, or I might see a Faery palace assuming there's one to see. Trouble is, I'm the only one who knows the Faeries are here, and they think I'm a threat to them because of that."

"Are you?"

David slapped his thighs. "I don't know. I don't mean to be. You're the first person I've told, and you probably don't believe me, either. Well, actually, I told Alec, but I didn't have any better luck with him than I'm havin' with you. Thing is, who *would* believe it? You grew up in the same rational world I did. Grown people don't believe in Faeries in this place and time."

"My granny did, and I think Uncle Dale might warm to the idea."

"If he ever warms to anything again," David muttered, once more fidgeting with his seatbelt. He paused, gnawing his lip, then continued. "Hmmm, maybe you could use your power – or whatever it was you tried to use that day at the lake – and try to, you know, read Uncle Dale. Maybe then you'd get something that would convince you."

In spite of the rain, Liz turned to stare at him. "You're serious!"

David nodded grimly. "You have no idea how serious. Believe me, I would love to have somebody to share this with. Only ... only I think I'd be putting you in danger if I did. The Sidhe might not like it and would be after you next."

"The Sidhe are –"

"The Irish Faeries," David replied more patiently than he felt. He paused again. "Hang on a minute, Liz; I've got something here ..." He reached into his knapsack, which rested in the footwell between his legs, and retrieved something small and brown, which he laid on the seat between them. "This is the book the fortuneteller gave me; it's called *The Secret Common-Wealth*. Got some stuff about Second Sight in there – stuff about the Faeries, too, though that part doesn't seem to be too accurate. But maybe it'll give you something to think about. Then again, maybe I shouldn't let you look at it."

Liz laid a hand possessively on the book. "Oh for heaven's sake, why not?"

David's expression clouded. "Might get you in trouble. The Sidhe said they'd get at me through ... through the people I care about."

"Me?"

David took a deep breath. "Of course I care about you, Liz. You're one of my best friends. Who else could I have trusted about this? Except Alec of course, and he's even more skeptical than you are." David felt his face starting to burn in what he realized was an acute case of embarrassment.

Liz glanced at him in surprise, then quickly back at the road, which was getting harder to see by the moment. "Well, I was wondering when you were going to admit that."

David cleared his throat. "That's why I want you to keep my runestaff. It's made of ash, which is supposed to ward off the Faeries – iron is too, and crosses, maybe, though I'm not sure they work. Might for you, though, you being more religious and all."

Liz smiled. "Well, if it'll make you feel better, I'll keep the staff. Can't hurt, can it?"

David smiled back. "I don't think so."

"So, how many times have you seen the ... Sidhe?" Liz asked bluntly. "Or should I say, do you think you've seen them?"

David slumped down in his seat again. "I haven't counted. But let's see: There was the first time, dogs at the window two different times – and the waterhorse at the lake. You saw that."

"That was scary," Liz agreed. "What do you think it was?"

"A kelpie, probably: a Scottish water monster. Either that or ... something worse. The Sidhe can make themselves visible when they want to, and can shape-shift as well, so it could've been one of them in some kind of disguise. Some of them are on my side, too; they're not all evil."

"They told you this?"

David frowned. "Look, Liz, if you're gonna be sarcastic, I'll shut up. I've held my peace this long; I can certainly continue."

Liz shook her head; her hair was like a sweep of auburn silk. "I don't know who I'm more worried about: you or Uncle Dale."

"Uncle Dale, I hope. I'm not likely to die of terminal Second Sight. But ... I may have to take the Sidhe up on their offer."

Liz slammed on the brakes and brought the truck to a skidding halt at the side of the road. She turned and looked straight at David. "Their offer? What offer? David, what have you done?"

"They want me to go with them to Faerie. You probably wouldn't know the difference if I did; they'd probably leave a changeling in my place."

Liz poked David in the ribs. "I'd know the difference, believe me.

David grinned.

To his surprise, Liz grinned back. "Tell you what," she said in her most practical and decisive voice, as she eased the truck back onto the highway. "Next time I see him, I *will* try to read Uncle Dale. Maybe then I'll get a clearer idea of what's going on. Something sure as heck is; you've been acting like a crazy man since the fair. Alec's noticed it; my mom has too –and she's only seen you twice but she thinks you're just in love with the mystery woman."

"Well, I'm not. That much I do know!"

Liz didn't reply for a long moment, then let out a breath. "I'm glad to hear that."

David grinned again. "Only woman in my life is my mama."

But he knew, suddenly, that was not quite true.

Fifteen minutes later, the pickup slipped and slithered up the Sullivans' driveway. Liz parked as close to the front porch as possible, and she and

David dashed frantically across the mushy yard – and still managed to arrive at the house half-drowned.

David knew something was wrong the instant they opened the door. It was too dark, for one thing, for in spite of the gloomy weather, no lights were on in the living room. The other thing was his mother. She was sitting in her chair by the television, her eyes open, but apparently seeing absolutely nothing.

He noticed then that her hair was soaked, as if she'd been out in the ongoing storm, and her shirt looked damp as well. She clasped a cup of coffee in her hands, but they shook so much that she had spilled part of it. Dark stains marked her pants leg.

"Ma!" David gasped. "What's happened?"

Behind him Liz closed the door softly and stood David's runestaff in the corner. Neither Big Billy nor Little Billy was anywhere to be seen.

His mother didn't say anything at all; rather, she simply looked up at David, horror on her face, tears running into wrinkles he had never noticed before. He could not read her thoughts, but he knew something awful was going on, for her blue eyes were open wide, imploring, and her mouth as well – though no sound came forth. She simply stared into space.

"Pa!" David shouted to the house at large. "Pa!"

Big Billy stomped into the room from the hall, wet about the shoulders of his khaki shirt. He was obviously shaken; his breath smelled of beer.

"What's wrong with her, Pa?"

Big Billy had brought a towel and was awkwardly trying to dry his wife's wet hair and hands. "It's Little Billy, son. He's in his room. Go see."

"Oh my God!" David exchanged anxious glances with Liz. "If anything's happened to him –"

He shouldered past his father, vaguely hearing him say, "Now Mama, it's all right. It's not your fault. It's nobody's fault."

David paused at the door to Little Billy's room, then took a breath and opened it into the half-dark, steeling himself, not knowing what to expect, but suddenly desperately glad that Liz had followed him.

His brother sat on the side of his bed, soaked to the skin. He was utterly still, save that he breathed shallowly. He didn't even blink; rather, his eyes were fixed on some empty point in the near distance. It was like the time they had seen the black dog, only ten times worse.

David rushed over to him and took him in his arms. "Little Billy, it's me, Davy. What's happened to you?"

Little Billy didn't reply.

"Good Lord, he's dripping wet," Liz cried, stepping closer. "Why isn't your father doing something?"

"'Cause Ma's messed up too, and he just doesn't know which way to go." David grasped his little brother's shoulders and shook him gently. His eyes were tingling again, and there was something weird about the way the boy was staring into space. "Little Billy," he called tentatively. Then: "Liz, turn on the lights."

Light flooded the room. David stared into his brother's eyes. Little Billy tried to flinch away, but David held him firm, forcing their gazes to meet – and saw what he had feared to see.

Beyond the frightened blue eyes that were Little Billy's, David caught a glimpse of other eyes: green and slightly slanted. He knew, then, that he looked upon a changeling.

The Sidhe had taken Little Billy.

"What's going on?" Liz demanded. "What's wrong?"

"Gettin' late, Liz. You'd best be goin'."

"It's four-thirty," Liz shot back. "That's hardly late. And I'm not goin' anywhere in the middle of this." She motioned toward the chaos in the living room. "I might be needed. You're obviously no good. What's happened?"

"The Faeries have taken Little Billy," David said heavily.

Liz stared at him, dumbfounded. "What're you saying? Little Billy's right in there. And he's sick – catatonic, I think."

"No."

"Yes!" Liz retorted and without seeming to think about it, slapped David hard on the cheek. "This is no time for fantasy!"

David's eyes smoldered as he grabbed her wrists. "I'm telling the truth, Liz," he snapped between gritted teeth. "The Sidhe have taken Little Billy and left one of their own children in his place. I believe that as much as I believe you're standing here!"

Liz backed away. "I'll go see to your mother."

"Yeah," David whispered, wilting, "I'd better get back to her, too. At least *she's* still in this world."

An instant later they were back in the living room. David's mother had buried her face in her hands and was weeping uncontrollably. Big Billy stood beside her, hands hanging helplessly. Liz took Joanne's coffee cup and set it on an end table.

"How did it happen, Pa?" David asked.

"I don't really know," Big Billy replied slowly. "I told Little Billy to go out in the yard to get the ax I'd left out there by the woodpile – and he didn't want to go, but I made him, told him there wasn't nothin' to be scared of at his age in his own backyard. Your ma told me not to make him go, but I told her there'd been enough foolishness around, and that I was gonna speak to you 'bout scarin' him with your fool stories."

"I never –" David began, but his father went on, "Anyhow, he didn't come back, and he didn't come back, and your ma come and asked me if I'd seen him. And then she looked out the window and seen him standin' out there in the rain by the woodpile lookin' up at the mountain, soaked to the skin. And she let out a holler and run on out there and grabbed him and started shakin' him."

"Did he say anything? *Has* he said anything?"

Big Billy shook his head. "Nothin' you could understand; just a lot of gobbledegook, like speakin' in tongues at church 'cept *right* when your ma got there and she said – Oh shit, I can't say this, boy." He bent his head, his breath catching.

"Say it, Pa!" For the first time David noticed that Big Billy was also crying.

"She said, 'Come to your mama,' and he looked up at her and said, 'You are not my mother.' And she busted out cryin' and come inside."

"How long ago was this?"

"Right before you come."

"Shoot," David spat. "It's my fault. If I hadn't –"

"We gotta call the hospital, boy," Big Billy interrupted. "You'd better do it, I don't think I can. This is all your ma needs."

David patted his father's arm. "Sure." He cast a baleful glance out the screen door at what little he could see of the sky. "You'd better head out, Liz."

Liz folded her arms. "I'm staying, David."

"Liz, this is a family matter."

"Oh, all right," she grumbled, and stomped to the door.

"I'm sorry," David murmured, "but I can't deal with anybody else right now. I'll get in touch with you later. But be careful."

"You sure I can't help?" Liz asked as she opened the door.

David handed her his runestaff and shook his head sadly. "No. Thanks." She stared at the staff, brow furrowed.

"Protection, remember?" David said simply, and closed the door behind her.

It was bad, he knew: to run her off like that. And maybe dangerous as well, what with the Sidhe now taking physical action against those he loved. But he could not be everywhere at once. At least Liz would be in the pickup, and that was steel, which should offer some protection. And she had his runestaff, which might help at other times – provided she remembered to carry it with her, which he doubted.

But what about his folks – and himself, for that matter? The car would help there as well – for most of the way. And once in town, once at the hospital, there would be too many people around – he hoped; that was all he could do. And after that? He just didn't want to contemplate.

Actually, he considered, he probably ought to stay at home, to look after things anyway. And draw off the attack, as it were – if there was another attack. Somebody had to stay, after all, and he didn't think Ailill would act again right away. Too many strange accidents would attract too much attention, which was exactly what the dark Faery's faction did not want.

Once again, he hoped.

He squared his shoulders and eased over to stand before his mother. "Ma," he whispered, "it'll be all right."

She turned a tear-stained face toward him. "You should've seen him, David: just standin' there in the rain, starin' at that mountain. And when he turned to me, just lookin' at me like I wasn't there, and said, 'You are not my mother,' I thought I would die. I swear; I just can't stand anything else. First you, and then Dale and now this; I just can't stand it." She was perilously close to screaming.

David knelt beside her and put his arm around her. "Okay, Ma, we'll get him to a hospital and find out what's wrong. Maybe it's just shock, or something – and we'll get something to calm you down, too."

"Don't worry about me," she sobbed. "All I want is my boy back. That's not Little Billy in there, David, not my Little Billy. I don't know what it is, but Little Billy's not in there. God knows I try to live a good life, but I must have sinned some way, for all this to be happening. You go look, David. That's not your brother in there; it's just a shell."

"He's been jumpy lately, Ma; he just saw something that scared him real bad. Hospital'll fix him up. May take a while, that's all." David knew he was lying extravagantly, but what else could he tell his mother? Not the truth, that was for certain.

Joanne was staring at the floor. "Shoot," she said, "I don't know if we should even bother takin' him to the doctor – much good they did poor old Dale. They'd just say there's nothin' they can do. Oh, you should have seen him, should have heard him, David, speakin' in tongues." She began to sob again.

David rose and crossed to the door, leaning against the frame. That was the second time they'd mentioned speaking in tongues. He thought for a moment, shutting out the panic in the room. There were three kinds of changelings, he recalled from what he had read in *The Secret Common-Wealth*: One was called a stock, which was just a piece of wood enchanted to look like a real person. A stock was what the Faeries used when they took somebody and wanted everybody to think he was dead, like what had happened to Reverend Kirk.

And sometimes they left one of their own old people that was about to die. But this obviously wasn't an old Faery; David's Second Sight had proved that; besides which he didn't think anybody could grow old in this part of Faerie. No one he had seen had looked older than about thirty, except Oisin, and he was a special case.

But sometimes, too, they left one of their own children. That was evidently what had happened here. The Sidhe had taken Little Billy and left one of their own, and it had spoken its native language in its fright. Why, it was probably just as scared as Little Billy had been, but it didn't know any English. What his mother thought she had heard must have been the changeling's thoughts amplified by its fear. Imagine being thrust into the world of men in the midst of a thundertorm! What kind of people would do that to one of their own children? Well, David had seen enough of the Sidhe to know something about their morality – or lack of it.

Big Billy's voice broke his reverie. "Call the hospital, boy, call the hospital."

"Okay, okay," David sighed, as he dialed the number to alert the medical center before returning to the living room.

"Just be calm, Mama, just be calm," he heard his father saying. "You get the hospital, boy?"

"Sure did," David nodded. "But I was just thinkin'," he added slowly, "that it might be better for me to stay here, do the evening chores, and keep an eye on things while you and Ma go with Little Billy – if that's all right with you."

"Yeah," Big Billy replied absently, "that'd be a good idea, I reckon."

"But you be careful, Pa. It's raining even harder than it was. Better take the pickup; there's gonna be bad weather tonight. And you call me the minute you hear anything, all right? And don't forget to let me know how Uncle Dale's doin'."

"All right. Good." Big Billy stumped over to his wife and took her by the shoulders. "Come on now, Mama."

"I'll take care of Little Billy," David called as the door slammed behind them.

"Poor little changeling," he whispered a moment later, when he returned to the room where that which wore his brother's shape still sat exactly where he had left it on the edge of the bed. It grinned an honest, childlike grin and did not resist as David began to strip off its wet clothing. David studied it, trying to will the Sight – he was finally beginning to learn how to turn it on and off. Apparently there were times and places it worked automatically: places where magic was strong or concentrated, he suspected. But sometimes, he had discovered, he could also summon it at will. As he tugged Little Billy's pajamas onto the changeling, he looked more closely at the boy and saw that other face: slimmer, more pointed of chin, the hair of unearthly fineness, the long-lashed lids that he knew covered eyes green and faintly slanted.

Yet this was somehow different; not quite like the other times he had experienced the Sight. He frowned, puzzled. Those other times he had seen the things of the Otherworld very clearly indeed. Or else he had glimpsed them as tenuously as things seen in a drifting fog. This time, however, it was not so much as if he looked on a shape — an actual form obscured by magic — as on the *memory* of a shape. There was magic afoot, all right, but magic of a type different from any he had encountered before.

He was still trying to figure things out when Big Billy came into the room, lifted the shell of his son, and carried him out to the truck.

Two hours later Big Billy called from the hospital.

"Everything all right, Pa?"

"I reckon so," Big Billy's voice crackled over the line, the connection even worse than usual. "Your ma's almost worse off than Little Billy, looks like; but they give her something to calm her down and put her in a room to sleep. Little Billy seems to be comin' round, but he's not talkin' much – or it's more like he was learnin' to talk all over again: askin' the names of things and stuff, real funny-like. I've heard of somebody bein' scared out of their growth, but I didn't think I'd ever see somebody scared out of their mind."

"Sorry you have to."

"Everything all right at home?"

"Power's flickered a time or two, but I've checked the oil lamps. You stayin' the night?"

"Looks like we'll have to. Lots of floodin' 'tween here an' home. Besides, they want to keep Little Billy under observation – treat him for shock. They think that he might've been hit by ball lightnin' or somethin'. Poor old Dale's a little better, though –I guess that's one good thing. But I tell you what, boy; I've had it with these know-nothin' doctors. Your ma and me have decided one thing: First thing tomorrow, we're bringin' 'em home – both of 'em. We can do as good as this hospital."

"You're probably right," David murmured.

"What was that?"

"Oh, nothing."

"I was a fool," Big Billy went on reflectively, "to ask a little boy to go out in the rain like that. A goddamn fool."

"Maybe so," David replied absently and hung up the phone.

The sudden silence made the very air seem empty. David frowned and ambled over to the refrigerator in search of something to quiet his growling stomach. Once full of coffee, cold roast beef, a peanut butter sandwich, and a handful of Ruffles, he began to pace the house, unable to stay in one place for more than a instant. The radio was full of static; the TV was out entirely; and reading demanded more concentration than he could muster.

He continued to pace, and when that became too much, ventured onto the front porch to watch the storm. Safe or unsafe, he didn't really care. It was raining as if it would never stop, and he stared at that silver-laced darkness for a long time before starting back inside. As he reached for the door handle, he stopped short. His runestaff was leaning in the corner by the door. Liz had left it for him. "Christ!" he whispered. "If anything happens to her –"

But there was nothing he could do about it now, he realized glumly, as he brought it inside and retreated to the sanctuary of his room. Whatever happened would happen.

He flopped down on his bed, ran his gaze blankly over his bookcase. Idly, he reached out and snared the worn blue copy of *Gods and Fighting Men*. He wished he'd had time to scour the local libraries, and the one at Young Harris as well, for more books on Celtic folklore, but there just hadn't been time. And forget about the Internet, which he couldn't access out here and hadn't found a way to ask Alec to check that wouldn't result in an argument or worse. Oh, he had prowled around in *The Secret Common-Wealth* a good bit, but all he could remember from that was something about iron and crosses, and he doubted that the latter of those were reliable. Still, the Faery boy – Fionchadd, or whatever his name was – had said that David was under some sort of protection, which he evidently was – and fairly powerful protection at that, else the Sidhe would've carried him off by now. Maybe the ring really was shielding him from afar. But even if he had the ring right now, what good would it do? He couldn't fancy it undoing what was already done. No, there must be other solutions, if only he could think of them.

He flipped through the pages of the book. Names and places once glorious to him flickered by. *And now I don't care! The magic is gone.* He stared at the long list of names in the glossary and thought about the changeling. "One of these people could be his father or his mother," he whispered. "I wonder where my little brother is sleeping now."

He slammed the covers.

   ⊛   ⊛   ⊛

Chapter XII

on the mountain

An hour later, David stood on the back porch staring out at the rain, barely noticing how it stung his face and arms where the T-shirt didn't cover. The rain was falling even harder, sluicing off the tin roof in cold silver sheets, turning the yard into bog, the driveway to a blood-colored river. The sorghum patch was all but flooded now; only a few stray stalks of derelict cane showed above the water. The sky hung heavy and almost pure black, save when lightning launched a barrage against the leaden clouds. Across the drive, the crosshatched shapes of trees and fences stuck up from the muck like frozen black corpses.

He sighed and returned to the kitchen to make a fresh pot of coffee. Another hour passed.

He couldn't take any more. Inaction was slowly driving him mad. Tension throbbed in the air like the omni-present thunder.

At a loss as to what to do, he slumped at the kitchen table, gazing sullenly out the window, watching the rain, the drops hard and bitter as his own despair. Last time he'd checked, the river bottoms looked like small lakes, and he could no longer see the mountains across the valley. Water was creeping across the Sullivan Cove Road, too, and he knew it was only a matter of time before it would become impassable, himself marooned. He tried to imagine what the waterfall up on Lookout Rock must look like, and shuddered. It had been raining virtually all day, without a letup – and that was all he needed.

He tried to remember bright clear skies and fresh green grass; soft warm winds and calm, cool water – not this demon-driven stuff. As if to taunt him, a gust of wind banged the screen door and forced its way inside, to chill him where he sat with a quarter-cup of cold coffee in his hand. The single overhead light cast knife-edged shadows around the room. He hugged himself, for the warmth had gone out of the kitchen, indeed from the whole house. It felt cold and clammy as winter.

The door banged again, and he jumped. *Probably the Sidhe come at last*, he told himself grimly. *And I think if they asked I'd go. Hell, I'll give 'em credit for one thing: they sure know how to get at me. Make my house an island, hide the sun, put my friends at a distance, my brother in some other world, and my favorite uncle barely in this. Shoot, what have I got to live for, anyway?* He slammed his fist on the table so hard that the sugar bowl came uncapped.

I'll do it. I'll give myself up to the Sidhe.

But even as the thought appeared, he knew that to even contemplate such a thing was madness! And where would he go? How did one find the Sidhe, anyway? The Straightway – or Track, or whatever it was? Well, it was a thing of the Sidhe, all right: one of their Places of Power – if it could be called a place. But he wasn't certain how to find it, nor did he know how to work it if he did. It might lead him to Faerie, or it might lead him somewhere else entirely, and the latter would do no one any good.

Bloody Bald? But it was an island, maybe half a mile from the nearest shore, and though he was a good swimmer, he didn't dare undertake such a venture in weather like this. He wondered, though, why he had never thought of visiting it before, in all his sixteen years. He'd been swimming in the cove more times than he could count, but never once had it occurred to him to venture out to the island – which was in plain sight from there. Nor, he realized, had anyone else he knew ever been there, either – or even proposed going there. Selective blindness like that could only be the magic of the Sidhe turning men's thoughts away. He shook his head; Bloody Bald was definitely out. With the weather gone wild, such a journey would simply be too perilous. A dead peace offering would be worthless. That left Lookout Rock. Lookout Rock was his own Place of Power; he'd even called it that when such things were only a game. It was nowhere near any place of the Sidhe that he knew about, but one could see Bloody Bald from there, at least on a clear night. That was it, then; he would go to Lookout Rock and offer himself to the Sidhe. He'd meet them but on his own ground, not like a beggar at the door.

Of course there was still the small matter of the weather. Rain. Wind. Thunder. Lightning. The odd bit of hail. Even the road up the mountain looked flooded. If he fell into the ditch, he could quite possibly drown.

Then again, there were certainly worse things than drowning. He had to die sometime, after all.

No, you fool! Don't think like that! he told himself – but was not convinced.

Of course drowning would solve one problem: With him dead, maybe the Sidhe would leave his folks alone.

Or would they? Had his family already become so tainted by the Otherworld, albeit all unknowing, that the Sidhe might consider them a threat, even with him gone? And there was still his ring out loose in the world: one more piece of unfinished business. He sighed. One thing was for sure: sitting around moping wouldn't improve things. He slumped over to the stove and refilled his cup with the last of the coffee. It was hot and black and bitter as gall. After a moment's thought, he snatched a handful of Oreos from an open package and headed for his room.

Grimly and methodically, he stripped and began to dress from the skin out in clothes more suitable for the bleak weather: warmer clothes, for the temperature had fallen with the rain so that it was sometimes perilously close to sleeting. Sleet! In Georgia! In August! Once again he recalled Oisin saying that Ailill was a lord of winds and tempests. If he'd had any doubts about that before, he certainly had none now.

He completed his kit with an ancient black rubber poncho that included a hood that far overhung his face, and with hiking boots that laced close about his ankles. As he passed his dresser, he paused, opened the top drawer, and removed two things: a handkerchief Liz had made him the previous Christmas, with his initials embroidered on it in blackwork Gothic; and a key fob Alec had given him with the Sullivan coat of arms enameled on one side and a blessing in Irish Gaelic on the other. He smiled wryly at the irony of the latter – he hadn't been into things Irish back then – and stuffed them into a shirt pocket, then closed the door behind him.

His gaze flickered around the kitchen, coming to rest at last on a comfortingly familiar object: his runestaff – the one Liz had left. It evidently held some kind of magic – or at least it had glowed when she had touched it. Well, maybe there was some good to magic after all. Sighing, he picked it up and slung the leather strap over his wrist, thought about taking an umbrella, then discarded the notion as ludicrous. The rain was nearly as horizontal as it was vertical.

The wind howled continuously, but the storm seemed to have abated – or so he thought, until lightning flashed hellishly right outside, and a mighty blast of thunder rattled the windows and doors like some dark beast trying to get in. Shades of *Forbidden Planet!* he thought, as he checked them, always looking beyond to see if something of that other world did not indeed pace about in the yard or on the porches seeking entrance. He wondered if the house would be safe, should his family, by some chance, make it home, but metal screens on doors and windows, iron locks and doorknobs had worked before – perhaps. He shrugged, drank the final swallow of the coffee, wincing at the flavor, and opened the back door.

The wind almost wrenched the knob from his grasp, but he caught it before the door could slam and was down the steps and into the yard before he could argue himself out of it. One thing was for sure – as he splashed across the sodden grass: He wouldn't leave any tracks. A glance up at the night sky made him wish for the witchlight of the Faery moon that had accompanied him when he'd gone to meet Oisin. Unfortunately, it was absent, but the rain itself imparted a sort of silver shimmer to the world that was almost as alien – though nowhere near as good to see by. *Well,* he thought, resigned, *it's uphill all the way. Long as I'm going uphill and don't run into trees, I'm on the road.*

Magic, he mused. He'd had enough of magic to last a lifetime. He was tired of tingling eyes and burning rings, of animals that talked, and of not being able to trust anything at face value, least of all his brother. That was the heart of the problem, too: not being able to trust anything. He could no longer be certain if a white animal was only a white animal, a friend only a friend. Even the rocks and trees were suspect now.

He dismissed that stream of reasoning as frivolous in light of the day's events. Trust? Ha! Who could trust him now? He'd lied to everyone he knew, so how could he expect them to believe him if he told the truth? Shoot, he wouldn't have believed them either, under the same conditions. It was Ailill's fault – his and Nuada's. And damn them both. Nuada was no better than Ailill. Yeah, he was doing the right thing, all right. Better to let the Sidhe have him and be done with it.

"You hear that, Silverhand?" he yelled into the darkness. "I'm gonna talk to you! Gonna meet you man to man. You guys want me, you can have me – but at a place of my choosing, and on my terms."

And with that, he started up the mountain.

The rain assailed him at once, soaking him in spite of the poncho. He tried to throw back his shoulders and walk erect and unafraid, but that notion lasted maybe ten steps before doubt settled in, weighing his shoulders down like the water that had already drenched them. Thunder rumbled like the evil laughter of giants, and the wind howled around his ears, forcing the rain into those few parts of his body that yet remained dry. He hunched over, pulled the hood of his poncho closer over his head, and tried not to breathe too heavily. Already the cold was making him sniffle. His glasses were utterly useless. *What the heck? I can see what I need to see without 'em. Almost don't need 'em anymore, anyway.* With that, he took them off, stuffed them into an inside pocket, and continued miserably onward.

He tried to blank his mind to all but the movements of his legs against the flow of water, and nearly succeeded. The wind seemed to swallow his thoughts as soon as he thought them and carry them away to roll among the thunderclouds, so that he had trouble recalling anything beyond the endless left-right, left-right, the tiny trickles of cold sweat oozing out here and there as he exerted himself against the wind and the ever more treacherous footing. It was probably stupid to remain on the road and not seek the meager shelter of the forest, but the forest did not appeal to him just then. He was already walking nearly blind, but at least on the road it was possible to tell where he was going.

For a good while he plodded onward, not knowing how long he had been away, nor caring; aware only of cold and the hiss of his breathing and the howling of the wind. He was half blind, half deaf, and soaked to the skin, his fingers numbing as the rain grew colder, his feet freezing, so that he was less and less certain where he stepped. His legs were getting tired too, as the water sometimes rose above his ankles even on the road. He had never tried walking uphill in a flood before – but then again, floods were rare in north Georgia. It was funny how someplace you'd been a thousand times could suddenly feel different – even threatening – when you experienced an aspect of it you hadn't encountered before.

He tried to sing – "The Old Walking Song" from *The Lord of the Rings* – but couldn't remember the words; then tried a sprightly John Denver tune, but the wind shrieked louder, and he quit.

He squinted at his watch, the green numerals barely visible in the gloom, and saw that it had stopped. He shook it furiously, saw the seconds blink forward a dozen numerals and stop again. Another try produced the same results, and he gave up. He could hardly make his legs move; shoot, could hardly *feel* his legs. He set himself a goal, then: a swirl of dark water thirty feet ahead that might mark a hidden boulder. Reaching it, he set another, and then another. There shouldn't be much further to go – if he didn't miss the landmarks and pass the turnoff entirely.

Another goal reached, then another. And then he brought his foot down on an unstable stone and staggered sideways, arms pinwheeling, his staff flying from suddenly loosened fingers to disappear beneath the torrent to his right

"No!" he shrieked, as he leapt after it, touched it, felt it slip from his grasp again.

All at once he was on the edge of the ditch that followed the road. It was deep there, and the incline steep. He felt the earth crumble beneath his feet, felt mud and stones carrying him down into turbulent water, felt his feet covered, his legs engulfed. He tried to jerk himself upright, but the ooze sucked him back against the bank so that he lay there winded, half buried in mud, half covered by water that rose above his waist and poured down upon his head. He could feel the current tugging relentlessly at his feet.

A long moment passed before he realized what had happened. He looked to his right and saw towering cliffs of darkness that would be blood-red clay in the daylight; but here, at night, they were bulwarks of sticky black muck that were already insinuating themselves greedily around him. He was slipping further into the water every second, too. And cold was seeping up at him through the ground itself; he could feel it enfolding him softly, softly. He realized, then, that if he didn't act very soon indeed he would drown or be entombed by mud. And fail his quest. The Faery boy had said David had the stuff of heroes in him. *Hero? Him? Ha!* He closed his eyes and lay still a moment longer.

And thought about heroes.

And then he thought about dying, and resolve awoke within him. Cuchulain would never have drowned in a ditch by the side of the road, no sir. He'd have boiled the water with his own fury. Finn would've laughed at it and dared it to touch him. Oisin would've pointed a finger and it would have been gone. Well, David Sullivan would not give up, either – not when he had business to attend to! The earth had already claimed one David Sullivan, and that was enough. What would David-the-Elder say now, if he could see him? *Get your butt up out of there, kid. You got better things to do than die in the dirt! I didn't teach you what I taught you to have it all end here in the mud.*

No, it wouldn't end here!

Ruthlessly David forced himself upright, feeling the mud pulling stubbornly at his back. His fingers brushed something smooth. His staff! He grasped it thankfully, poured his strength into it, used it to lever himself the rest of the way up. Water swirled about his thighs, and he almost lost his balance, but he anchored the staff in the earth again – and clambered out of the ditch.

Once back on the road, he paused breathlessly, letting the rain strip the worst of the mud from his body. A glance back down the way he had come was like sighting into a long black tunnel full of ancient spiderwebs blending into a shiny floor. Scowling, he turned his gaze uphill, took a step that way. Another landmark set; another goal to accomplish. Slowly he became aware of a pulse of warmth from somewhere around his right hand. He stared at it numbly – and noticed a faint light issuing from where he clutched his runestaff: a pale ruddy radiance that glowed but did not illuminate, rather like phosphorescence. He recalled, then, how the staff had glowed when he had given it to Liz that time in the woods. "Things have Power because you give them Power," Oisin had said. Well, this was certainly Power. Maybe it only required the presence of a little real magic to awaken more. That was interesting, too, but he didn't have time to waste on speculation. His eyes were tingling. Magic was afoot.

The glow neither spread nor intensified, but the warmth did, seeping slowly up his hand through his arm and across his chest, where he felt it loosen a construction that lay about his heart: a tightness he had not noticed until it vanished. From there, the warmth continued both downward into his legs and up into his head. When it reached his eyes, his vision cleared and he saw ahead the break in the trees where the narrow trail branched off the road, leading to Lookout Rock. He had almost reached his goal.

And when he gained the place itself, David *knew* that magic was afoot, for the clouds were torn away like gossamer before a torch, and the witchmoon showed overhead. He could see the familiar stars as well: Cygnus high in the northwest, his favorite constellation after Orion. He raised his runestaff in salute, half-fearing, half-expecting to see the wings of the sky-swan flap in response. Stranger things had happened of late. And then he laughed. It was a good sign that such a notion had occurred to him; it meant his brain was working again.

Taking a deep breath, he walked over to the precipice and stood as close as he dared to the edge, listening to the roar of the waterfall behind him, drumming on the rocks like the low song of the hosts of night on the march. Straining his ears, he could hear the faint cries of bats, nightjars, and whippoorwills. Warily he glanced down, but the shapes twisted and blurred, showing first clouds, then moonlit mountains, then clouds again.

Bloody Bald reared up straight across from him like a beacon of white in the eerie light. He tried to summon the Sight, to conjure again the castle he knew was there. Nothing changed. Whatever glamour hid Lugh's palace was more powerful than Second Sight. Perhaps only at dusk and dawn did it reveal itself to mortal eyes.

So how does one summon the Sidhe? he wondered. *Stand up here and yell "Here I am; come get me?"* But he was less sure of himself now. Did he even want to go through with it at all? Well, he'd come this far, and the Sidhe were obviously waiting for him – or somebody was – else they wouldn't have been fooling with the weather. Slowly he raised his ash staff above his head, gripping it with two hands. The wind whipped his hood away, slapping damp strands of hair across his face.

"Silverhand!" he yelled into air that still shook with the thunders of the mortal world. It almost seemed that he could see the word hanging visible in the sky, as uncertain as he was.

"Silverhand!" he cried again, and put more force into his voice, but the sound still seemed muffled.

He took another breath, filled his lungs to their depths, as if for a long dive, steeled his throat and vocal cords, and yelled a third time: *"Silverhand!"*

The name sprang forth, hard and clear into the night. It felt as if it had ripped his throat asunder as it burst out like the report of a rifle; he could almost see the air spring aside in surprise at the presumption of its volume; could hear it echo from mountains and rocks, heard even above the falls: "***Silverhand, Silverhand,*** *Silverhand* ..."

He sat down then – and waited, watching the lightning that played among the lowlands like lost stars.

Nothing happened.

He leaned back, arms braced behind him with the staff between ... and abruptly jerked back upright when a pain stabbed through his right hand. Something had struck it – something hard and sharp. *Snake*, instinct supplied.

He twisted around from reflex to see an ice-white raven placidly preening its feathers behind him, its ivory beak the instrument of his distress.

The raven cocked his head at him. "Silverhand," it croaked.

"You?" David asked.

"Raven," replied the raven.

"Raven?"

"Raven."

"I called Silverhand," David snapped. "Nuada of the Silver Hand." He was in no mood to talk to a bird. Not when his resolve was weakening by the instant.

"Messenger," said the raven.

David folded his arms and looked away. "I need to talk to Nuada."

"Forbidden," said the raven.

"Why?"

216

"Lugh's law."

David stood up and paced back and forth, precariously close to the edge, then faced the raven again. It remained implacable. He gestured around at the night. "So, what is all this?"

"Power."

"Whose Power? Ailill's? Nuada's? *Lugh's?*"

"Enemy! Enemy!" the raven squawked, abruptly agitated. Even as David opened his mouth to frame another question, it spread its wings and took flight.

David found himself cast into shadow. A darkness passed overhead, eclipsing the starlit sky, then was gone. He jerked his head up, frowning. Cygnus still blazed. A check of another part of the sky showed Corona Borealis, which the Welsh called Caer Arianrhod, the Castle of the Silver Wheel. It reminded him of the ring. And then his eyes took fire, and he was once more plunged into darkness.

A sound reached his ears with that darkness: a concussion of the air, as of vast wings flapping. David looked up to see the raven fluttering frantically about, not ten feet above his head. But beyond it, shadowing half the sky, were the outstretched pinions and dagger talons of a vast black eagle – fully forty feet from wing tip to wing tip.

There are no eagles in Georgia that big.

The eagle dipped its wings. Once. Twice. Slowly, almost deliberately. And each time those wings moved, blue lightning arced and crackled among the inky feathers at their tips, setting the creature now in such high relief that David was certain he could see every vane of every plume cut out against the heavens; now plunging it into darkness so profound it was like a jagged rip in the sky itself.

And the size kept shifting: forty feet, then scarcely larger than a real eagle, then dispersed across the sky so far and thin that the stars showed through its substance, then forty feet again.

A bolt of lightning struck at it from somewhere, briefly outlining it in glory.

Its size stabilized at that, but the eagle continued to float in the air, ominously aloof, still too impossibly huge to fly.

There are no eagles in the world *like that!* David corrected himself, as he blinked eyes he felt certain must themselves be blazing. A few yards below it, the raven fluttered in small, confused circles, trapped, looking for escape – out –

Or up –

Or down.

The smaller bird folded its wings and dove toward the sheer cliff face beyond David's feet, where it disappeared into the gloom below. The eagle wheeled lazily and followed, dropping in pursuit like a stone. David could feel displaced air whip his face as the eagle fell past his vantage point. He peered cautiously over the edge.

Both eagle and raven were lost to sight in the shadow of the mountain. But a brief, high cry cut the night, and the eagle rose alone, climbing like smoke into the midnight blue sky. And then it turned its baleful red gaze toward David.

A blast of heat seared his face – and suddenly he was running: across rocks, over fallen tree trunks, toward the sheltering boughs of the forest. He barely made it. For as he dived into that protective darkness – still clutching his runestaff – he heard the *whoosh* of wings, felt hot breath on his neck, smelled again the odor of sulfur – though this time it was mixed with blood. Pain cut across his shoulders like a whip. A harsh cry exploded in his ears like the snapping of a branch from a tree: a nonhuman cry that yet registered first surprise, then pain, then rage.

Instinctively, David reached back to feel inside his shirt collar, but the pain had already passed: vanished as quickly as it had come. He did find a rent in the fabric, but there was none of the expected sticky ooze of blood on his fingers when he looked at them, only a thin smear of some black powder like soot.

It's the ring! Wherever it is, it's still working. It saved me, he thought as he passed deeper into the woods, still fearing to hear at any moment the sound of wings or to feel talons or beak come at him out of the air to pierce his flesh and rend his life from him

Or take him away to Faerie where, he now realized, he did not want to go.

But there was no sound in the night save his own breathing; nothing unusual showing against the sky in those few glimpses he got of it.

Sometime later he emerged from the woods on the bank above the logging road that led down to his house, though much farther up the mountain than he'd expected.

The eagle was waiting for him there, perched in the sturdy branches of the same ancient oak whose shelter he had just abandoned. As he scrambled down into the roadbed, the bird glided soundlessly toward him, talons outstretched, seeming to grow longer, sharper, more terrifyingly pointed as they filled his vision.

Instinctively, he raised his runestaff above his head, held it horizontally between his hands.

To his surprise, the eagle retreated, rising to hover impossibly slowly just out of reach above his head, wings masking the sky, claws like knives.

He fully expected it to fall upon him, to smash him to a bloody, mangled pulp. Certainly it had mass enough to overpower him with ease.

Yet it did not. It simply hung there, upheld by some uncanny, unfelt wind.

David gritted his teeth and prayed, as he continued to hold the staff aloft. *Things have Power because you give them Power.* Oisin's words chimed in his mind, seeming to spread, to resonate throughout his body. *Iron and ash are some protection. Iron and ash. Iron and ash. Power. Power. Power.* He felt the staff grow warm.

Suddenly, beyond the eagle, David saw a vaster whiteness flash down from the night sky, to fall straight upon the back of his adversary. He felt the eagle's shadow spread to engulf the world and stumbled backward onto the ground, eyes closed in absolute terror, staff still fixed firmly in his hands.

But the expected suffocating weight did not fall upon him. Rather, there was one brief, strangled cry, and then –

Nothing.

When he opened his eyes again, the eagle was gone. Where it had been, Cygnus the Swan glittered in the sky. A yard to his right a white feather five feet long glimmered, fading from existence even as he gawked at it.

He ran: wildly, madly, unaware when the rains returned. Relief? Fear? Both? He didn't know; he simply buried his rational mind and let instinct rule. He was back in the forest, he realized at one point, for branches poked him painfully and tore brutally at his clothes and skin. The rain had slackened, but only by comparison to its former fury. He tried to stop, to think, to compose himself. But it was hard, so hard. And it was so dark he could barely see where he was going.

A foot caught on a fallen branch and sent him sprawling. He retained his hold on the staff, but his other arm flailed outward, its fingers grabbing vainly at the twigs that clutched back at him. One slipped through his grasp; another broke off in his fist. He fell heavily, winded, the staff beneath him. For a moment he lay motionless and gasping, trying vainly to regain some semblance of self-control.

Something warm touched his cheek, and he looked up, squinting into the gloom. Nothing there. But he knew he had felt something. Something very like a summer breeze.

Fear stabbed at him, but vanished even as he flinched away, for there had been no threat in that touch, though he had no idea how he knew that.

As if in answer to that realization, he noticed a sparkle of light in the forest ahead of him. Even as he watched, it grew brighter – moment

219

by moment, second by second – until at last he was looking into a circle of light, almost like daylight, perhaps twenty feet across. He sat up, brushed his fingers across his clothes. They were dry; the mud flaked away as he slapped at it. He fumbled his glasses out of his pocket and put them on, then realized they were filthy and tried to clean them on his shirt – to no avail.

"Seeing is not really necessary when you've important things to hear," came a familiar voice from a few scant feet ahead of him. "In fact, it is not really necessary at all."

David stared stupidly at the multi-lobed leaves of the branch still clutched in his fist.

It was oak.

Oisin!

"It will not last long," Oisin murmured, from where he sat on a tree stump between two more oaks, looking exactly as he had looked the last time David had seen him. "For it takes much Power for me to send my spirit roving in a form you can discern, and more to provide an appropriate setting for any sort of conversation. But I did not come to discuss metaphysics. You have summoned me, I surmise, in a time of distress."

"Actually, it was an accident," David admitted, embarrassed. "But I'm glad you came." He scrambled to his feet and took a hesitant step forward, then knelt at Oisin's feet.

"You are not wearing the ring," Oisin said mildly. "Nor do I sense it anywhere about you."

David exhaled. His lips quivered. He looked down at the ground. "I'm sorry, Oisin, I'm sorry!" he burst out. "I strayed onto a Straight Track, and a Faery boy started chasing me, and then all at once I ran off the Track, or fell off, or something, and when I came to, the ring was gone. And now the Sidhe are after my family."

Suddenly he was crying, his tears falling on the warm, dry leaves. Nor did he fight those tears.

Oisin said nothing for perhaps a minute, then laid both hands on David's head. "This tale is known to me already, David; and though it distresses me, yet there is hope. For though you do not have the ring, I do not believe the Sidhe have it either. It does not answer my call, yet I can sense its protection still upon you, which would not be the case if anyone else had claimed it for his own, unless that one were very powerful indeed – more powerful than Ailill. *He* does not have it; of that, I am certain; you would not be standing here now if he did. For though you have Power, you cannot stand against him. Therefore, the ring must still remain in your world, perhaps not far from where you lost it. Before all else, David, seek the ring, for at least it will prevent further misfortune."

David shook his head. "Further misfortune? How much more misfortune can there be? I've already lost my brother and Uncle Dale." He looked up at Oisin. "Is there anything I can do to help them? I went up to the mountain tonight to give myself up to Nuada. But ... something happened."

"I know – and I likewise find that strange. But to answer your question about your kinsmen: I fear I have no good news for you there. Both of their lives are bound about with Power: Power beyond my skill to break, for only those who create such bonds may sever them. More to the point, Lugh has forbidden my further intervention; only the fact of my previous promise to you allows me to come here now, and at that it is but part of me you see before you. Thus, I fear I can say little that will give you comfort, except to remind you that there is always a solution to such problems if only it can be found; it is one of the Laws of Power. But knowledge of that solution must come from within yourself, David; not so much from any Power which you possess – though you have more than a little – but from those other things that make you the person you are: your own ingenuity and determination. I can see the threads of fate patterning your destiny even as we speak." Here he raised his arms into the air as if weaving some web of sunlight and wind. "Yet more than one pattern can be woven from the same threads. Use your head, but follow your heart. The Sidhe are not as unlike mortal men as they would have you think."

"You say I have Power?"

"It is as I have said, and as I suspect you are learning: Things indeed have Power because you give them Power. How do you think you stayed Ailill long enough for Nuada to come to your aid?"

"I ... don't know. I was praying for Power, thinking about it, anyway. Hoping more than I've ever hoped before. I think I felt something ... strange, but I thought it was just the staff. After all, it *is* made of iron and ash."

"And well made it is, too. Both ash and iron were factors, but most of what sustained you against the eagle was your own Power working through those things: The power of determination, of fear, and of belief. It may be difficult for you to understand, but perhaps I should tell you."

"Tell me what?" David asked eagerly.

Oisin cleared his throat. "I told you I did not come to discuss metaphysics, yet I see that yours is the sort of mind that will not rest until these questions are answered, so listen well."

He cleared his throat again, then: "There are Worlds and Worlds, David Sullivan, of which this is but one. There are others that touch this one, even as Faerie does, and others that touch Faerie as well, but not this. Power is a part of all these Worlds, though mortal men seem to have forgotten that. Earth and Water, Air and Fire: of these the Worlds are made. Earth is matter; Air is spirit, more or less. The two are often linked together – though more so in your World than in Faerie, for both are passive principles. By themselves they are useless; they need something to bind them together and give them life. And such are the active principles: Water, which binds matter together – you would call it energy, I think – and Fire, which does the same for spirit. Power is simply Fire – a force acting on spirit, like emotion or imagination or will to continue existing – bent to a certain purpose."

"Oh-kay, I think I understand that much – maybe," David said slowly. "But how can a piece of wood have Power?"

"I was coming to that. The main difference between the Worlds is in the proportion and distribution of the four elements. In your world, Air spirit is confined almost exclusively to living things; inanimate objects may also contain it – but that Air can only be awakened by other Air and its attendant Fire and those must come from without – such as your own Fire, for instance. In other words, your Power awakened the Power of the staff and added to it. These are hard things to understand, I know, and they become harder the more you study them. There are realms of almost pure matter, for instance, and realms of almost pure spirit. Faerie differs from your World mostly in the relative amounts of Fire and Earth: There is more of Fire in Faerie, more of Earth in the Lands of Man. That is why the Sidhe command Power so easily, but also why many of them fear the World of Men, for just as the Sidhe may send their Power through the Walls between the Worlds and into the Lands of Men, so the substance of the Lands of Men may break through into Faerie."

"And iron and ash are two of those things, right?"

Oisin shook his head. "Not entirely. Ash is ... The closest word is *sacred*, though *damned* might serve as well or better. Ash contains almost no Air, but what it does contain in profligate amounts – amounts all out of proportion to the amount of Air that is present within it – is Fire: so much that it is both a temptation and a threat. Used properly, it can do wonders; improper use can lead to disaster.

"I will give you an example of the latter. When the Sidhe – the Danaans, rather – first came to their World, there were no ash trees in Faerie. Then someone brought a single ash seed from the Lands of Men to see how it would thrive in the soil of that World. They planted it in Aelfheim, and there it grew into an ash tree as tall as the sky. Too late those folk realized that it was drawing the very substance from that

World, and reaching into others as well. Finally there was only the tree and the Straightways, and then, when the tree touched them: *nothing*. Aelfheim was no more. So now ash is forbidden: a thing of great Power that the Sidhe must perforce avoid.

"As for the power of iron: Iron is a curious thing as well, and almost as difficult to explain, for I have no proper words for the ideas. Iron does not exist in Faerie, and that is fortunate, for in iron alone among metals the fires of the Worlds' first making never completely cool, though it may seem otherwise to mortal men. Yet the mere presence of the Power that is in the Sidhe can call forth that flame again. To the Sidhe, therefore, iron is eternally red-hot. And to make it worse, that heat may sometimes pass to that which iron touches, if left long enough. It is like the ash I told you of: Enough iron in your world in one place can burn through the barriers between your World and ours. And once it breaks through, it begins to consume the very stuff of Faerie. Those steel rails that once lay on your family's land broke into Tir-Nan-Og like a veil of flame, and the land there still lies hot long after they have gone. So hot, in fact, that even the Power of the Straightways is disrupted – and theirs is another kind of Power entirely. Fortunately the Ways are strong, and the burning slow, else your World might not long survive."

"So it's heat that keeps the Sidhe from touching iron?"

Oisin nodded. "Though they may touch it briefly, even as you might pass your hand through a candle flame and not be burned – if you are quick enough."

"Can it kill? Is its touch fatal?"

Oisin sighed restlessly. "That, too, is hard to answer, for one must first ask, 'What is fatal?' Life and death are not precisely the same with your kind and with the Sidhe. In your world the body controls the spirit to a great degree. The opposite is true in Faerie: There, the spirit controls the body; there, one who has the skill may alter the form he wears. It is all related to that difference in proportion I told you of. And there is another factor as well: The spirits of mortal men are usually bound to the substance of their world alone. The Sidhe may wrap their spirits in the substance of either World in either place. But when wearing the substance of the World of Men, the Sidhe are bound to that World's laws and may therefore be as easily slain by iron as any ordinary mortal. When such occurs, that body, at least, dies and the spirit is forced to flee; but without the strength of its physical substance to sustain it, it must find its way through the Walls Between the Worlds before it can wrap itself in its original substance – and that does not always happen.

"On the other hand, if, while wearing the substance of Faerie, one should be wounded by iron, the fire wrought by that wound would gradually consume that body. One who wore it would almost certainly be forced to flee the pain of that consumption and be forced to build another body – which can be a long, difficult – and agonizing – process. But even then, the wound rarely completely heals; it would be as if the spirit itself were scarred. One so wounded must spend eternity in torment, or else follow the Ways to other ... places, where the laws that govern such things are different. Nuada is one of the few to overcome that curse, and even he must wear an arm of metal. If anyone ever understands even a tenth part of the laws that rule the Worlds, he will be a learned man indeed." A pause, then: "Someday you may get a chance to walk those other Roads and find that out for yourself. The Sidhe do not own them."

David looked puzzled.

Oisin smiled. "It is confusing, I know. But there is no time to say more, for Lugh watches me closely. I have told you little that would be of real use to you, though much on which you may reflect. As for aiding your kinsmen, the only thing I can tell you to do is hope."

Oisin rose, straightened, and stretched. "I am sorry that I could be of no more help. But remember that every use of Power has a counter. If your kinsmen are no better for this meeting, at least they are no worse, for both may live indefinitely as they are. And you have Power of your own to see you through, and a greater power than that, even, in your two young friends. Do not underestimate them."

David released the breath he had been holding unawares. "How is it you know these things?"

Oisin smiled again. "Magic, of course – or Power. Power calls to Power, and spirit may cast shadows the same as matter. With us such things are as obvious as the falling of leaves in autumn. Now, be gone! Take the Straightway home; it crosses the road uphill from here. Step on it and enjoy what you find. I do not think you need to fear the Sidhe tonight, for the things of this world are often reflected in that, and while I sense Ailill's hand in this storm, it is not entirely of his making. The Sidhe cannot completely close off their World from yours, and this storm will be felt even in Faerie as a scattering of raindrops among the flowers. Now go!"

And Oisin was simply not there.

David stood alone in darkness and in rain.

Funny, David realized, a short while later, he had rarely been higher up the mountain than the turnoff to Lookout Rock – though the road continued for at least another mile, both uphill and down. And the Track certainly ran near the mountain's foot, so it must cross up here somewhere. With that in mind, he trudged on up the mountain. Rain bit at him again, yet its force was diminished, and eventually the road made a sharp turn to the east, and he could barely make out something glimmering faintly golden among the raindrops ahead. As he drew nearer, he saw that it was indeed a Straight Track: a slash of summer day painted across the wet Georgia night with a brush of magic. Had the Sight not wakened his eyes, he would have crossed it unaware.

As he stepped into that narrow belt, night became day indeed, though he could see the rain splashing into darkness on either side. The air smelled good, and the trees were dry where they overhung the Track. The way was narrow – only five or six feet wide – but David didn't care: the grass was soft, the air sweet and warm. And the sun! The sun was shining! Or something was – maybe not the sun, for the light was too rich, like the light of early morning or of twilight, or of the two entwined.

It took but a breath to make a decision, and David set off down the mountainside, sliding sometimes at steep places, but without concern or injury. At some point, he ripped off his muddy poncho and cast it aside, as an almost irrational joy welled up inside him. He had no more answers than heretofore, but now he could face his problems. It was as though the forced stagnation of his inaction had been shattered. The air elemental had won free again, by whatever name one wished to call that air – *Fire*, or whatever.

And so he followed daylight to the bottom of the mountain, to the place where the Track crossed the highway. From there it was only a short jog home. The rains returned, but they had lost their force and their cold. A new gentleness permeated the drops, and overhead glimpses of sky – *real* sky – showed among the clouds.

He met his father in the backyard, dressed in his heaviest raincoat. Before he knew it, he found himself enfolded by Big Billy's thick arms in a bear hug so strong and fierce he had to gasp for breath.

"I was just goin' out to hunt for you, boy," Big Billy rumbled. "I tried to call home and couldn't get nobody, and got to worryin', so I just come on back – roads wasn't as bad as they said they was. An' when I found you gone, it scared me to death, let me tell you. Where you been?" There was no trace of anger in his words.

"Just out walkin' in the rain, Pa. I just couldn't stand stayin' in the house any longer."

Big Billy laughed. "You're a bigger fool than I am, then, but right now I don't much care."

"You're nobody's fool, Pa. If there's a fool in the family, it's me."

Big Billy looked curiously at his son, then grinned and shrugged. "Let's not argue over that, boy. I promised I'd get back to your ma before the night's over." He glanced at the sky. "Looks like the weather might be breakin'." He laid a heavy arm across David's shoulders and turned toward the house. "How're you at makin' coffee, boy? I sure could use a cup."

David grinned as well. "Better'n you are." The grin widened. He had won a victory of sorts against the Sidhe – and against his own fears and doubt in the bargain – and those were both things to be proud of. Now if he could figure out how to cure Uncle Dale, and rescue Little Billy, and protect his family and friends, and –

No! he told himself firmly. *Not now, not tonight.*

But as he stepped onto the porch, he thought he heard the rumble of distant thunder and the flapping of unseen wings.

 PART IV

Prologue V

In Tir-nan-og
(high summer)

If *there is anything I would rather do than fly,* thought Ailill, *it is to run. And if there is anything I would rather do than run in my own shape, it is to do so in the shape of a stag. And if there is anything I would rather do than that, it is to set myself in a contest of speed with a beast of a different kind.*

Thus it happened that Ailill, in the form of a fine black stag, had for some time been racing alongside a young white stallion he had lately acquired. They had begun their contest in a secluded, close-grown forest of lacy, tree-high ferns, where sureness of foot had been as important as speed. But now they burst out into the hot copper sunlight of a narrow meadow full of high, sharp-edged grass from which spiky clusters of wine-red flowers rose on knobby stalks. Somewhere within that cover a griffin belled. Lightning flashed from Ailill's antlers at that, startling the white. And with that, their contest began in earnest.

At first neither showed an advantage, but at last the horse's longer legs began to tell and put it a body-length ahead. Ailill redoubled his efforts, then; masking the stag's fear of the open with his own desire for victory – and thus was almost upon the meadow's farther edge before he knew it. The white slowed abruptly and swung away to the right, chasing the sunlight, but Ailill did not change course and suddenly found himself beneath the low, sprawling limbs and spraddle-fingered leaves at the shadowy fringe of an oak wood.

As he paused there, gasping, the muffled clomping of hooves reached his ears. *Better not to be seen as I am*, he thought, as he called the horse to him and abandoned hide and antlers in favor of his own form, clothing his brief nakedness in a sleeveless hunting tunic and baggy breeches of tawny velvet quickly spun from a handful of grass. So it was that when that unknown rider urged his gold-coated stallion through one final scrim of mold-webbed leaves and entered the meadow, what met that rider's eyes was an elegant black-haired man sitting bareback on an equally elegant white horse, both of which were breathing heavily, and one of which looked somewhat guilty in the bargain.

"I am ... surprised to see you here, Silverhand," Ailill called, with uncharacteristic hesitation, when he recognized the other rider.

"I am surprised to see you in your own shape anywhere at all these days," Nuada replied. "But I would rather see it than certain others you sometimes affect — to no good purpose, or success either, I might add."

Ailill refused to be baited. "Are you not afraid, Nuada, that something might happen to your pet mortal while you are wandering around here in the woods?"

"The thing most likely to happen to him is you!" Nuada retorted. "And you I am watching very closely — as doubtless you observed when you sought to answer a summons not meant for you."

"You cannot always protect the mortal boy." Ailill chuckled. "And when I have the ring, it will not matter."

Nuada frowned. "You realize, of course, that Lugh knows about the changeling. *Displeased* would not be too strong a word to describe his reaction."

"That does not disturb me," Ailill replied complacently.

"Does it disturb you, then, that such activities are not, perhaps, entirely appropriate for an ambassador? I would remind you yet again that you are a guest in this land, and a guest who makes himself unwelcome in Tir-Nan-Og is a fool indeed. Be warned, Ailill: If you dwell in Lugh's land, you are bound by Lugh's laws; for you are here by his grace, not by your right. This is not Annwyn, or even Erenn. You may not pick and choose among the inhabitants of the Lands of Men as pleases you."

"I think I have heard enough from you today," Ailill snapped. "In fact, I think I have heard enough from you for a very long time indeed!"

"You will hear as much as it pleases me to tell you," Nuada flared, his eyes flashing dangerously.

"Then I shall have to see to it that you tell me nothing more!" Ailill shouted. He slapped both fists closed before him — and with his right hand withdrew from his left hand a sword: a sword born of Power alone — a fire sword that blazed in the forest like the burning blood of rubies.

Weapon in hand, Ailill laughed — and jabbed his heels into the stallion's white flanks. Blood burst forth as the beast leapt toward Nuada, who sat his own horse, unarmed.

Nuada jerked the gold smoothly aside as Ailill swung the sword. The blade sizzled past his head, but the smell of burning hair filled the air. The grass between them smoldered.

Ailill spun about in his seat, eyes narrowed into slits. He raised the sword again. Lightning flashed down to greet it, wrapping it in a nimbus of Power. He smiled.

In that instant Nuada set his own fists together and likewise called forth a blade new-forged of Faery magic: a blade of cold blue ice. And in the thick, still air of Tir-Nan-Og the two met: An arc of red flame intersected one of frosty blue.

... once ...

... twice ...

Then, with a crackling hiss, Nuada's sword shattered into fragments that burned away to nothing even as they fell.

But as Ailill continued his downward stroke, something swished past his ear and clanged like a warning bell on the fiery hilt of his blade: a dagger cast from among the dark trees behind them. Indeed, it struck so cleanly that Ailill's blade flew hissing through empty air, even as Nuada swung his horse another step to the side.

Both Nuada and Ailill whirled about to see a dark woman richly clad in burgundy and scarlet urging a steel-gray horse between the needlelike leaves of a stand of giant club moss that flanked the narrow opening from which she was emerging. A black crow sat on the high pommel before her; an empty dagger sheath hung from her side. A moment later a second, larger figure joined her, this one dressed in an amber robe, a glittering golden circlet on hair like topaz spun into silk.

"My lord Ard Rhi," Nuada inclined his head toward the man. "Morrigu."

Ailill did not follow his example.

"Airgetlam," Lugh acknowledged, with an absent nod before turning to stare at Ailill. "And the troublemaker from Erenn. You I am glad to see, Nuada. But it would seem that some do not hold such favorable inclinations toward you, else they would not violate the peace of my realm." The King of the Sidhe glanced at the Mistress of Battles beside him.

"Nor the Rules of Battle, either, Ard Rhi," the woman added, turning her icy gaze upon Ailill. "There may be no combat involving Power unless I sanction it, Windmaster. Combat is sacred; do you forget that? In combat a man risks all the gifts he has been given, and such gifts are not to be risked capriciously. You have called me a fool, but at least I still honor the trust that has been laid upon me – as you, apparently, do not."

"Ailill may have called you a fool, Morrigu," Lugh added, "but he has thought me one." He deliberate ignored the look of fury that burned on Ailill's face. "From Beltane to Lughnasadh have I listened to his ranting, and since then my realm has been vexed by the contention he has caused. I have been thinking for a while what I might do to end his conniving. I have even been in touch with Finvarra, his brother and king."

"And?"

"Finvarra said to follow my own judgment. And now I see that judgment will not be delayed."

"And what judgment is that?" Ailill sneered.

"To order you to cease your meddling in the Lands of Men and release the mortal boy you have taken as a changeling," Lugh replied calmly. "Do this at once, or face exile from Tir-Nan-Og."

"I will not," Ailill shot back. "David Sullivan is a presumptuous mortal who has made a mockery of me and my son. I claim the right to vengeance upon him."

Lugh did not respond.

"The boy knows about us," Ailill went on. "He is a threat to your realm; do you not see?"

"I see a short-sighted fool who has spent too much time in Annwyn, where the Ways to the Lands of Men open onto older times than here," Lugh snapped. "And now I have heard enough of these matters. As for you, Ailill, you are no longer welcome in my realm."

"The Way to Erenn is perilous this time of year," Ailill smirked. "And, besides, I am the only one who knows where the mortal child is hidden."

"You are no longer welcome in my realm," Lugh repeated, as the gold-cloaked members of his guard rode from the forest and surrounded Ailill Windmaster with swords as bright as sunlight.

Chapter XIII

choices
(saturday, august 15)

"**Let's** see, St. Charles Place with three houses: that's $1500 you owe me." Liz looked up at Alec and smiled a smug, close-mouthed smile that reduced her eyes to slits and made her look like a large, self-satisfied cat – rather like the one that was slinking (illegally) among their feet as they clustered around the kitchen table at David's house.

Alec groaned. "Well, I'll just have to mortgage my railroads, I guess; I don't have that kind of cash."

David laughed – the first time he'd really loosened up in what felt like ages. He leaned back from the table and folded his arms across his chest, peering at his friends over the tops of what were becoming largely redundant glasses – an unexpected positive side-effect of the Sight, he supposed. Alec was frantically checking values on the back of his Monopoly cards while Liz held out a demanding hand.

"I really owe you two a lot," David said abruptly. He felt rather silly getting into one of his maudlin moods in the middle of a Monopoly game, but when those moods came, they came, and it was generally better to let them out and get it over with.

"Yeah, I know," Liz shot back. "You still owe me fifty bucks from the last time you landed on Boardwalk. If I hadn't given you credit, you'd be out of the game."

"That's not what I meant, and you know it! It's just that I'm glad you guys could come up here to help me baby-sit the invalids so my folks could go to the movies. They really needed a night out by themselves – haven't had one in ages, and with all the crises lately –"

233

"We know why we're here," Alec huffed. "Now – you gonna play, or not?" He stuck out his tongue as he handed Liz a stack of multicolored paper. She snatched it away with exaggerated haste.

"Oh, yeah, suppose so." David sighed, as he rolled the dice. "Shoot! Seven! That puts me ... where? On Alec's property. Damn! There goes my $200 for passing GO. Can I owe you one more round, Liz?"

"With interest?"

"You won't make another round, my lad," Alec chuckled. "The worm has turned."

"The wind has too," Liz noted with a shudder. "Listen to it howl."

"It's done nothing but blow all summer," David muttered. "When it hasn't been raining, I mean."

"That's what it's supposed to do," Alec observed dryly. "By definition."

David glared at his friend. "Well, it's blown *really* hard this month."

Liz cocked her head to the right. "Remember the wind that came up while we were swimming last week? The time we saw that horse – or whatever it was? This reminds me of that."

"It does, a little," David agreed, suddenly wary.

"Dang!" Alec said. "It's getting worse too: loud enough to wake the dead."

"Don't say that!" David hissed. "Least not around here."

"Oh, come on!"

"Okay! Okay! I will try to function solely in the real world for just this one night. No forays into ... strangeness."

Alec nodded. "Good enough. You have seemed to have your act together a little better the last couple of days – but I'm still worried about you."

"He's got a right to act weird," Liz retorted, "what with all he's been through." She got up and went to the stove to reheat the hot chocolate. "Hmm, it's nearly eleven o'clock," she said, frowning at the pan. "When'll your folks be back?"

"Heck if I know. They were goin' to a triple feature – at the drive-in, no less."

"Uh-oh," Alec smirked, eyes a-twinkle. "You're liable to end up with another little brother."

"Alec!"

"Well, you could!"

"Shows what you know, McLean. Besides, that's the least of my worries."

"I'll agree with that." Alec regarded the board. "You're losing, kiddo. But, then, Liz always has been lucky at games. Better not teach her how to play strip poker – or have you already?"

Liz pointedly ignored Alec's remark. "You know, this is the longest-winded wind I ever heard," she murmured, peering past the checked window curtains. "Must be blowing in around something – only the trees aren't bending or anything. It almost sounds like somebody crying."

David felt a shiver run down his spine. He rubbed his finger where the ring should have been. It itched a lot. "Now you mention it, it does sound like crying," he agreed cautiously, intensely aware that his eyes had started tingling. "Like – like some old lady carrying on at a funeral," he finished.

The wind subsided abruptly, fading away to an eerie whine.

"Where does your mom keep the cocoa?" Liz called from the counter. "There's not enough in the pan for each of us to have a cup; I'll have to make more."

"In the cabinet above the stove."

Liz checked, then turned expressively. "Not there."

"Oh fiddle," David grumbled. "Let me look." He rummaged among the canned goods, finally digging out a new can of Hershey's.

The wind kicked up again.

Liz shot David a meaningful glance, one eyebrow raised, as he passed her the chocolate. "It really does sound like somebody crying. You don't have any neighbors I don't know about, do you?"

David rolled his eyes and twitched the curtain aside – and began slowly backing away, arms held out rigid from his sides, fingers stretched taut.

"David!" Liz cried. "What is it?"

His voice was barely a whisper. "Look for yourself!"

Liz squinted through the glass pane; a puzzled expression crossed her face. "I don't see anything."

"Alec, you look. Please!"

David had backed across the room and was leaning hard against the freezer. Alec opened the back door and peered through the screen. Liz was still squinting out the window, as if trying to discern the cause of David's discomfort.

"What am I supposed to see?" Alec asked, as he started to unhook the screen door.

David leapt across the room to grab the handle against Alec's push. "No!" he shouted. "Don't! You'll let it in!"

Alec frowned at his friend uncertainly. "Let what in?"

David stared at him incredulously. "You don't see it? You really don't see it?"

"I see you, half crazy and if you're acting, you're doing a damn fine job."

"You don't see a woman in white standing in our backyard, not ten feet from the steps? She's the one who's howling."

"David, for the last time: No, I don't. You're putting us on."

"I do see a bright patch of moonlight there," Liz ventured.

David slumped down at the table and buried his face in his hands.

"What is it you thought you saw?" Liz asked.

David opened one eye distrustfully and gazed up at Liz from between his fingers. "A banshee, Liz. A real banshee. And from everything I know and have read, it almost has to have come for Uncle Dale's life."

She did not reply for a long, thoughtful moment, during which she stood absolutely still, brow furrowed, lips pressed thin and taut. "Well, I do hear the wailing," she admitted finally, "so at least that much is real – and the more I hear, the less it sounds like the wind."

"Liz, not you, too!" Alec groaned. He reached for the door again.

David sprang up faster than even he could have imagined. He grabbed his friend by the shoulders, jerked him roughly back, spun him around and slammed him against the doorjamb, his arms locked tight behind him. Their faces were inches apart. David's gaze burned into Alec's; his breath hissed so hot on Alec's cheek he could feel it reflected back on his own.

"Believe me, Alec! For God's sake, believe me: I've got Second Sight, I can see it. When my uncle dies tonight, *then* will you believe me?"

"Dammit, David, I'd like to believe you," Alec rasped through gritted teeth. "But banshees don't exist! If I could see for even a second whatever it is you think you see, I'd believe I think. But I can't take something like that on faith."

"If you could see –" David paused, as a memory played across his mind. Then: "Alec, stand on my feet."

"Huh?"

Realization dawned on Liz's face. "Do it, Alec, do what he says."

Alec shook his head angrily. "What are you guys talking about?"

"Dammit, I'm gonna make you see, McLean," David growled. "Now stand on my feet." He swung Alec around so that he faced the yard and forced his friend's chin onto his shoulder.

"David, if this is some kind of game –"

"Oh, believe me, bro, it's no game. Now, put both your feet on my feet."

"Sullivan, if you don't let me go –"

"Alec, as you are my friend, my best friend, stand on my feet!"

"Just do what he says, Alec! Trust him."

"Okay! Okay!"

"Do it, Alec!" Liz shouted.

Okay! Give me a break, will you?"

David felt Alec's whole weight ease upon his feet. "Damn, you're heavy," he muttered. With his left hand he shifted his hold on his friend's tense body and freed his right, then slapped that hand firmly atop Alec's dark, spiky hair and said, very clearly, "*Everything between my hands and my feet is within my power! Now see, Alec, see!*"

And Alec saw.

David knew from the shudder that ran through his friend's body that he saw. He could feel Alec's heart skip a beat and his body go slack as he ceased fighting David's hold. After perhaps ten breaths, David removed his hand. Alec staggered back, white-faced, to fall heavily into a chair.

"I don't doubt you anymore," he gasped at last.

"I don't think I need to see," Liz whispered as she closed the inside door. "The book was right, then, wasn't it?"

David nodded. "Okay, now that you've seen, what do we do?"

"Do?" Liz yipped. "What can we do against a banshee? There wasn't anything about them in *The Secret Common-Wealth*."

Alec looked confused. "The secret what?"

"It's a book." David sighed. "The fortuneteller gave it to me. I loaned it to Liz."

Alec's face clouded.

"She was more likely to get something out of it."

Alec nodded reluctantly. "I understand – I guess." Then, after a pause: "But there's nothing in it about banshees, you said? They just stay till they've done their job; is that it?"

David nodded agreement. "More or less. But I can't just sit around and wait. I've got to do something!" He slammed the table with his fist. The Monopoly houses scattered.

"You can't go up against that," Alec protested. "You'd be crazy to try."

"Well, I'm not just gonna sit here and listen to it howl until Uncle Dale dies!" David shot back. "That's for damned sure! It's my fault he was hurt, so it's for me to set right. The Faeries are after me. I know that sounds crazy, but you've seen the banshee; you'll just have to accept that now. They shot Uncle Dale with a Faery arrow I know it looks like he's had a stroke, but he hasn't."

Alec was biting his knuckles – a clear sign that he had way too much to assimilate at once. "Does this mean," he began finally, looking up, "that what you said about the water-horse, about the ring, all of that is ... true?"

"Yeah," David answered simply, "it is."

"But you're the folklore student. Don't you know what to do?"

David shrugged. "That's just it, Alec. I *should* know. I've always bragged about it – but I can't think of anything at all. Nobody ever does anything about banshees."

"I wish she'd just go away," Liz murmured. "That wailing could drive you bonkers in short order." She slapped her hands over her ears and paced the length of the room.

"She will." David sighed. "As soon as my uncle is dead."

"What *are* banshees, anyway?" Alec asked at last. "I have to admit I've prowled around on the net a bit, but I never got that far."

David frowned and cleared his throat, trying to regain at least a modicum of control. "That depends. The term is from *bean sidhe*, which is Gaelic for *woman fairy*. According to some people, they're the ghosts of young women of particular families who have died under unpleasant or unconventional circumstances. Each family is supposed to have one. I suppose I should be flattered: Ours would have had to come from Ireland."

The wailing continued, though at a lower pitch.

"Did you see her face?" Alec ventured. "Was she human? I was afraid to look for more than a second."

David shrugged again. "I couldn't tell. At least she wasn't the Scottish kind; they're ugly. But, oh God, folks, I know this sounds terrible, and I know I just said the exact opposite but ... but the worst thing about this is that part of me really could be tempted to just sit here and let nature – if you can call it that – take its course. I mean, it doesn't look like there's anything I can do about it, and at least some of this friggin' waiting and wondering would be over."

"Except," Alec put in. "I smell an 'except'."

David chuckled grimly, "Yeah, except for something Oisin told me. Never mind who he is; I'll tell you later if we get out of this. Anyway, he told me that there is a solution, but that it lies in me, in my own Power as the Faeries call it. Trouble is, I can't think of a thing. None of the books I've looked at mention cures for elf-shot. Yet I was led to believe there was something I could do."

Liz went back to the window, flicked the curtain aside, and glanced out. "That spot of moonlight has moved closer," she announced.

"Reckon it'll try to come in the house?" Alec wondered through a shiver.

"I don't think so," David replied. "The screen door ought to hold it."

"I sure hope so," Liz said, through a shiver of her own. "It is steel, after all. Steel mesh, anyway."

Alec sat straight up. "Does it have to have your uncle's life?" He asked suddenly.

David stared at him. "What do you mean? He's the one who's dying."

"I know. But has anyone ever tried to outwit a banshee by killing somebody else before the intended victim expired? Just theoretically, you understand."

"Alec!" David snapped. "Nobody's gonna be killed here. I'm not that crazy – and I sincerely hope you're not."

"I was thinking about the cat."

David picked up the cat from its accustomed place by the stove and rubbed its head so that it purred. He looked meaningfully into its green eyes, then scowled. "My guess is that it has to be human." His eyes took on a faraway look. "But Little Billy is *not* human – but he's not an animal either. And he's –"

"What do you mean, 'he's not human?'" Alec interrupted. "Of course he's human!"

"No, he's not!" David shot back. "He's a changeling: a Faery child, left in place of my brother. You'll have to trust me on that, McLean. You've seen enough now to know I'm telling the truth. Or would you like another look over my shoulder?

Alec put up his hands, a screen before his face. "No thanks! One was more than enough!"

"So!" David muttered. His mouth hardened in resolve.

"David!" Alec cried, grabbing his friend's arm as he pushed past. "You're not going to kill your brother!"

"No, I'm not going to *kill* him," David retorted, knocking Alec's hand away. "I finally have a plan – if it'll work."

With that, he turned and made his way to his bedroom, which, with Uncle Dale having taken over Little Billy's former room, he now shared with the changeling. It was sleeping peacefully, as it always did, except when it had to be fed, bathed, or changed. It had given up trying to talk and didn't even walk much anymore, as if it had abandoned hope of adapting to a world not its own. David was genuinely sorry for it. Poor thing; the shock of changing worlds, bodies, and families all at the same time must have been unimaginable. So much for Faery morality.

He paused beside the bed, his resolve weakening, then squared his shoulders and picked up the small sleeping form, not bothering to bring the blanket that wrapped it. The changeling moaned and stretched. David was surprised at how light it had become. It had lost visible weight in the few days it had been in his world, and its face looked shrunken – both its real face and the phantom face it wore when David's eyes tingled. David backed out of the room with the changeling in his arms.

"Davy!" Liz gasped. "No!"

"If you don't want to watch, then don't," David snapped. "Maybe you should stay with Uncle Dale till this is over." He nodded toward his uncle's room. "Unless you'd like a look over my shoulder, just for proof. This is not my brother. Let me repeat that: not my brother."

"No, thanks," she whispered as she drew away. "But I'm not gonna hide in the dark, either. You can do whatever you think you have to. But remember that I'm gonna be watching. And if it even looks like you're gonna do anything ... permanent, well, we'll see about that."

David did not reply, but he stared at Liz for a long moment before heading back to the kitchen.

Alec skipped quickly aside when his friend strode over to one of the drawers and pulled out a long-bladed butcher knife.

"You two can join me or not," David told them. "Either way, I'll be responsible."

"Actually, I think this makes us accessories." Alec sighed under his breath.

David ignored him and headed for the door. "If anything happens, just remember: iron and ash."

"Will we be able to see anything?" Alec called.

"I dunno. You might. Try is all I can say. Maybe you've still got some of the Sight on you."

And with that, David opened the back door, shouldered the screen aside without looking beyond, and eased onto the porch.

The banshee stood a scant two strides from the bottom steps. Her mouth was open, her lips pulled back from her gums, showing uncannily white teeth. A low moan issued from her throat and set David's bones to vibrating. For the first time he got a good look at her.

Although the banshee stood in the yard and he on the porch three feet higher, their eyes were level with each other. She was tall – inhumanly tall – and clad in long white robes with flowing sleeves that trailed away to vapor at the edges. Her arms were raised at her sides and twitched slowly to a kind of unheard rhythm, the fingers long, pale, and very, very thin. Her hair, too, was white; unbound, it flowed free in the night air, no strand quite touching another, and it fell to below her waist. And when David finally dared look fully upon her face, it seemed close kin to a skull, though some semblance of its former beauty clung yet about it. The skin was nearly transparent, and he could see dark shadows beneath the cheekbones and darker hollows that housed the eyes: eyes that burned round and red like living flame. Those eyes alone had nothing of beauty. Only hatred: hatred of life.

David straightened his shoulders, shifting the changeling so that it was cradled awkwardly in the crook of his left arm, then eased himself down to a wary crouch, though his gaze never left the banshee's face. He freed his right hand and took a firmer grip on the knife.

"Greetings, banshee," he said tentatively, realizing even as he spoke that he had no idea how to greet such a being, and feeling like an utter idiot the moment the words escaped him. His eyes burned so much with the Sight that he felt they might take fire in his head; he could feel tears forming in them.

The banshee remained where she was, but her gaze slid down to meet his, the movements as jerky and uncertain as a lizard's.

For a moment it seemed to David that the flesh fell away from her face and he truly looked upon an empty skull with flaming eyes.

"Greetings, Banshee of the Sullivans," he began again, swallowing hard. "Looks like you've had a long journey tonight – but I'm afraid it'll do you no good. I can't let you have what you came for."

The banshee's wailing faltered. She looked – there was no other word for it – confused.

David coughed and laid the changeling before him on the porch floor, then knelt beside it. "I have a child here, a *Faery* child. I don't know if it has a soul or not, but I guess I'll find out real soon unless some things change right quick. I have no doubt that this knife – this *iron* knife – will have some effect on it." He raised his voice and looked up, his gaze searching the darkness beyond the banshee. "You hear me? I'm going to kill the changeling! The Sidhe took my brother; I claim this life for me and my kin!"

And with that, he lifted the blade.

The banshee took a half step forward and extended its arms. Its fingers caressed the air.

David jerked the knife toward it in a warning gesture; his eyes flashed. "Back off! I may try to kill the dead before this is over!"

He glanced down at the changeling. Its eyes were open: blue on green, though the green now predominated. And by some trick they reflected a hint of the red gleam from those other eyes.

"I'm not kiddin', banshee! Go back to Ireland and leave Dale Sullivan in peace! I don't want to hurt this ... whatever it is. Really I don't. But I will if I have to, because I know my uncle is real, half alive or not; and I know he doesn't deserve what your kind have done to him."

David suddenly realized he had not been addressing the banshee as much as an unseen host he imagined lurking in the looming darkness beyond.

The banshee took another step; the hem of her robe brushed the bottom step.

241

The knife rose higher.

"*Stop!*" came a voice from the shadows by the barn.

David's head jerked up.

The banshee likewise turned; its wild hair flowed like water about its shoulders. The keening had quieted to a low, thin hiss, like wind between skeletal trees.

A woman stepped into the light before the door: A beautiful, pale-skinned woman clothed in deep blue-gray – a black-haired woman of the Sidhe.

"Who are you talkin' to?" David demanded. "Me, or the banshee of the Sullivans?"

"I speak to you both," the woman replied. David could see that rage wrapped her like a cloud, though he was unsure of its focus.

She stepped closer, even as the banshee stepped back to regard her. They faced each other across the backyard, ten feet apart. David snatched up the changeling and eased to the top of the steps.

"Do not harm my child!" the woman cried. Then, turning to face the banshee, she extended a pointed finger. "Banshee, be gone! I would speak with this one in private."

The towering figure did not move.

David laughed in spite of himself. "Seems like she won't listen to you, either," he called. "But I'm still not satisfied. Lady, is this your child?"

The Faery woman looked David up and down, her fair face dark with anger and contempt. "It is."

"Then what's he doing here?"

"Ailill stole him from me."

"But you let him be stolen. You haven't tried to get him back. The child is sick, woman. He's probably gonna die anyway. I'm just gonna speed him along a little."

"Not by iron! Not wielded by mortal hand!"

David shrugged. "Talk to the banshee."

The woman turned her head the merest fraction. "The banshee does not concern me. All I desire is my child's safety."

"Then why don't you just take him?" David challenged. "All you have to do is help me first." He knelt again and laid the changeling lengthwise before him then set the flat of the knife against its throat. It did not flinch. David was scared as hell.

The Faery woman stepped forward and stretched her hands toward the still form, brushing her fingertips across its face – then jerked them back as though burned, to hold them clenched at her sides. "I may not!" she spat. "And not because of that flimsy shard of iron! I touched my child with Power to learn what manner of binding was laid upon him and bitter indeed was that learning. It is as I feared: Ailill has bound him to the substance of this World by some means that is beyond my Power to break – likely beyond any Power but his own."

"I don't believe you," David replied coldly, forcing his voice to remain calm.

The woman glared at him. "Believe it, mortal! I would not lie about such things, not with iron pricking at my little one's throat. I have not the Power to set his proper shape again upon him nor to restore a mind that has already been broken once by the switching of Worlds. Were I now to take him back to Faerie, ensorcelled as he is, it could bring upon him a madness in which he would have to dwell through countless ages – perhaps through all eternity. That I dare not risk."

David shrugged. "Sure you can. He may die anyway."

"I cannot take the child," the woman repeated. "And you would be a fool to harm him, for then you would have made another enemy in Faerie, which I do not think you either desire or need."

A long pause, then: "That's true," David conceded. "But what about Uncle Dale? Surely you could cure him."

The woman shook her head. "Ailill's influence is at work there as well. I might do as much harm as good, even were it not forbidden."

"Forbidden?"

"Lugh has exiled Ailill and –"

David's breath caught in his throat. "*Exiled?*"

The Faery's face hardened. "Exiled. He leaves tonight. Lugh no longer cares what damage the Windy One has done in your World; he only wants him gone from Tir-Nan-Og. Meanwhile, he has forbidden the rest of us to interfere with mortals. He feels too much has passed between the Worlds already. I court his wrath by coming here."

"But aren't you interfering now, just by talking to me?"

"I fear for the life of my child more than I fear my king."

"So, what difference would it make if you were to interfere again?"

"Talk is one thing; action is another. The first, Lugh might forgive; the second, he would not. I play a game as dangerous as the one you play, and for higher stakes. Do not forget that."

David nodded grimly, then took a deep breath. "Well," he said thoughtfully. "If you can talk but not act, tell me two things, and I'll promise not to harm the changeling."

"Ask. But be warned, I may not be able to answer. Ailill's Power is involved here, and I truly do not know its limits."

Another deep breath. "First, how can I drive off this –" David gestured at the banshee "– thing?"

The Faery woman cast a scornful glance at the apparition. "I can banish the spirit for a time, but she will return if your kinsman does not recover. She is bound to do that."

"Unless Uncle Dale is healed?"

The woman nodded. "It is as I have said."

"You're certain you can't heal him?"

Another nod.

"And there's nothing I can do?"

"Nothing."

David considered the statement for a moment.

"You had another question?" the woman snapped.

"Is there no way I can get my brother back?"

The woman grimaced – a strange expression on her inhumanly beautiful face. "No, it is impossible. The changeling now wears the substance of your World as well as the form, and even so does your brother wear the substance of Faerie. Only by bringing them face to face in the bodies that now clothe them might they return to their proper Worlds."

"Damn," David groaned. "So all you have to do is get the real Little Billy back from Ailill or take this one to him? Seems like you could do that. Why haven't you?"

"Do you think if it were that simple I would not have done so?" the woman flared. "As I told you, my child would go mad if I returned him to Faerie and did not effect the change very quickly, which is certainly not a given. Also, I respect the laws of my king. Finally, finding your brother is no simple matter. Ailill has hidden him so that I cannot find him – perhaps in some secret place, perhaps in a form not his own. He could be wearing your brother as a ring upon his hand for all I know."

"I'd know," David snorted.

"Ha!" the woman shot back scornfully. "If I cannot find him, do you suppose you could?"

"I could try. I'm alleged to be protected, after all."

"It is impossible, I say. Besides, the Way to Faerie is closed to you."

David's brow creased in thought. "Is there no other way? Couldn't Lugh grant me a boon or something? Couldn't I go to the Straight Track and ask him?"

The woman's face was impassive. "You might stand there a thousand years and get no answer. Lugh is angry, as angry as I have ever seen him, because of the contention that has been caused in his realm over you. What you desire might be within his power, but he will not listen to you. He will not listen to mortal men at all."

"Nobody?"

"Fool of a mortal," the woman raged. "Do you not think that I would tell you if it were anything you could possibly achieve? Ailill's quarrel with Nuada and Lugh is none of my doing. I hold no ill will toward you and your kin. I want only my child's safety. I —"

"Wait a minute!" David broke in. "Did you just say you would tell me if it was anything I could possibly achieve? Does that mean there is something that can be done? At least theoretically?"

The woman took a deep breath. "Among mortals Lugh will only listen to heroes. To them only will he grant boons."

"So all I need to do is become a hero?" David replied sarcastically. "Well, that sounds simple enough."

Fire flashed angrily in the woman's eyes. "Say no such things in ignorance, boy. There *is* a Trial of Heroes, but it has been a very great while since a mortal man has undertaken it. Still, if you would assay it, you must act tonight, before Ailill leaves Lugh's realm, and with him the knowledge you seek."

"We both seek, you mean."

"You have no time for talk, mortal," the woman said sharply. "There is a chance — a bare chance — you might succeed and thus fulfill both our desires. But if it is your intention to dare the Trial of Heroes, you must begin now. I myself will relay the word to those in Faerie, for the Trial is a thing both ancient and sacred, and even Lugh must abide by it. Half of one mortal hour I will give you to decide, and then I must be gone. If you truly would attempt the Trial, tell me, and I will set the Rite in motion."

David took a deep breath. "But how will I know what to do? What kind of trial are we talkin' about? I mean, I'm not a hero; I'm not even an adult. If I thought it was something I could do, I'd do it, just to have an end to all this this Faery stuff."

"The Trial consists of three parts," the woman said. "A Trial of Knowledge, a Trial of Courage, and a Trial of Strength. No more than this may I say. Little more than that do I know."

"But —"

"Time passes, boy, and death hovers near — or have you forgotten? I await your decision." The Faery woman drew herself up to her full height and folded her arms across her breasts.

Both she and David faced the banshee then. The latter had dwindled to a mere patch of pale light, barely distinguishable from moonglow.

The Faery woman said something in a tongue David did not understand, and the glimmer winked out.

"She has made a long trip in vain," the woman observed.

"I hope she doesn't have to do it again," David sighed, as he withdrew the knife from the changeling's throat and slipped it into his belt. He picked up the limp form and cast one last look toward the place where the Faery woman had stood, but she too had disappeared.

Another sigh, and he turned back toward the house, where he leaned for a long moment against the doorjamb, having suddenly realized that he had a serious decision to make – the most serious in his life, in fact, for two lives hinged directly on it – and little time in which to make it.

Alec raised an inquiring eyebrow as David reentered the kitchen.

David glanced around the room, confused. "Where's Liz?" he asked, as he passed the changeling to his friend and laid the knife on the kitchen table.

Alec inclined his head toward the hall. "Soon as the ... light vanished, she went to check on Uncle Dale." He paused. "How'd it go?"

"I have a reprieve ... I think,"

Alec gaped. "You mean you really accomplished something with that stunt?"

"The changeling's mother came. We ... reached an accommodation. Didn't you see?"

Alec shook his head. "Not much. But what do you mean by 'an accommodation?' Do you mean you may have a solution?"

David nodded slowly. "I think so, but it's not over yet. I've got a tough decision to make and fast – and I have to see Uncle Dale."

He met Liz coming out of Uncle Dale's room. "He seems to be a little better," she said. "Is the ... she ... you know, gone?"

"Until she comes back – which, I hope, won't be for a very long time. Now come on, I have work to do. I have to go look in on Uncle Dale one last time. And then I have to go out to the Track."

"The Track ... ?"

David flashed them a guarded glance. "I don't have much time, folks, I'll tell you as soon as I can."

"You know, I never did get a chance to read Uncle Dale," Liz mused as they opened the door into the old man's room. He was sitting propped up in bed where Liz had left him, and though his eyes were closed, a sort of vague agitation about him told David he wasn't asleep.

"Uncle Dale," he called softly. "Uncle Dale – Liz, turn on that little light over there." He motioned to a nightstand. "Uncle Dale, can you hear me?"

The old man opened his left eye and tried to speak, but the words were slurred and indistinguishable.

"Don't try to talk, just nod."

The old man nodded; the movements were jerky – like the movements of the banshee.

"Uncle Dale, do you have any idea about what's been goin' on with the banshee and all?"

"David!" Liz cried.

"As close to that world as he's been tonight, I think he's aware anyway. You know about the banshee, don't you, Uncle Dale?"

The old man nodded again.

"Okay, then. Good. Look, I may have a way to cure you if it'll work. I don't know if it will – but I'm gonna make the attempt. And if I fail ... Well, you won't be any worse off than you are, all right?"

Uncle Dale looked at him and nodded again. David saw the muscles in his wasted neck and jaw grow taut. The old man's mouth contorted awkwardly, and a string of grunts and groans passed his lips, but he finally managed to wring out one single intelligible phrase. "Go ... now ... or I die." And with that he closed his eyes again and fell back against the pillows.

David needed no more help with his decision.

Chapter XIV

The Lord of the Trial

Alec tapped gently on the screen door, then eased onto the back porch, where David was sitting on the steps staring out at the yard. David had explained to him and Liz about the Trial of Heroes then asked for some time alone to get his head straight. "You ready?" Alec asked.

David shook his head and glanced sideways at his friend. "Not really. But you know what I've been goin' through now, don't you?"

Alec shook his head in turn. "No, but I don't think I ever will. It's too much, Davy – too much to assimilate this fast."

David sat up straight, squared his shoulders, and clapped his hands on his knees decisively. "Well, I can't put this off any longer; I've got to get goin' – though I haven't a clue how I'm gonna get through this."

Alec extended a hand toward David to help him up. "I'm sure we'll think of something."

A flush of anger crossed David's face as he took Alec's hand. "*We?* Who is *we?*"

Alec looked surprised. "Why, you and me and Liz, of course; who'd you think?"

David froze where he stood. "Alec, don't you see what's goin' on, yet? Don't you remember what I've been saying to anybody who would listen for the last two weeks? It's the ring, Alec, the friggin' ring. It protects me. Even though I don't have it, it still protects *me*" – David thumped his chest "– against the Faeries. But it doesn't protect you – or Liz, or anybody else – unless I have it on. You know about Little Billy and Uncle Dale now; you could find one of those magic arrows sticking out of your chest just as easy as Uncle Dale did."

"We're your friends, Davy," Alec said quietly.

David's face was grim. "This is my fight."

Alec's face went as hard as David had ever seen it. "Dammit, David, I've already had one fight with you tonight 'cause I was wrong. Am I gonna have to have another one now 'cause I'm right? 'Cause let me tell you one thing, Mister Sullivan: Protected or not, you take the battle to the Sidhe on their own turf like you're threatening to do, I'm gonna be right there with you – and so will Liz, I guaran-damn-tee you."

David had slumped against one of the porch posts, hands in his pockets, still gazing at the yard.

Alec laid an arm across his shoulders and drew him toward the door. "What're you crying for, bro?"

David looked up and smiled. "'Cause I'm not alone anymore."

"I really wish you folks would change your minds," David grumbled a few minutes later, as he riffled the kitchen drawers in search of the longest, sharpest knives he could find. He doubted they would be of much use, but maybe they would at least provide some psychological protection.

"I mean, I appreciate your concern and all," he continued. "But this is for real, folks. You may be risking your lives – has that really sunk into you? Even your good Baptist soul, Liz."

"We've already been over this," Alec replied, reaching out to grasp his friend's arm so that David turned to look at him. Alec stared him straight in the eyes. "If you go, Liz and I go. Is that clear?"

David didn't say anything, but he studied Alec's face for a long moment, then shifted his gaze to Liz.

"You don't know what you're gettin' into, folks," he whispered.

"I doubt you do either, David Sullivan," Liz shot back. "Besides, the fortuneteller told me and Alec to keep an eye on you – and you wouldn't want to disappoint a lady, would you?"

David snorted. "I've already disappointed a lot of ladies. Now you go get the changeling dressed. Alec, go in the living room and get my runestaff – you didn't happen to bring yours, did you?"

"Matter of fact, I did. Liz asked me to, for some reason. It's in her truck."

"Better get it, then. And when you get back, check in that drawer for some duct tape. Oughta be a big roll in there."

It was not an imposing group that assembled in the Sullivans' backyard a short while later, but it was an interesting-looking one, especially for north Georgia in August. Since they had no idea what they would be facing, they had tried to anticipate a variety of possibilities and conditions and had dressed and equipped themselves accordingly. It was not much of a problem for Alec and David, for they were close enough to a size that they could wear each other's clothes; thus, they both wore jeans, hiking boots (Alec in David's second best pair), and sweatshirts under nylon parkas. It was summer, and by rights hot even in the mountains, but they had no way of guessing what sort of weather they would encounter on their way to Tir-Nan-Og or wherever they wound up going and didn't want to freeze before they had gone two miles. "We can always take off stuff," David had said.

Equipping Liz had proved more of a problem, but a raid on David's mother's closet had produced a sweater and cammo fatigues, a pair of high boots that were more or less her size, and a leather coat that looked sturdy. A slightly more purposeful image was provided by their armament: hunting knives pilfered from Big Billy's stash, and the make-do spears Alec and Liz carried, which they had contrived by lashing and taping butcher knives to their runestaffs. None of them had any notion how to use such weapons, but ... it just felt better. Not once had any of them proposed taking any of the numerous guns with which the house was stocked. Somehow, they knew, such weapons would neither be useful nor appreciated.

Alec and Liz wore backpacks hastily stuffed with food from the Sullivans' stores. David carried the changeling. Though he wore a sheathed knife at his hip and another in his boot top, he was otherwise devoid of protection, for he had chosen to rely on his own Power and whatever dubious protection the ring – wherever it was – still afforded him. Frankly, he doubted that weapons of any kind would be needed in the Trial but he couldn't say why he thought that.

They hesitated at the top of the steps, uncertain how to proceed, but just as David was about to voice his uncertainty, the Faery woman stepped from the shadows between the barn and the car shed. Alec and Liz squinted, as though they were aware of something yet were unable to make their eyes focus on anything. To David, however, the image was crystal clear.

"Have you decided?" the woman demanded.

"I have," David replied grimly.

The woman nodded. "By the look of things, I know your choice."

David cleared his throat and felt the changeling twitch in his arms.

"I have set the Rites in motion," the woman informed him. "You are to go immediately to the Straightway and there await what transpires."

A thought struck David, and he cursed himself for not thinking of it sooner. "What about Uncle Dale? We can't leave him alone; one of us will have to stay here."

"If you will permit it," the Faery woman replied, "I will look after the old man in your absence, and my child as well."

"I don't know," David countered hesitantly. "Can I trust you?"

"Your success in this means as much to me as it does to you," the woman retorted. "Remember that."

"But don't we need to take the changeling with us? You said it and my brother had to be brought face to face."

"If you are victorious in the Trial of Heroes, I am informed that will not be necessary."

"But how will you know whether or not we win?"

"I will know," the woman assured them, as she made a certain sign in the air and without actually touching its flesh lifted the changeling from David's uncertain arms. "Of that you may be very sure indeed."

"So we've got to go to this Straight Track, or Straightway, or whatever it is?" Alec asked a moment later, as they trudged up the hill behind the house.

David nodded. "Yeah, and that's the only part I'm clear about, too. This is apparently a very ancient and serious ritual. In fact, come to think of it, the Sidhe seem to have a fairly ritualistic approach to life as a whole. I guess when you're immortal you need structure or everything goes to chaos – especially when you consider that some folks think the Sidhe used to be gods or angels or something. Screwy as it sounds, too – given how petty and malicious they seem sometimes – I think they're basically just really remote and indifferent – most of the time, anyway. Just a little too concerned with their own affairs to care about us one way or the other. Kind of like the way we treat chimpanzees."

Alec stared at him, as if amazed at the sudden gush of words. David met the look his friend gave him and smiled wryly. He was scared to death, and so, he suspected, were Alec and Liz. And Alec, at least, surely knew he was talking to keep his mind off what was approaching.

"I mean, just think about it," David went on rapidly as a rush of ideas took fire in his brain. "Immortality sounds great to us mortals, but it has to be complicated if you're livin' it. I mean, you could go crazy just trying to divide your property among your offspring, or trying to get some property *to* divide, for that matter. There's only so much land, after all, but I assume there are more and more Sidhe all the time, since they can't really die, and they pretty clearly have kids. And if you made an enemy, it could be for eternity. Think about that! Or what about marriage? You could get bored with the best of mates in a thousand years."

Alec could only roll his eyes and shrug.

Liz merely shrugged.

"You're stalling, man," Alec said finally.

"I am," David agreed. And then he could delay no longer.

A moment later they turned left into the woods, and a moment after that, they reached the first of the briars. David strode straight in among them.

Liz and Alec, however, hung back.

"We're not going into *that*, are we?" Liz yelped.

David spun around in place, confused. "Into what? There're some briars here, but nothing major, nothing to worry about."

"Are you crazy?" Alec all but shouted. "There's a wall of thorns ten feet high and thick as ... as a hedge, not two feet in front of you!"

David glanced over his shoulder. The briars were there all right, but only waist high. And though there was an abundance of them between the trees, they were hardly impassable.

Illusion, he realized. Or glamour.

"Close your eyes," he said aloud. "Walk straight ahead until I tell you to stop. They're not there, not like you see them. I think they're part of the magic that keeps people from getting on the Track."

"If you say so," Alec muttered. "But it seems to me that thorns like this would draw attention themselves."

"I think they may look like ... you see them because we're deliberately seeking the Track now."

"If you say so," Alec repeated.

"I don't see that we've got any choice but to believe him," Liz countered. "We're on his ground now."

"Thanks." David chuckled under his breath. "Now, let's get goin'." With that, he turned and marched forward into the thicket, glancing frequently behind him to see how Alec and Liz progressed. They had closed their eyes as David had instructed and were fumbling their way slowly along, with Alec swearing frequently – and uncharacteristically

— as the thorns caught at his unprotected hands. Liz, having had more foresight, wore leather gloves.

"Maybe another ten feet to the trail," David called.

An instant later they were clear of the barrier.

David was immediately struck anew by the otherness of the place when they arrived: so different from the rest of the forest, as though the alien glamour it wore on certain nights never entirely faded and flared to life anew when the Faerie moon shone full among the trees and the Tuatha de Danaan walked or rode upon it.

"I wish I'd brought a Coke or something," Liz grumbled.

"Too late for that now," Alec sighed. "I've got half a Hershey bar, if that'll help."

"You just wait," David snorted. "Soon as things start happenin' you'll forget all about being hungry. You may never be hungry again."

Liz frowned. "What do you mean by that?"

"This is serious business, Liz; haven't I got that through to you yet? *You might not come back.* Some Faery lord might take a fancy to you and —"

"Oh, hush."

"They tended to like blonds, though ..."

Alec and Liz raised their eyebrows in unison. Only then did David recall his own fair hair.

"How will we know what to do?" Alec whispered.

David shrugged. "We were told to come here and wait — so we wait. Last time I heard bells and saw lights ..." He paused, glancing around the surrounding woods. "But I have no idea what you folks might see. It could be anything or nothing. From what I can tell, the Sidhe pretty much choose who sees them most of the time. Apparently, the only people who can see the things of Faerie of their own free will are people with Second Sight, like me and it doesn't always work the same even then. Sometimes I can control it; sometimes I can't. I sure hope you see something, though, 'cause it's gonna be a pain if you have to go through this blind — never mind the danger. Little Billy just whimpered and kept askin' who I was talkin' to, so he evidently didn't see anything, but he did hear the bells and the singing — that's what started it all, in fact. Maybe it'll be the same for you — assuming they don't just send a dragon or something."

"Whatever they're gonna do, I wish they'd hurry," Alec muttered.

David glanced over his shoulder. Far away he could make out the familiar glow of the mercury vapor light by his house, its lonesome point of blue radiance miraculously fighting its way among the trunks of oak and pine and maple. It represented reality to him: his world by birth, if not precisely by preference.

It was also home.

But up ahead things were different, Oh, the trees were the still the same, the sparse undergrowth exactly as it should have been, the slope of the land itself comfortingly familiar. But close to the ground a faint golden glimmer overlaid a narrow strip of ground maybe ten feet wide that stretched out of sight to their left and right. The Straight Track: The road to Tir-Nan-Og.

"See anything?" David ventured.

Alec squinted. "I'm not sure – maybe a little glow or something out there between those two pine trees."

"Liz?"

"Yeah, maybe a kind of goldish glitter sorta overlying the ground – not like it was really touching it, though."

"Well," David sighed, "at least you can see something"

With that, he stepped onto the strip, moving by instinct toward the center. His friends joined him there, their makeshift spears towering above them like pikes, giving the whole tableau martial air. Wordlessly they clasped hands with each other. David reached over and planted a firm, wet and very impulsive kiss on Liz's cheek. "Take care, whatever happens. I couldn't stand to lose you."

"I think it's happening," Alec murmured, pointing with his staff, as his gaze followed the Track up the mountainside.

David and Liz followed Alec's direction.

An armored man sat on horseback a short way up the glowing trail.

He was not tall – certainly not as tall as either Nuada or Ailill – but whatever he lacked in height he more than made up in presence; for it seemed, in some odd way that had nothing to do with light, that he glowed. His regalia was impressive, too, for he was clothed from head to foot in close-fitting mail that reflected the golden glimmer of the Track. Over his shoulders hung an open-sided tabard of deep blue-gray velvet, while a boar-crested helm crowned his head, its long, intricately worked cheek-guards and nasal obscuring the upper half of his face – all save the eyes. What little mouth was visible above a clean-shaven chin looked full and very, very grim. The man was mounted on a huge, long-limbed horse whose flanks shone like blued steel. A naked sword lay crossways on the saddle before him, a burning white flame in the light of the witchmoon that already shone above.

The man glared at the companions as he paced his steed forward.

David flinched under that gaze but stood his ground. His mouth was suddenly dry.

"Who has come to dare the Trial of Heroes?" the man cried, his surprisingly young-sounding voice amplified by some acoustical trick of his helm and the Track.

David swallowed, straightened, and tried to look taller than he was: more a man and not so much a half-grown teen. "I have ... sir."

The man nodded. "Do you dare it alone, or with companions?"

David's breath hissed; he heard Alec and Liz inhale sharply. He'd been afraid it would come to this. He had hoped – seriously hoped – that he would have to go alone, that his friends would be spared what would certain be an ordeal, and one from which they might very well not return. Not that he didn't want them along, or anything like that. But he didn't dare risk them.

"Alone," he said.

"Together," came his friends' voices behind him, louder.

"No!" David cried.

"Three are mightier than one!" Liz shot back.

"One is mightiest of the three," Alec added.

"*Do you go alone, or with companions?*" the man demanded.

David grimaced. There was no time for argument, no time for delay. "With companions," he replied through gritted teeth.

"Then they had best not travel blind," the Lord of the Trial retorted. "For not all those you meet may wish to be seen." And with that, in one smooth, swift gesture, he leveled his sword at them. A burst of light blazed from its point to strike full in their faces.

David cried out, though less from fear for himself than for his friends. He heard Liz scream and Alec grunt out something unintelligible. And then the light was gone. He could tell by the way his friends blinked and stared that they now saw with more than human sight.

"The Trial of Heroes has begun," the man said. "The Trial is for David alone, but if any one of you completes the test and comes before Lugh Samildinach, High King for this time in Tir-Nan-Og, it will be as if David himself has won. But know you, Alec McLean and Liz Hughes, that this is *David's* trial. *He* is the leader; his decisions are the ones that must stand. You may offer advice and help where it is needed, but neither of you must act without David's consent, for it is *his* knowledge, *his* courage, *his* strength that are being tested here, not your own. Let the Trial of Heroes now begin. When you can no longer see me, follow the Track uphill."

With that, he wheeled his horse around and was simply ... gone.

Chapter XV

of knowledge and courage

Alec shrugged his shoulders. "After you."

David sighed, planted his runestaff on the leafy mould ahead of him, and strode forward on the Straight Track. Alec and Liz flanked him on either side.

The Track ran steadily uphill for a considerable distance, illuminated by the light of a moon that was now full, though it should not have been. At first David was uncertain whether they were even on the Track, for the characteristic golden glow had faded, and the forest itself seemed no different. There was none of the unnaturally healthy plant life he remembered from his earlier encounters, none of those shifts in quality of light or air. But when he stepped to the side of the trail and tried to thrust a hand between two pine trees that grew close to what he supposed was the edge, his fingers met resistance, and he knew then, that for good or ill, they must remain with the Track until the end.

Alec noticed it first: how their every step sent traceries of sparks scintillating among the thick blue-green mosses that had begun replacing the pine straw beneath their feet – sparks that haloed outward and then died away again. They were pale at first, and almost colorless; but gradually they increased in brilliance as the hikers progressed. Eventually patterns began to appear, outlined by those sparks, forming and reforming more quickly than the eye could follow: lozenges and elaborate flourishes like Arabic calligraphy, and sickening spirals of interlaced beasts that disappeared if looked at too directly or too long. The colors changed as well, became stronger and more intense, varying from red close to

257

the hikers' feet through the whole spectrum into violet at the margin of the Track. Eventually, however, the familiar golden yellow that David remembered began to dominate and finally became pervasive, disrupted only by flashes of other hues.

The farther they walked, the more excited the sparks became, and the less confined to the area about their feet, so that for a time they walked knee-deep in a glittering cloud of floating motes that eventually curved up more than head high on either side, obscuring any clear view save straight ahead.

After a while that part of the growth that was still visible beside them began to alter as well. At first the change was marked simply by a gradual disappearance of the scruffy weeds that were a familiar but unremarkable adjunct to any normal forest, then of the taller shrubs, and finally of the pine trees themselves. In their place came taller, thicker trees, with limbs that branched forth higher from the ground. The leaves were still recognizable as oak and ash and maple, but they were unnaturally large and shiny, and there was a greater degree of uniformity among them, as though each leaf had been freshly struck from the same die.

And then there were the briars that looped and whirled and wove about those trunks like thorny snakes, to form an impenetrable screen of red stems that were sometimes as thick as David's arms, and which often bore serrated six-inch thorns the color of new-cast bronze.

Eventually, the floating motes within which they walked became even more agitated, rising first to their waists, then to their shoulders, so that they appeared only as disembodied heads bobbing along on a sea of light, with their make-do spears sticking up like the masts of becalmed ships and the briars looming over them like the arms of hungry sea beasts.

Finally the mist rose above Liz's head – she first because she was shortest. A few strides farther along, David disappeared, and then Alec. They could still see their route, however – sense it, rather – rising straight and true; but now a deep-pitched ringing sounded in their ears with every step. Bitter cold bit into them, then fiery heat, then cold again.

Not too soon for any of them, the mist began to dissipate, at last revealing a lighter spot ahead illuminated by what looked like bright moonlight. As one they quickened their steps.

Directly before them, the wood gave way to a wide, grassy clearing through which the Track ran like a ribbon of golden fog. The trees fell away, but the briars remained, twisting and spiraling amid the tall, blue-shadowed grass – but now those thick stems were studded with satiny roses as big as a man's head. Even in the moonlight the saw-toothed leaves on those briars shone green as emeralds, but the blossoms they bore were black.

Liz reached out to touch one of the blooms, but David hauled her back, though he too felt a strong compulsion to caress those silky petals and to breathe the heady fragrance of the black roses of Faerie. Instead, he reached into the haze upon the ground, picked up something he had just seen fall there, and held it up for Liz's inspection: an iridescent wedge of butterfly's wing, sapphire-blue, veined with silver – and smoothly cut along one side. He pressed it against the edge of one of those onyx petals and saw it fall into two parts, as if sliced by a razor. A raised eyebrow was his only comment.

They moved on quickly after that, avoiding any contact with the roses – and soon entered another wood exactly like the first.

For a long time they walked in silence.

"Neat!" Liz cried abruptly, her words shaking David from the reverie into which he had fallen.

Without really being aware of it, they had passed from the wood into a beautiful green meadow maybe a quarter of a mile across, through which the Track showed as a withered strip of amber against neatly cropped grass the color of polished jade. They could barely make out the dark line of more forest on the other side. Thirty yards away to their right grazed three low-slung beasts that looked something like armadillos and something like turtles – except that they stood man-high at their armored shoulders and had heavy, spiked clubs at the ends of their longish tails. More than anything else (as Alec, in fact, remarked), they resembled the extinct Pleistocene armadillos called glyptodonts, though not exactly. The sun flashed on bright spiral patterns lacquered on their shells –

The sun!

But it had been night when they left: nearly midnight. What was the sun doing out? They couldn't have been walking so long; David was not even tired. In fact, he couldn't recall ever feeling better in his life. A sweet odor tickled his nostrils, and he inhaled deeply, appreciatively, noticing, as Liz and Alec followed him into the meadow, the waxy yellow petals and sooty black stamens of a vast profusion of huge poppies that grew alongside the trail. David regarded the animals warily and the flowers with equal caution, wishing he could see better, especially near the front feet of the most distant beast – though he had to admit his vision, with or without glasses, was nearly perfect now.

"We need to boogie," David whispered. "Those things don't look like they could move very fast or see very well, but I think we'd be safer if we got by them as quickly as possible. Just don't breathe any more deeply than you have to, okay?"

Liz frowned. "Is there something you're not telling us? Wouldn't it be better to sneak by?"

David shook his head. "I don't think so. I've got a suspicion this is more dangerous than it seems. Take a breath. Doesn't that air smell sweet? But doesn't it make you sleepy, too? Now look at that critter furthest to the right. Doesn't that look like a deer carcass to you – sort of a deer, anyway? I don't think these guys are vegetarians. I think they wait for the flowers to put animals to sleep and then feast on their bodies. If we run, the flowers will have as less time to affect us."

"Wizard of Oz," Alec supplied.

David nodded. "Exactly."

Without another word Alec and Liz followed David's purposeful jog across the clearing. One of the beasts raised a bone-cased head and took a tentative step forward as they passed, but the friends crossed the distance safely and shortly found themselves once more beneath the limbs of a forest.

The companions slowed again just inside the wood. The trees around them were low and sprawling, very much like live oaks, even to the pale beards of what in their own world would have been Spanish moss. The leaves were too small and too regular, however, and the whorled bark seemed as much carved as natural. The silence was disquieting too, for even when the leaves brushed against one another they made no sound.

They walked for a long time in that eerie silence. David felt marvelous – physically – but tension was growing stronger in him by the instant. He was tired of keeping his guard up, of having to be wary every moment, suspicious of every sight and sound – and even smell – and all the while knowing what would happen if he failed.

It was night again when they emerged into the next open space – night, or dark, anyway. A sound reached them there, as from a great distance: a sort of hissing roar that spoke of waves on some distant shore. Unfortunately, they could see little beyond the expanse of long grass that surrounded them, though the sharp-edged blades flickered alternately all white and all black as a brisk breeze teased them beneath the blue-white disk of the witchmoon.

Shapes moved out there in the dark: hunched shapes taller than a horse, with smooth, pale skins and vast staring eyes that glowed orange and never blinked, and that went sometimes on two legs, sometimes on four; and which now and then leapt high above the grass, displaying tri-forked tails. And there were other shapes as well: things too tall and spindly to be of the world David knew, or too quick, or – he shuddered – too impossibly huge.

The place was alive: Even the ground seemed animate, for it pulsed under their feet as if the earth sought to relay to them the secrets of that unseen sea. David found himself straining his ears, expecting to hear the cry of gulls – but the only sound was the soft rasp of their own breathing and the steady, hypnotic hiss of the phantom Faerie ocean.

They passed quietly. Nothing threatened them, but eyes watched their every step. And three lumbering shapes entered that place as they left it.

Another wood.

Another meadow.

Daylight.

Closer together now, and their feet no longer struck sparks as they strode along – among ferns, this time. But the air was becoming thicker by the instant, clogging their senses, so that the simple act of breathing became an effort, and maintaining even a walking pace all but wore them out. David could feel his vitality draining away like air from a spent balloon. They moved more sluggishly with every step. The air itself seemed to push against them. A blink seemed to take an hour, a single breath half a day. A dragonfly flew past them so slowly they could count the copper spots that dotted wings like vitrified night.

Sunset, and red shadows upon the bracken.

And still they walked.

Night.

And sunrise again, and the air grew thinner.

But it was dark again before they could move normally. And then light once more.

There were bushes to left and right, and then trees, and then bushes again.

And dark and light.

And dark and light again, alternating with mind-searing rapidity, so that David lost all sense of time, and the world narrowed to the Track that continued as it had: running dead straight, and now absolutely level, though the frightened ghost of logic that lingered in the back of his mind told him that if the geography of Faerie in any way paralleled that of his own world they should have long since crested whatever mountain they had been climbing, descended into the valley beyond, and now be going uphill again. But the Track was obviously much farther from his own world now, or the heart of Faerie much nearer. He wondered where they were: in Tir-Nan-Og itself, or in another realm, or in some timeless space between, where the only certainty was a strip of glowing gold.

Light. Dark. Light. Dark.

Woods. Fields. Small streams.

Flowers. Another forest.

Abruptly they found themselves standing beneath a full moon on copper sands at the edge of a vast, still lake perhaps half a mile across: a lake whose waters gave forth a peculiar, unpleasant odor that was nevertheless vaguely familiar – almost like blood. *Exactly* like blood, in fact. David saw that the surface of that dark lake glinted red and that the countless small wavelets that licked the copper shore moved with a strange greasy languor that did nothing to assuage his anxiety.

But the worst thing was the Track.

Ahead lay not only the familiar strip of light, but a crossroads at which *three* Tracks converged, one a continuation of that on which they traveled, one breaking off at a sharp angle to either side.

The way to the left bent steeply back uphill toward the woods they had just departed, but long before it passed into that leafy barrier it became hedged about with a threatening wall of thorns that appeared more than capable of rending the flesh from the bones of anyone or anything careless enough to brush against them. To the right, the upward slope was gentler. Short grass pierced the copper sand there, giving way perhaps twenty yards away to a field of white lilies that glowed eerily in the half-light: lilies that became more and more plentiful as they receded, so that at the limits of sight they seemed to form a line of light at the edge of the trees.

And ahead ...

The Track ahead was *not* straight. For the first time it failed to run laser-true before them. Instead it bent and twisted like the writhings of a wounded serpent as it continued into that disturbing lake, where it manifested as a vague red-tinged burnishing beneath the surface.

They halted where they stood, despair clouding all their faces.

David caught his breath, shoulders sagging. "Well hell!" he groaned.

"So, Davy, which way?" Alec dared at last.

David shook his head. "I don't know. Straight ahead seems out, for obvious reasons. Of the other two, my instinct says left. That looks like the most difficult path, and thus the one most likely to test us."

Alec followed David's gaze in that direction, but then turned to look toward the right-hand trail. "Maybe," he mused. "But what seems obvious might be *too* obvious. This path seems to be the least dangerous and therefore might be the most dangerous. So far we've seen nothing that's actively threatening. We've had no decisions to make and had no indication that any part of the Trial had begun, much less been completed. I think this is the first test. It's the first time there's been a decision to make. But if you ask me, the right-hand path seems best."

Liz had said nothing since stepping onto the beach, but her forehead was wrinkled in perplexity. "I don't think either of you are right," she murmured. "This place reminds me of a song my granny used to sing – the one who taught me how to read vibrations. I think she called it 'Thomas the Rhymer.' It's about this fellow who runs into the Queen of Elfland and is carried away by her. Funny how I never thought of it before, given our recent adventures. But the part I'm talking about seems to fit this place perfectly – a little too perfectly, I might add." She closed her eyes and recited:

> *"Oh, see you not that broad, straight road,*
> > *that lies across the lilied way?*
> *That is the path of wickedness,*
> > *though the road to Heaven, some also say.*
> *And see you not the narrow road,*
> > *that's thickly walled with thorns and briars?*
> *That is the path of righteousness,*
> > *though to that end but few aspires.*
> *And see you not that pretty road,*
> > *that winds across the ferny way?*
> *That is the road to fair Elfland,*
> > *where you and I must go today."*

She opened her eyes. "It's too close, Davy: too close for it not to be the way."

David shook his head. "I don't know; I just don't know. It still doesn't quite fit. That's a lake of blood out there, not a 'ferny way.'"

"That's true," Liz conceded. "But there's another verse a little farther on that runs like this:

> *"For all a day and all a night,*
> > *they rode through red blood to the knee,*
> *And saw they neither sun nor moon,*
> > *but heard the roaring of the sea."*

"Now, that's interesting," David mused. "It looks like there're logical reasons for following all three routes. There's supposed to be a Test of Knowledge, a Test of Courage, and a Test of Strength. This seems to be the Test of Knowledge. But what if I'm wrong?"

"Then you'll be wrong," Alec replied matter-of-factly. "Won't be the first time."

"But it might be the last – probably *will* be the last. I just remembered what the fortuneteller told me."

Alec scowled at him. "Which was?"

"That if I choose the wrong road at the end, there may be no more roads for me at all."

Liz looked at him for a long moment. "It's your decision," she said finally. "Because whatever else we do, we have to follow one of these routes. But the Lord of the Trial said to follow the Track, not follow the *Straight* Track, so we at least have the option of taking the crooked road. It may not even be crooked; it may only seem that way to confuse us."

David squared his shoulders "Okay, Liz. It seems wrong to my way of thinking, but one thing I do know about the Sidhe is that, though they're devious, they don't lie. Their riddles are subtle, but there's always a solution. In fact, I don't think they *dare* cheat. They use words like an artist uses a brush – only a really good artist can make you see more than one set of pictures at the same time."

"Whatever it is, you'd better decide fast," Alec broke in. "'Cause we've got company." He dipped his head upslope.

David followed his friend's gaze – to see three hulking shapes shouldering their way out of the woods fifty yards behind them. Branches squealed across painted shells; blunt, low-held heads swung from side to side with ominous deliberation; heavy front claws scraped upon the sand as the shell-beasts came full upon the beach. Red lights shone deep within their tiny eyes, increasing in brilliance as they turned toward the travelers.

"David, hurry!" Liz cried.

"They've been tracking us!" Alec whispered. "They *are* meat eaters. Make it fast, Sullivan."

David glanced desperately about. "I guess we'd better continue on ahead and hope the creatures won't follow us into the lake. If nothing else, we can wait them out. Alec, lend me your staff. I want to know where I'm going."

Alec, somewhat hesitantly, did as requested, and with staff in hand, David stepped onto the crooked road, hearing, rather than seeing, his friends fall into step behind him.

Though they did not seem to move rapidly at all, the shell-beasts somehow gained five yards.

With some trepidation David eased the staff into the substance ahead of him, probing a bottom he could not see and did not want to visualize. To his amazement, the liquid – he could no longer bring himself to think of the stuff as water – drew away from the wood for roughly a foot on either side, to form a sort of trough, with the faint gleam of the Track superimposed on the copper sand at the bottom. Encouraged, he took a step, then another, planting the staff ahead of himself again, and then once more. Alec followed, with Liz bringing up the rear, her staff also borne low before her. Thus fortified, they marched into the tenuous rift formed by the untested Power of the makeshift spears of iron and ash that a would-be boy sorcerer had once made so his friends would think he was strange.

The Track twisted to their right almost immediately, then to the left, and the trough grew deeper. They had to trace their way along with the staffs, ever fearful of losing their unlikely guide. It was slow going, and – with the knowledge of the beasts behind them – nerve-wracking.

A glance over his shoulder told David that the beasts had already reached the edge. One lowered its nose toward the ruddy liquid but withdrew at once, as though burned. The other two shambled up behind it. One edged a tentative claw into the fluid, then jerked it back and shook it violently.

"I don't think those things like the lake," David whispered. "They're still prowlin' around on the shore. Maybe they'll stop following us now."

"I hope so," Liz murmured, likewise looking back. "They creep me out more than anything else we've seen. It's almost like they're – I don't know – *aware*, or something."

"Purposeful?" David suggested.

"Strange behavior for carnivores, though," Alec observed. "You'd think they'd like blood."

David raised an eyebrow. "Maybe it's not blood."

"Or maybe they can't swim."

Alec's brow furrowed "Maybe not. They're heading back toward the woods."

David squinted across the glistening surface to where, indeed, the shell-beasts were ambling toward the shelter of the dark forest.

Liz whistled her relief. "Giving up, you reckon?"

"Maybe so," David replied. "And while they're doing that, we need to put as much distance between us and them as we can."

"I'll drink to that!"

"Hush, Alec. What a thing to say here!"

"Let's move it, kids," David said firmly, and returned his attention to their route, leading them forward at a quicker pace than they had maintained heretofore.

By the time the travelers reached what seemed to be the middle of the sanguine lake, the walls of red liquid had risen above their heads, towering in an uneasy, jellylike tension that set all their nerves vibrating like saws struck by a hammer.

Wet copper sand squished beneath their feet, smooth as a plate, marked by neither rock nor weed nor living thing, only by the Track itself. Before them was nothing but the roiling wall of dark red, here flickering purple in the reflected blue-white light of the witchmoon, there foaming to pink where it withdrew before David's staff.

David hastened his pace again, as unease rose within him like the quivering walls to either side. He kept the staff before him, sweeping the viscous liquid ahead with a kind of grim determination, wondering how long his luck would hold; wondering, more to the point, when those awful walls would come crashing down around him and his friends. He dared not look back, not even to see their faces, for he feared to see the way collapse behind him, as he knew it must be doing from the thick splashing sounds that followed in their wake; and feared, as well, to know how closely peril stalked as they threaded a path so narrow the walls brushed their shoulders on either side, spreading alarming red stains up the sleeves of their jackets.

They walked for a long time, fearful, the rank smell of blood in their nostrils, the sickening squish of bloody sand beneath their feet. But finally – sooner than David had expected – the walls began to lower again, and the bottom to slope upward.

A moment later, the three friends stood once more upon dry sand. The Track continued on its twisted way across that beach before straightening itself at the edge of the inevitable line of trees.

David paused at the last turn and glanced back toward the lake.

And looked upon a trail that ran perfectly straight.

And on a helmed and armored figure sitting on horseback in the exact middle of it, scarcely three yards behind them. No hoof-prints marred the sand behind that man.

The Lord of the Trial.

The Lord raised his sword and flourished it once in the air as if in salute, then paced the horse closer, so that David stood virtually face to nose with the animal. The rider regarded him for a moment, then spoke. "Hear me, David Kevin Sullivan, and know that you have passed the Test of Knowledge – not by knowing which road to take, but by knowing when to trust another's judgment above your own."

David found himself grinning in spite of himself, and turned impulsively to embrace a startled Liz. "You did it, girl. One down."

He stopped suddenly and stared at the ground, uncomfortably aware of how foolish he must look before this Lord of Power. But when he glanced up again, the man was gone. There was only the lake and the shell-beasts still prowling about the opposite shore.

"Once more into the breach," Alec said.

"I'm afraid so," David sighed. "Let's get movin'."

The wood before them was darker than any they had yet seen, and more stately, beginning possibly ten yards ahead with a palisade of tall, red-trunked trees, each of almost identical thickness and height, so that the overall effect was of the colonnade before a temple. The Track passed between two trees slightly thicker than the rest, their twined branches meeting in a pointed arch high above their heads, as if marking a gateway.

From moonlight, they passed into gloom. The trail began to slope downhill, too, and that slope increased as trees clustered closer to the Track and more undergrowth filled the spaces between, effectively locking them into a tunnel in which the only illumination was the light cast by the Track itself.

Down and down and down, but continuing straight, if ever more steeply, so that at times they had to sit down and scoot along on their backsides or risk a foolhardy plunge into the blackness ahead.

Down and down and down.

The way became darker as well, until even the Track shrank to the faintest of glimmers.

Darker and darker and darker.

Somewhere behind them, three hulking shapes ranked themselves shoulder to shoulder at the juncture of three Straight Tracks and stretched their short necks skyward. One by one their mouths opened, revealing gray-white linings. Together they sent a shrill, keening cry wavering across what was not in any wise water.

On the opposite bank, three similar shapes pricked their tiny, bone-shielded ears in response and lumbered from the shadows of the forest, moving with absolute precision toward three sets of human footprints that showed beneath the glimmer of the Straight Track where it emerged from the lake of blood.

Darker and darker and darker.

Not until David felt fresh, cool air on his face did he realize how close the air had become in the tree-tunnel that had enclosed them. Up ahead, the way lightened and the path turned level again. Unable to restrain himself, David bolted toward that light.

Only Alec's flying tackle saved him from disaster. His friend's arms wrapped around his hips from behind, pitching David forward onto his knees, his arms scraping along rough rock. The breath whooshed from his lungs; the smell of wet stone and decaying leaves filled his nostrils.

"You really like running into thin air, don't you?" Alec grunted.

"What?" David gasped, confused – until his vision adjusted to the new light in which they found themselves.

It was light in fact – but only by comparison to the darkness through which they had lately passed. For the night sky still soared above them, and the Faerie moon, which never seemed to set, rode once more at the zenith.

And directly in front of them, inches from David's nose, a vast gulf opened in the land, looking as deep as the sky was high: a yawning black abyss between matching cliffs that fell unbelievably steep on either side. The jagged silhouettes of evergreens crowned those cliffs, and the narrow rocky ledge on which the friends had halted thrust out above the terrible darkness of the rift like shelf fungus on an ancient tree. David looked at the rift with dread. It was not particularly wide – a hundred feet at the outside. But there was no way across.

The Straight Track simply ended there, breaking cleanly off into empty air.

On the opposite face, etched brightly by the moonlight, the topmost branches of pale-barked trees rose above a stone archway composed of three immense rough-hewn boulders. The glow of the Track resumed there and continued through the opening. But in the empty distance between ... Nothing.

"Damn!" Alec spat. "It was the wrong turn; it must have been. We can't go on from here."

"No, it wasn't," Liz shot back. "It couldn't have been. The Lord of the Trial said we'd passed the first test."

David squinted into the darkness. "Then there has to be a way across."

He struggled to his feet, but as he did, he lost his grip on the staff he'd still been carrying. The end with the iron butcher knife lashed to it fell into the darkness above the gulf.

"No!" David yelped, grabbing frantically after it.

But it did not topple into the giddy darkness below them; rather, the staff rested in apparent defiance of gravity with two-thirds of its length lying unsupported above the abyss. The air rang with a gentle *ping* like the tinkling of a glass wind chime.

And from the point of the knife sparks began to appear: a panoply of glittering motes borne into the night that spread in all directions until at last they limned, faint but clear, the shape of the most insubstantial of bridges arching across the chasm to butt neatly against a ledge on the opposite cliff. It was appallingly steep – almost a true half-circle, like an oriental bridge – and frightfully narrow no more than a foot and a half wide. Nor was there any rail. A bridge it was, but a perilous one: scarcely more than a glimmer in the air.

"We can't cross that!" Liz groaned.

"We've no choice, the way I see it," came David's choked reply. "And, besides, we can't go back. Those shell-things may still be back there – or others like them."

Fear had begun to coil in the pit of David's stomach as the dark places of his mind began to creep open. He couldn't do it. He knew he couldn't. The bridge was too steep, too narrow, too *high!* His hidden fear – the one thing he had never revealed even to Alec – was upon him: the terror of bridges. High places were fine; he could wander around the ledges on Lookout Rock completely unafraid. But being high up and unsupported, with nothing but empty space below him: that set his gut to writhing and his balls to seeking sanctuary inside his body. Unfortunately, he had no choice.

And the bridge itself – so tenuous it was barely there – surely it would not support his weight. David reached cautiously down and snared the staff, fearing that the whole span would collapse at the slightest touch, or that the faint traceries that defined it would wink out.

Neither event occurred. What disconcerted him, however, was the way he could feel the whole structure tremble at that most delicate of touches. Would it support his weight? Would it support any of their weights?

For a dozen breaths neither of them spoke. None of them dared admit what they knew they must.

Finally Alec broke the silence. "All right, who's first?"

David drew a ragged breath, his face pale as death. "Me, of course."

"Not necessarily," Liz countered behind him.

David whirled around. "What do you mean?"

"I was thinking," she began," which you don't seem to be doing."

David opened his mouth for a scathing reply, tension or fear having made him reckless, but Liz cut him off. "No, David, let me finish. Be rational. This is a really shaky bridge. It might not bear our weight."

"Which is why I should go first," David retorted. "I'm heaviest. If it'll hold me, it'll hold you."

"Which is why the lightest should go first," Liz shot back. "Meaning me. One of us has to get through. If the heaviest goes first, and it breaks, none of us will make it. If the lightest goes first, there's a greater chance somebody'll get through. Remember the conditions: As long as one of us succeeds, the Trial will be a success."

"But it has to be David's decision," Alec pointed out.

"Right. So David can decide. But I've told him what I think."

David had scarcely heard the argument. Either way, first or last, meant traversing that frightful gulf. That was what he most feared.

"David!" Alec's voice was sharp.

"Oh, right." David's forehead furrowed as he paced the narrow ledge – fearless now, where only a few feet beyond he knew he would be quaking jelly.

"I don't like either option, but you're right, Liz: Lightest should go first. That's my decision. Uh, Liz, you *are* the lightest, aren't you?"

"That's what I just said."

"Well, it doesn't hurt to be sure."

"I weigh a hundred and seven pounds, David."

"I was just makin' sure."

Liz shook her head suspiciously. "And you, Master McLean?"

"One thirty-five."

"Davy?"

"One forty-one."

Liz raised an eyebrow. "But Alec's taller."

"Only by three inches – and I'm more muscular."

Alec glared at him.

"This is *not* the time to play macho-man," Liz snapped.

"Right," David agreed. "Okay, Liz, take off. I'd suggest hands and knees."

"Next time remind me to bring a rope," Alec muttered.

"Next time I will," David replied archly.

Liz approached the juncture of bridge and ledge cautiously – *and* set one foot tentatively upon the sparkling surface. David saw it tremble in response to that most minimal of contacts. He also saw her breath catch. "I don't know if any of us can make it," she called back.

"One of us has to. Otherwise the Trial will end. And there has to be a possibility of victory."

"Okay, but none of you start until I get across. All the way across."

With that, Liz knelt on all fours and braced her staff crossways between her two hands. She slid one hand onto the narrow span before her, then the other.

One knee. Two.

The bridge shook. David could see the glimmer scintillate.

One foot. Five feet. Ten. Twenty.

Liz was halfway across.

"Oh no," she called as she reached the apex. "It's downhill now, and that's going to be even harder." She flattened herself onto her stomach and scooted, her elbows and knees hooked around the angled edges. The staff she kept crossways in front of her, forcing it downward against the substance of the bridge so that whatever small bit of extra friction was thereby generated would help slow her descent. It worked for several feet, but halfway down the far slope she began to slide. One foot slipped sideways into air. She screamed and ground the staff into the bridge even more forcefully – which slowed her enough for her to right herself. The last third of her descent was more falling than sliding – and then she found herself lying facedown on the opposite ledge.

"You okay?" David shouted, obviously terrified.

Liz stood up and dusted herself off. "Scrapes and bruises. Watch out for the downslope; it's slick as glass."

David rolled his eyes.

Meanwhile, Alec had knelt down onto all fours and eased onto the span. He'd had the foresight to remove his shoes and socks, figuring the extra grip bare skin would provide might come in useful, especially as he'd left the staff with David and wouldn't have it to use for balance.

Disgusting, David thought, when he saw the ease with which Alec accomplished the crossing. This time there was no slipping.

"What're you waiting for?" Alec yelled, when he had reached the other side. "It's easy. Easy as falling off a –" He clapped a hand on his mouth.

"A log?" David called back, trying to mask his fear with levity. But it was no use; he was petrified. Never in his life had anything so completely unnerved him as the prospect of crossing that hundred-foot span. A glance over the edge of the cliff showed nothing but blackness: no bottom, nothing. Suppose there *was* no bottom; suppose it just went on forever. He could imagine that, too: imagine fear knotting his whole body more and more tightly into itself until he simply winked out of existence in this universe and popped out again somewhere else and kept on falling ...

"Come on, David!"

Finally he said it. "I'm scared!"

"Scared? *You?*" Alec snorted. "I've seen you scale ledges higher than this up on Lookout with even thinking about it."

"But I knew where the bottom was, and I had solid ground under my feet."

"David!"

"I've never told anybody this, Alec. Bridges scare me. Haven't you ever noticed how I always speed up on bridges?"

He could see Alec's mouth drop open as realization dawned upon him.

"You've got to cross, David!"

"Okay, okay! Just give me a minute."

"Come *now*, David! *Now,* or you'll never do it."

"I think the bridge is fading!" Liz shouted in such genuine alarm that David could detect it even across the gulf between them. In spite of his concern, a part of him wondered at the ease with which he had been able to hear across the distance.

"It is!" Alec cried.

"*Now, David! Now!*"

David stared at the bridge. It was indeed becoming more transparent by the moment. Darkness showed through the nearer end.

"David! Behind you!" Alec's voice carried shrill across the void.

David spun around.

An armored head three feet wide thrust through the undergrowth not ten yards up the slope.

"*Now, David. Now!*"

The shell-beast advanced. Slowly. Methodically. Its eyes never left David. Moonlight glittered on the pearlescent whorls painted on its carapace.

"David!"

David glanced back at the bridge, then at the creature. It took a step.

For no logical reason, he faced it, crouching warily before it, the make-do spear poised in one hand.

Another step. Eyes never leaving its quarry.

"This ends now!" David shouted, even as he hurled the spear at the beast.

It struck in the flaccid, grainy hide at the juncture of neck and shell, and remained there, bobbing up and down. The merest puncture it looked, yet thick, evil-smelling blood welled out below the shaft. The acrid scent of burning flesh filled the air as the wrinkled skin around the wound began to blacken and curl away. The creature reared onto its stubby hind legs and screamed, a cry that tortured the silence like a dull sword thrust slowly into rusty metal.

David stood in frozen awe.

The creature collapsed back onto front feet that could no longer support its weight. No trace of light showed in its eyes. Its fellows began lumbering toward it.

David rushed forward and seized the spear, wrenching it from the surprisingly yielding flesh. The stench was nearly overpowering.

All at once he was on the bridge.

It gave beneath his weight in a way that made his stomach churn. He was certain he felt one knee slip through. But he was moving; that was the important thing: crab-crawling his way across as his friends had done, staff pushed before him. He could feel the substance slick beneath the heels of his palms and smooth against his chest. Close before his eyes was a complexity of slowly moving lights defining the surface, glowing lines connecting the major nexi. But even as he looked, even as he scooted forward and up, the lights began to pale. Whole lines winked out. More and more space showed between.

Somehow he was in the middle. Downhill was a slide – he'd seen that – but his nerve was frozen. He could not go forward, and he could not go back, for there *was* no back. Ahead, not fifty feet, David could see the eager, expectant faces of his friends. But he dared not relinquish control. And to make matters worse, his grip was slipping – and not straight ahead, either; the sharp angles that marked the shoulders of the span were rounding. The cross-section was becoming circular! And David could feel himself shifting sideways.

"David!"

"Loosen up! Let go! Slide!"

He closed his eyes, released his grip the merest fraction, gave himself the gentlest of forward nudges with his feet ...

An instant later he felt Alec's arms around him, pulling him to safety. Nothing had ever felt so warm, so welcoming, or so solid.

"You made it, old man!" Alec grinned.

David sank to the ground, shuddering uncontrollably. "I did, didn't I?" His breath was coming fast; he flung himself backward, chest heaving, staring up at the distant, star-filled sky.

A face swung into view above him: neither Alec nor Liz. A face half-masked by an intricate helm.

"You have passed the Trial of Courage," said the Lord of the Trial. "Not by defeating the Watcher or crossing the bridge, but by allowing your friends to precede you, knowing they might have to complete your quest alone and trusting them enough to believe they would. It takes courage to put one's fate in another's hands."

David sat up and glanced back at the bridge. And was not surprised to see that it had vanished. Where it had abutted the other side, two shell-beasts were now feasting on the flesh of their fellow. A chill shook him, then another.

"What *are* those things?" he gasped.

"Watchers? Guardians? Keepers, perhaps?" the Lord replied. "By iron alone may they be slain. You are now at the fringe of Tir-Nan-Og itself; there is no further need for them to shadow you. Your last Trial will be of another sort entirely. It awaits you through the arch."

Alec laid an arm across David's shoulders and pointed to the ground beneath them, where the golden glitter of the Straight Track still lay. It was brighter than it had ever been.

When they looked up, The Lord of the Trial was gone.

"Two down," Alec panted.

"And one to go: the Trial of Strength, I would guess."

"Quicker begun, quicker ended," Liz sighed.

"Right," David sighed in turn as he heaved himself up. "So, onward, children onward and into the breach."

The trilithon gate reared before them, more than a little evocative of Stonehenge, and then they were under it. Ahead stretched an arching passage in the wood. It was dark, but from where they stood they could already see light at the far end.

By some unspoken agreement they began to run.

An instant later, they burst out into the blazing sunlight of a grassy glade maybe a quarter mile across. Ahead, looming above even the highest of the trees on the far side, David could, for the first time, make out the shape that had haunted his dreams: the impossibly slender cone of this World's Bloody Bald. He could not reckon the distance, however, for though the mountain appeared tiny, he was able to make out the smallest detail of the faceted, sharp-buttressed towers and pearly walls, the gold-laced pinnacles and high-arched windows, and the riotously tumbling gardens and ominous forests that enwrapped it.

"Neat!" Alec cried.

"And restful," Liz added. "This place, I mean."

"Not for long, I'm sure," David put in. But even he had to admit it was a beautiful glade. The brilliant green grass beside the Track was as short as a well-tended lawn. Small bushes bearing thick spiky leaves, and gray boulders crudely carved with scowling human faces were scattered about in artful clumps, each accenting some slight hill or hollow. At no place were all of them visible at once. Still, the Track continued onward, and they followed it reluctantly, wanting to stop and rest but knowing they did not dare.

Through the middle of the glade flowed a small stream maybe twenty feet across, neatly bisecting the Track. A narrow strip of fine silver sand bordered it on either side. They paused there, wondering what hidden perils might lurk beneath its innocuous surface. Though shallow, it flowed rapidly and was remarkably clear. Yellow and red rocks flashed on its bottom, and once David thought he saw the flickering silver forms of a school of tiny, blue-finned fish dart past. He *did* see a hand-sized octopus almost as green and transparent as fine jade.

The air was still. Empty. No sound disturbed the peace of that place save the gentle gurgle of the stream.

And then one other sound.

For, issuing from the woods ahead, came an almost subliminal jingling, accompanied by a low-pitched buzz that finally resolved into the howl of warpipes at full cry.

Chapter XVI

The Stuff of Heroes

The sky darkened abruptly, as if masked by clouds, though none showed to mar that pristine vault. Black shadows crowded in among the distant trees. The sun still shone, but its light lacked strength and conviction. It was like predawn twilight and early evening and the eerie half-light of a solar eclipse all at once, and yet like none of those things.

Alec tugged on David's jacket sleeve, gesturing toward the line of trees straight ahead, his mouth agape in wonder. David nodded, for he too had seen what approached.

Light.

A body of ghostly yellow-white radiance more like phosphor-escence than anything else David had seen, except that it was pale at the center and scintillated into colors at the edge. But, like phosphorescence, the light did not illuminate; rather, there was the dark forest on the one hand, the light on the other, and an almost-tangible interface between.

As the light drew nearer, the jingle of bells likewise increased in volume. The ground trembled as if many horses trod upon it, and the sound of pipes, too, grew louder. And then voices joined with that skirling: men's voices singing of battle and of war – or at least that was how it sounded, though the language was strange. Warpipes howled in that music like thunder in the mountains on a hot summer day. And though David could not make out the words of the song, they filled him with wonder and with dread.

Alec pointed to the Track ahead of them. Its edges had begun to glow even more brightly, eventually flaring into a brilliance like white flame

— as white as the star-shaped flowers that sprang up alongside it in the vanguard of the Sidhe at their riding. Shapes slowly took form in that nimbus of light, winking in and out among the trees at the edge of the meadow: shapes that could only be the Sidhe themselves.

The whole Host of Faerie seemed to be part of that riding, their actual forms and faces sometimes all but lost amid the panoply of glittering jewels and metals, brightly patterned fabrics and richly woven textures, furs and feathers, banners and pennants and musical instruments, swords and spears and helms, and thin golden staffs bearing strange carved and gilded insignia that glowed with their own light and cast their glow about the host.

The singing grew louder still, and more drivingly intense. But now a darker motif wove its way into the melody, and the rhythmic jingle of the horses' bells altered in its wake. There was a new hint of tambourine and drum in the music, and of someone playing a harp, but the strings were plucked high and strange, almost a discord.

One by one the Host of the Sidhe forded the stream and continued up the Straight Track toward the mortals. Closer and closer they came, and still they sang.

When the last of the host cleared the trees and came full into David's sight, he forgot Alec, forgot Liz, almost forgot Little Billy and Uncle Dale. For the company parted and he saw who rode centermost among the Host of Faerie: Ailill, his enemy.

Ailill sat a young white stallion whose golden mane hung halfway to the ground, and it seemed to David that tiny flames issued from the horse's nostrils and that its hooves struck sparks from the mossy turf. Ailill himself was dressed in black and silver, save for a band of red jewels about his head and the wide border of embroidered red-and-silver eagles that edged his cloak. Arrogance showed cold on his handsome features, but the ornate silver scabbard that hung by his side was empty.

A company of twenty grim-faced warriors rode close about the Lord of Winds. The horses they bestrode were black. Each man bore a black lance pointing skyward, and each wore a black cloak wrapped tightly around him. Black mail gleamed on throat and legs and arms. Plain black helms capped heads of black hair. Their mouths were open, and they sang with the others: their voices now high and clear, now dark and ominous.

Hope awoke within David when he saw who rode point to the armored company: hope when he'd had a near-brush with hopelessness. It was a silver-armed figure in white and gold, the golden fringe of whose snowy cloak swept the earth: Nuada of the Silver Hand.

The Morrigu was there too: the Mistress of Battles. A crow sat on the saddle before her, black as her unbound hair. Her tight, low-cut gown was red as blood, and its trailing sleeves were lined with satin that flickered like flame. She was beautiful the way a slim-tipped dagger is beautiful.

But then David looked at Ailill, and saw that the dark Faery was glaring back at him, his eyes all but glowing with hate.

The song ended abruptly, cut off on a single note, as a life may end on a lone sword thrust. Someone began to pluck a harp one string at a time, soft and sad and strange.

Alec slipped David his runestaff. He accepted it with a grunt of thanks and held it braced before him in his two hands as he squared his shoulders and strode forward to meet that company. He knew he must look ridiculous to stand thus before such a host, bruised and dirty as he was – but he knew he had no choice but to brazen it out, though his heart felt cold as arctic lead.

Nuada reined his horse to a halt. The armed company that accompanied him slowed as one until they too had stopped. Indeed, they stood so still they looked frozen.

David looked up into the glittering gaze of the Faery lord, glanced back at Ailill, then took a deep breath and addressed Nuada.

"Hail, Lord of Faerie," he cried, and choked for a moment as new fear welled up inside him.

"Hail, mortal lad," Nuada returned wryly. "You seem to have a facility for meeting the Danaans at their Riding."

"His business is with me, Silverhand," Ailill snapped.

"And what business is that?" Nuada retorted sharply. "You are an exile now – or soon will be. You have had doings enough with mortal men."

Ailill ignored him, but fire blazed in the dark eyes beneath his dark hair, as he folded his arms across the bronze eagle's head that comprised the pommel of his saddle and leveled his gaze upon David. "You are a fool, then, are you not? More so than I had ever guessed, to challenge the Danaans to the Trial of Heroes. Two Trials you have passed, so I have heard, but the Trial of Strength yet awaits you. And that Trial I claim for myself, as is my right. Your challenge was directed at me, was it not? Even if you did not so state it?"

David gulped. "I suppose so."

"Then it is mine to choose the nature of that Trial. You have come too far to go back now, and your fate is upon you, though not in the manner I had planned. No matter. The end will be the same. I am the champion of Erenn, you see; I am –"

"You are my prisoner until I rid my lands of you," a now-familiar voice interrupted from behind the mortals. "*I* determine what you are and what you are not, what you will do and what you will not."

Tom deitz

David whirled around, to see the Lord of the Trial casually pacing his steed up the Track toward the company.

When he had almost reached the host, the Lord lifted his helmet and handed it to a young man in gold and crimson livery who rode forward to receive it. A circlet of interlaced gold gleamed forth upon the long, fair hair thus revealed. Alone of all that company, the Lord seemed to glow.

A rustling murmur caused David to turn again toward the host, to see them kneel as one body in obvious obeisance to the shining figure that loomed before them.

"The Ard Rhi," someone whispered.

The Ard Rhi! David thought. *The High King:* Lugh Samildinach himself, High King of the Sidhe in Tir-Nan-Og. Lugh was the Lord of the Trial!

Ailill glared at the mounted figure that faced him. "Nevertheless, the Rules do not forbid me to contest with the boy," he snarled, "for the Rule of the Trial is beyond even the Law of Lugh Samildinach. But I was about to add that the Trial of Strength would not be with me, but with my son." He raised his head and shouted, "Fionchadd, attend me!"

A buzz arose from the assembled multitude, which quickly parted as a green-clad figure rode from where it had ridden unobtrusively among the ranks. It was a youth, David saw, seemingly little older than himself: golden-haired and lightly, if neatly, built – almost his own size, in fact.

The boy removed the long-peaked cap that shadowed his face, and David gasped as he recognized the clean-chiseled features beneath it. It was the same boy who had shot Uncle Dale. And now he realized that it was also the same half-glimpsed face that had belonged to the Faery runner who had chased him what seemed like a very long time ago. That race had started all this, in fact – all the bad part of it, anyway. The boy's face flushed with emotions David could not read. "What is it you would have of me ... Father?"

Ailill's face was hard as rock. "Twice I sent you on missions for me, missions a mere child could have accomplished – yet you failed," he said coldly. "But third time pays for all, and by the Rule of Three you owe me a third. I demand you avenge your honor."

"You are correct, for once," Lugh agreed, in a voice that allowed no argument, "though not in the manner of honor. The Trial must be a fair contest, a striving among equals. Your son and David are of a size and almost of an age, allowing for the difference between the Worlds. And Oisin's ring is lost in the Lands of Men and has no power here. Yes, Ailill, I think you have the right of it: Third time pays for all. Do you agree?"

Ailill glared at Lugh, his mouth hardened to a thin, arrogant line.

"Even I must bow to the Trial of Heroes; for that which rules it is mightier than anyone here."

Lugh ignored the glare and turned his gaze toward the Morrigu. "Mistress of Battles?"

The Morrigu inclined her head a fraction. "Long it is since we have observed the Rite. Yet it must be done in accord with strictest honor or not at all. Fionchadd is the most fit opponent. If it is David's will to try with him, so let it be."

Lugh turned again toward David. "Is it so?"

David stared at the boy – what was his name? Fionchadd? – then at Alec and Liz, both of whose faces mirrored bewildered concern. He felt dead. Numb. He stood as if paralyzed, ten steps from ... What? Doom? Or immortality? He could remain in Faerie; that had always been an option. Surely with eternity for the search he could find Little Billy. But what about Uncle Dale? And Liz and Alec? Did he have the right to make such preposterous decisions for them? Doom one and – Well, if he aborted the quest now, the three of them could be friends forever – maybe in Liz's case more than friends. Not until that moment had he realized how much he loved them.

And with that last realization, he found that the decision was made.

"I choose the Trial of Strength with Fionchadd," he said at last, his mouth dry as dust, for all that he knew he had in fact defeated, or at least eluded, his incipient adversary at least once.

Lugh glared down at David. "You do not look very strong," he observed. "What can you do?"

David hesitated barely an instant, as for once the right words came to him. "I can run and wrestle and swim."

"He can indeed," Fionchadd agreed. "And since he has already bested me at the first two, for my part I would try with him at swimming."

Lugh nodded, then spoke in a voice clear as a trumpet: "As Lord of the Trial, and in spite of what Ailill may say, it is my duty to decide the form of the Trial of Strength, and this is my decision: Let it be as Fionchadd wills. Having competed already at running and wrestling, let the final Trial be swimming."

Lugh looked Ailill straight in the eye then. "But I have a stake in this as well," he continued. "The Trial will be a test of strength and will. If David wins, he will gain that which he seeks, and the desire for such gain is a mighty incentive indeed. But what if Fionchadd wins? Then I owe the mortal no boons. He and his friends will be doomed to eternity as my guests in Tir-Nan-Og – but you, Ailill, will have paid no price for the suffering you have caused – yet you are not without guilt. Therefore let it also be a contest to the death. It is *Fionchadd's* death I claim if he loses. On him I lay the death of iron: a time of torment in the Dark Realm from which only his strength of will may free him."

A hush filled the ranks. Even the harp stopped for an instant. "As you will have it, Ard Rhi," Fionchadd said quietly.

Ailill's face turned white. "Fool of a boy!" he hissed. "Twice fool, and thrice."

The Morrigu silenced him with a glance. "It is not your decision. The Rite has been set in motion."

David looked around uncertainly. "But ... there's nowhere here to swim."

Lugh smiled wryly. "A small matter in Tir-Nan-Og. Do you see that stream? That will become your river. That you will swim, this bank to the other."

"But how?" David blurted out, trying not to ponder what he had just heard. "The stream's maybe twenty feet across. Why, I could wade it!"

"Not if you are no higher than my finger is long," Lugh chuckled.

David's mouth dropped open. "You mean you'll shrink us?"

"Or expand the land around you," Lugh replied with an absent shrug. "It comes to the same thing. Sometimes I myself am not certain which occurs. Now let the contestants come stand by the stream, and we will end this matter.

Lugh's gaze swept the assembly. "Morrigu, shape-shifting is an art you practice almost as frequently as Ailill, and to somewhat more pleasing effect; can you shift a man's size as easily as his form?"

The dark-haired woman stepped forward, a disquieting smile upon her fair face. "That I can do, Lord, and that I will do most gladly."

Lugh nodded. "David Sullivan, Fionchadd MacAilill, come forward," he commanded.

David glanced at Alec and Liz. Alec smiled sadly and stuck out his hand. David took it and squeezed it, but went on to enfold his friend in a hearty hug.

Liz he likewise hugged, regretfully aware of how nice her body felt against his. As he broke away, he was surprised when she pulled him back and kissed him firmly on the mouth.

A moment later David was standing on the sand at the side of the stream, water lapping about the toes of his hiking boots. Fionchadd strode over to stand at his side. The boy's face was grimly emotionless. David could not imagine what thoughts hid behind those emerald eyes. Was the Faery boy favorably disposed toward him, as David had some reason to suspect, or was he truly an enemy? And what was the relationship between the boy and Ailill? Father and son, certainly, but was that love between them, or hatred, or some curious combination of the two?

"Prepare yourselves," the Morrigu intoned.

Prepare yourselves? David had no idea what that meant. He glanced at Fionchadd for a cue, then realization dawned: The Faery boy had already sat down and was tugging off the thigh-high green boots he wore beneath his short green tunic. David felt his face both heating and coloring. *Well, of course! One can't very well win a race like this fully clothed!* But ... he had brought nothing to swim in, and there were people around – *women* around – *Liz, for heaven's sake!* A corner of his mind knew that bathing suits were a recent innovation; that in olden times people had customarily swum bare-assed, but still – But still, when you really got down to it, modesty seemed an insignificant thing when lives were at stake. Reluctantly he unzipped his jacket.

A moment later he stood beside Fionchadd, blushing furiously in his tighty-whiteies. The Faery boy had stripped to the skin, but seemed totally unconcerned about his nudity. David tried to assess his opponent without really looking at him. The Faery was an inch or two taller than he and more finely boned, but long, smooth muscles wrapped his arms and legs, and the firm, graceful curves of his chest and shoulders hinted at the sort of strength that was good for endurance.

David wondered suddenly if he *could* win. So far the trappings of the contest had distracted him from the thought that should have been uppermost in his mind: Victory. It was for Little Billy, he did this, and Uncle Dale, and now for Liz and Alec.

"Face me!" came the unexpectedly harsh voice of the Morrigu. "Look me in the eyes! Both of you! Now!"

David found he had no choice but to obey. The Power in the woman's voice seemed easily the equal of Lugh's, perhaps even stronger in its own way.

The eyes he gazed into were gray. Gray as evening. Gray as the steel of swords. Gray as cannons and arrows and unpolished armor. Gray as the netherworld of death.

The Morrigu blinked or David did. And he stood again beside Fionchadd, looking down at the ridiculously small stream, utterly confused.

Lugh's voice rang loud in their ears. "When I give the word, you will dive forward. The change will come upon you at that time."

David's gaze sought his friends. Alec gave him a thumbs-up. Liz blew him a kiss. He grinned in spite of himself.

"Ready."

He tensed, then crouched bent-kneed, poised for a long, shallow dive. The notion of throwing himself with full force into what appeared to be three inches of water was daunting. But that was logic, and logic was not the pillar of stability it once had been.

"*Now!*"

David's body took over for him – for which he was grateful. He flung himself forward, fully expecting to feel the sharp stones of the streambed impact his chest and drive the air from his lungs. Instead, there was a brief sensation of falling, like a dive from a great height – and suddenly he was in deep water, twenty yards or more offshore.

There was a commotion beside him – no, in *front* of him – as Fionchadd wasted no time in forging ahead. David had to fight an urge to pause and gaze skyward to see if the towering forms of the Sidhe looked down upon him from on high. But there was no time for that now. Fionchadd was already two body-lengths ahead and pulling away. David gave himself over to the task at hand.

Though he was certainly not a trained swimmer, he had nevertheless been swimming since he was a child, when David-the-Elder had told him that he had a natural gift for it. Water thus held no terrors for him, and he often swam far out into the lake. He'd also raced Alec and the rest of the MacTyrie Gang, but always in fun, never for any stakes more serious than a pizza or a CD or a stolen beer.

And then he quit thinking and simply let his body take over. Stroke. Stroke. Kick. Kick. *Breathe.* Stroke. Stroke. Kick. Kick. *Breathe.*

He was gaining. But not fast enough.

Ahead he could see Fionchadd's supple form gliding smoothly through the water, barely disturbing the surface as he plunged his narrow hands into it.

Stroke. Stroke. Kick. Kick. *Breathe.*

They were into the current now, and it was all either of them could do to keep from being overwhelmed by it – especially when vast waves appeared as if from nowhere, towering high above their heads before crashing down upon them.

A particularly large example fell directly on him, plunging him far under water. Something brushed against a foot, but he tried not to think what it might be – and certainly not about that small, green octopus. And then he was on the surface again, and Fionchadd not as far ahead as heretofore.

More waves, and then the waters smoothed, and then waves again, bearing him upward, higher and higher, then plunging him down once more. Up and down. Up and down. It was like swimming in a stormy sea.

A wave crashed upon him, harder than any before, and he felt himself knocked half senseless, felt himself drifting nervelessly toward the stream-bed, as bubbles trickled from his mouth to tickle his nose. His lungs hurt. His head hurt. He was drowning.

Drowning in two feet of water.

He remembered what Fionchadd had said about the Stuff of Heroes and how David was himself of that substance. From somewhere images came unbidden in his mind: Beowulf in his contest with Brecca amid the monsters of a cold northern ocean; Leander, who had dared the Hellespont each night for love of a woman whose very name was Hero; Bran the Blessed who had *waded* the Irish Sea.

Ruthlessly he kept his arms and legs in motion. Ruthlessly he kicked his way upward, ignoring the pain in his lungs, the buzz in his ears, the red blur that filled his eyes.

He broke through to the surface. He rolled onto his back, coughing, dragging in long, blessedly cool breaths of sweet air. He looked for Fionchadd, but the boy was nowhere in sight.

Despair filled him – until he saw the Faery's head break water near his own, victim of the same monster wave. For an uncertain moment their gazes met, and then both set forth again. But Fionchadd had lost most of his advantage; David was nearly neck and neck with him now, and the Faery seemed to be tiring.

David tried to ration his energy yet maintain his pace. The shore was in sight: a thin dark line seen through a wet blur of water and hair that continually obscured his vision. But he was tiring, falling farther and farther behind. He needed an incentive, he realized, and so he once again set his imagination free to conjure images – dark images, this time: the things he most feared, the things he knew would happen if he failed:

Uncle Dale lying in bed, head rocked loosely back, eyes staring at nothing, a thin line of spittle trickling from his open mouth, while the banshee stood beside him, her rictor smile greedy upon her face.

Little Billy a bodiless wraith of hopeless fear, torn from his own world, maybe even his own shape; a disembodied child-voice crying in the wind: "Davy! Davy! Davy!"

Alec and Liz clad in the extravagant garb of Faerie, besotted on Faery wine, eyes dulled by an endless succession of days wherein nothing ever changed.

His parents wondering how two sturdy sons could have vanished without a trace.

Fionchadd.

Fionchadd, who would die if he won. Well, he'd wanted to kill him when he saw the elf-arrow stuck in Uncle Dale's chest, so now was the chance to even that score. But they had also made a sort of peace on that occasion. "When this song is ended, let us be friends," the boy had said. Well, there was still one more verse. And, much as he hated to admit it, the boy still owed him one.

They were even now, neck and neck, and the shoreline was close, maybe fifty yards away. David took a breath and withdrew into himself, summoning energy from every nerve, every muscle, every cell. And from one thing more: his rage. He had never entirely set that latter free, but now he did: freed it and sent it spreading fire throughout his body.

And his body obeyed, knifing fiercely through the water, each movement born of the deadly flame of anger that now drove him on, each flame consumed thrusting him closer to his goal.

Pulling him ahead of Fionchadd.

David glanced sideways, saw a look of true, incredulous fear cross the Faery boy's face.

That was what finally did it: the fact that the boy considered his own defeat a real possibility. A final show of strength would do it.

Now! David told his body, and every part of him unified into one whole, as he poured his last precious reserves of energy into the effort.

Sand brushed his fingertips.

Another stroke.

Again.

And then he was scrambling to his feet, to fling himself breathlessly against the coarse sand of the shore. Panting like a bellows, he flopped onto his back, chest heaving, eyes glazed. Somehow he was his own size again.

But had he won? An eerie silence hung in the air.

"Way to go, Davy! You did it!" familiar voices cried at last. A feeling strangely like elation filled his mind, replacing those darker images that had pushed him to ... to *victory,* he supposed. But he was too tired to think, too numb to move.

Warm, tanned hands gripped his arms as someone helped him sit up. Other hands forced a drink into his mouth: a spicy richness that sent new fire racing through his body as soon as it touched his lips, so that he was finally able to rise shakily to his feet. Someone draped a tabard across his shivering shoulders. He fingered the fabric absently. Velvet. Midnight-blue and gray.

"Hold!" a voice thundered. "The Trial is not ended!"

Chapter XVII

The Justice of Lugh

Not *ended!* David's thoughts were awhirl. *Not ended! What* –?

"It was a trial to the *death,*" came Lugh's voice, sounding very, very grim. "No life has yet been taken. You, Alec McLean, give your comrade that iron blade I see fixed to your staff. Fionchadd's life is his."

Someone – Alec? – thrust a knife into David's hand. He raised his head groggily, staring stupidly at the length of slightly rusty metal set in a worn wooden handle.

Two of the black-clad guards pulled Fionchadd upright. The Faery boy's body sagged between them, dripping wet, his eyes as unfocused as David's. Water sheened his white skin; he breathed in great shuddering gasps. With obvious effort, Fionchadd stretched a trembling arm toward David. "You have won fairly. My life is yours. And know that ... that I bear you no ill will, for my fate is my own doing. My song is over."

Still half dazed, David felt someone leading him forward. One of the guards pulled Fionchadd's head back, exposing his throat. David could see the pulse beating there as he raised the knife until the blade hovered just above that smooth flesh. He felt Fionchadd's breath brush hot against the back of his hand, saw the boy close his eyes in resignation. He set his mouth, biting his lips to keep them from trembling. Was he really doing this? He was human, mortal, *civilized.* Could he really kill a man like this? And not just a man, a man he in some sense knew, had talked to; who had possessed a whole long and complex life before their meeting but who would have no life at all afterward save perhaps an eternity of pain.

"No!" he cried and flung the knife to the sand.

"It is a strong man," Lugh said, "who can set an enemy free, perhaps to face him again someday. By taking that risk, you have passed your final Trial."

"By this you have cost me the last of my honor!" Ailill snarled behind him.

David whirled around – just in time to see the dark Faery wrench Liz's makeshift spear from her grasp. Pain darkened Ailill's face as white smoke poured from between his fingers; the smell of charring flesh filled the air all in the instant before Ailill spurred his horse to a brutal charge straight at David.

The company fell back, shouting in alarm.

David stood frozen, staring at black-clad death bearing down upon him. He screamed. Other voices shouted in his head. "No!" he heard Liz and Alec yell as one.

Time slowed.

David saw Ailill on the white horse, the smoking hand that grasped the spear, the glittering eyes of the Faery lord. The blade pointed straight at his heart burned red hot as Ailill's fury awakened it.

And he couldn't move.

He absolutely could not move.

There was no sound save the snorting of the horse and the pounding of hooves on the sand.

And still the spear came on.

Although David could not move, the horse could – and did, though in an unexpected manner. Something, a small stone perhaps, upset its balance, so that it broke its gait.

Fire flashed across David's side. He looked down to see the velvet tabard slashed crossways and a thin line of red oozing from a long, clean cut across his ribs.

Two screams rang in his ears.

And the pain was gone.

He turned, stared – and saw Fionchadd lying on the sand beside him. The boy's eyes were open, but Liz's knife-pointed runestaff protruded from his pale, still chest. The tiniest hint of white smoke spiraled upward from the wound to mark the sky. A single rivulet of blood trickled across the white flesh to stain the sand.

David wanted to protest, to say "No! This isn't how it was supposed to end! I'd forgiven him!" But his jaw locked. He felt his gorge start to rise and clamped a hand across his mouth as he jerked his gaze away.

Silence hung in the air like a threat of thunder.

Wordlessly, Nuada dismounted and with his silver hand yanked the spear from Fionchadd's wound and tossed it to Alec. Then, moving with deliberate precision, as if he had all the time in the world, he spread his white cloak across the boy's body. Only then did he turn to face Ailill.

"Madman!" he whispered.

"Idiot!" a woman's voice shrieked.

"Fool!"

"Murderer!" The cries were a rising tide of anger.

"*Kinslayer!*"

"Kinslayer!" another voice took up the call, and then others joined in a chant that rang across the clearing: "Kinslayer! Kinslayer! Kinslayer!"

Despair washed across Ailill's face: despair and horror – and finally fear. His pride broke, and he spurred the horse to a gallop and made toward the Straight Track, where it lay across the empty glade.

But even he flashed past, David caught a blur of movement to his left and saw Alec thrust his makeshift spear directly into the Faery lord's face

Ailill's eyes stretched wide in horror as the instinctive fear of iron came upon him. He flinched away, sending the startled horse rearing beneath him. Though he held the reins firmly, he was unprepared when the horse bucked sideways. That move unbalanced him, and he slipped from the saddle. But he was on his feet again as soon as he struck the earth: afoot, and running for the Track.

But another stood there before him, appearing from nowhere as though she'd simply stepped out of the air: a black-haired, blue-clad woman with, beside her, an empty-eyed child in yellow pajamas. Straight in front of Ailill she stood: proud and fierce, barring his way with her very presence.

Yet she was no fear-cowed Faery woman this time, but a great warrior-queen of the Tuatha de Danaan. Vengeance was in her gaze and triumph in her carriage as her fingers worked before her.

Ailill found his way blocked by a shimmering wall of swirling flame that leapt man-high from the tall grass about him and spread to either side in an arc only a madman would try to pass. An intricate, cage-like mesh of icicles took form within that barrier, through which the colored fires leapt and wove, constantly melting and refreezing, even as the flames were extinguished and rekindled.

And so Ailill stood confounded, facing arcane fire on the one hand and the fires of iron that could bind him in torment on the other. Reluctantly he turned and stumbled forward to stand before the king, head bowed.

Without a word, Nuada moved to stand behind Ailill, as though he feared he might attempt some new ploy.

"So it is to be my justice at last," Lugh said. His stern gaze swept the crowd, "Then hear you all the justice of Lugh Samildinach, High King for this Time in Tir-Nan-Og!"

Lugh's gaze bored into the dark Faery. "You, Ailill, are a fool. For even as you pass from my realm, you still contrive plots and deceptions. It was a plot of yours that started this trouble, for you should never have made that bargain with the mortal boy. But having made it, you should have stayed by it – so any honorable man would have done. And now a plot of yours has finished it again, as is fitting, but that gamble has cost you a son: a high price to pay for victory. And worse, because the purse from which it was paid was your son's, not your own. Nor is that the worst of your offenses, for you have been guilty of another crime as well: a crime against my own house."

"My lord, I have not – !" Ailill protested.

Lugh motioned the Faery woman forward. She responded instantly, bringing the surrogate Little Billy with her.

"Now we all know," Lugh began, "that you took a changeling. The proof of that we see before us. Is this not so?"

Ailill made no move to answer Lugh's allegation.

"No matter," Lugh continued. "We all know the truth of it. We also know that we Danaans could use some of the hot blood of mortals to heat our own. But you took that changeling without my consent; indeed, you flaunted it in my face, even to refusing to return the boy when I commanded it, thereby setting your will above my own, for which you earned this exile. And what is even worse is that you left one of our own in the child's stead when a log would have served as well. What could have possessed you to do such a thing?"

Ailill's eyes narrowed. "Were you indeed as well studied in the ways of men as you claim, Ard Rhi," he spat, "you would know that mortal men have more ways of looking at illness now than when we were mighty in the land. Had I left a stock in the boy's place, they might have grasped the heart of our deception, and that would have made trouble for us far beyond what stealing this boy would cause. I had to use a child of our own people."

Lugh drew himself up to his full height. His fingers grasped his jeweled reins so tightly that they snapped, sending a rain of sapphires and topazes glittering to the ground. "Is it this you are telling me, Ailill?" he thundered: "That you deemed a child of the Danaans to be of less value than a child of mortal men? *I know the last number of the people I rule,* do not forget that. Did you truly think that I would overlook the theft of a trueborn scion of Faerie? No, Dark One, you have been too much in your own counsel, for though you took the child, and the mother all unwilling, you failed to inquire closely enough as to who that woman might be – and in that you erred grievously."

"A woman is a woman," Ailill spat. "A child is a child."

"A woman may also be a daughter of a king," Lugh replied quietly. "Not all of my kindred choose to remain at court."

Ailill's face went white beneath his ruby circlet.

Lugh smiled. "You had best not give an heir to the Danaan King as a changeling without that king's consent. I have my own plans for his fosterage."

Laughter sounded like bells at that, but Ailill's face flushed red.

"Yes, Windmaster," Lugh continued, "your true nature shines forth at last. I do not know what we will do with you, but we will see whether we can lessen the harm you have already wrought." He stretched upward in the stirrups, shading his gaze with a hand. "Unfortunately, I do not see the human child anywhere about."

Oblivious to the pain it cost, Lugh jerked the ash spear from Alec's hand and leveled its still-glowing tip at Ailill's heart, as two guards grabbed the dark Faery on either side. "*Now, where is the boy?*"

Ailill glared at him and muttered something in a low voice. A spell, David knew instinctively and probably a very Powerful one, for the crowd fell silent, and the very air itself seemed at once to thicken and go flat, as if Ailill's words were too potent for mere air to contain them.

The white horse that Ailill had ridden so proudly only a short while earlier stamped its feet as if disturbed by the presence of so much Power. It danced sideways, its eyes rolling in fright, its tongue lolling from its mouth. All at once it snorted and reared up, fell heavily to earth, and reared again – and remained standing on its hind legs, as it suddenly became a naked five-year-old boy with white-blond hair and bright blue eyes. Confused recognition broke forth on that small face, as Little Billy stood there staring wide-eyed, as though not quite believing he had won free from the horse-shape that had enwrapped him.

David could contain himself no longer. He ran forward, knelt before his brother, and gathered him into his arms. "Little Billy, it's me, Davy!"

"Davy! Davy!" Little Billy cried in turn, as tears wet both their faces.

Lugh also smiled as he saw the blue-clad woman kneel and embrace her own child – whose eyes, too, blazed with renewed life. And they were his own green eyes now, shining joyfully in his own face.

David hugged his brother tightly. Somebody handed him a cloak, and he threw it around his brother's shoulders. Alec casually returned David's T-shirt and jeans, and while the attention of the crowd was diverted, David slipped them on beneath his tabard, which he retained.

Lugh cleared his throat. "We still have things to consider," he announced, "including whether or not banishment is sufficient punishment for our rebellious ... associate here. He has slain his son, a grievous thing indeed, but I wonder whether that loss is enough?"

The blue-clad woman stepped forward at that, resting a hand on the pommel of Lugh's saddle. "Majesty," she began, "may I offer my counsel in this?"

"I am always glad to hear your advice, daughter," Lugh replied.

"Well, then," the woman said, "since Ailill is so fond of shape-shifting, let me take him into my care and lay on him the shape of a black horse and make of him a mount for my son to ride until he be of an age to bear arms." She smiled triumphantly at Ailill, but there was warning in her smile.

"There is great justice in this," Lugh agreed. "So shall it be."

"I will assist," Nuada broke in quickly. "The more locks there are on that spell the better. Perhaps the Ard Rhi might even provide one as well ..."

"Aye," Lugh agreed promptly. "But we can discuss the subtleties of this matter later. It will give Ailill more time in which to contemplate his crimes."

The woman's eyes caught David's and lingered there a moment before flickering over Alec and Liz and Little Billy. She smiled cryptically. "So be it then. I think, too, that these fine folk will be dealing with the Danaans again – perhaps more than they like."

"I hope not," Lugh sighed, "but I fear you are correct. We have seldom met with mortals so lively in the last few centuries. Now," the High King continued, "are there any other boons to be craved, while I seem to be holding court?" His gaze rested on David.

David opened his mouth. "I –"

"I crave a boon, Ard Rhi," Ailill broke in.

Lugh raised an eyebrow. "You?"

"I would ask one thing, and as it has a bearing on the death of my son, it is a thing I have a right to know."

"And what is that?"

"Never in five hundred years have I missed a blow, not with sword nor spear nor lance. How is it, then, since the ring of Oisin lies lost and useless in the Lands of Men, that my blow not only missed but found the wrong target?"

"Perhaps it was your choice of mounts," Lugh replied. "Or perhaps you are simply not as skilled as once you were."

"Or perhaps it is because the ring is *not* lost and useless," came the voice of Nuada. The silver-armed Faery reached into the breast of his tunic and drew out something round that glittered in the sun of Tir-Nan-Og. "I too have more shapes than one, Ailill, but the shape of a white trout may sometimes be more useful than that of a black eagle when one travels the Lands of Men."

Nuada turned toward Lugh. "Long have I watched Ailill, Lord; seeking to learn exactly how grave a threat he posed to our relations with the Lands of Men. And so I perforce watched David, too. Thus it happens that I was a trout in the stream into which David fell when the ring's Power broke him free of the Straightway. The chain parted in that fall and the ring rolled into the water where I was. It was then a simple thing for me to swallow while the boy lay unknowing. The ring is not a thing entirely of our understanding, Lord, for we did not make it. I feared my feasting might cost me, but it did not, for I bore David no ill will, nor did I claim the ring for my own. Until this Riding I have kept it in an iron box, which this silver arm allows me to handle."

Nuada stepped forward and returned the silver band to David. "I am sorry, David Sullivan, for much ill has befallen you because of this ring. And in truth I thought for a time to return it to you. But until you actually give it to another of your own volition, it is yours, regardless of who holds it. And until that time, you, at least, are under its protection."

"But why didn't you give it back?" David cried. "You put me through bloody hell for no good reason!"

"So I did," replied Nuada. "For I see a time not far off – much closer, in fact, than even I had guessed – when we will need someone to serve our cause among mortals – not as a traitor; I would not ask that of anyone, but as an ambassador. You, David Sullivan, I thought might be that person. I sensed Power alive in you from our first meeting, which I thought strange, since Power normally slumbers in your kind unless awakened by some outside force. My curiosity was aroused. And when I learned you had somehow acquired the Sight as well –"

"I thought that was because I looked between my legs at a funeral procession," David broke in.

Nuada smiled faintly and shook his head. "What would we do without Reverend Kirk? But no, that is doubtful. Oh, it may have been the spark, for the Laws of Power are capricious, but I think something else was at work there – though I still have not been able to set a name to what that might have been."

"I can set a name to it," a female voice inserted harshly. "For that name is mine."

"Morrigu?" Nuada stared incredulously at the red-clad Mistress of Battles.

"And why not? I, too, see war a-making between Faerie and the Lands of Men, and I do not like the odds. I, too, think an advocate among humans might be useful to ward off such a conflict. Indeed, I have often been in that World of late seeking such a one – even more frequently than you, Airgetlam, though my preferred shape is that of crow. And on one of those occasions I happened to see a burial in progress, and our young friend here regarding those proceedings from between his legs. The foolishness of his position called to my mind the equally foolish phrases the Scotsman had set down in that book of his. And since I already knew who that boy was – the thrice great-grandson of a mortal man with whom I once had lain – I could not resist a small test of my own. There was Power in him already, for it is the heritage of his house. It was thus a simple thing for me to call it forth again in the form of the Second Sight, so as to see of what metal the boy is made."

"And which metal is it?" Lugh asked.

"I have not decided," Morrigu replied. "Iron, perhaps, for the fires of the world's first making certainly flame in him. Or maybe gold, for the glory of learning which never fades from him. Or possibly silver, for the power a ring of that metal once had over him."

"Or maybe mercury, for the way he slipped through Ailill's fingers," Lugh suggested. "Or lead like a fisherman's sinker, for the net of plots that seem to be tangled about him."

"Perhaps," said the Mistress of Battles. "Or perhaps he is not the one we need at all."

David found himself blushing in spite of himself, but then he realized he had forgotten something: the most important thing – the reason he had come here!

"Milord Ard Rhi? I ... I mean Your ... Majesty?"

Lugh turned his face toward him. "Speak, mortal boy."

"I ... well ... this is all very interesting, but you do recall why I went through all this in the first place: so that I could crave a boon of you?"

Lugh raised an eyebrow. "That is also my recollection."

David squared his shoulders. "I have a boon, then ... I mean, I crave a boon."

Lugh's eyes twinkled in a way that made him look both old and young at once. "Ask, and if it be a just thing and within my Power to grant, I will."

"I ask that you – or someone skilled in Faery magic – please heal my Uncle Dale. He was wounded by a –"

"By a Faery arrow," the High King finished. "This I know. But you yourself have already effected the cure of your uncle. For one of the Laws of Power states that if a man be wounded by a thing of Power forged in a World not his own, so long as he not die of that wound it has power over him only so long as he whose Power is in that weapon lives."

David looked confused.

Nuada eased up beside him and pointed to the white-draped body of Fionchadd. "With the death of the slayer, the spell itself is slain. The death of Ailill's son, who was the instrument of your uncle's wound, has broken the Power of the arrow within him. The old man sleeps the sweet sleep of mortals. When he awakes tomorrow, he will be healed."

David was so relieved he couldn't reply, though he heard Alec vent a startled, "Cool!" It was still unreal to him; all of it was. It would take a while to sort things out. But now he thought he actually had that while.

"Thanks," he said at last, but only after Liz had elbowed him in the ribs to remind him.

Lugh regarded David keenly. "I would speak to you now, mortal lad. And I think I would like to speak to you again in a few years' time, when you have gained more wisdom. For I begin to see something of what Nuada saw in you: more an ally than a foe, and truly something of a hero as well. But the time for that is not yet. Until then, you do pose a problem. It is customary to blind those who look upon the folk of my realm unbidden, and I could do that now ..." He raised his hand, then hesitated. "But I have always thought that rather – shall we say – shortsighted, so I will simply lay a ban on all of you that you may speak of nothing you have seen or heard today to any dweller of your World except yourselves."

Lugh surveyed the host one final time, then grasped the ragged ends of the broken reins in one closed fist. A nod of his head, a narrowing of his eyes, and the break was mended. He shook the leather strips experimentally, setting the bells upon them to jingling. "Now, unless someone else has a boon to crave, let us proceed," he cried. "It seems we no longer have need to ride to the Eastern Sea, for Ailill will not be leaving after all. But there is still time to make that journey today, if we depart at once. If anyone objects to such an outing, let that voice be heard." He fixed Ailill with a burning stare. "I believe I will lead the procession a while since both my guard and my daughter will be otherwise occupied." Then, almost as an afterthought: "Nuada, since you are so fond of mortals, you may escort our guests back to their own World."

Nuada nodded and remounted. From somewhere three white horses appeared, saddled and bridled with red leather. Nuada motioned David and his companions to mount, which they did with ease by virtue of the Power of that place. "These horses never tire, never lose their way, and never throw a rider," Nuada informed them. "Even if that rider has never sat a horse."

Nuada shook his reins; the bells chiming softly as the smaller procession formed. Somewhere the harp music began again; somewhere else was the dull buzz of warpipes coming up to cry and a tentative run on a chanter.

David had held his peace as long as he could, then urged his horse close beside that of the High King. "Can I come back next year and watch?" he asked.

The Ard Rhi raised an eyebrow. "With your lips bound, what have we to fear from your eyes? If you are at the right place and time, mayhap you will see us."

Lugh turned once more to face the milling host. "Now let us ride, Lords and Ladies of the Tuatha de Danaan and folk of Tir-Nan-Og!"

Nuada's small company watched as the greater host passed down the Straight Track that had been David's road to Faerie. David looked down at the head of his brother, who sat in the saddle before him, wearing the yellow pajamas the changeling had previously worn. He ruffled his brother's hair. "How've you been, kid?"

"Sleepy," Little Billy replied through a yawn. "Real sleepy." He paused. "And I've gotta get Pa's ax."

"You can get it in the morning," David chuckled.

Alec whistled. "That was something else!"

"That's an understatement," Liz agreed, nodding.

"Three are mightier than one," David grinned.

"But one is mightiest of the three!" Alec and Liz cried in unison.

David scratched his finger where the ring once again was set and watched the Sidhe ride away: a line of glittering lights against the edge of the forest, for it was twilight again. He also saw a smaller party ride closer by, re-entering the wood from which they had first emerged. Amid that company rode Ailill, under heavy guard, with Lugh's daughter on one of the black horses, closest to him of all.

The Dark Faery said nothing as he passed, but his eyes betrayed his thoughts, and Nuada sighed before he set his horse onto the Straight Track. Ailill would take some watching.

epilogue

in the lands of men
(sunday, august 16)

david stood staring at Uncle Dale's wound. Little remained of it now: only a tiny white circle that was rapidly darkening to the color of the old man's flesh. His kinsman's face was relaxed, his breathing peaceful.

Quietly, David turned and reached for the doorknob.

A cough behind him made him freeze. "Thank you, boy," rasped a wonderfully familiar voice.

David whirled around and dashed back to the bedside. The old man's words were thick, but clear; he raised his arm – his *right* arm – high enough to pat David on the hand. His grip was weak but firm, and there was warmth in the hand. "You'd better not tell yore folks 'bout me," Uncle Dale murmured. "You don't know nothin' 'bout this, but I'll be better in the mornin'."

"Whatever you say," David grinned. "Whatever you say – and thanks for holdin' out."

"I knew you could do it, boy. I never doubted."

A moment later he was snoring.

David grinned again and stole from the room. A glance into his own room across the hall showed Little Billy likewise asleep. The little boy would remember nothing of his time in Faerie, so Nuada had told him. That and the journey home would seem like a dream. His last clear memory would be of lightning.

David glanced at the clock on the wall as he rejoined his friends in the kitchen. It was a little after one. Time had passed, but not enough. How much time had they spent in Faerie? he wondered. Days and days, it had seemed – and yet no time at all. He found himself looking at the ring. *The circle of Time that encloses all things:* another thing Nuada had referenced.

Car doors slammed in the yard. Laughter floated in from outside. David and Alec and Liz exchanged knowing looks and began a mad scramble back to the dining table.

"Let's see, you'd landed on Boardwalk again, hadn't you, David?" Liz chuckled as they reclaimed their places.

"Oh no! Not that old ploy," David shot back. "Why look, Liz, your hotels are all over the floor, and I bet you don't remember where they were, do you?"

"Want to bet, David Sullivan?"

"Now, Liz, you know I'm not a gambling man," David laughed – and rolled the dice.

meet the author:

photo by Beth Wheeler

tom deitz grew up in Young Harris, Georgia, and earned bachelor and master of arts degrees from the University of Georgia. His major in medieval English and his fondness for castles, Celtic art and costumes led Mr. Deitz to the Society for Creative Anachronism, of which he is still a member. He terms himself a "fair-to-middlin" artist. (You can be the judge, as his illustrations enliven the part pages of this collector's edition of *Windmaster's Bane*.) His books reflect his knowledge of Celtic lore and a tenuous grounding in current reality.

now, in the author's own words, how this book came to be:

the book you hold in your hand began as a short story written in late spring or early summer of 1980 or 81. I remember the time of year because I'd used my income tax refund to take a creative writing class offered by the University of Georgia's adult education program. (I'd recently moved from Young Harris where I'd been getting my feet wet in the "real world," back to Athens, Georgia, where I'd begun dating a certain young lady.) And I remember taking off a week in August to hibernate and write like a mad man for about a week, crouched over the typewriter in a little attic bedroom. In that time I produced what probably amounts to about half the text of the current novel.

"I also remember how that genesis story – basically David in the barn loft being deviled by his kid brother, and the first encounter with the Sidhe – all but wrote itself, and changed very little from draft to draft, with the obvious addition of the first "Lookout Rock" scene. Still, David's dialog with Little Billy about the funeral procession and the hearse is almost exactly the same as when I first wrote it.

"And I remember that the darned thing wouldn't leave me alone, and that I rewrote it three times before I ever sent it to a publisher. Each time it got longer, and each time I trimmed the timeline further. In the original version, the story took place over an entire year, with one chapter per month — which was a format that, while it gave me some structure on which to hang visuals and "atmospheric effects"(things like autumn leaves and snow), also required me to spend a lot of time explaining why nothing had happened since the last chapter. I also kept having to ask my country-reared mother what status corn would be in during the "David and Little Billy first meet the Sidhe" scene, because the time of year in which that scene was set kept changing.

"Eventually I got it down to six weeks, and that kept my characters sufficiently off balance that they couldn't ever quite get a handle on one crisis before another kicked in.

"There were a lot of other changes, too, notably of the ending. *Especially* of the ending, in fact, since the first publisher of this book, Avon, wanted "more fantasy." That's why the book acquired a prologue set entirely in Faerie: because otherwise nothing overtly fantastic happens for about fifty pages and the publisher wanted to assure readers that the thing was, in fact, fantasy. So I must give credit where credit is due: to Ms. Chris Miller of Avon Books, who not only bought this book, but shaped it as well.

"In any case, I was lucky enough to have the book debut at the World Science Fiction Convention in Atlanta in 1986, and it's done well for me, by and large. As is common in the fantasy field, it generated sequels, though I'd planned none. But sequels gave me a chance to get to know my characters better, to create additional new characters, and to add to the various worlds of which they were a part. They also gave me a chance to watch those characters grow up. And they all gave me a chance to take my own country and invest it with magic — an idea, I am proud to say, I borrowed from the late North Carolina writer, Manly Wade Wellman.

"And so I wrote more of what I came to call "The Adventures of David Sullivan," and eventually got him through a degree in English at the University of Georgia (though never into grad school, which he certainly would have attended.)

"And then, in the way of many good things, the realities of publishing changed and David's adventures came to an end.

"But he's always been there in the back of my mind — he and his friends. He had to be, because I realized at some point that in creating David and Liz and Alec and the rest of the Mactyrie Gang, I was essentially creating the friends I wished I had had in high school, and David foremost among them. I'm not him – the main things we had/have in common is being bright, somewhat flakey, lads growing up in a situation where such things are both misunderstood and undervalued, and the fact that we both wear glasses. In fact, personality-wise I'm much more like Alec.

"But enough of that. A few years back I was lucky enough (that word again), through the good auspices of author Sharyn McCrumb, to come in contact with High Country Publishers – and to find that they were interested in reprinting this, my first and favorite novel. More time passed; contracts were sent and signed; the whole MS was scanned into a computer; and I had a chance to go over it with a mental fine-toothed comb (as detailed in the introduction).

Tom Deitz as SCA Herald

"The rest, as they say, is history."

hiscorical noce

AS IS probably evident to the reader, *Windmaster's Bane* owes a considerable debt to the folklore and mythology of Ireland and Scotland. What is perhaps less obvious is the debt it owes to the folklore of an entirely different culture: the Cherokee Indians of the southeastern United States. It was Cherokee folklore that provided the collaborative evidence that solidified my notion that one could, indeed, write a "Celtic fantasy" set in the Appalachian Mountains.

There is the matter of the piled stone fortifications on Fort Mountain, for instance. Those structures are usually attributed to Prince Madoc of Wales, who supposedly founded a colony in Mobile, Alabama in the year 1170, and later worked his way inland. The Cherokees, however, attribute those ruins to the "moon-eyed people." It was my efforts to learn more about these mysterious folk that first led me to James Mooney's *Myths of the Cherokee*. Alas, Mooney's book provided little illumination on the matter of the "moon-eyed people" – but it had something better: the Nunnehi.

According to Mooney, the Cherokees believed in a race of (usually invisible) spirit people called the Nunnehi, a word meaning something like "the immortals" or "the people who live everywhere." In particular, the Nunnehi lived in "townhouses" high in the mountains or under water. They were fond of music and dancing, and often helpful to humans – at least to the Cherokee, on whose side they fought as recently as the mid-nineteenth century. With the Nunnehi I had both a link to the Sidhe of Irish mythology and to Tir-Nan-Og, the paradise to the west. The rest, as they say, is history.

Tom Deitz
Athens, Georgia
12 April 1986
and
Oakwood, Georgia
06 January 2006

Welcome to books from
INGALLS PUBLISHING GROUP!

BOOKS from the Ingalls family of imprints, including
High Country Publishers and Claystone Books,
provide novels and nonfiction of the highest quality
for readers of all ages.

We invite you to visit the websites
for Ingalls Publishing Group and for this book:

Ingallspublishinggroup.com
Highcountrypublishers.com
www.windmastersbane.com

For information about Tom Deitz,
the writing of this book and other books in the
Tales of David Sullivan series and
links to other relevant sites,
visit the website for this book.

www.windmastersbane.com

Enjoy!